GREAT GHOST STORIES

GREAT GHOST STORIES

Selected by R. Chetwynd-Hayes and Stephen Jones

CARROLL & GRAF PUBLISHERS
NEW YORK

GREAT GHOST STORIES

Carroll & Graf Publishers
An Imprint of Avalon Publishing Group Inc.
245 West 17th Street
New York, NY 10011

AVALON
publishing group incorporated

The arrangement of this collection is copyright © Stephen Jones and the
estate of Ronald Chetwyd-Hayes 2004.

First Carroll & Graf edition 2004

Library of Congress Cataloging-in-Publication Data is available.

ISBN: 0-7867-1363-1

Typesetting design by Bill Walker
Printed in the United States of America
Distributed by Publishers Group West

In Celebration of
RONALD CHETWYND-HAYES
(1919–2001)
A man who knew his ghosts.

❧ CONTENTS ❧

ACKNOWLEDGEMENTS

Special thanks to Linda Smith, Richard Chizmar, Herman Graf, Claiborne Hancock, Marsha DeFilippo, Chuck Verrill, Mike Ashley, Paul McAuley, Les Edwards, Val Edwards, Seamus A. Ryan and Dorothy Lumley for helping make this anthology possible.

The Editors gratefully acknowledge permission to publish the following copyright material:

Foreword copyright © Stephen Jones 2004.

Introduction copyright the estate of R. Chetwynd-Hayes 2004.

'The Night Walkers' copyright © Sydney J. Bounds 1979. Originally published in *The Fifteenth Fontana Book of Great Ghost Stories*. Reprinted by permission of the author and the author's agent, Cosmos Literary Agency.

'The Reaper's Image' copyright © Stephen King 1969. Originally published in *Startling Mystery Stories,* Spring 1969. Reprinted by permission of the author and the author's agent, Darhansoff, Verrill, Feld-man.

'Housewarming' copyright © Steve Rasnic Tem 1982. Originally published in *The Eighteenth Fontana Book of Great Ghost Stories*. Reprinted by permission of the author.

'The Ferries' copyright © Ramsey Campbell 1982. Originally published in *The Eighteenth Fontana Book of Great Ghost Stories*. Reprinted by permission of the author.

'The Fetch' copyright © Tina Rath 1983. Originally published in *The*

EDITORS' NOTE

FOREWORD

In a writing career that spanned four decades, Ronald Chetwynd-Hayes published thirteen novels, but he is best remembered today as the author of more than 200 short stories, collected in over twenty-five volumes in various languages around the world. Often combining horror and humour, these highly original tales of ghosts, vampires, werewolves and even more extraordinary creatures have been adapted into movies (From Beyond the Grave and The Monster Club), television (Rod Serling's Night Gallery), radio (The Price of Fear) and other media.

It is perhaps less well known that Ron was also a prolific and erudite anthologist.

During the late 1960s and '70s, the horror field was experiencing one of its occasional resurgences in popularity. Publishers were climbing over themselves to produce anthology series, and in 1964 the British paperback imprint Fontana Books hired acclaimed short story writer Robert Aickman to edit *The Fontana Book of Great Ghost Stories*, which collected together obscure tales by well-known masters of the macabre. The first volume was an instant success, quickly going into several reprints, and Aickman went on to edit another seven annual volumes. Meanwhile, Fontana added *The Fontana Book of Great Horror Stories* series, edited by Christine Bernard and later Mary Danby, and *European Tales of Terror* and *Oriental Tales of Terror* both edited by J.J. Strating, to its list.

The publisher perpetuated the latter series in the early 1970s by asking Ron to edit *Cornish Tales of Terror, Scottish Tales of Terror* (under his pseudonym "Angus Campbell") and *Welsh Tales of Terror.* The contents were eclectic, and the books sold well.

When Aickman finally tired of being an editor, Ron was inevitably offered the job and continued *The Fontana Book of Great Ghost Stories* for a further twelve volumes. He not only chose to reprint classic and esoteric stories of the supernatural but, recognising the changes that were happening in horror publishing at that time, he began including newer stories by established names like Ramsey Campbell, Brian Lumley, Sydney J. Bounds, James Turner, Mary Williams and Rosemary Timperley, as well as giving such newcomers as Steve Rasnic Tem, Garry Kilworth, Tony Richards, Rick Kennett, Tina Rath, Rick Ferrira, Peter A. Hough and Roger F. Dunkley, amongst others, an opportunity to shine. Because of budgetary restrictions, Ron also made sure that he also included one of his own stories in each volume.

However, perhaps his biggest *coup* as an editor was obtaining the first British publication of Stephen King's story 'The Reaper's Image' for the 17th volume.

The series was so successful that Ron simultaneously edited a further two volumes for Fontana, *Tales of Terror from Outer Space and Gaslight Tales of Terror*, as well as compiling six volumes of *The Armada Monster Book* for the publisher's children's imprint. He was also the editor of a one-off anthology, *Doomed to the Night*, for hardcover publisher William Kimber in 1978.

By the mid-1980s, the horror field was changing again, and sales of anthologies—especially those containing traditional Victorian and Edwardian ghost stories—began to slow down. Reprints became more infrequent, and the old-fashioned wraiths and spectres of a century before could not compete with the modern terrors of such bestsellers as King and James Herbert.

The Fontana Book of Great Ghost Stories was cancelled after the 20th volume appeared in 1984. Although Ron did not agree with the decision, he understood it from a commercial viewpoint. His more genteel phantoms were simply unable to co-exist in a world that was only interested in reading about children with psychic powers and mutant vermin.

However, as an author he continued to write exactly the kind of stories that he always wanted to, and his work was collected in a number of hardcover editions aimed principally at the library market. Although he would dearly have loved to have inherited the legendary *Pan Book of Horror Stories* (in which he began his career as a horror writer), he never edited another anthology again.

But, as always, the wheel of taste moves on, and those classic tales that Ron so carefully selected for his twelve volumes of *The Fontana Book of Great Ghost Stories* are once again popular, with numerous small press imprints around the world churning out collectible and highly-priced editions devoted to obscure and long-dead authors.

It therefore seems only fitting that this present volume should collect together twenty-five stories that reflect the scholarship and discernment that Ronald Chetwynd-Hayes brought to his editorship of that series of books more than a quarter of a century ago.

I trust that over the following pages you will discover some tales and authors which may be unfamiliar to you; and afterwards, as Ron would have said, may you never hear invisible footsteps following you down the stairs.

Happy shuddering.

Stephen Jones
London, England
February, 2003

INTRODUCTION

R. Chetwynd-Hayes

Having published numerous books of my own, all dealing in some way with the supernatural; read voraciously every publication dealing with the subject that has fallen into my greedy hands; corresponded with, interviewed and visited ghost hunters; those who had reason to believe they were haunted; I must surely now—with all due modesty—be entitled to classify myself as an expert in this genre.

But—I am still not entirely certain what a ghost is.

According to my calculations there are three possibilities to choose from. A disembodied spirit. A personality residue. A time image. I have very grave doubts about the first, as to my knowledge no one has held a conversation with a ghost. I know all about Parson Rudall and 'The Botathen Ghost', having included the story in *Cornish Tales of Terror,* but that momentous event took place some three hundred years ago; the distant past is a foreign country, they speak a different language there. But of course I may be wrong and am quite willing to be convinced.

A personality residue? Maybe. A fragment of the ego that due to some pressure experienced during life, has managed to survive that holocaust we call death and for a while can manifest to certain people at certain times? This phenomenon would have a limited memory recall, brief periods of awareness, governed possibly by a dimly-realised single emotion. I should imagine solitary people would be more inclined to leave this particular hair-raising morsel behind them, than those who had lived gregarious lives.

A time image is my favourite. Thought waves which have become impregnated in the woodwork, atmosphere, etc., and can be transformed into the likeness of their dead creator. I have often pondered on the possibility that our descendants will be able to watch our antics on a kind of super-television set. It is a sobering thought.

Having re-read my learned discourse on the types of ghosts one may encounter in this haunted vale of tears, I find that I missed one out: the fear ghost. The most common, I suspect.

Let us take a hypothetical example. You move into a house that has the reputation of being haunted by an old man carrying a lighted candle. While the sun shines through the nylon curtains you can afford to laugh at this nonsensical idea and even talk bravely of blowing his candle out, should he put in an appearance. But when long shadows creep across the garden and strange shapes appear in obscure corners, a little grey snake uncoils in your brain. You may possibly remember that someone (me) once said that every house harbours at least one ghost, even if the living inhabitants are too blind to see it. It is conceivable that you will recollect that the same person maintained that few people can boast of mounting the stairs without *something* walking very close behind them. Such reflections are not comforting when you are seated in an empty house that has the reputation of being haunted by an old man carrying a lighted candle—and the chances are that sooner or later you will see him.

Why? The answer is simple. Atmosphere, plus a generous helping of fear, will make your brain project the image it expects to see. Now, I am going to take this blood-curdling conjecture one stage further. Is it not possible that one or more people can create a fear ghost that becomes part of the surroundings and is later seen by someone who is—at first—not particularly frightened? Imagine—you may be on the receiving end of someone else's fear.

'The Four-Fifteen Express' by Amelia B. Edwards undoubtedly deals with a time-ghost. Here we have an apparently flesh-and-blood man, entering a train carriage and conducting a conversation about events which belong in the past. There would be nothing unusual about this, were it not for the fact . . . But I have no intention of spoiling your fun. Read the story.

The ghost in 'On the Brighton Road', by Richard Middleton, has the same unconventional code of behaviour and deserves to be continuously bumped off, whenever a suitable occasion occurs.

I suppose Ambrose Bierce's most famous story is 'Incident at Owl Creek', which has had the distinction of being made into two films and a radio play. I have not included it here, because it has been reprinted so many times, and in any case it is not a ghost story. But 'The Moonlit Road' is, and a very gripping one into the bargain. It has a terrifying depth and intensity and I think comes a good second to its more famous predecessor.

'The Whittakers Ghost' which I found in an old bound volume of *Argosy* dated 1879, has the apparition wandering around the garden.

Sabine Baring-Gould died in 1924 at the age of ninety. Apart from being a well-known novelist and short-story writer, he is also responsible for the hymns 'Onward Christian Soldiers' and 'Now the Day is Over'. 'The Leaden Ring' proves he knew how to tell a good ghost story as well. May this serve as a lesson to any spoilt young lady who is thinking of giving her boyfriend the brush-off.

In 'The Tapestried Chamber' by Sir Walter Scott, my sympathies were entirely with General Browne who decided that one night spent in Woodville Castle was enough and: *to seek in some less beautiful country, and with less dignified friend, forgetfulness of the painful night which he had passed . . .*

In other words, he put his running shoes on. So would I.

In my opinion Joseph Sheridan Le Fanu was the greatest of

Victorian ghost-story writers. There are three or four close runners-up, but he had the gift of writing good prose without boring the reader. 'Ghost Stories of the Tiled House' is an excellent example of what I mean. One feels that if these stories are not true—they jolly well should be. At the same time I am not certain that old Sally should have been allowed to entertain her young mistress with such gruesome tales while preparing her for bed. Would the young lady have slept soundly after listening to the old woman relate: . . . *He drew the curtain at the side of the bed, and saw Mrs Prosser lying, as for a few seconds he mortally feared, dead, her face being motionless, white, and covered with cold dew; and on the pillow, close beside her head, and just within the curtains, was the same white, fattish hand, the wrist resting on the pillow, and the fingers extended towards his temple with a slow, wavy motion?*

Ugh!

'The Dead Smile' by F. Marion Crawford is a dreadful tale, a real piece of juicy macabre. Read this:

And he went in alone and saw that the body of Sir Vernon Ockram was leaning upright against the stone wall, and that his head lay on the ground near by with his face turned up, and the dried leathern lips smiled horribly at the dried-up corpse, while the iron coffin, lined with black velvet, stood open on the floor.

And very nice too.

To my knowledge, Daniel Defoe wrote only two ghost stories. 'The Apparition of Mrs. Veal', which has been grossly over-exposed, and 'The Ghost of Dorothy Dingley', which I have included here. I must say both stories are told in a most convincing fashion and one is inclined to believe that they might well be true. Dorothy is a very active ghost and able to climb over stiles, terrify well-spoken schoolboys and chat up verbose clergymen. The trouble is the wretched man does not tell us what she said. But it is an entertaining period piece.

That indefatigable writer of Victorian ghost stories, Anon, has come up with another terrifying nightmare, 'The Dead Man of Varley

Grange'. It was published some time in the 1880s, but who the author was I have not the faintest idea. But I suspect he was a well-endowed young gentleman with a military background and a welcome visitor at country houses, where he scared the pants off his fellow guests by relating gruesome stories. Of course I might be wrong. Anon could well have been a respectable middle-aged lady who hugged her ghastly secret—pandering to the public's depraved taste—of her bombazine-clad bosom. I must say, the house guests are a pretty tough lot, for after witnessing this:

We all turned round, and there . . . stood a man leaning over the rail of the gallery, staring down at us.

. . . He had a long tawny beard, and his hands, that were crossed before him, were nothing but skin and bone. But it was his face that was so unspeakably dreadful. It was livid—the face of a dead man!

Three characters exclaim:

"It must be a delusion of our brains," said one.

"Our host's champagne," suggested another.

"A well-organised hoax," opined a third.

I will concede that four of them:

. . . received by the morning post—so they stated—letters of importance which called them up to town by the very first train.

Even so, the remainder decided to sweat it out.

'John Charrington's Wedding' by E. Nesbit was first published in 1893 in a collection called *Grim Tales*. Some people may say that getting married is a grim business at the best of times, but Mr. Charrington's belated appearance at the church was enough to send the most resilient of brides running home to mother. I find myself wondering what took place between the unhappy couple when they were shut up in the carriage together.

We gather that Roger Bateson had not been married very long when he set out in 'The Night Walkers' by Sydney J. Bounds to explore an old canal, and his matrimonial problems were not improved by *what* walked the banks and clearly desired company. The story borders on the horrific, but is none the worse for that. I can now understand why some of our canals have been so sadly neglected in recent years.

Many years ago I read a story, the plot of which haunted my sleeping and waking hours, although I was unable to remember either title or author. I know now it was 'Brickett Bottom' by Amyas Northcote. It was first published by John Lane in a book called *In a Ghostly Company* in 1922. In more respects than one it is a haunting little story, with a simple plot that leads us gently to a terrifying climax. One is inclined to wonder if Mr. Northcote had read Ambrose Bierce's *Mysterious Disappearances,* which had been published sometime during the 1890s. Certainly he seems to owe a considerable debt to the episode that Bierce headed 'Charles Ashmore's Trial', but I do not hold that against him. Writers have been feeding off each other since the days of Shakespeare. With one exception, of course.

I have included 'The Water Ghost of Harrowby Hall, by John Kendrick Bangs because I like my collections to have at least one humorous story. And this is very funny. What does one do with a ghost who comes up from the sea every Christmas Eve and soaks everything—and everyone—about her? Oglethorpe works out a simply splendid solution that might be worth remembering should you ever find yourself in his predicament.

Which brings me to 'The Reaper's Image' by Stephen King, the world-famous author of *Carrie, The Shining, 'Salem's Lot* and other superb masterpieces. A nicely subtle slice of the macabre that opens up more than one line of conjecture and is apt to put one off antique mirrors for life.

I take pleasure in presenting 'Christmas Eve in the Blue Chamber' by Jerome K. Jerome. There is an uncle who says: *"I don't want to make you fellows nervous,"* in a peculiarly impressive, not to say bloodcurdling, tone of voice: a statement that is more optimistic than accurate. He then goes on to say that the blue room is haunted by the ghost of a sinful man who once killed a Christmas carol singer with a lump of coal. He also seems to have disposed of an entire German band, a meritorious act for which he was never thanked. I classify this one as a disembodied spirit with good intentions.

Steve Rasnic Tem has made quite a name for himself on both sides of the Atlantic and now enjoys the reputation of being a fantasy writer of merit. 'Housewarming' is a subtle study of mounting terror. Poor Judith undoubtedly creates her own fear-ghost—and one that will be around for a long time. I can offer no comfort to the reader. This kind of situation could happen to anyone—and probably will. 'Housewarming' is a plot I would dearly have liked to have thought of first, and now I can only gnash my teeth in pure envy.

I do not know if Ramsey Campbell had in mind the thought of receiving someone else's fear when he wrote 'The Ferries'. Possibly not, but it is one explanation as to why Berry experienced what he did, after being in close proximity with a very frightened uncle. Let me state without reservation that 'The Ferries' is a brilliant, imaginative stab of macabre, guaranteed to arrest your interest from the very first word, while making you extremely wary of shadows, unexplained pools of water and ships in bottles, for the rest of your life.

Until I read 'The Fetch' by Tina Rath, I was not aware that there is another name for a Doppelgänger. The ghost of yourself. Very nasty. Sir Walter Scott is said to have been haunted by his Doppelgänger (or Fetch) prior to his death and maintained it was seated in an armchair watching him. Miss Rath has concocted an intricate plot that involves a violent husband, a shrinking wife and a scheming female, to say nothing of the Fetch, which insists on standing under the pines at the end of the garden. For good measure there is a nice—or nasty—surprise at the end.

'Guests from Gibbet Island' by Washington Irving was written over 180 years ago, but is still intensely readable today. The author of *Rip Van Winkle* knew how to make full use of his whimsically humorous style in telling a ghost story, which in no way detracts from its overall chilling effect. Here is a sample:

. . . there, at a table, on which burned a light as blue as brimstone, sat the three guests from Gibbet Island, with halters round their necks, and bobbing their cups together, as they were hob-a-nobbing, and trolling the old Dutch freebooters' glee, since translated into English:

For three merry lads be we,
And three merry lads be we:
I on the land, and thou on the sand,
And Jack on the gallows-tree.

In 'The Tryst' by Garry Kilworth, the heroine's imagination *seemed to unfold like a black-paper beast into something barely recognisable.* The cottage where Rebecca is planning to meet her lover has two windows *that burned in the evening sunlight: the eyes of a man on the point of death.* The cottage has a reputation; Rebecca has been told the story; she is alone; the atmosphere builds up and . . .

Guy De Maupassant is possibly one of the greatest short story writers of all time, although much of his later work betrayed signs of approaching madness. Personally, I think some of his supernatural stories are more horrible than horrific, but 'An Apparition' must be listed among the top ten most terrifying ghost stories ever written. The spectre who pleaded to have her long hair combed, the unsolved mystery as to why she haunted that long, locked room, the subtle hint of tragedy—perhaps a crime—all combine to intrigue and chill.

Brian Lumley writes the kind of story that should have some future anthologist rubbing his hands with glee, particularly when it is out of copyright and he can get it for nothing. 'Aunt Hester' is a prime example. An exceptionally gifted lady, who might not be everyone's idea of a favourite maiden aunt, but not lacking a certain chilling charm. Needless to say, the climax is really horrifying.

Tony Richards always turns in a first-class story, but with 'Our Lady of the Shadows' he has really excelled himself. Set in Paris, the sounds, smells and buildings of the city become as real as Monday morning to the engrossed reader. The first sentence rivets one's attention: *In any other city in the world, the discovery of Mary-Jane Palmer's body floating in the river would have been sad, and disquieting, that was all.*

The action flows back and forth across the city, carrying with it Mary-Jane Palmer, who gradually becomes aware of the horror which is pursuing her. We know she is doomed, but at the same time hope she will in some way escape. And of course there is the insatiable hunger to know why? How? Surely in the distant future, someone will say: "They don't write 'em like *this* anymore."

Lastly, there is my own 'She Walks on Dry Land' which for a change I have set in the Regency period. Well—why not? I like to write about arrogant earls that ride into lonely villages and get their deserts after hitting the innkeeper over the head with a riding crop.

It must have been fun being an arrogant earl back in 1812.

So—twenty-five stories, every one written by a well-established and in some cases world-famous author. All written with the deliberate intention of scaring the living daylights out of the reader. I sincerely hope and pray this intention is realised.

May black angels keep watch at your bed.

THE FOUR-FIFTEEN
EXPRESS

Amelia B. Edwards

The events which I am about to relate took place between nine and
ten years ago. Sebastopol had fallen in the early spring, the peace
of Paris had been concluded since March, our commercial relations
with the Russian empire were but recently renewed; and I, returning
home after my first northward journey since the war, was well pleased
with the prospect of spending the month of December under the hospitable and thoroughly English roof of my excellent friend, Jonathan
Jelf, Esq., of Dumbleton Manor, Clayborough, East Anglia. Travelling
in the interests of the well-known firm in which it is my lot to be a
junior partner, I had been called upon to visit not only the capitals of
Russia and Poland, but had found it also necessary to pass some weeks
among the trading ports of the Baltic; whence it came that the year was
already far spent before I again set foot on English soil, and that,
instead of shooting pheasants with him, as I had hoped, in October, I
came to be my friend's guest during the more genial Christmas-tide.

My voyage over, and a few days given up to business in Liverpool
and London, I hastened down to Clayborough with all the delight of a
school-boy whose holidays are at hand. My way lay by the Great East
Anglian line as far as Clayborough station, where I was to be met by

one of the Dumbleton carriages and conveyed across the remaining nine miles of country. It was a foggy afternoon, singularly warm for the 4th of December, and I had arranged to leave London by the 4:15 express. The early darkness of winter had already closed in; the lamps were lighted in the carriages; a clinging damp dimmed the windows, adhered to the door-handles, and pervaded all the atmosphere; while the gas-jets at the neighbouring book-stand diffused a luminous haze that only served to make the gloom of the terminus more visible. Having arrived some seven minutes before the starting of the train, and, by the connivance of the guard, taken sole possession of an empty compartment, I lighted my traveling-lamp, made myself particularly snug, and settled down to the undisturbed enjoyment of a book and a cigar. Great, therefore, was my disappointment when, at the last moment, a gentleman came hurrying along the platform, glanced into my carriage, opened the locked door with a private key, and stepped in.

It struck me at the first glance that I had seen him before—a tall, spare man, thin-lipped, light-eyed, with an ungraceful stoop in the shoulders, and scant grey hair worn somewhat long upon the collar. He carried a light waterproof coat, an umbrella, and a large brown japanned deed-box, which last he placed under the seat. This done, he felt carefully in his breast-pocket, as if to make certain of the safety of his purse or pocket-book, laid his umbrella in the netting overhead, spread the waterproof across his knees, and exchanged his hat for a travelling-cap of some Scotch material. By this time the train was moving out of the station and into the faint grey of the wintry twilight beyond.

I now recognized my companion. I recognized him from the moment when he removed his hat and uncovered the lofty, furrowed, and somewhat narrow brow beneath. I had met him, as I distinctly remembered, some three years before, at the very house for which, in all probability, he was now bound, like myself. His name was Dwerri-house, he was a lawyer by profession, and, if I was not greatly mistaken, was first cousin to the wife of my host. I knew also that he was a man eminently "well-to-do," both as regarded his professional and private means. The Jelfs entertained him with that sort of observant courtesy which falls to the lot of the rich relation, the children made much of him, and the old butler, albeit somewhat surly 'to the general', treated him with deference. I thought, observing him by the vague mixture of lamplight and twilight, that Mrs. Jelf's cousin looked all the worse for the three years' wear and tear which had gone over his head since our last meeting. He was very pale, and had a restless light in his eye that I did not remember to have observed before. The anxious lines, too, about his mouth were deepened, and there was a cavernous, hollow look about his cheeks and temples which seemed to speak of sickness or sorrow. He had glanced at me as he came in, but without any gleam of recognition in his face. Now he glanced again, as I fancied, somewhat doubtfully. When he did so for the third or fourth time I ventured to address him.

"Mr. John Dwerrihouse, I think?"

"That is my name," he replied.

"I had the pleasure of meeting you at Dumbleton about three years ago."

"I thought I knew your face," he said; "but your name, I regret to say—"

"Langford—William Langford. I have known Jonathan Jelf since we were boys together at Merchant Taylors', and I generally spend a few weeks at Dumbleton in the shooting season. I suppose we are bound for the same destination."

"Not if you are on your way to the manor," he replied. "I am travelling upon business—rather troublesome business, too—while you, doubtless, have only pleasure in view."

"Just so. I am in the habit of looking forward to this visit as to the brightest three weeks in all the year."

"It is a pleasant house," said Mr. Dwerrihouse.

"The pleasantest I know."

"And Jelf is thoroughly hospitable."

"The best and kindest fellow in the world!"

"They have invited me to spend Christmas week with them," pursued Mr. Dwerrihouse, after a moment's pause.

"And you are coming?"

"I cannot tell. It must depend on the issue of this business which I have in hand. You have heard perhaps that we are about to construct a branch line from Blackwater to Stockbridge."

I explained that I had been for some months away from England, and had therefore heard nothing of the contemplated improvement.

Mr. Dwerrihouse smiled complacently.

"It *will* be an improvement," he said, "a great improvement. Stockbridge is a flourishing town, and needs but a more direct railway communication with the metropolis to become an important centre of commerce. This branch was my own idea. I brought the project before the board, and have myself superintended the execution of it up to the present time."

"You are an East Anglican director, I presume?"

"My interest in the company," replied Mr. Dwerrihouse, "is threefold. I am a director, I am a considerable shareholder, and, as head of the firm of Dwerrihouse, Dwerrihouse and Craik, I am the company's principal solicitor."

Loquacious, self-important, full of his pet project, and apparently unable to talk of any other subject, Mr. Dwerrihouse then went on to tell of the opposition he had encountered and the obstacles he had overcome in the cause of the Stockbridge branch. I was entertained with a multitude of local details and local grievances. The rapacity of one squire, the impracticability of another, the indignation of the rector whose glebe was threatened, the culpable indifference of the Stockbridge townspeople, who could *not* be brought to see that their most vital interests hinged upon a junction with the Great East Anglian line; the spite of the local newspaper, and the unheard-of difficulties attending the common question, were each and all laid before me with a circumstantiality that possessed the deepest interest for my excellent fellow-traveller, but none whatever for myself. From these, to my despair, he went on to more intricate matters: to the approximate expenses of construction per mile; to the estimates sent in by different contractors; to the probable traffic returns of the new line; to the provisional clauses of the new act as enumerated in Schedule D of the company's last half-yearly report; and so on and on and on, till my head ached and my attention flagged and my eyes kept closing in spite of every effort that I made to keep them open. At length I was roused by these words:

"Seventy-five thousand pounds, cash down."

"Seventy-five thousand pounds, cash down," I repeated, in the liveliest tone I could assume. "That is a heavy sum."

"A heavy sum to carry here," replied Mr. Dwerrihouse, pointing significantly to his breast-pocket, "but a mere fraction of what we shall ultimately have to pay."

"You do not mean to say that you have seventy-five thousand pounds at this moment upon your person?" I exclaimed.

"My good sir, have I not been telling you so for the last half-hour?" said Mr. Dwerrihouse, testily. "That money has to be paid over at half-past eight o'clock this evening, at the office of Sir Thomas's solicitors, on completion of the deed of sale."

"But how will you get across by night from Blackwater to Stockbridge with seventy-five thousand pounds in your pocket?"

'To Stockbridge!" echoed the lawyer. "I find I have made myself very imperfectly understood. I thought I had explained how this sum only carries us as far as Mallingford—the first stage, as it were, of our journey—and how our route from Blackwater to Mallingford lies entirely through Sir Thomas Liddell's property."

"I beg your pardon," I stammered. "I fear my thoughts were wandering. So you only go as far as Mallingford tonight?"

"Precisely. I shall get a conveyance from the Blackwater Arms. And you?"

"Oh, Jelf sends a trap to meet me at Clayborough! Can I be the bearer of any message from you?"

"You may say, if you please, Mr. Langford, that I wished I could have been your companion all the way, and that I will come over, if possible, before Christmas."

"Nothing more?"

Mr. Dwerrihouse smiled grimly. "Well," he said, "you may tell my cousin that she need not burn the hall down in my honour *this* time, and that I shall be obliged if she will order the blue-room chimney to be swept before I arrive."

"That sounds tragic. Had you a conflagration on the occasion of your last visit to Dumbleton?"

"Something like it. There had been no fire lighted in my bedroom since the spring, the flue was foul, and the rooks had built in it; so when I went up to dress for dinner I found the room full of smoke and the chimney on fire. Are we already at Blackwater?"

The train had gradually come to a pause while Mr. Dwerrihouse was speaking, and, on putting my head out of the window, I could see the station some few hundred yards ahead. There was another train before us blocking the way, and the guard was making use of the delay to collect the Blackwater tickets. I had scarcely ascertained our position when the ruddy-faced official appeared at our carriage door.

"Tickets, sir!" said he.

"I am for Clayborough," I replied, holding out the tiny pink card.

He took it, glanced at it by the light of his little lantern, gave it back, looked, as I fancied, somewhat sharply at my fellow-traveller, and disappeared.

"He did not ask for yours," I said, with some surprise.

"They never do," replied Mr. Dwerrihouse; "they all know me, and of course I travel free."

"Blackwater! Blackwater!" cried the porter, running along the platform beside us as we glided into the station.

Mr. Dwerrihouse pulled out his deed-box, put his travelling-cap in his pocket, resumed his hat, took down his umbrella, and prepared to be gone.

"Many thanks, Mr. Langford, for your society," he said, with old-fashioned courtesy. "I wish you a good-evening."

"Good-evening," I replied, putting out my hand.

But he either did not see it or did not choose to see it, and, slightly lifting his hat, stepped out upon the platform. Having done this, he moved slowly away and mingled with the departing crowd.

Leaning forward to watch him out of sight, I trod upon something which proved to be a cigar-case. It had fallen, no doubt, from the pocket of his waterproof coat, and was made of dark morocco leather, with a silver monogram upon the side. I sprang out of the carriage just as the guard came up to lock me in.

"Is there one minute to spare?" I asked, eagerly. "The gentleman who traveled down with me from town has dropped his cigar-case; he is not yet out of the station."

"Just a minute and a half, sir," replied the guard. "You must be quick."

I dashed along the platform as fast as my feet could carry me. It was a large station, and Mr. Dwerrihouse had by this time got more than half-way to the farther end.

I, however, saw him distinctly, moving slowly with the stream. Then, as I drew nearer, I saw that he had met some friend, that they were talking as they walked, that they presently fell back somewhat from the crowd and stood aside in earnest conversation. I made straight for the spot where they were waiting. There was a vivid gas-jet just above their heads, and the light fell full upon their faces. I saw both distinctly—the face of Mr. Dwerrihouse and the face of his companion. Running, breathless, eager as I was, getting in the way of porters and passengers, and fearful every instant lest I should see the train going on without me, I yet observed that the newcomer was considerably younger and shorter than the director, that he was sandy-haired, moustachioed, small-featured, and dressed in a close-cut suit of Scotch tweed. I was now within a few yards of them. I ran against a stout gentleman, I was nearly knocked down by a luggage-truck, I stumbled over a carpet-bag; I gained the spot just as the driver's whistle warned me to return.

To my utter stupefaction, they were no longer there. I had seen them but two seconds before—and they were gone! I stood still; I looked to right and left; I saw no sign of them in any direction. It was as if the platform had gaped and swallowed them.

"There were two gentlemen standing here a moment ago," I said to a porter at my elbow; "which way can they have gone?"

"I saw no gentlemen, sir," replied the man.

The whistle shrilled out again. The guard, far up the platform, held up his arm, and shouted to me to 'come on!'

"If you're going on by this train, sir," said the porter, "you must run for it."

I did run for it, just gained the carriage as the train began to move, was shoved in by the guard, and left, breathless and bewildered, with Mr. Dwerrihouse's cigar-case still in my hand.

It was the strangest disappearance in the world; it was like a transformation trick in a pantomime. They were there one moment—palpably there, talking, with the gaslight full upon their faces—and the next moment they were gone. There was no door near, no window, no staircase; it was a mere slip of barren platform, tapestried with big advertisements. Could anything be more mysterious?

It was not worth thinking about, and yet, for my life, I could not help pondering upon it—pondering, wondering, conjecturing, turning it over and over in my mind, and beating my brains for a solution of the enigma. I thought of it all the way from Blackwater to Clayborough. I thought of it all the way from Clayborough to Dumbleton, as I rattled along the smooth highway in a trim dog-cart, drawn by a splendid black mare and driven by the silentest and dapperest of East Anglian grooms.

We did the nine miles in something less than an hour, and pulled up before the lodge-gates just as the church clock was striking half-past seven. A couple of minutes more, and the warm glow of the lighted hall was flooding out upon the gravel, a hearty grasp was on my hand, and a clear jovial voice was bidding me "welcome to Dumbleton."

"And now, my dear fellow," said my host, when the first greeting was over, "you have no time to spare. We dine at eight, and there are people coming to meet you, so you must just get the dressing business over as quickly as may be. By the way, you will meet some acquaintances; the Biddulphs are coming, and Prendergast (Prendergast of the Skirmishers) is staying in the house. Adieu! Mrs. Jelf will be expecting you in the drawing-room."

I was ushered to my room—not the blue room, of which Mr. Dwerrihouse had made disagreeable experience, but a pretty little bachelor's chamber, hung with a delicate chintz manteau. I tried to be expeditious, but the memory of my railway adventure haunted me. I could not get free of it; I could not shake it off. It impeded me, it worried me, it tripped me up, it caused me to mislay my studs, to mistie my cravat, to wrench the buttons off my gloves. Worst of all, it made me so late that the party had all assembled before I reached the drawing-room. I had scarcely paid my respects to Mrs. Jelf when dinner was announced, and we paired off, some eight or ten couples strong, into the dining-room.

I am not going to describe either the guests or the dinner. All provincial parties bear the strictest family resemblance, and I am not aware that an East Anglian banquet offers any exception to the rule. There was the usual country baronet and his wife; there were the usual country parsons and their wives; there was the sempiternal turkey and haunch of venison. *Vanitas vanitatum.* There is nothing new under the sun.

I was placed about midway down the table. I had taken one rector's wife down to dinner, and I had another at my left hand. They talked across me, and their talk was about babies; it was dreadfully dull. At length there came a pause. The entrées had just been removed, and the turkey had come upon the scene. The conversation had all along been of the languidest, but at this moment it happened to have stagnated altogether. Jelf was carving the turkey; Mrs. Jelf looked as if she was trying to think of something to say; everybody else was silent. Moved by an unlucky impulse, I thought I would relate my adventure.

"By the way, Jelf," I began, "I came down part of the way today with a friend of yours."

"Indeed!" said the master of the feast, slicing scientifically into the breast of the turkey. "With whom, pray?"

"With one who bade me tell you that he should, if possible, pay you a visit before Christmas."

"I cannot think who that could be," said my friend, smiling.

"It must be Major Thorp," suggested Mr.s Jelf.

I shook my head.

"It was not Major Thorp," I replied; "it was a near relation of your own, Mrs. Jelf."

"Then I am more puzzled than ever," replied my hostess. "Pray tell me who it was."

"It was no less a person than your cousin, Mr. John Dwerrihouse."

Jonathan Jelf laid down his knife and fork. Mrs. Jelf looked at me in a strange, startled way, and said never a word.

"And he desired me to tell you, my dear madam, that you need not take the trouble to burn the hall down in his honour this time, but only to have the chimney of the blue room swept before his arrival."

Before I had reached the end of my sentence I became aware of something ominous in the faces of the guests. I felt I had said something which I had better have left unsaid, and that for some unexplained reason my words had evoked a general consternation. I sat confounded, not daring to utter another syllable, and for at least two whole minutes there was dead silence round the table. Then Captain Prendergast came to the rescue.

"You have been abroad for some months, have you not, Mr. Langford?" he said, with the desperation of one who flings himself into the breach. "I heard you had been to Russia. Surely you have something to tell us of the state and temper of the country after the war?"

I was heartily grateful to the gallant Skirmisher for this diversion in my favour. I answered him, I fear, somewhat lamely; but he kept the conversation up, and presently one or two others joined in, and so the difficulty, whatever it might have been, was bridged over—bridged over, but not repaired. A something, an awkwardness, a visible constraint remained. The guests hitherto had been simply dull, but now they were evidently uncomfortable and embarrassed.

The dessert had scarcely been placed upon the table when the ladies left the room. I seized the opportunity to select a vacant chair next Captain Prendergast.

"In Heaven's name," I whispered, "what was the matter just now? What had I said?"

"You mentioned the name of John Dwerrihouse."

"What of that? I had seen him not two hours before."

"It is a most astounding circumstance that you should have seen him," said Captain Prendergast. "Are you sure it was he?"

"As sure as of my own identity. We were talking all the way between London and Blackwater. But why does that surprise you?"

"Because," replied Captain Prendergast, dropping his voice to the lowest whisper—"because John Dwerrihouse absconded three months ago with seventy-five thousand pounds of the company's money, and has never been heard of since."

John Dwerrihouse had absconded three months ago—and I had seen him only a few hours back! John Dwerrihouse had embezzled seventy-five thousand pounds of the company's money, yet told me that he carried that sum upon his person! Were ever facts so strangely incongruous, so difficult to reconcile? How should he have ventured again into the light of day? How dared he show himself along the line? Above all, what had he been doing throughout those mysterious three months of disappearance?

11

Perplexing questions these—questions which at once suggested themselves to the minds of all concerned, but which admitted of no easy solution. I could find no reply to them. Captain Prendergast had not even a suggestion to offer. Jonathan Jelf, who seized the first opportunity of drawing me aside and learning all that I had to tell, was more amazed and bewildered than either of us. He came to my room that night, when all the guests were gone, and we talked the thing over from every point of view; without, it must be confessed, arriving at any kind of conclusion.

"I do not ask you," he said, "whether you can have mistaken your man. That is impossible."

"As impossible as that I should mistake some stranger for yourself."

"It is not a question of looks or voice, but of facts. That he should have alluded to the fire in the blue room is proof enough of John Dwerrihouse's identity. How did he look?"

"Older, I thought; considerably older, paler, and more anxious."

"He has had enough to make him look anxious, anyhow," said my friend, gloomily, "be he innocent or guilty."

"I am inclined to believe that he is innocent," I replied. "He showed no embarrassment when I addressed him, and no uneasiness when the guard came round. His conversation was open to a fault. I might almost say that he talked too freely of the business which he had in hand."

"That again is strange, for I know no one more reticent on such subjects. He actually told you that he had the seventy-five thousand pounds in his pocket?"

"He did."

"Humph! My wife has an idea about it, and she may be right—"

"What idea?"

"Well, she fancies—women are so clever, you know, at putting themselves inside people's motives—she fancies that he was tempted, that he did actually take the money, and that he has been concealing himself these three months in some wild part of the country, struggling possibly with his conscience all the time, and daring neither to abscond with his booty nor to come back and restore it."

"But now that he has come back?"

"That is the point. She conceives that he has probably thrown himself upon the company's mercy, made restitution of the money, and, being forgiven, is permitted to carry the business through as if nothing whatever had happened."

"The last," I replied, "is an impossible case. Mrs. Jelf thinks like a generous and delicate-minded woman, but not in the least like a board of railway directors. They would never carry forgiveness so far."

"I fear not; and yet it is the only conjecture that bears a semblance of likelihood. However, we can run over to Clayborough tomorrow and see if anything is to be learned. By the way, Prendergast tells me you picked up his cigar-case."

"I did so, and here it is."

Jelf took the cigar-case, examined it by the light of the lamp, and said at once that it was beyond doubt Mr. Dwerrihouse's property, and that he remembered to have seen him use it.

"Here, too, is his monogram on the side," he added—"a big J transfixing a capital D. He used to carry the same on his note-paper."

"It offers, at all events, a proof that I was not dreaming."

"Ay, but it is time you were asleep and dreaming now. I am ashamed to have kept you up so long. Good-night."

"Good-night, and remember that I am more than ready to go with you to Clayborough or Blackwater or London or anywhere, if I can be of the least service."

"Thanks! I know you mean it, old friend, and it may be that I shall put you to the test. Once more, good-night."

So we parted for that night, and met again in the breakfast-room at half-past eight next morning. It was a hurried, silent, uncomfortable meal; none of us had slept well, and all were thinking of the same subject. Mrs. Jelf had evidently been crying, Jelf was impatient to be off, and both Captain Prendergast and myself felt ourselves to be in the painful position of outsiders who are involuntarily brought into a domestic trouble. Within twenty minutes after we had left the breakfast-table the dog-cart was brought round, and my friend and I were on the road to Clayborough.

"Tell you what it is, Langford," he said, as we sped along between the wintry hedges, "I do not much fancy to bring up Dwerrihouse's name at Clayborough. All the officials know that he is my wife's relation, and the subject just now is hardly a pleasant one. If you don't much mind, we will take the 11:10 to Blackwater. It's an important station, and we shall stand a far better chance of picking up information there than at Clayborough."

So we took the 11:10, which happened to be an express, and, arriving at Blackwater about a quarter before twelve, proceeded at once to prosecute our inquiry.

We began by asking for the station-master, a big, blunt, businesslike person, who at once averred that he knew Mr. John Dwerrihouse perfectly well, and that there was no director on the line whom he had seen and spoken to so frequently.

"He used to be down here two or three times a week about three months ago," said he, "when the new line was first set afoot; but since then, you know, gentlemen—"

He paused significantly.

Jelf flushed scarlet.

"Yes, yes," he said, hurriedly; "we know all about that. The point now to be ascertained is whether anything has been seen or heard of him lately."

"Not to my knowledge," replied the station-master.

"He is not known to have been down the line any time yesterday, for instance?"

The station-master shook his head.

"The East Anglian, sir," said he, "is about the last place where he would dare to show himself. Why, there isn't a station-master, there isn't a guard, there isn't a porter, who doesn't know Mr.

Dwerrihouse by sight as well as he knows his own face in the looking-glass, or who wouldn't telegraph for the police as soon as he had set eyes on him at any point along the line. Bless you, sir! There's been a standing order out against him ever since the 25th of September last."

"And yet," pursued my friend, "a gentleman who traveled down yesterday from London to Clayborough by the afternoon express testifies that he saw Mr. Dwerrihouse in the train, and that Mr. Dwerrihouse alighted at Blackwater station."

"Quite impossible, sir," replied the station-master, promptly.

"Why impossible?"

"Because there is no station along the line where he is so well known or where he would run so great a risk. It would be just running his head into the lion's mouth; he would have been mad to come nigh Blackwater station; and if he had come he would have been arrested before he left the platform."

"Can you tell me who took the Blackwater tickets of that train?"

"I can, sir. It was the guard, Benjamin Somers."

"And where can I find him?"

"You can find him, sir, by staying here, if you please, till one o'clock. He will be coming through with the up express from Crampton, which stays at Blackwater for ten minutes."

We waited for the up express, beguiling the time as best we could by strolling along the Blackwater road till we came almost to the outskirts of the town, from which the station was distant nearly a couple of miles. By one o'clock we were back again upon the platform and waiting for the train. It came punctually, and I at once recognized the ruddy-faced guard who had gone down with my train the evening before.

"The gentlemen want to ask you something about Mr. Dwerrihouse, Somers," said the station-master, by way of introduction.

The guard flashed a keen glance from my face to Jelf's and back again to mine.

"Mr. John Dwerrihouse, the late director?" said he, interrogatively.

"The same," replied my friend. "Should you know him if you saw him?"

"Anywhere, sir."

"'Do you know if he was in the 4:15 express yesterday afternoon?"

"He was not, sir."

"How can you answer so positively?"

"Because I looked into every carriage and saw every face in that train, and I could take my oath that Mr. Dwerrihouse was not in it. This gentleman was," he added, turning sharply upon me. "I don't know that I ever saw him before in my life, but I remember *his* face perfectly. You nearly missed taking your seat in time at this station, sir, and you got out at Clayborough."

"Quite true, guard," I replied; "but do you not also remember the face of the gentleman who traveled down in the same carriage with me as far as here?"

"It was my impression, sir, that you traveled down alone," said Somers, with a look of some surprise.

"By no means. I had a fellow-traveller as far as Blackwater, and it was in trying to restore him the cigar-case which he had dropped in the carriage that I so nearly let you go on without me."

"I remember your saying something about a cigar-case, certainly," replied the guard; "but—"

"You asked for my ticket just before we entered the station."

"I did, sir."

"Then you must have seen him. He sat in the corner next the very door to which you came."

"No, indeed; I saw no one."

I looked at Jelf. I began to think the guard was in the ex-director's confidence, and paid for his silence.

"If I had seen another traveler I should have asked for his ticket," added Somers. "Did you see me ask for his ticket, sir?"

"I observed that you did not ask for it, but he explained that by saying—" I hesitated. I feared I might be telling too much, and so broke off abruptly.

The guard and the station-master exchanged glances. The former looked impatiently at his watch.

"I am obliged to go on in four minutes more, sir," he said.

"One last question, then," interposed Jelf, with a sort of desperation. "If this gentleman's fellow-traveller had been Mr. John Dwerrihouse, and he had been sitting in the corner next the door by which you took the tickets, could you have failed to see and recognize him?"

"No, sir; it would have been quite impossible."

"And you are certain you did *not* see him?"

"As I said before, sir, I could take my oath I did not see him. And if it wasn't that I don't like to contradict a gentleman, I would say I could also take my oath that this gentleman was quite alone in the carriage the whole way from London to Clayborough."

"Why, sir," he added, dropping his voice so as to be inaudible to the station-master, who had been called away to speak to some person close by, "you expressly asked me to give you a compartment to yourself, and I did so. I locked you in, and you were so good as to give me something for myself."

"Yes; but Mr. Dwerrihouse had a key of his own."

"I never saw him, sir; I saw no one in that compartment but yourself. Beg pardon, sir; my time's up."

And with this the ruddy guard touched his cap and was gone. In another minute the heavy panting of the engine began afresh, and the train glided slowly out of the station.

We looked at each other for some moments in silence. I was the first to speak.

"Mr. Benjamin Somers knows more than he chooses to tell," I said.

"Humph! Do you think so?"

"It must be. He could not have come to the door without seeing him; it's impossible."

"There is one thing not impossible, my dear fellow."

17

"What is that?"

"That you may have fallen asleep and dreamed the whole thing."

"Could I dream of a branch line that I had never heard of? Could I dream of a hundred and one business details that had no kind of interest for me? Could I dream of the seventy-five thousand pounds?"

"Perhaps you might have seen or heard some vague account of the affair while you were abroad. It might have made no impression upon you at the time, and might have come back to you in your dreams, recalled perhaps by the mere names of the stations on the line."

"What about the fire in the chimney of the blue room—should I have heard of that during my journey?"

"Well, no; I admit there is a difficulty about that point."

"And what about the cigar-case?"

"Ay, by Jove! There is the cigar-case. That *is* a stubborn fact. Well, it's a mysterious affair, and it will need a better detective than myself, I fancy, to clear it up. I suppose we may as well go home."

A week had not gone by when I received a letter from the secretary of the East Anglian Railway Company, requesting the favour of my attendance at a special board meeting not then many days distant. No reasons were alleged and no apologies offered for this demand upon my time, but they had heard, it was clear, of my inquiries anent the missing director, and had a mind to put me through some sort of official examination upon the subject. Being still a guest at Dumbleton Hall, I had to go up to London for the purpose, and Jonathan Jelf accompanied me. I found the direction of the Great East Anglian line represented by a party of some twelve or fourteen gentlemen seated in solemn conclave round a huge green baize table, in a gloomy board-room adjoining the London terminus.

Being courteously received by the chairman (who at once began by saying that certain statements of mine respecting Mr. John Dwerrihouse had come to the knowledge of the direction, and that they in consequence desired to confer with me on those points), we were placed at the table, and the inquiry proceeded in due form.

I was first asked if I knew Mr. John Dwerrihouse, how long I had been acquainted with him, and whether I could identify him at sight. I was then asked when I had seen him last. To which I replied, "On the 4th of this present month, December, 1856." Then came the inquiry of where I had seen him on that fourth day of December; to which I replied that I met him in a first-class compartment of the 4:15 down express, that he got in just as the train was leaving the London terminus, and that he alighted at Blackwater station. The chairman then inquired whether I had held any communication with my fellow-traveller; whereupon I related, as nearly as I could remember it, the whole bulk and substance of Mr. John Dwerrihouse's diffuse information respecting the new branch line.

To all this the board listened with profound attention, while the chairman presided and the secretary took notes. I then produced the cigar-case. It was passed from hand to hand, and recognized by all. There was not a man present who did not remember that plain cigar-case with its silver monogram, or to whom it seemed anything less than entirely corroborative of my evidence. When at length I had told all that I had to tell, the chairman whispered something to the secretary; the secretary touched a silver hand-bell, and the guard, Benjamin Somers, was ushered into the room. He was then examined as carefully as myself. He declared that he knew Mr. John Dwerrihouse perfectly well, that he could not be mistaken in him, that he remembered going down with the 4:15 express on the afternoon in question, that he remembered me, and that, there being one or two empty first-class compartments on that especial afternoon, he had, in compliance with any request, placed me in a carriage by myself. He was positive that I remained alone in that compartment all the way from London to Clayborough. He was ready to take his oath that Mr. Dwerrihouse was neither in that carriage with me, nor in any compartment of that train. He remembered distinctly to have examined my ticket at Blackwater; was certain that there was no one else at that time in the carriage; could not have failed to observe a second person, if there had been one; had that second person been Mr. John Dwerrihouse, should have quietly double-locked the door of the carriage and have at once given information to the Blackwater station-master. So clear, so decisive, so ready, was Somers with this testimony, that the board looked fairly puzzled.

"You hear this person's statement, Mr. Langford," said the chairman. "It contradicts yours in every particular. What have you to say in reply?"

"I can only repeat what I said before. I am quite as positive of the truth of my own assertions as Mr. Somers can be of the truth of his."

"You say that Mr. Dwerrihouse alighted at Blackwater, and that he was in possession of a private key. Are you sure that he had not alighted by means of that key before the guard came round for the tickets?"

"I am quite positive that he did not leave the carriage till the train had fairly entered the station, and the other Blackwater passengers alighted. I even saw that he was met there by a friend."

"Indeed! Did you see that person distinctly?"

"Quite distinctly."

"Can you describe his appearance?"

"I think so. He was short and very slight, sandy-haired, with a bushy moustache and beard, and he wore a closely fitting suit of grey tweed. His age I should take to be about thirty-eight or forty."

"Did Mr. Dwerrihouse leave the station in this person's company?"

"I cannot tell. I saw them walking together down the platform, and then I saw them standing aside under a gas-jet, talking earnestly. After that I lost sight of them quite suddenly, and just then my train went on, and I with it."

The chairman and secretary conferred together in an undertone. The directors whispered to one another. One or two looked suspiciously at the guard. I could see that my evidence remained unshaken, and that, like myself, they suspected some complicity between the guard and the defaulter.

"How far did you conduct that 4:15 express on the day in question, Somers?" asked the chairman.

"All through, sir," replied the guard, "from London to Crampton."

"How was it that you were not relieved at Clayborough? I thought there was always a change of guards at Clayborough."

"There used to be, sir, till the new regulations came in force last midsummer, since when the guards in charge of express trains go the whole way through."

The chairman turned to the secretary.

"I think it would be as well," he said, "if we had the day-book to refer to upon this point."

Again the secretary touched the silver hand-bell, and desired the porter in attendance to summon Mr. Raikes. From a word or two dropped by another of the directors I gathered that Mr. Raikes was one of the under-secretaries.

He came, a small, slight, sandy-haired, keen-eyed man, with an eager, nervous manner, and a forest of light beard and moustache. He just showed himself at the door of the board room, and, being requested to bring a certain day-book from a certain shelf in a certain room, bowed and vanished.

He was there such a moment, and the surprise of seeing him was so great and sudden, that it was not till the door had closed upon him that I found voice to speak. He was no sooner gone, however, than I sprang to my feet.

"That person," I said, "is the same who met Mr. Dwerrihouse upon the platform at Blackwater!"

There was a general movement of surprise. The chairman looked grave and somewhat agitated.

"Take care, Mr. Langford," he said; "take care what you say."

"I am as positive of his identity as of my own."

"Do you consider the consequences of your words? Do you consider that you are bringing a charge of the gravest character against one of the company's servants?"

"I am willing to be put upon my oath, if necessary. The man who came to that door a minute since is the same whom I saw talking with Mr. Dwerrihouse on the Blackwater platform. Were he twenty times the company's servant, I could say neither more nor less."

The chairman turned again to the guard.

"Did you see Mr. Raikes in the train or on the platform?" he asked. Somers shook his head.

"I am confident Mr. Raikes was not in the train," he said, "and I certainly did not see him on the platform."

The chairman turned next to the secretary.

"Mr. Raikes is in your office, Mr. Hunter," he said. "Can you remember if he was absent on the 4th instant?"

"I do not think he was," replied the secretary, "but I am not prepared to speak positively. I have been away most afternoons myself lately, and Mr. Raikes might easily have absented himself if he had been disposed."

At this moment the under-secretary returned with the day-book under his arm.

"Be pleased to refer, Mr. Raikes," said the chairman, "to the entries of the 4th instant, and see what Benjamin Somers's duties were on that day."

Mr. Raikes threw open the cumbrous volume, and ran a practiced eye and finger down some three or four successive columns of entries. Stopping suddenly at the foot of a page, he then read aloud that Benjamin Somers had on that day conducted the 4:15 express from London to Crampton.

The chairman leaned forward in his seat, looked the under-secretary full in the face, and said, quite sharply and suddenly:

"Where were *you*, Mr. Raikes, on the same afternoon?"

"*I,* sir?"

"You, Mr. Raikes. Where were you on the afternoon and evening of the 4th of the present month?"

"Here, sir, in Mr. Hunter's office. Where else should I be?"

There was a dash of trepidation in the under-secretary's voice as he said this, but his look of surprise was natural enough.

"We have some reason for believing, Mr. Raikes, that you were absent that afternoon without leave. Was this the case?"

"Certainly not, sir. I have not had a day's holiday since September. Mr. Hunter will bear me out in this."

Mr. Hunter repeated what he had previously said on the subject, but added that the clerks in the adjoining office would be certain to know. Whereupon the senior clerk, a grave, middle-aged person in green glasses, was summoned and interrogated.

His testimony cleared the under-secretary at once. He declared that Mr. Raikes had in no instance, to his knowledge, been absent during office hours since his return from his annual holiday in September.

I was confounded. The chairman turned to me with a smile, in which a shade of covert annoyance was scarcely apparent.

"You hear, Mr. Langford?" he said.

"I hear, sir; but my conviction remains unshaken."

"I fear, Mr. Langford, that your convictions are very insufficiently based," replied the chairman, with a doubtful cough. "I fear that you dream dreams, and mistake them for actual occurrences. It is a dangerous habit of mind, and might lead to dangerous results. Mr. Raikes here would have found himself in an unpleasant position had he not proved so satisfactory an alibi."

I was about to reply, but he gave me no time.

"I think, gentlemen," he went on to say, addressing the board, "that we should be wasting time to push this inquiry further. Mr. Langford's evidence would seem to be of an equal value throughout. The testimony of Benjamin Somers disproves his first statement, and the testimony of the last witness disproves his second. I think we may conclude that Mr. Langford fell asleep in the train on the occasion of his journey to Clayborough, and dreamed an unusually vivid and circumstantial dream, of which, however, we have now heard quite enough."

There are few things more annoying than to find one's positive convictions met with incredulity. I could not help feeling impatience at the turn that affairs had taken. I was not proof against the civil sarcasm of the chairman's manner. Most intolerable of all, however, was the quiet smile lurking about the corners of Benjamin Somers's mouth, and the half-triumphant, half-malicious gleam in the eyes of the under-secretary. The man was evidently puzzled and somewhat alarmed. His looks seemed furtively to interrogate me. Who was I? What did I want? Why had I come here to do him an ill turn with his employers? What was it to me whether or not he was absent without leave?

Seeing all this, and perhaps more irritated by it than the thing deserved, I begged leave to detain the attention of the board for a moment longer. Jelf plucked me impatiently by the sleeve.

"Better let the thing drop," he whispered. "The chairman's right enough; you dreamed it, and the less said now the better."

I was not to be silenced, however, in this fashion. I had yet something to say, and I would say it. It was to this effect: that dreams were not usually productive of tangible results, and that I requested to know in what way the chairman conceived I had evolved from my dream so substantial and well-made a delusion as the cigar-case which I had had the honour to place before him at the commencement of our interview.

"The cigar-case, I admit, Mr. Langford," the chairman replied, "is a very strong point in your evidence. It is your *only* strong point, however, and there is just a possibility that we may all be misled by a mere accidental resemblance. Will you permit me to see the case again?"

"It is unlikely," I said, as I handed it to him, "that any other should bear precisely this monogram, and yet be in all other particulars exactly similar."

The chairman examined it for a moment in silence, and then passed it to Mr. Hunter. Mr. Hunter turned it over and over, and shook his head.

"This is no mere resemblance," he said. "It is John Dwerrihouse's cigar-case to a certainty. I remember it perfectly; I have seen it a hundred times."

"I believe I may say the same," added the chairman; "yet how account for the way in which Mr. Langford asserts that it came into his possession?'

"I can only repeat," I replied, "that I found it on the floor of the carriage after Mr. Dwerrihouse had alighted. It was in leaning out to look after him that I trod upon it, and it was in running after him for the purpose of restoring it that I saw, or believed I saw, Mr. Raikes standing aside with him in earnest conversation."

Again I felt Jonathan Jelf plucking at my sleeve.

"Look at Raikes," he whispered; "look at Raikes!"

I turned to where the under-secretary had been standing a moment before, and saw him, white as death, with lips trembling and livid, stealing towards the door.

To conceive a sudden, strange, and indefinite suspicion, to fling myself in his way, to take him by the shoulders as if he were a child, and turn his craven face, perforce, towards the board, were with me the work of an instant.

"Look at him!" I exclaimed. "Look at his face! I ask no better witness to the truth of my words."

The chairman's brow darkened.

"Mr. Raikes," he said, sternly, "if you know anything you had better speak."

Vainly trying to wrench himself from my grasp, the under-secretary stammered out an incoherent denial.

"Let me go," he said. "I know nothing—you have no right to detain me—let me go!"

"Did you, or did you not, meet Mr. John Dwerrihouse at Blackwater station? The charge brought against you is either true or false. If true, you will do well to throw yourself upon the mercy of the board and make full confession of all that you know."

The under-secretary wrung his hands in an agony of helpless terror.

"I was away!" he cried. "I was two hundred miles away at the time! I know nothing about it—I have nothing to confess—I am innocent—I call God to witness I am innocent!"

"Two hundred miles away!" echoed the chairman. "What do you mean?"

"I was in Devonshire. I had three weeks' leave of absence—I appeal to Mr. Hunter—Mr. Hunter knows I had three weeks' leave of absence! I was in Devonshire all the time; I can prove I was in Devonshire!"

Seeing him so abject, so incoherent, so wild with apprehension, the directors began to whisper gravely among themselves, while one got quietly up and called the porter to guard the door.

"What has your being in Devonshire to do with the matter?" said the chairman. "When were you in Devonshire?"

"Mr. Raikes took his leave in September," said the secretary, "About the time when Mr. Dwerrihouse disappeared."

"I never even heard that he had disappeared till I came back!"

"That must remain to be proved," said the chairman. "I shall at once put this matter in the hands of the police. In the meanwhile, Mr. Raikes, being myself a magistrate and used to deal with these cases, I advise you to offer no resistance, but to confess while confession may yet do you service. As for your accomplice—"

The frightened wretch fell upon his knees.

"I had no accomplice!" he cried. "Only have mercy upon me—only spare my life, and I will confess all! I didn't mean to harm him! I didn't mean to hurt a hair on his head! Only have mercy upon me, and let me go!"

The chairman rose in his place, pale and agitated. "Good heavens!" he exclaimed, "what horrible mystery is this? What does it mean?"

"As sure as there is a God in heaven," said Jonathan Jelf, "it means that murder has been done."

"No! no! no!" shrieked Raikes, still upon his knees, and cowering like a beaten hound. "Not murder! No jury that ever sat could bring it in murder. I thought I had only stunned him—I never meant to do more than stun him! Manslaughter—manslaughter—not murder!"

Overcome by the horror of this unexpected revelation, the chairman covered his face with his hand and for a moment or two remained silent.

"Miserable man," he said at length, "you have betrayed yourself."

"You made me confess! Your urged me to throw myself upon the mercy of the board!"

"You have confessed to a crime which no one suspected you of having committed," replied the chairman, "and which this board has no power either to punish or forgive. All that I can do for you is to advise you to submit to the law, to plead guilty, and to conceal nothing. When did you do this deed?"

The guilty man rose to his feet, and leaned heavily against the table. His answer came reluctantly, like the speech of one dreaming.

"On the 22nd of September!"

On the 22nd of September! I looked in Jonathan Jelf's face, and he in mine. I felt my own paling with a strange sense of wonder and dread. I saw his blanch suddenly, even to the lips.

"Merciful heaven!" he whispered. *"What was it, then, that you saw in the train?"*

※　　※　　※

What was it that I saw in the train? That question remains unanswered to this day. I have never been able to reply to it. I only know that it bore the living likeness of the murdered man, whose body had then been lying some ten weeks under a rough pile of branches and brambles and rotting leaves, at the bottom of a deserted chalk-pit about half-way between Blackwater and Mallingford. I know that it spoke and moved and looked as that man spoke and moved and looked in life; that I heard, or seemed to hear, things related which I could never otherwise have learned; that I was guided, as it were, by that vision on the platform to the identification of the murderer; and that, a passive instrument myself, I was destined, by means of these mysterious teachings, to bring about the ends of justice. For these things I have never been able to account.

As for that matter of the cigar-case, it proved, on inquiry, that the carriage in which I traveled down that afternoon to Clayborough had not been in use for several weeks, and was, in point of fact, the same in which poor John Dwerrihouse had performed his last journey. The case had doubtless been dropped by him, and had lain unnoticed till I found it.

Upon the details of the murder I have no need to dwell. Those who desire more ample particulars may find them, and the written confession of Augustus Raikes, in the files of *The Times* for 1856. Enough that the under-secretary, knowing the history of the new line, and following the negotiation step by step through all its stages, determined to waylay Mr. Dwerrihouse, rob him of the seventy-five thousand pounds, and escape to America with his booty.

In order to effect these ends he obtained leave of absence a few days before the time appointed for the payment of the money, secured his passage across the Atlantic in a steamer advertised to start on the 23rd, provided himself with a heavily loaded 'life-preserver', and went down to Blackwater to await the arrival of his victim. How he met him on the platform with a pretended message from the board, how he offered to conduct him by a short cut across the fields to Mallingford, how, having brought him to a lonely place, he struck him down with the life-preserver, and so killed him, and how, finding what he had done, he dragged the body to the verge of an out-of-the-way chalk-pit, and there flung it in and piled it over with branches and brambles, are facts still fresh in the memories of those who, like the connoisseurs in De Quincey's famous essay, regard murder as a fine art. Strangely enough, the murderer, having done his work, was afraid to leave the country. He declared that he had not intended to take the director's life, but only to stun and rob him; and that, finding the blow had killed, he dared not fly for fear of drawing down suspicion upon his own head. As a mere robber he would have been safe in the States, but as a murderer he would inevitably have been pursued and given up to justice. So he forfeited his passage, returned to the office as usual at the end of his leave, and locked up his ill-gotten thousands till a more convenient opportunity. In the meanwhile he had the satisfaction of finding that Mr. Dwerrihouse was universally believed to have absconded with the money, no one knew how or whither.

Whether he meant murder or not, however, Mr. Augustus Raikes paid the full penalty of his crime, and was hanged at the Old Bailey in the second week in January, 1857. Those who desire to make his further acquaintance may see him any day (admirably done in wax) in the Chamber of Horrors at Madame Tussaud's exhibition, in Baker Street. He is there to be found in the midst of a select society of ladies and gentlemen of atrocious memory, dressed in the close-cut tweed suit which he wore on the evening of the murder, and holding in his hand the identical life-preserver with which he committed it.

ON THE BRIGHTON ROAD

Richard Middleton

Slowly the sun had climbed up the hard white downs, till it broke with little of the mysterious ritual of dawn upon a sparkling world of snow. There had been a hard frost during the night, and the birds, who hopped about here and there with scant tolerance of life, left no trace of their passage on the silver pavements. In places the sheltered caverns of the hedges broke the monotony of the whiteness that had fallen upon the coloured earth, and overhead the sky melted from orange to deep blue, from deep blue to a blue so pale that it suggested a thin paper screen rather than illimitable space. Across the level fields there came a cold, silent wind which blew a fine dust of snow from the trees, but hardly stirred the crested hedges. Once above the skyline, the sun seemed to climb more quickly, and as it rose higher it began to give out a heat that blended with the keenness of the wind.

It may have been this strange alternation of heat and cold that disturbed the tramp in his dreams, for he struggled for a moment with the snow that covered him, like a man who finds himself twisted uncomfortably in the bed-clothes, and then sat up with staring, questioning eyes. "Lord! I thought I was in bed," he said to himself as he took in the vacant landscape, "and all the while I was out here." He stretched his limbs, and, rising carefully to his feet, shook the snow off his body. As he did so the wind set him shivering, and he knew that his bed had been warm.

"Come, I feel pretty fit," he thought. "I suppose I am lucky to wake at all in this. Or unlucky—it isn't much of a business to come back to." He looked up and saw the downs shining against the blue like the Alps on a picture-postcard. "That means another forty miles or so, I suppose," he continued grimly. "Lord knows what I did yesterday. Walked till I was done, and now I'm only about twelve miles from Brighton. Damn the snow, damn Brighton, damn everything!" The sun crept higher and higher, and he started walking patiently along the road with his back turned to the hills.

"Am I glad or sorry that it was only sleep that took me, glad or sorry, glad or sorry?" His thoughts seemed to arrange themselves in a metrical accompaniment to the steady thud of his footsteps, and he hardly sought an answer to his question. It was good enough to walk to.

Presently, when three milestones had loitered past, he overtook a boy who was stooping to light a cigarette. He wore no overcoat, and looked unspeakably fragile against the snow. "Are you on the road, guv'nor?" asked the boy huskily as he passed.

"I think I am," the tramp said.

"Oh! Then I'll come a bit of the way with you if you don't walk too fast. It's a bit lonesome walking this time of day." The tramp nodded his head, and the boy started limping along by his side.

"I'm eighteen," he said casually. "I bet you thought I was younger."

"Fifteen, I'd have said."

"You'd have backed a loser. Eighteen last August, and I've been on the road six years. I ran away from home five times when I was a little 'un, and the police took me back each time. Very good to me, the police was. Now I haven't got a home to run away from."

"Nor have I," the tramp said calmly.

"Oh, I can see what you are," the boy panted; "you're a gentleman come down. It's harder for you than for me." The tramp glanced at the limping, feeble figure and lessened his pace.

32

"I haven't been at it as long as you have," he admitted.

"No, I could tell that by the way you walk. You haven't got tired yet. Perhaps you expect something the other end?"

The tramp reflected for a moment. "I don't know," he said bitterly, "I'm always expecting things."

"You'll grow out of that," the boy commented. "It's warmer in London, but it's harder to come by grub. There isn't much in it really."

"Still, there's the chance of meeting somebody there who will understand—"

"Country people are better," the boy interrupted. "Last night I took a lease of a barn for nothing and slept with the cows, and this morning the farmer routed me out and gave me tea and toke because I was so little. Of course, I score there; but in London, soup on the Embankment at night, and all the rest of the time coppers moving you on."

"I dropped by the roadside last night and slept where I fell. It's a wonder I didn't die," the tramp said. The boy looked at him sharply.

"How do you know you didn't?" he said.

"I don't see it," the tramp said, after a pause.

"I tell you," the boy said hoarsely, "people like us can't get away from this sort of thing if we want to. Always hungry and thirsty and dog-tired and walking all the time. And yet if anyone offers me a nice home and work my stomach feels sick. Do I look strong? I know I'm little for my age, but I've been knocking about like this for six years, and do you think I'm not dead? I was drowned bathing at Margate, and I was killed by a gypsy with a spike; he knocked my head right in, and twice I was froze like you last night, and a motor cut me down on this very road, and yet I'm walking along here now, walking to London to walk away from it again, because I can't help it. Dead! I tell you we can't get away if we want to."

The boy broke off in a fit of coughing, and the tramp paused while he recovered.

"You'd better borrow my coat for a bit, Tommy," he said, "your cough's pretty bad."

"You go to hell!" the boy said fiercely, puffing at his cigarette; "I'm all right. I was telling you about the road. You haven't got down to it yet, but you'll find out presently. We're all dead, all of us who're on it, and we're all tired, yet somehow we can't leave it. There's nice smells in the summer, dust and hay and the wind smack in your face on a hot day; and it's nice waking up in the wet grass on a fine morning. I don't know, I don't know—" he lurched forward suddenly, and the tramp caught him in his arms.

"I'm sick," the boy whispered—"sick."

The tramp looked up and down the road, but he could see no houses or any sign of help. Yet even as he supported the boy doubtfully in the middle of the road a motor car suddenly flashed in the middle distance, and came smoothly through the snow.

"What's the trouble?" said the driver quietly as he pulled up. "I'm a doctor." He looked at the boy keenly and listened to his strained breathing.

"Pneumonia," he commented. "I'll give him a lift to the infirmary, and you, too, if you like."

The tramp thought of the workhouse and shook his head "I'd rather walk," he said.

The boy winked faintly as they lifted him into the car.

"I'll meet you beyond Reigate," he murmured to the tramp. "You'll see." And the car vanished along the white road.

All the morning the tramp splashed through the thawing snow, but at midday he begged some bread at a cottage door and crept into a lonely barn to eat it. It was warm in there, and after his meal he fell asleep among the hay. It was dark when he woke, and started trudging once more through the slushy roads.

Two miles beyond Reigate a figure, a fragile figure, slipped out of the darkness to meet him.

"On the road, guv'nor?" said a husky voice. "Then I'll come a bit of the way with you if you don't walk too fast. It's a bit lonesome walking this time of day."

"But the pneumonia!" cried the tramp, aghast.

"I died at Crawley this morning," said the boy.

THE MOONLIT ROAD

Ambrose Bierce

I. STATEMENT OF JOEL HETMAN, JR.

I am the most unfortunate of men. Rich, respected, fairly well educated and of sound health—with many other advantages usually valued by those having them and coveted by those who have them not—I sometimes think that I should be less unhappy if they had been denied me, for then the contrast between my outer and my inner life would not be continually demanding a painful attention. In the stress of privation and the need of effort I might sometimes forget the somber secret ever baffling the conjecture that it compels.

I am the only child of Joel and Julia Hetman. The one was a well-to-do country gentleman, the other a beautiful and accomplished woman to whom he was passionately attached with what I now know to have been a jealous and exacting devotion. The family home was a few miles from Nashville, Tennessee, a large, irregularly built dwelling of no particular order of architecture, a little way off the road, in a park of trees and shrubbery.

At the time of which I write I was nineteen years old, a student at Yale. One day I received a telegram from my father of such urgency that in compliance with its unexplained demand I left at once for home. At the railway station in Nashville a distant relative awaited me to apprise me of the reason for my recall: my mother had been barbarously murdered—why and by whom none could conjecture, but the circumstances were these:

My father had gone to Nashville, intending to return the next afternoon. Something prevented his accomplishing the business in hand, so he returned on the same night, arriving just before the dawn. In his testimony before the coroner he explained that having no latchkey and not caring to disturb the sleeping servants, he had, with no clearly defined intention, gone round to the rear of the house. As he turned an angle of the building, he heard a sound as of a door gently closed, and saw in the darkness, indistinctly, the figure of a man, which instantly disappeared among the trees of the lawn. A hasty pursuit and brief search of the grounds in the belief that the trespasser was someone secretly visiting a servant proving fruitless, he entered at the unlocked door and mounted the stairs to my mother's chamber. Its door was open, and stepping into black darkness he fell headlong over some heavy object on the floor. I may spare myself the details; it was my poor mother, dead of strangulation by human hands!

Nothing had been taken from the house, the servants had heard no sound, and excepting those terrible fingermarks upon the dead woman's throat—dear God! That I might forget them!—no trace of the assassin was ever found.

I gave up my studies and remained with my father, who, naturally, was greatly changed. Always of a sedate, taciturn disposition, he now fell into a so deep dejection that nothing could hold his attention, yet anything—a footfall, the sudden closing of a door—aroused in him a fitful interest; one might have called it an apprehension. At any small surprise of the senses he would start visibly and sometimes turn pale, then relapse into a melancholy apathy deeper than before. I suppose he was what is called a 'nervous wreck'. As to me, I was younger then than now—there is much in that. Youth is Gilead, in which is balm for every wound. Ah, that I might again dwell in that enchanted land! Unacquainted with grief, I knew not how to appraise my bereavement; I could not rightly estimate the strength of the stroke.

One night, a few months after the dreadful event, my father and I walked home from the city. The full moon was about three hours above the eastern horizon; the entire countryside had the solemn stillness of a summer night; our footfalls and the ceaseless song of the katydids were the only sound, aloof. Black shadows of bordering trees lay athwart the road, which, in the short reaches between, gleamed a ghostly white. As we approached the gate to our dwelling, whose front was in shadow, and in which no light shone, my father suddenly stopped and clutched my arm, saying, hardly above his breath:

"God! God! What is that?"

"I hear nothing," I replied.

"But see—see!" he said, pointing along the road, directly ahead.

I said: "Nothing is there, Come, Father, let us go in—you are ill."

He had released my arm and was standing rigid and motionless in the centre of the illuminated roadway, staring like one bereft of sense. His face in the moonlight showed a pallor and fixity inexpressibly distressing. I pulled gently at his sleeve, but he had forgotten my existence. Presently he began to retire backward, step by step, never for an instant removing his eyes from what he saw, or thought he saw. I turned half round to follow, but stood irresolute. I do not recall any feeling of fear, unless a sudden chill was its physical manifestation. It seemed as if an icy wind had touched my face and enfolded my body from head to foot; I could feel the stir of it in my hair.

At that moment my attention was drawn to a light that suddenly streamed from an upper window of the house: one of the servants, awakened by what mysterious premonition of evil who can say, and in obedience to an impulse that she was never able to name, had lit a lamp. When I turned to look for my father he was gone, and in all the years that have passed no whisper of his fate has come across the borderland of conjecture from the realm of the unknown.

※　※　※

II. STATEMENT OF CASPAR GRATTAN

Today I am said to live; tomorrow, here in this room, will lie a sense-less shape of clay that all too long was I. If any one lift the cloth from the face of that unpleasant thing it will be in gratification of a mere morbid curiosity. Some, doubtless, will go further and inquire, "Who was he?" In this writing I supply the only answer that I am able to make—Caspar Grattan. Surely, that should be enough. The name has served my small need for more than twenty years of a life of unknown length. True, I gave it to myself, but lacking another I had the right. In this world one must have a name; it prevents confusion, even when it does not establish identity. Some, though, are known by numbers, which also seem inadequate distinctions.

One day, for illustration, I was passing along a street of a city, far from here, when I met two men in uniform, one of whom, half pausing and looking curiously into my face, said to his companion, "That man looks like 767." Something in the number seemed familiar and hor-rible. Moved by an uncontrollable impulse, I sprang into a side street and ran until I fell exhausted in a country lane.

I have never forgotten that number, and always it comes to memory attended by gibbering obscenity, peals of joyless laughter, the clang of iron doors. So I say a name, even if self-bestowed, is better than a number. In the register of the potter's field I shall soon have both. What wealth!

Of him who shall find this paper I must beg a little consideration. It is not the history of my life; the knowledge to write that is denied me. This is only a record of broken and apparently unrelated memo-ries, some of them as distinct and sequent as brilliant beads upon a thread, others remote and strange, having the character of crimson dreams with interspaces blank and black—witch-fires glowing still and red in a great desolation.

Standing upon the shore of eternity, I turn for a last look landward over the course by which I came. There are twenty years of footprints fairly distinct, the impressions of bleeding feet. They lead through poverty and pain, devious and unsure, as of one staggering beneath a burden—

"Remote, unfriended, melancholy, slow."

Ah, the poet's prophecy of Me—how admirable, how dreadfully admirable!

Backward beyond the beginning of this *via dolorosa*—this epic of suffering with episodes of sin—I see nothing clearly; it comes out of a cloud. I know that it spans only twenty years, yet I am an old man.

One does not remember one's birth—one has to be told. But with me it was different; life came to me full-handed and dowered me with all my faculties and powers. Of a previous existence I know no more than others, for all have stammering intimations that may be memories and may be dreams. I know only that my first consciousness was of maturity in body and mind—a consciousness accepted without surprise or conjecture. I merely found myself walking in a forest, half-clad, footsore, unutterably weary and hungry. Seeing a farmhouse, I approached and asked for food, which was given me by one who inquired my name. I did not know, yet knew that all had names. Greatly embarrassed, I retreated, and night coming on, lay down in the forest and slept.

The next day I entered a large town which I shall not name. Nor shall I recount further incidents of the life that is now to end—a life of wandering, always and everywhere haunted by an overmastering sense of crime in punishment of wrong and of terror in punishment of crime. Let me see if I can reduce it to narrative.

I seem once to have lived near a great city, a prosperous planter, married to a woman whom I loved and distrusted. We had, it sometimes seems, one child, a youth of brilliant parts and promise. He is at all times a vague figure, never clearly drawn, frequently altogether out of the picture.

One luckless evening it occurred to me to test my wife's fidelity in a vulgar, commonplace way familiar to every one who has acquaintance with the literature of fact and fiction. I went to the city, telling my wife that I should be absent until the following afternoon. But I returned before daybreak and went to the rear of the house, purposing to enter by a door with which I had secretly so tampered that it would seem to lock, yet not actually fasten. As I approached it, I heard it gently open and close, and saw a man steal away into the darkness. With murder in my heart, I sprang after him, but he had vanished without even the bad luck of identification. Sometimes now I cannot even persuade myself that it was a human being.

Crazed with jealousy and rage, blind and bestial with all the elemental passions of insulted manhood, I entered the house and sprang up the stairs to the door of my wife's chamber. It was closed, but having tampered with its lock also, I easily entered, and despite the black darkness soon stood by the side of her bed. My groping hands told me that although disarranged it was unoccupied.

"She is below," I thought, "and terrified by my entrance has evaded me in the darkness of the hall."

With the purpose of seeking her I turned to leave the room, but took a wrong direction—the right one! My foot struck her, cowering in a corner of the room. Instantly my hands were at her throat, stifling a shriek, my knees were upon her struggling body; and there in the darkness, without a word of accusation or reproach, I strangled her till she died!

There ends the dream. I have related it in the past tense, but the present would be the fitter form, for again and again the somber tragedy re-enacts itself in my consciousness—over and over I lay the plan, I suffer the confirmation, I redress the wrong. Then all is blank; and afterward the rains beat against the grimy window-panes, or the snows fall upon my scant attire, the wheels rattle in the squalid streets where my life lies in poverty and mean employment. If there is ever sunshine I do not recall it; if there are birds they do not sing.

There is another dream, another vision of the night. I stand among the shadows in a moonlit road. I am aware of another presence, but whose I cannot rightly determine. In the shadows of a great dwelling I catch the gleam of white garments; then the figure of a woman confronts me in the road—my murdered wife! There is death in the face; there are marks upon the throat. The eyes are fixed on mine with an infinite gravity which is not reproach, nor hate, nor menace, nor anything less terrible than recognition. Before this awful apparition I retreat in terror—a terror that is upon me as I write. I can no longer rightly shape the words. See! They—

Now I am calm, but truly there is no more to tell: The incident ends where it began—in darkness and in doubt.

Yes, I am again in control of myself: "the captain of my soul." But that is not respite; it is another stage and phase of expiation. My penance, constant in degree, is mutable in kind: one of its variants is tranquility. After all, it is only a life-sentence. "To Hell for life"—that is a foolish penalty: the culprit chooses the duration of his punishment. Today my term expires.

To each and all, the peace that was not mine.

✳ ✳ ✳

III. STATEMENT OF THE LATE JULIA HETMAN, THROUGH THE MEDIUM BAYROLLES

I had retired early and fallen almost immediately into a peaceful sleep, from which I awoke with that indefinable sense of peril which is, I think, a common experience in that other, earlier life. Of its unmeaning character, too, I was entirely persuaded, yet that did not banish it. My husband, Joel Hetman, was away from home; the servants slept in another part of the house. But these were familiar conditions; they had never before distressed me. Nevertheless, the strange terror grew so insupportable that conquering my reluctance to move I sat up and lit the lamp at my bedside. Contrary to my expectation this gave me no relief; the light seemed rather an added danger, for I reflected that it would shine out under the door, disclosing my presence to whatever evil thing might lurk outside. You that are still in the flesh, subject to horrors of the imagination, think what a monstrous fear that must be which seeks in darkness security from malevolent existences of the night. That is to spring to close quarters with an unseen enemy—the strategy of despair!

Extinguishing the lamp I pulled the bedclothing about my head and lay trembling and silent, unable to shriek, forgetful to pray. In this pitiable state I must have lain for what you call hours—with us there are no hours, there is no time.

At last it came—a soft, irregular sound of footfalls on the stairs! They were slow, hesitant, uncertain, as of something that did not see its way; to my disordered reason all the more terrifying for that, as the approach of some blind and mindless malevolence to which there is no appeal. I even thought that I must have left the hall lamp burning and the groping of this creature proved it a monster of the night. This was foolish and inconsistent with my previous dread of the light, but what would you have? Fear has no brains; it is an idiot. The dismal witness that it bears and the cowardly counsel that it whispers are unrelated. We know this well, we who have passed into the Realm of Terror, who skulk in eternal dusk among the scenes of our former lives, invisible even to ourselves, and one another, yet hiding forlorn in lonely places; yearning for speech with our loved ones, yet dumb, and as fearful of them as they of us. Sometimes the disability is removed, the law suspended: by the deathless power of love or hate we break the spell—we are seen by those whom we would warn, console, or punish. What form we seem to them to bear we know not; we know only that we terrify even those whom we most wish to comfort, and from whom we most crave tenderness and sympathy.

Forgive, I pray you, this inconsequent digression by what was once a woman. You who consult us in this imperfect way—you do not understand. You ask foolish questions about things unknown and things forbidden. Much that we know and could impart in our speech is meaningless in yours. We must communicate with you through a stammering intelligence in that small fraction of our language that you yourselves can speak. You think that we are of another world. No, we have knowledge of no world but yours, though for us it holds no sunlight, no warmth, no music, no laughter, no song of birds, nor any companionship. O God! What a thing it is to be a ghost, cowering and shivering in an altered world, a prey to apprehension and despair!

No, I did not die of fright: the Thing turned and went away. I heard it go down the stairs, hurriedly, I thought, as if itself in sudden fear. Then I rose to call for help. Hardly had my shaking hand found the door-knob when—merciful heaven!—I heard it returning. Its footfalls as it remounted the stairs were rapid, heavy and loud; they shook the house. I fled to an angle of the wall and crouched upon the floor. I tried to pray. I tried to call the name of my dear husband. Then I heard the door thrown open. There was an interval of unconsciousness, and when I revived I felt a strangling clutch upon my throat—felt my arms feebly beating against something that bore me backward—felt my tongue thrusting itself from between my teeth! And then I passed into this life.

No, I have no knowledge of what it was. The sum of what we knew at death is the measure of what we know afterward of all that went before. Of this existence we know many things, but no new light falls upon any page of that; in memory is written all of it that we can read. Here are no heights of truth overlooking the confused landscape of that dubitable domain. We still dwell in the Valley of the Shadow, lurk in its desolate places, peering from brambles and thickets at its mad, malign inhabitants. How should we have new knowledge of that fading past?

What I am about to relate happened on a night. We know when it is night, for then you retire to your houses and we can venture from our places of concealment to move unafraid about our old homes, to look in at the windows, even to enter and gaze upon your faces as you sleep. I had lingered long near the dwelling where I had been so cruelly changed to what I am, as we do while any that we love or hate remain. Vainly I had sought some method of manifestation, some way to make my continued existence and my great love and poignant pity understood by my husband and son. Always if they slept they would wake, or if in my desperation I dared approach them when they were awake, would turn toward me the terrible eyes of the living, frightening me by the glances that I sought from the purpose that I held.

On this night I had searched for them without success, fearing to find them; they were nowhere in the house, nor about the moonlit lawn. For, although the sun is lost to us for ever, the moon, full-orbed or slender, remains to us. Sometimes it shines by night, sometimes by day, but always it rises and sets, as in that other life.

I left the lawn and moved in the white light and silence along the road, aimless and sorrowing. Suddenly I heard the voice of my poor husband in exclamations of astonishment, with that of my son in reassurance and dissuasion; and there by the shadow of a group of trees they stood—near, so near! Their faces were toward me, the eyes of the elder man fixed upon mine. He saw me—at last, at last, he saw me! In the consciousness of that, my terror fled as a cruel dream. The death-spell was broken: Love had conquered Law! Mad with exultation I shouted—I *must* have shouted, "He sees, he sees: he will understand!" Then, controlling myself, I moved forward, smiling and consciously beautiful, to offer myself to his arms, to comfort him with endearments, and, with my son's hand in mine, to speak words that should restore the broken bonds between the living and the dead.

Alas! Alas! His face went white with fear, his eyes were as those of a hunted animal. He backed away from me, as I advanced, and at last turned and fled into the wood—whither it is not given to me to know.

To my poor boy, left doubly desolate, I have never been able to impart a sense of my presence. Soon he, too, must pass to this Life Invisible and be lost to me for ever.

THE WHITTAKERS GHOST

G.B.S.

The following ghost story has been told me, word for word, by an eye-witness, and is authenticated by persons of recognized position.

—G.B.S.

My name is Anna Ducane, and I had two sisters, Hélène and Louise. About twenty years ago we lived with our parents on our Canadian farm in the neighbourhood of Montreal, that is to say, within about thirty miles of that city. Our life was a very quiet, uneventful one. From time to time we visited among our neighbours in the country, or spent a few days, shopping and sight-seeing, "in town" with our parents; but our excitements were simple and few, and a brood of ducks would serve us for conversation for a week. It is needful to say we enjoyed perfect health, and were all three of us strong, good-natured, and useful girls, who could turn our hands to most household employments, and a good many outdoor jobs as well—having a rather supercilious contempt of affectation and what we called "fine-ladyism."

All this I mention at the outset, because I wish to show that we were women to whom anything like nerves was unknown. At the time I speak of, Hélène and I, who are twins, were nearly two-and-twenty, and Louise was about nineteen.

It was in the end of August that we received an unexpected and delightful invitation to spend some weeks in Montreal, at Whittakers, the house of an old Major Whittaker, who, with his two sisters, resided on a very pretty property on the outskirts of the town. Lucy Whittaker, their niece, had been at school with us in Hamilton, and her return from a visit to Europe was the reason for our invitation to her uncle's house. At first our mother declared she could not think of sending all three of us to stop in a town house; but Lucy wrote and insisted that none should remain behind. There was plenty of space, if we did not mind sharing one big room, like the ward of a hospital, which she was busy preparing for us.

So one evening early in September we found ourselves welcomed to Whittakers by Lucy, looking prettier than ever in a wonderful Parisian dress, the like of which none of us had ever seen. It quite cast into the shade all the elaborate preparations, the flouncings, frillings, and ironings, which had engrossed us all for the last fortnight.

But Lucy was just her own self, despite her smart new wardrobe, and she and Louise became at once as inseparable as they had been at school, while Hélène and I fell straightway in love with the old Miss Whittakers, Miss Sara and Miss Hesba. They were different from any old ladies we had ever known; more refined in looks and manners than our country neighbours, and accomplished in many curious arts which now scarcely survive, such as tambour work, and painting on velvet, and playing the harp. We wanted at once to learn everything they could teach us, and thought that our three weeks' visit would never suffice if we did not begin immediately to be initiated into these mysteries, which were to render us of fresh importance and attractiveness when we should return home.

So we threw ourselves into all sorts of employments with a will, and the days flew by rapidly. Lucy and Louise were generally out of doors together, either in the big, old-fashioned garden behind the house, where they chattered and picked fruit and whispered their secrets by the hour, or in the town itself; sight-seeing and promenading under the protection of a young relation of our hosts', Harry Leroy, who was, like ourselves, visiting Whittakers for the first time.

A word here about Major Whittaker, who, though not wanting in the hospitality and geniality of a host, somehow was very little seen by his visitors: except at eight o'clock, morning and evening, when he regularly read prayers to his assembled household, and at the two meals that followed. He never appeared downstairs, but spent his time in a little study over the porch, where, if the door stood accidentally open, the passer-by might see him hard at work on his life's object, a Harmony of the Four Gospels, over which he had been poring for years. I never knew anything of his past history—how he came by his military title, when he had left the army, or what had given him the very strong and peculiar religious opinions which he held. These opinions were enforced upon the household morning and evening at family prayers, when the Major's long extempore petitions sometimes kept us half an hour at a time upon our knees.

A fortnight of our time at Whittakers had passed very pleasantly, and we were beginning to think, with reluctance, that in another week or so we must be returning home. I mentioned this one afternoon to Miss Hesba as we sat at our painting. She scouted the idea at once, declaring that as long as we cared to stay, and the fine weather continued, we must not think of leaving them.

But even as she spoke, Miss Sara got up and looked anxiously out of the window, for it seemed as if the splendid weather was about to break. Clouds had been creeping up since the morning, and a wet-sounding, whistling wind was beginning to haunt the chimneys, and to rattle the red leaves of the maples.

The two younger girls, and Harry Leroy, came in from the garden, and, to our surprise, old Major Whittaker himself appeared from the regions above, shivering as if with cold. "Shut the windows," he said, "and don't go out any more this evening." For we generally spent the hour before and after prayers and supper in the verandah.

We did not heed his words particularly at the time, and soon he went away to his study again.

We spent the early part of the evening pleasantly enough, part-singing at the piano. Then came prayers and supper as usual, and then, as we re-crossed the hall from the dining-room, some one of us suggested that we should go out upon the steps of the front door and watch the storm which was rapidly coming up, and the clouds which dashed across the full moon, hanging like a red globe over the St. Lawrence.

I do not think either host or hostesses saw us, and we had quite forgotten the Major's counsel that we should not go out again that evening. We left the hall door ajar, and stood out upon the gravel in front of the house, we four girls and young Mr. Leroy.

In order that the following circumstances may be clearly understood, I must explain a little the topography of Whittakers. It was a long, two-storeyed house, standing a little back from the road which ran into Montreal, and its entrance was not unlike that of many modern English villas. It had two wooden gates, both opening upon the road, which always stood wide, and these were connected by a semicircular sweep of gravel in front of the house, edged with laurels and shrubs. The big garden, orchard, and fields were all behind the house, which in front approached within about fifty yards of the highway. The hall door of Whittakers stood always open during our visit—it was two leaves of battered, weather-stained oak, and on its outside were the marks whence two large knockers had evidently been removed. We had remarked their removal before, and Mr. Leroy had said he supposed the rattle of the knockers had interfered with the Harmony of the Four Gospels in the study above.

As we stood upon the gravel walk we all five distinctly heard the noise of a heavy carriage approaching from the town along the road in front of us, apparently having two, or even four horses, and driven at a great pace. We could not see it for the laurels which intervened between us and the road on either side, but we knew it was rapidly drawing near the gate. Its approach interested us, for it was now nearly ten o'clock, and a visitor at such an hour was unheard of. But if not coming to Whittakers, whither could the carriage be going? For it was the last house of any importance for miles along that way.

We stepped back into the doorway, and found ourselves suddenly caught and dragged in by old Major Whittaker, who, trembling with excitement, and with his queer flowered dressing-gown fluttering round him, as though he had been just aroused from bed, somehow whirled us all into the hall, and banged-to the great leaves of the door with a noise that made the house shake.

But above all the rattle of chains and bars—for the old man was busy securing the door as if for a siege—we heard the approach of the carriage, which, as we expected, turned in at the gate and drew up, with a crack of the whip and a splutter of gravel when the horses were sharply pulled in at the hall steps.

We all five heard it; and so, I am sure, did Major Whittaker and his sisters, who had also come out into the hall. Not one of us dared say anything, for we were awed by the intensity of excitement which characterized every movement of our host.

A moment afterwards the old door was almost battered in by a furious assault upon it with the iron knocker, and, looking in each other's faces, we all recollected simultaneously that *there was no knocker there.* "Let us pray," said Major Whittaker's voice above the noise. We all knelt down where we were, while he poured forth a long, rambling prayer, in which he entreated to be delivered from some evil and ghostly influence; but we were all too frightened and excited to listen much. Lucy and Louise were both crying and receiving an undercurrent of consolation from Harry Leroy, while our host prayed on in a high, unnatural tone. The hammering on the front door continued at intervals.

However, these grew longer and longer, and at last the sound ceased altogether. Not so the prayers, for though I was longing to get away to our room, which also looked to the front, to see if the carriage remained at the door, the old Major kept us quite half an hour, without any reference to the usual family worship, which had been punctually performed as usual two hours before.

When at last we retired to our room our first rush, of course, was to the window, but all that was to be seen was the moon riding high in the sky, and the storm clouds sweeping past—no trace of a carriage or its occupants anywhere. Of course we lay awake till morning, discussing the extraordinary event, and Lucy came creeping in to sleep with Louise, too frightened to remain by herself.

I ought to explain that she was almost as much a stranger to Whittakers as we were, having been lately left an orphan to the charge of her uncle, who had at first sent her on a tour with some friends to Europe. Consequently the bombardment of the house by the ghost and the spectre knocker (for we were convinced that what we had heard was supernatural) was as terrible to her as to us.

The next morning it seemed as if all the pleasure of our visit was gone, and—a straw will show which way the wind blows—on some reference being made to our return home, I was struck, but not altogether astonished, to find that no opposition was made to our carrying out our intention, even by Miss Hesba. The two old ladies were evidently miserable and ill-at-ease about something, and though no allusion was made to the occurrence of the night before, it was in all our minds, and rose up between us and all enjoyment.

Our pleasant morning employments were not resumed, for the Misses Whittaker were closeted upstairs with their brother, and we younger ones preferred keeping all together in the garden, where the sun shone and we seemed to be out of the supernatural influence which invested the gloomy old place. Harry Leroy confided to us that he had investigated the front of the house, and that traces of the wheels of a heavy vehicle and the hoof-marks of a pair of horses were distinctly visible upon the gravel!

By-and-by, when we came in to early dinner, Miss Sara took me aside, and, twisting her watch-guard about in her hands from nervousness, explained that she and her brother thought perhaps it would be better, "under the unfortunate circumstances," that our visit to Whittakers should end as soon as possible. Without actually saying so, she gave me to understand that the annoyance of the previous evening was not by any means over.

I was glad of her plain speaking, for though I did not personally mind the "ghost," as we had already taken to call this disturbing influence, among ourselves, I could not bear the change which had so suddenly fallen upon the previously cheerful household. Besides, I dreaded its effect upon Louise, who was of a very excitable temperament. So I gladly arranged with Miss Sara to have a note ready for my mother, to be sent that afternoon by a special messenger, to prepare her for our unexpected return home, as soon as four disengaged places could be obtained in the stage, which in those days was the means of communication between Montreal and our nearest village. Four places—for I persuaded Miss Whittaker to let us take Lucy with us. I could not bear the idea of leaving the girl companionless, though her aunt said, with a sigh: "Lucy is one of us, and must learn to bear this as we do!"

That night we again all slept together in the big front bedroom. I must mention that I had not told any of the others of Miss Sara's hint that possibly the ghost was not yet laid to rest, for, I thought, we had talked over the matter quite enough. So I incited Lucy to tell us some of her European experiences, and we all went to sleep in the middle of her description of Cologne Cathedral.

We must have slept about two hours or so, when I was awakened by a sharp pinch from Hélène, and called out, "What are you doing?" before I opened my eyes. Her answer, "Hush! It is here in the room!" woke me up thoroughly. I saw her face looking, pale in the dim light, towards the window, a large bow, which occupied the whole end of the room to the right hand of our bed. Louise and Lucy slept in another bed on our left, and consequently farther from the window.

I followed the direction of her looks with my eyes, but without stirring, for her words had given me an uncomfortable kind of thrill. There, behind the big dressing-table, which stood in the centre of the bow-window, but well into the room, leaving a considerable space clear behind it, I saw a tall veiled figure, which something told me at once was not human. It was muffled from head to foot in trailing, grey garments, and something was wrapped about its head, but from its long, swinging strides—for it paced to and fro in the little enclosure between window and table—I guessed it to be a male figure, though the garments were womanly, or perhaps monkish. At first it did not appear to notice us, but presently it began somewhat to slacken its regular walk, and turning its hooded head towards us, seemed to be intently regarding us. My hand was tightly locked in Hélène's, and I know the same thought was in both our minds: "What if it comes into the open part of the room, and near either of the beds?"

Suddenly a little gasp from the other bed told us that the other girls were also awake (it was too dark to see their faces), and Louise's voice broke the intense silence. In that Name to which all powers must yield, she commanded it to be gone.

This from Louise, the most timid and nervous of us all! I forgot the ghost in my amazement, and turned to look at her, as she sat up in bed, a trembling little white figure.

A moment after, when I looked to the window, the ghost *was* gone. Louise had exorcized it. She was crying bitterly now, and shaking all over. Hélène and I jumped up and crowded round her, patting and soothing her until her sobbing ceased.

"I don't know what put it into my head to do it, I'm sure," she explained; "but I had been looking at the dreadful thing so long: long before any of you woke—and at last I felt I should go mad if I did not speak. I could see his eyes quite plainly, like two lamps, looking me through and through, and I knew it was I who must speak to him."

By-and-by, when we were all a little calmer, I told the girls of Miss Sara's confidence to me, and also of our arrangement to return home as soon as our journey could be settled. Lucy cried out that she could not be left behind, and hugged me when I said that, of course, she was to go with us, for as long as she liked to stay. "I can never come back to this dreadful house," she declared; and would take no comfort from the suggestion, which I had picked up from Miss Sara's conversation, that long intervals, sometimes of years, elapsed between these ghostly visitations.

So the night wore away, and with earliest dawn we were all glad to rise, and get through some of our packing, so as to shorten as much as possible our stay in the haunted bed-chamber.

After breakfast, Hélène and I took Miss Whittaker aside, and told her the events of the night. They impressed, but evidently did not astonish her, and her only question when we finished was, "Did the figure attempt to approach any of you?"

"No," I answered; "though Louise declares its face and burning eyes were distinctly turned upon her."

Our hostess sighed, but made no comment, and my twin-sister and I went away upstairs to finish the preparations for our departure, for it was decided we were to leave Whittakers that day at noon. These were soon completed, and Hélène and I were about to descend to spend the last hour or two with the old ladies, when Lucy and Louise, who had been round the garden for the last time, rushed up the oak staircase and into the room, and I saw in a moment, by their disordered looks, that they had seen something more.

Yes, the ghost had again appeared, and the girls were still shaking with nervousness when they told their story.

"It was in the box-walk," said Louise,"and Mr. Leroy was with us. Lucy went away for a few minutes, just as we reached the end, to pick herself some nuts in the shrubbery, and Mr. Leroy began telling me how sorry he was our party was to be broken up, and might he come and see us at home. I said "of course," and just then we felt something close behind us (we were standing side-by-side), and, thinking it was Lucy, we turned and saw the horrible figure at our elbow, laying a hand upon the arm of each of us! An instant afterwards it was gone, but Lucy, who was coming up from the other end of the walk, had also plainly seen it, its back being towards her; so it was no imagination."

No, it was no imagination. I told the whole story to Miss Whittaker before we left the house. This time the poor old lady broke down completely, and, wringing her hands, accused herself of bringing ruin upon two young lives. Then, seeing my astonishment, she was obliged to explain that it was a sign, too fatally proved to be true, of approaching death, when the veiled figure laid his hand upon any person to whom he chose to show himself. Her words sank like lead into my heart.

There is little more to tell.

Our little Louise fell ill of a strange low fever, soon after our return to the farm, and before Christmas she had left us for ever. Harry Leroy never paid his contemplated visit, for he, too, died, by the accidental discharge of his gun, a few weeks after we parted from him. The only happy consequence of our stay at Whittakers was Lucy's marriage to a neighbour of ours, who wedded her from our house, and by-and-by took her south, so that for some time we lost sight of her, and heard no news of her relations. When we met again she told us her uncle had died quietly one evening, after completing his life's work—the Harmony of the Four Gospels. Her aunts had shut up the house, which was their own, and had gone to live beyond Hamilton. I never saw them again; nor did I see much more of Lucy, for our own family removed at this time to England, and our Canadian ties were broken.

Whether the curse still lies upon the old house, or whether the house itself still stands, I know not, but the foregoing is a true and unexaggerated account of what we underwent there.

THE LEADEN RING

S. Baring-Gould

"It is not possible, Julia. I cannot conceive how the idea of attending the county ball can have entered your head after what has happened. Poor young Hattersley's dreadful death suffices to stop that."

"But, Aunt, Mr. Hattersley is no relation of ours."

"No relation—but you know that the poor fellow would not have shot himself if it had not been for you."

"Oh, Aunt Elizabeth, how can you say so, when the verdict was that he committed suicide when in an unsound condition of mind? How could I help his blowing out his brains, when those brains were deranged?"

"Julia, do not talk like this. If he did go off his head, it was you who upset him by first drawing him on, leading him to believe that you liked him, and then throwing him over as soon as the Hon. James Lawlor appeared on the *tapis*. Consider: what will people say if you go to the assembly?"

"What will they say if I do not go? They will immediately set it down to my caring deeply for James Hattersley, and they will think that there was some sort of engagement."

"They are not likely to suppose that. But really, Julia, you were for a while all smiles and encouragement. Tell me, now, did Mr. Hattersley propose to you?"

"Well—yes, he did, and I refused him."

"And then he went and shot himself in despair. Julia, you cannot with any face go to the ball."

"Nobody knows that he proposed. And precisely because I do go everyone will conclude that he did not propose. I do not wish it to be supposed that he did."

"His family, of course, must have been aware. They will see your name among those present at the assembly."

"Aunt, they are in too great trouble to look at the paper to see who were at the dance."

"His terrible death lies at your door. How you can have the heart, Julia . . ."

"I don't see it. Of course, I feel it. I am awfully sorry, and awfully sorry for his father, the admiral. I cannot bring him to life again. I wish that when I rejected him he had gone and done as did Joe Pomeroy, marry one of his landlady's daughters."

"There, Julia, is another of your delinquencies. You lured on young Pomeroy till he proposed, then you refused him, and in a fit of vexation and mortified vanity he married a girl greatly beneath him in social position. If the ménage proves a failure you will have it on your conscience that you have wrecked his life and perhaps hers as well."

"I cannot throw myself away as a charity to save this man or that from doing a foolish thing."

"What I complain of, Julia, is that you encouraged young Mr. Pomeroy till Mr. Hattersley appeared, whom you thought more eligible, and then you tossed him aside; and you did precisely the same with James Hattersley as soon as you came to know Mr. Lawlor. After all, Julia, I am not so sure that Mr. Pomeroy has not chosen the better part. The girl, I day say, is simple, fresh, and affectionate."

"Your implication is not complimentary, Aunt Elizabeth."

"My dear, I have no patience with the young lady of the present day, who is shallow, self-willed, and indifferent to the feelings and happiness of others, who craves excitement and pleasures, and desires nothing that is useful and good. Where now will you see a girl like Viola's sister, who let concealment, like a worm i' the bud, feed on her damask cheek?" Nowadays a girl lays herself at the feet of a man if she likes him, turns herself inside out to let him and all the world read her heart."

"I have no relish to be like Viola's sister, and have my story— a blank. I never grovelled at the feet of Joe Pomeroy or James Hattersley."

"No, but you led each to consider himself the favoured one till he proposed, and then you refused him. It was like smiling at a man and then stabbing him to the heart."

"Well—I don't want people to think that James Hattersley cared for me—I certainly never cared for him—nor that he proposed; so I shall go to the ball."

Julia Demant was an orphan. She had been kept at school till she was eighteen, and then had been removed just at the age when a girl begins to take an interest in her studies, and not to regard them as drudgery. On her removal she had cast away all that she had acquired, and had been plunged into the whirl of Society. Then suddenly her father died—she had lost her mother some years before—and she went to live with her aunt, Miss Flemming. Julia had inherited a sum of about five hundred pounds a year, and would probably come in for a good estate and funds as well on the death of her aunt. She had been flattered as a girl at home, and at school as a beauty, and she certainly thought no small bones of herself.

Miss Flemming was an elderly lady with a sharp tongue, very outspoken, and very decided in her opinions; but her action was weak, and Julia soon discovered that she could bend the aunt to do anything she willed, though she could not modify or alter her opinions.

In the matter of Joe Pomeroy and James Hattersley, it was as Miss Flemming had said. Julia had encouraged Mr. Pomeroy, and had only cast him off because she thought better of the suit of Mr. Hattersley, son of an admiral of that name. She had seen a good deal of young Hattersley, had given him every encouragement, had so entangled him, that he was madly in love with her; and then, when she came to know the Hon. James Lawlor, and saw that he was fascinated, she rejected Hattersley with the consequences alluded to in the conversation above given.

Julia was particularly anxious to be present at the country ball, for she had been already booked by Mr. Lawlor for several dances, and she was quite resolved to make an attempt to bring him to a declaration.

On the evening of the ball Miss Flemming and Julia entered the carriage. The aunt had given way, as was her wont, but under protest.

For about ten minutes neither spoke, and then Miss Flemming said, "Well, you know my feelings about this dance. I do not approve. I distinctly disapprove. I do not consider your going to the ball in good taste, or, as you would put it, in good form. Poor young Hattersley . . ."

"Oh, dear Aunt, do let us put young Hattersley aside. He was buried with the regular forms, I suppose?"

"Yes, Julia."

"Then the rector accepted the verdict of the jury at the inquest. Why should not we? A man who is unsound in his mind is not responsible for his actions."

"I suppose not."

"Much less, then, I who live ten miles away."

"I do not say that you are responsible for his death, but for the condition of mind that led him to do the dreadful deed. Really, Julia, you are one of those into whose head or heart only by a surgical operation could the thought be introduced that you could be in the wrong. A hypodermic syringe would be too weak an instrument to effect such a radical change in you. Everyone else may be in the wrong, you—never. As for me, I cannot get young Hattersley out of my head."

"And I," retorted Julia with asperity, for her aunt's words had stung her—"I, for my part, do not give him a thought."

She had hardly spoken the words before a chill wind began to pass round her. She drew the Barege shawl that was over her bare shoulders closer about her, and said, "Auntie! Is the glass down on your side?"

"No, Julia; why do you ask?"

"There is such a draught."

"Draught!—I do not feel one; perhaps the window on your side hitches."

"Indeed, that is all right. It is blowing harder and is deadly cold. Can one of the front panes be broken?"

"No. Rogers would have told me had that been the case. Besides, I can see that they are sound."

The wind of which Julia complained swirled and whistled about her. It increased in force; it plucked at her shawl and slewed it about her throat; it tore at the lace on her dress. It snatched at her hair, it wrenched it away from the pins, the combs that held it in place; one long tress was lashed across the face of Miss Flemming. Then the hair, completely released, eddied up above the girl's head, and the next moment was carried as a drift before her, blinding her. Then—a sudden explosion, as though a gun had been fired into her ear; and with a scream of terror she sank back among the cushions. Miss Flemming, in great alarm, pulled the check-string, and the carriage stopped. The footman descended from the box and came to the side. The old lady drew down the window and said: "Oh! Phillips, bring the lamp. Something has happened to Miss Demant."

The man obeyed, and sent a flood of light into the carriage. Julia was lying back, white and senseless. Her hair was scattered over her face, neck, and shoulders; the flowers that had been stuck in it, the pins that had fastened it in place, the pads that had given shape to the convolutions lay strewn, some on her lap, some in the rug at the bottom of the carriage.

"Phillips!" ordered the old lady in great agitation, "tell Rogers to turn the horses and drive home at once; and do you run as fast as you can for Dr. Crate."

A few minutes after the carriage was again in motion, Julia revived. Her aunt was chafing her hand.

"Oh, Aunt!" she said, "are all the glasses broken?"

"Broken—what glasses?"

"Those of the carriage—with the explosion."

"Explosion, my dear!"

"Yes. That gun which was discharged. It stunned me. Were you hurt?"

"I heard no gun—no explosion."

"But I did. It was as though a bullet had been discharged into my brain. I wonder that I escaped. Who can have fired at us?"

"My dear, no one fired. I heard nothing. I know what it was. I had the same experience many years ago. I slept in a damp bed, and awoke stone deaf in my right ear. I remained so for three weeks. But one night when I was at a ball and was dancing, all at once I heard a report as of a pistol in my right ear, and immediately heard quite clearly again. It was wax."

"But, Aunt Elizabeth, I have not been deaf."

"You have not noticed that you were deaf."

"Oh! But look at my hair; it was that wind that blew it about."

"You are labouring under a delusion, Julia. There was no wind."

"But look—feel how my hair is down."

"That has been done by the motion of the carriage. There are many ruts in the road."

They reached home, and Julia, feeling sick, frightened, and bewildered, retired to bed. Dr. Crate arrived, said that she was hysterical, and ordered something to soothe her nerves. Julia was not convinced. The explanation offered by Miss Flemming did not satisfy her. That she was a victim to hysteria she did not in the least believe. Neither her aunt, nor the coachman, nor Phillips had heard the discharge of a gun. As to the rushing wind, Julia was satisfied that she had experienced it. The lace was ripped, as by a hand, from her dress, and the shawl was twisted about her throat; besides, her hair had not been so slightly arranged that the jolting of the carriage would completely disarrange it. She was vastly perplexed over what she had undergone. She thought and thought, but could get no nearer to a solution of the mystery.

Next day, as she was almost herself again, she rose and went about as usual.

In the afternoon the Hon. James Lawlor called and asked after Miss Flemming. The butler replied that his mistress was out making calls, but that Miss Demant was at home, and he believed was on the terrace. Mr. Lawlor at once asked to see her.

He did not find Julia in the parlour or on the terrace, but in a lower garden to which she had descended to feed the goldfish in the pond.

"Oh! Miss Demant," said he, "I was so disappointed not to see you at the ball last night."

"I was very unwell; I had a fainting fit and could not go."

"It threw a damp on our spirits—that is to say, on mine. I had you booked for several dances."

"You were able to give them to others."

"But that was not the same to me. I did an act of charity and self-denial. I danced instead with the ugly Miss Burgons and with Miss Pounding, and that was like dragging about a sack of potatoes. I believe it would have been a jolly evening, but for that shocking affair of young Hattersley which kept some of the better sort away. I mean those who knew the Hattersleys. Of course, for me that did not matter, we were not acquainted. I never even spoke with the fellow. You knew him, I believe? I heard some people say so, and that you had not come because of him. The supper, for a subscription ball, was not atrociously bad."

"What did they say of me?"

"Oh!—if you will know—that you did not attend the ball because you liked him very much, and were awfully cut up."

"I—I! What a shame that people should talk! I never cared a rush for him. He was nice enough in his way, not a bounder, but tolerable as young men go."

Mr. Lawlor laughed. "I should not relish to have such a qualified estimate made of me."

"Nor need you. You are interesting. He became so only when he had shot himself. It will be by this alone that he will be remembered."

"But there is no smoke without fire. Did he like you—much?"

"Dear Mr. Lawlor, I am not a clairvoyante, and never was able to see into the brains or hearts of people—least of all of young men. Perhaps it is fortunate for me that I cannot."

"One lady told me that he had proposed to you."

"Who was that? The potato-sack?"

"I will not give her name. Is there any truth in it? Did he?"

"No."

At the moment she spoke there sounded in her ear a whistle of wind, and she felt a current like a cord of ice creep round her throat, increasing in force and compression; her hat was blown off, and next instant a detonation rang through her head as though a gun had been fired into her ear. She uttered a cry and sank upon the ground.

James Lawlor was bewildered. His first impulse was to run to the house for assistance; then he considered that he could not leave her lying on the wet soil, and he stooped to raise her in his arms and to carry her within. In novels young men perform such a feat without difficulty; but in fact they are not able to do it, especially when the girl is tall and big-boned. Moreover, one in a faint is a dead weight. Lawlor staggered under his burden to the steps. It was as much as he could perform to carry her up to the terrace, and there he placed her on a seat. Panting, and with his muscles quivering after the strain, he hastened to the drawing-room, rang the bell, and when the butler appeared, he gasped: "Miss Demant has fainted; you and I and the footman must carry her within."

"She fainted last night in the carriage," said the butler.

. When Julia came to her senses, she was in bed attended by the housekeeper and her maid. A few moments later Miss Flemming arrived.

"Oh, Aunt! I have heard it again."

"Heard what, dear?"

"The discharge of a gun."

"It is nothing but wax," said the old lady. "I will drop a little sweet-oil into your ear, and then have it syringed with warm water."

"I want to tell you something—in private."

Miss Flemming signed to the servants to withdraw.

"Aunt," said the girl, "I must say something. This is the second time that this has happened. I am sure it is significant. James Lawlor was with me in the sunken garden, and he began to speak about James Hattersley. You know it was when we were talking about him last night that I heard that awful noise. It was precisely as if a gun had been discharged into my ear. I felt as if all the nerves and tissues of my head were being torn, and all the bones of my skull shattered—just what Mr. Hattersley must have undergone when he pulled the trigger. It was an agony for a moment perhaps, but it felt as if it lasted an hour. Mr. Lawlor had asked me point blank if James Hattersley had proposed to me, and I said, 'No.' I was perfectly justified in so answering, because he had no right to ask me such a question. It was an impertinence on his part, and I answered him shortly and sharply with a negative.

"But actually James Hattersley proposed twice to me. He would not accept a first refusal, but came next day bothering me again, and I was pretty curt with him. He made some remarks that were rude about how I had treated him, and which I will not repeat, and as he left, in a state of great agitation, he said, 'Julia, I vow that you shall not forget this, and you shall belong to no one but me, alive or dead.' I considered this great nonsense, and did not accord it another thought. But, really, these terrible annoyances, this wind and the bursts of noise, do seem to me to come from him. It is just as though he felt a malignant delight in distressing me, now that he is dead. I should like to defy him, and I will do it if I can, but I cannot bear more of these experiences—they will kill me."

Several days elapsed.

Mr. Lawlor called repeatedly to enquire, but a week passed before Julia was sufficiently recovered to receive him, and then the visit was one of courtesy and of sympathy, and the conversation turned upon her health, and on indifferent themes.

But some few days later it was otherwise. She was in the conservatory alone, pretty much herself again, when Mr. Lawlor was announced.

Physically she had recovered, or believed that she had, but her nerves had actually received a severe shock. She had made up her mind that the phenomena of the circling wind and the explosion were in some mysterious manner connected with Hattersley.

She bitterly resented this, but she was in mortal terror of a recurrence; and she felt no compunction for her treatment of the unfortunate young man, but rather a sense of deep resentment against him. If he were dead, why did he not lie quiet and cease from vexing her?

To be a martyr was to her no gratification, for hers was not a martyrdom that provoked sympathy, and which could make her interesting.

She had hitherto supposed that when a man died there was an end of him; his condition was determined for good or for ill. But that a disembodied spirit should hover about and make itself a nuisance to the living, had never entered into her calculations.

"Julia—if I may be allowed so to call you—" began Mr. Lawlor, "I have brought you a bouquet of flowers. Will you accept them?"

"Oh!" she said, as he handed the bunch to her, "how kind of you. At this time of the year they are so rare, and Aunt's gardener is so miserly that he will spare me none for my room but some miserable bits of geranium. It is too bad of your wasting your money like this upon me."

"It is no waste, if it affords you pleasure."

"It is a pleasure. I dearly love flowers."

"To give you pleasure," said Mr. Lawlor, "is the great object of my life. If I could assure you happiness—if you would allow me to hope—to seize this opportunity, now that we are alone together . . ."

He drew near and caught her hand. His features were agitated, his lips trembled, there was earnestness in his eyes.

At once a cold blast touched Julia and began to circle about her and to flutter her hair. She trembled and drew back. That paralyzing experience was about to be renewed. She turned deadly white, and put her hand to her right ear. "Oh, James! James!" she gasped. "Do not, pray do not speak what you want to say, or I shall faint. It is coming on. I am not yet well enough to hear it. Write to me and I will answer. For pity's sake do not speak it." Then she sank upon a seat—and at that moment her aunt entered the conservatory.

On the following day a note was put into her hand, containing a formal proposal from the Hon. James Lawlor; and by return of post Julia answered with an acceptance.

There was no reason whatever why the engagement should be long; and the only alternative mooted was whether the wedding should take place before or after Easter. Finally, it was settled that it should be celebrated on Shrove Tuesday. This left a short time for the necessary preparations. Miss Flemming would have to go to town with her niece concerning a trousseau, and a trousseau is not turned out rapidly any more than an armed cruiser.

There is usually a certain period allowed to young people who have become engaged to see much of each other, to get better acquainted with one another, to build their castles in the air, and to indulge in little passages of affection, vulgarly called "spooning." But in this case the spooning had to be curtailed and postponed.

At the outset, when alone with James, Julia was nervous. She feared a recurrence of those phenomena that so affected her. But, although every now and then the wind curled and soughed about her, it was not violent, nor was it chilling; and she came to regard it as a wail of discomfiture. Moreover, there was no recurrence of the detonation, and she fondly hoped that with her marriage the vexation would completely cease.

In her heart was deep down a sense of exultation. She was defying James Hattersley and setting his prediction at naught. She was not in love with Mr. Lawlor; she liked him, in her cold manner, and was not insensible to the social advantage that would be hers when she became the Honourable Mrs. Lawlor.

The day of the wedding arrived. Happily it was fine. "Blessed is the bride the sun shines on," said the cheery Miss Flemming; "an omen, I trust, of a bright and unruffled life in your new condition."

All the neighbourhood was present at the church. Miss Flemming had many friends. Mr. Lawlor had fewer present, as he belonged to a distant county. The church path had been laid with red cloth, the church decorated with flowers, and a choir was present to twitter. "The voice that breathed o'er Eden."

The rector stood by the altar, and two cushions had been laid at the chancel steps. The rector was to be assisted by an uncle of the bridegroom who was in Holy orders; the rector, being old-fashioned, had drawn on pale-grey kid gloves.

First arrived the bridegroom with his best man, and stood in a nervous condition balancing himself first on one foot, then on the other, waiting, observed by all eyes.

Next entered the procession of the bride, attended by her maids, to the 'Wedding March' in *Lohengrin,* on a wheezy organ. Then Julia and her intended took their places at the chancel step for the performance of the first portion of the ceremony, and the two clergy descended to them from the altar.

"Wilt thou have this woman to thy wedded wife?"

"I will."

"Wilt thou have this man to thy wedded husband?"

"I will."

"I, James, take thee, Julia, to my wedded wife, to have and to hold . . ." and so on.

As the words were being spoken, a cold rush of air passed over the clasped hands, numbing them, and began to creep round the bride, and to flutter her veil. She set her lips and knitted her brows. In a few moments she would be beyond the reach of these manifestations.

When it came to her turn to speak, she began firmly: "I, Julia, take thee, James . . ." but as she proceeded the wind became fierce; it raged about her, it caught her veil on one side and buffeted her cheek, it switched the veil about her throat, as though strangling her with a drift of snow contracting into ice. But she persevered to the end.

Then James Lawlor produced the ring, and was about to place it on her finger with the prescribed words: "With this ring I thee wed . . ." when a report rang in her ear, followed by a heaving of her skull, as though the bones were being burst asunder, and she sank unconscious on the chancel step.

In the midst of profound commotion, she was raised and conveyed to the vestry, followed by James Lawlor, trembling and pale. He had slipped the ring back into his waistcoat pocket. Dr. Crate, who was present, hastened to offer his professional assistance.

In the vestry Julia rested in a Glastonbury chair, white and still, with her hands resting in her lap. And to the amazement of those present, it was seen that on the third finger of her left hand was a leaden ring, rude and solid as though fashioned out of a bullet. Restoratives were applied, but fully a quarter of an hour elapsed before Julia opened her eyes, and a little colour returned to her lips and cheek. But, as she raised her hands to her brow to wipe away the damp that had formed on it, her eye caught sight of the leaden ring, and with a cry of horror she sank again into insensibility.

The congregation slowly left the church, awestruck, whispering, asking questions, receiving no satisfactory answers, forming surmises all incorrect.

"I am very much afraid, Mr. Lawlor," said the rector, "that it will be impossible to proceed with the service today; it must be postponed till Miss Demant is in a condition to conclude her part, and to sign the register. I do not see how it can be gone on with today. She is quite unequal to the effort."

The carriage which was to have conveyed the couple to Miss Flemming's house, and then, later, to have taken them to the station for their honeymoon, the horses decorated with white rosettes, the whip adorned with a white bow, had now to convey Julia, hardly conscious, supported by her aunt, to her home.

No rice could be thrown. The bell-ringers, prepared to give a joyous peal, were constrained to depart.

The reception at Miss Flemming's was postponed. No one thought of attending. The cakes, the ices, were consumed in the kitchen.

The bridegroom, bewildered, almost frantic, ran hither and thither, not knowing what to do, what to say.

Julia lay as a stone for fully two hours; and when she came to herself could not speak. When conscious, she raised her left hand, looked on the leaden ring, and sank back into senselessness.

Not till late in the evening was she sufficiently recovered to speak, and then she begged her aunt, who had remained by her bed without stirring, to dismiss attendants. She desired to speak with her alone. When no one was in the room with her, save Miss Flemming, she said in a whisper: "Oh, Aunt Elizabeth! Oh, Auntie! Such an awful thing has happened. I can never marry Mr. Lawlor, never. I have married James Hattersley; I am a dead man's wife. At the time that James Lawlor was making the responses, I heard a piping voice in my ear, an unearthly voice, saying the same words. When I said: "I, Julia, take you, James, to my wedded husband"—you know Mr. Hattersley is James as well as Mr. Lawlor—then the words applied to him as much or as well as to the other. And then, when it came to the giving of the ring, there was the explosion in my ear, as before—and the leaden ring was forced on to my finger, and not James Lawlor's golden ring. It is of no use my resisting any more. I am a dead man's wife, and I cannot marry James Lawlor."

Some years have elapsed since that disastrous day and that incomplete marriage.

Miss Demant is Miss Demant still, and she has never been able to remove the leaden ring from the third finger of her left hand. Whenever the attempt has been made, either to disengage it by drawing it off or by cutting through it, there has ensued that terrifying discharge as of a gun into her ear, causing insensibility. The prostration that has followed, the terror it has inspired, have so affected her nerves, that she has desisted from every attempt to rid herself of the ring.

She invariably wears a glove on her left hand, and it is bulged over the third finger, where lies the leaden ring.

She is not a happy woman, although her aunt is dead and has left her a handsome estate. She has not got many acquaintances. She has no friends; for her temper is unamiable, and her tongue is bitter. She supposes that the world, as far as she knows it, is in league against her.

Towards the memory of James Hattersley she entertains a deadly hate. If an incantation could lay his spirit, if prayer could give him repose, she would have recourse to none of these expedients, even though they might relieve her, so bitter is her resentment. And she harbours a silent wrath against Providence for allowing the dead to walk and to molest the living.

THE TAPESTRIED CHAMBER

Sir Walter Scott

About the end of the American war, when the officers of Lord Cornwallis's army, which surrendered at Yorktown, and others, who had been made prisoners during the impolitic and ill-fated controversy, were returning to their own country to relate their adventures and repose themselves after their fatigues, there was amongst them a general officer, to whom Miss S. gave the name of Browne, but merely, as I understood, to save the inconvenience of introducing a nameless agent in the narrative. He was an officer of merit, as well as a gentleman of high consideration for family and attainments.

Some business had carried General Browne upon a tour through the western counties, when, in the conclusion of a morning stage, he found himself in the vicinity of a small country town, which presented a scene of uncommon beauty, and of a character peculiarly English.

The little town, with its stately old church, whose tower bore testimony to the devotion of ages long past, lay amidst pastures and cornfields of small extent, but bounded and divided with hedgerow timber of great age and size. There were few marks of modern improvement. The environs of the place intimated neither the solitude of decay nor the bustle of novelty; the houses were old, but in good repair; and the beautiful little river murmured freely on its way to the left of the town, neither restrained by a damn nor bordered by a towing-path.

Upon a gentle eminence, nearly a mile to the southward of the town, were seen, amongst many venerable oaks and tangled thickets, the turrets of a castle as old as the wars of York, and Lancaster, but which seemed to have received important alterations during the age of Elizabeth and her successor. It had not been a place of great size; but whatever accommodation it formerly afforded was, it must be supposed, still to be obtained within its walls; at least, such was the inference which General Browne drew from observing the smoke arise merrily from several of the ancient wreathed and carved chimney-stalks. The wall of the park ran alongside of the highway for two or three hundred yards; and through the different points by which the eye found glimpses into the woodland scenery it seemed to be well stocked. Other points of view opened in succession—now a full one of the front of the old castle, and now a side glimpse at its particular towers, the former rich in all the bizarrerie of the Elizabethan school, while the simple and solid strength of other parts of the building seemed to show that they had been raised more for defence than ostentation.

Delighted with the partial glimpses which he obtained of the castle through the woods and glades by which this ancient feudal fortress was surrounded, our military traveller was determined to enquire whether it might not deserve a nearer view, and whether it contained family pictures or other objects of curiosity worthy of a stranger's visit, when, leaving the vicinity of the park, he rolled through a clean and well-paved street and stopped at the door of a well-frequented inn.

Before ordering horses to proceed on his journey, General Browne made enquiries concerning the proprietor of the chateau which had so attracted his admiration, and was equally surprised and pleased at hearing in reply a nobleman named whom we shall call Lord Woodville.

How fortunate! Much of Browne's early recollections, both at school and at college, had been connected with young Woodville, whom, by a few questions, he now ascertained to be the same with the owner of this fair domain. He had been raised to the peerage by the decease of his father a few months before, and, as the General learned from the landlord, the term of mourning being ended, was now taking possession of his paternal estate, in the jovial season of merry autumn, accompanied by a select party of friends, to enjoy the sports of a country famous for game.

This was delightful news to our traveller. Frank Woodville had been Richard Browne's fag at Eton, and his chosen intimate at Christ Church; their pleasures and their tasks had been the same; and the honest soldier's heart warmed to find his early friend in possession of so delightful a residence, and of an estate, as the landlord assured him with a nod and a wink, fully adequate to maintain and add to his dignity. Nothing was more natural than that the traveler should suspend a journey which there was nothing to render hurried to pay a visit to an old friend under such agreeable circumstances.

The fresh horses, therefore, had only the brief task of conveying the General's travelling-carriage to Woodville Castle. A porter admitted them at a modern Gothic lodge, built in that style to correspond with the castle itself, and at the same time rang a bell to give warning of the approach of visitors. Apparently the sound of the bell had suspended the separation of the company, bent on the various amusements of the morning, for, on entering the court of the chateau, several young men were lounging about in their sporting-dresses, looking at and criticizing the dogs, which the keepers held in readiness to attend their pastime. As General Browne alighted, the young lord came to the gate of the hall, and for an instant gazed as at a stranger upon the countenance of his friend, on which war, with its fatigues and its wounds, had made a great alteration. But the uncertainty lasted no longer than till the visitor had spoken, and the hearty greeting which followed was such as can only be exchanged betwixt those who have passed together the merry days of careless boyhood or early youth.

"If I could have formed a wish, my dear Browne," said Lord Woodville, "it would have been to have you here, of all men, upon this occasion, which my friends are good enough to hold as a sort of holiday. Do not think you have been unwatched during the years you have been absent from us. I have traced you through your dangers, your triumphs, your misfortunes, and was delighted to see that, whether in victory or defeat, the name of my old friend was always distinguished with applause."

The General made a suitable reply, and congratulated his friend on his new dignities, and the possession of a place and domain so beautiful.

"Nay, you have seen nothing of it as yet," said Lord Woodville, "and I trust you do not mean to leave us till you are better acquainted with it. It is true, I confess, that my present party is pretty large, and the old house, like other places of the kind, does not possess so much accommodation as the extent of the outward walls appears to promise. But we can give you a comfortable old-fashioned room, and I venture to suppose that your campaigns have taught you to be glad of worse quarters."

The General shrugged his shoulders and laughed. "I presume," he said, "the worst apartment in your chateau is considerably superior to the old tobacco-cask in which I was fain to take up my night's lodging when I was in the bush, as the Virginians call it, with the light corps. There I lay, like Diogenes himself, so delighted with my covering from the elements that I made a vain attempt to have it rolled on to my next quarters; but my commander for the time would give way to no such luxurious provision, and I took farewell of my beloved cask with tears in my eyes."

"Well, then, since you do not fear your quarters," said Lord Woodville, "you will stay with me a week at least. Of guns, dogs, fishing-rods, flies and means of sport by sea and land, we have enough and to spare; you cannot pitch on an amusement, but we will find the means of pursuing it. But if you prefer the gun and pointers, I will go with you myself, and see whether you have mended your shooting since you have been amongst the Indians of the back settlements."

The General gladly accepted his friendly host's proposal in all its points. After a morning of manly exercise, the company met at dinner, where it was the delight of Lord Woodville to conduce to the display of the high properties of his recovered friend, so as to recommend him to his guests, most of whom were persons of distinction. He led General Browne to speak of the scenes he had witnessed; and as every word marked alike the brave officer and the sensible man, who retained possession of his cool judgement under the most imminent dangers, the company looked upon the soldier with general respect, as on one who had proved himself possessed of an uncommon portion of personal courage—that attribute, of all others, of which everybody desires to be thought possessed.

The day at Woodville Castle ended as usual in such mansions. The hospitality stopped within the limits of good order; music in which the young lord was a proficient, succeeded to the circulation of the bottle; cards and billiards, for those who preferred such amusements, were in readiness; but the exercise of the morning required early hours, and not long after eleven o'clock the guests began to retire to their several apartments.

The young lord himself conducted his friend, General Browne, to the chamber destined for him, which answered the description he had given of it, being comfortable, but old-fashioned. The bed was of the massive form used in the end of the seventeenth century, and the curtains of faded silk, heavily trimmed with tarnished gold. But then the sheets, pillows and blankets looked delightful to the campaigner, when he thought of his "mansion, the cask." There was an air of gloom in the tapestry hangings which, with their worn-out graces, curtained the walls of the little chamber, and gently undulated as the autumnal breeze found its way through the ancient lattice-window, which pattered and whistled as the air gained entrance. The toilet, too, with its mirror, turbaned, after the manner of the beginning of the century, with a coiffure of murrey-coloured silk, and its hundred strange-shaped boxes, providing for arrangements which had been obsolete for more than fifty years, had an antique, and in so far a melancholy aspect. But nothing could blaze more brightly and cheerfully than the two large wax candles; or if aught could rival them, it was the flaming, bickering faggots in the chimney, that sent at once their gleam and their warmth through the snug apartment, which, notwithstanding the general antiquity of its appearance, was not wanting in the least convenience that modern habits rendered either necessary or desirable.

"This is an old-fashioned sleeping-apartment, General," said the young lord, "but I hope you find nothing that makes you envy your old tobacco-cask."

"I am not particular respecting my lodgings," replied the General; "yet were I to make any choice, I would prefer this chamber by many degrees to the gayer and more modern rooms of your family mansion. Believe me, that when I unite its modern air of comfort with its venerable antiquity, and recollect that it is your lordship's property, I shall feel in better quarters here than if I were in the best hotel London could afford."

"I trust—I have no doubt—that you will find yourself as comfortable as I wish you, my dear General," said the young nobleman; and once more bidding his guest good night, he shook him by the hand and withdrew.

The General once more looked round him, and internally congratulating himself on his return to peaceful life, the comforts of which were endeared by the recollection of the hardships and dangers he had lately sustained, undressed himself, and prepared himself for a luxurious night's rest.

Here, contrary to the custom of this species of tale, we leave the General in possession of his apartment until the next morning.

The company assembled for breakfast at an early hour, but without the appearance of General Browne, who seemed the guest that Lord Woodville was desirous of honouring above all whom his hospitality had assembled around him. He more than once expressed surprise at the General's absence, and at length sent a servant to make enquiry after him. The man brought back information that General Browne had been walking abroad since an early hour of the morning, in defiance of the weather, which was misty and ungenial.

"The custom of a soldier," said the young nobleman to his friends; "many of them acquire habitual vigilance, and cannot sleep after the early hour at which their duty usually commands them to be alert."

Yet the explanation which Lord Woodville thus offered to the company seemed hardly satisfactory to his own mind, and it was in a fit of silence and abstraction that he awaited the return of the General. It took place near an hour after the breakfast bell had rung. He looked fatigued and feverish. His hair, the powdering and arrangement of which was at this time one of the most important occupations of a man's whole day, and marked his fashion as much as, in the present time, the tying of a cravat, or the want of one, was disheveled, uncurled, void of powder, and dank with dew. His clothes were huddled on with a careless negligence remarkable in a military man, whose real or supposed duties are usually held to include some attention to the toilet; and his looks were haggard and ghastly in a peculiar degree.

"So you have stolen a march upon us this morning, my dear General," said Lord Woodville; "or you have not found your bed so much to your mind as I had hoped and you seemed to expect. How did you rest last night?"

"Oh, excellently well—remarkably well—never better in my life!" said General Browne rapidly, and yet with an air of embarrassment which was obvious to his friend. He then hastily swallowed a cup of tea, and, neglecting or refusing whatever else he was offered, seemed to fall into a fit of abstraction.

"You will take the gun today, General?" said his friend and host, but had to repeat the question twice ere he received the abrupt answer, "No, my lord; I am sorry I cannot have the honour of spending another day with your lordship; my post-horses are ordered, and will be here directly."

All who were present showed surprise, and Lord Woodville immediately replied, "Post-horses, my good friend! What can you possibly want with them, when you promised to stay with me quietly for at least a week?"

"I believe," said the General, obviously much embarrassed, "that I might, in the pleasure of my first meeting with your lordship, have said something about stopping here a few days; but I have since found it altogether impossible."

"That is very extraordinary," answered the young nobleman. "You seemed quite disengaged yesterday, and you cannot have had a summons today, for our post has not come up from the town, and therefore you cannot have received any letters."

General Browne, without giving any further explanation, muttered something of indispensable business, and insisted on the absolute necessity of his departure in a manner which silenced all opposition on the part of his host, who saw that his resolution was taken, and forbore all further importunity.

"At least, however," he said, "permit me, my dear Browne, since go you will or must, to show you the view from the terrace, which the mist, that is now rising, will soon display."

He threw open a sash-window and stepped down upon the terrace as he spoke. The General followed him mechanically, but seemed little to attend to what his host was saying, as, looking across an extended and rich prospect, he pointed out the different objects worthy of observation. Thus they moved on till Lord Woodville had attained his purpose of drawing his guest entirely apart from the rest of the company, when, turning around upon him with an air of great solemnity, he addressed him thus:

"Richard Browne, my old and very dear friend, we are now alone.

Let me conjure you to answer me upon the word of a friend and the honour of a soldier. How did you in reality rest during last night?"

"Most wretchedly indeed, my lord," answered the General, in the same tone of solemnity; "so miserably, that I would not run the risk of such a second night, not only for all the lands belonging to this castle, but for all the country which I see from this elevated point of view."

"This is most extraordinary," said the young lord, as if speaking to himself; "then there must be something in the reports concerning that apartment." Again turning to the General, he said, "For God's sake, my dear friend, be candid with me and let me know the disagreeable particulars which have befallen you under a roof where, with consent of the owner, you should have met nothing save comfort."

The General seemed distressed by this appeal, and paused a moment before he replied. "My dear lord," he at length said, "what happened to me last night is of a nature so peculiar and so unpleasant, that I could hardly bring myself to detail it even to your lordship, were it not that, independent of my wish to gratify any request of yours, I think that sincerity on my part may lead to some explanation about a circumstance equally painful and mysterious. To others, the communication I am about to make might place me in the light of a weak-minded, superstitious fool, who suffered his own imagination to delude and bewilder him; but you have known me in childhood and youth, and will not suspect me of having adopted in manhood the feelings and frailties from which my early years were free." Here he paused, and his friend replied:

"Do not doubt my perfect confidence in the truth of your communication, however strange it may be," replied Lord Woodville; "I know your firmness of disposition too well to suspect you could be made the object of imposition, and am aware that your honour and your friendship will equally deter you from exaggerating whatever you may have witnessed."

"Well, then," said the General, "I will proceed with my story as well as I can, relying upon your candour, and yet distinctly feeling that I would rather face a battery than recall to my mind the odious recollections of last night."

He paused a second time, and then perceiving that Lord Woodville remained silent and in an attitude of attention, he commenced, though not without obvious reluctance, the history of his night adventures in the Tapestried Chamber.

"I undressed and went to bed, so soon as your lordship left me yesterday evening; but the wood in the chimney, which nearly fronted my bed, blazed brightly and cheerfully, and, aided by a hundred exciting recollections of my childhood and youth, which had been recalled by the unexpected pleasure of meeting your lordship, prevented me from falling immediately asleep. I ought, however, to say that these reflections were all of a pleasant and agreeable kind, grounded on a sense of having for a time exchanged the labour, fatigues and dangers of my profession for the enjoyments of a peaceful life, and the reunion of those friendly and affectionate ties which I had torn asunder at the rude summons of war.

"While such pleasing reflections were stealing over my mind, and gradually lulling me to slumber, I was suddenly aroused by a sound like that of the rustling of a silken gown and the tapping of a pair of high-heeled shoes, as if a woman were walking in the apartment. Ere I could draw the curtain to see what the matter was, the figure of a little woman passed between the bed and the fire. The back of this form was turned to me, and I could observe, from the shoulders and neck, it was that of an old woman, whose dress was an old-fashioned gown, which, I think, ladies call a sacque—that is, a sort of robe completely loose in the body, but gathered into broad plaits upon the neck and shoulders, which fall down to the ground, and terminate in a species of train.

"I thought the intrusion singular enough, but never harboured for a moment the idea that what I saw was anything more than the mortal form of some old woman about the establishment, who had a fancy to dress like her grandmother, and who, having perhaps, as your lordship mentioned that you were rather straitened for room, been dislodged from her chamber for my accommodation, had forgotten the circumstance and returned by twelve to her old haunt. Under this persuasion I moved myself in bed and coughed a little, to make the intruder sensible of my being in possession of the premises. She turned slowly round, but, gracious Heaven! My lord, what a countenance did she display to me! There was no longer any question what she was, or any thought of her being a living being. Upon a face which wore the fixed features of a corpse were imprinted the traces of the vilest and most hideous passions which had animated her while she lived. The body of some atrocious criminal seemed to have been given up from the grave, and the soul restored from the penal fire, in order to form, for a space, a union with the ancient accomplice of its guilt. I started up in bed, and sat upright, supporting myself on my palms, as I gazed on this horrible spectre. The hag made, as it seemed, a single and swift stride to the bed where I lay, and squatted herself down upon it, in precisely the same attitude which I had assumed in the extremity of horror, advancing her diabolical countenance within a yard of mine, with a grin which seemed to intimate the malice and the derision of an incarnate fiend."

Here General Browne stopped, and wiped from his brow the cold perspiration with which the recollections of his horrible vision had covered it.

"My lord," he said, "I am no coward. I have been in all the mortal dangers incidental to my profession, and I may truly boast that no man ever knew Richard Browne dishonour the sword he wears; but in these horrible circumstances, under the eyes, and, as it seemed, almost in the grasp, of an incarnation of an evil spirit, all firmness forsook me, all manhood melted from me like wax in the furnace, and I felt my hair individually bristle. The current of my life-blood ceased to flow, and I sank back in a swoon, as very a victim to panic terror as ever was a village girl or a child of ten years old. How long I lay in this condition I cannot pretend to guess.

"But I was roused by the castle clock striking one, so loud that it seemed as if it were in the very room. It was some time before I dared open my eyes, lest they should again encounter the horrible spectacle. When, however, I summoned courage to look up, she was no longer visible. My first idea was to pull my bell, wake the servants, and remove to a garret or a hay-loft, to be ensured against a second visitation. Nay, I will confess the truth, that my resolution was altered, not by the shame of exposing myself, but by the fear that, as the bell-cord hung by the chimney, I might, in making my way to it, be again crossed by the fiendish hag, who, I figured to myself, might be still lurking about some corner of the apartment.

"I will not pretend to describe what hot and cold fever-fits tormented me for the rest of the night, through broken sleep, weary vigils, and that dubious state which forms the neutral ground between them. A hundred terrible objects appeared to haunt me; but there was the great difference betwixt the vision which I have described and those which followed, that I knew the last to be deceptions of my own fancy and over-excited nerves.

"Day at least appeared, and I rose from my bed ill in health and humiliated in mind. I was ashamed of myself as a man and a soldier, and still more so at feeling my own extreme desire to escape from the haunted apartment, which, however, conquered all other considerations; so that, huddling on my clothes with the most careless haste, I made my escape from your lordship's mansion, to seek in the open air some relief to my nervous system, shaken as it was by this horrible encounter with a visitant, for such I must believe her, from the other world. Your lordship has now heard the cause of my discomposure, and of my sudden desire to leave your hospitable castle. In other places I trust we may often meet; but God protect me from ever spending a second night under that roof!"

Strange as the General's tale was, he spoke with such a deep air of conviction, that it cut short all the usual commentaries which are made on such stories. Lord Woodville never once asked him if he was sure he did not dream of the apparition, or suggested any of the possibilities by which it is fashionable to explain supernatural appearances, as wild vagaries of the fancy or deceptions of the optic nerves. On the contrary, he seemed deeply impressed with the truth and reality of what he had heard; and, after a considerable pause, regretted, with much appearance of sincerity, that his early friend should in his house have suffered so severely.

"I am the more sorry for your pain, my dear Browne," he continued, "that it is the unhappy, though most unexpected, result of an experiment of my own. You must know that, for my father and grandfather's time, at least, the apartment which was assigned to you last night had been shut on account of reports that it was disturbed by supernatural sights and noises. When I came, a few weeks since, into possession of the estate, I thought the accommodation which the castle afforded for my friends was not extensive enough to permit the inhabitants of the invisible world to retain possession of a comfortable sleeping-apartment. I therefore caused the Tapestried Chamber, as we call it, to be opened, and, without destroying its air of antiquity, I had such new articles of furniture placed in it as became the modern times. Yet, as the opinion that the room was haunted very strongly prevailed among the domestics, and was also known in the neighbourhood and to many of my friends, I feared some prejudice might be entertained by the first occupant of the Tapestried Chamber, which might tend to revive the evil report which it had laboured under, and so disappoint my purpose of rendering it a useful part of the house. I must confess, my dear Browne, that your arrival yesterday, agreeable to me for a thousand reasons besides, seemed the most favourable opportunity of removing the unpleasant rumours which attached to the room, since your courage was indubitable, and your mind free of any preoccupation on the subject. I could not, therefore, have chosen a more fitting subject for my experiment."

"Upon my life," said General Browne, somewhat hastily, "I am infinitely obliged to your lordship—very particularly indebted indeed. I am likely to remember for some time the consequences of the experiment, as your lordship is pleased to call it."

"Nay, now you are upset, my dear friend," said Lord Woodville. "You have only to reflect for a single moment, in order to be convinced that I could not augur the possibility of the pain to which you have been so unhappily exposed. I was yesterday morning a complete sceptic on the subject of supernatural appearances. Nay, I am sure that, had I told you what was said about the room, those very reports would have induced you, by your own choice, to select it for your accommodation. It was my misfortune, perhaps my error, but really cannot be termed my fault, that you have been afflicted so strangely."

"Strangely indeed!" said the General, resuming his good temper; "and I acknowledge that I have no right to be offended with your lordship for treating me like what I used to think myself, a man of some firmness and courage. But I see my post-horses are arrived, and I must not detain your lordship from your amusement."

"Nay, my old friend," said Lord Woodville, "since you cannot stay with us another day, which, indeed, I can no longer urge, give me at least half an hour more. You used to love pictures, and I have a gallery of portraits, some of them by Vandyke, representing ancestry to whom this property and castle formerly belonged. I think that several of them will strike you as possessing merit."

General Browne accepted the invitation, though somewhat unwillingly. It was evident he was not to breathe freely or at ease till he left Woodville Castle far behind. He could not refuse his friend's invitation, however; and the less so, that he was a little ashamed of the peevishness which he had displayed towards his well-meaning entertainer.

The General, therefore, followed Lord Woodville through several rooms, into a long gallery hung with pictures, which the latter pointed out to his guest, telling the names, and giving some account of the personages whose portraits presented themselves in progression. General Browne was but little interested in the details which these accounts conveyed to him. They were, indeed, of the kind which are usually found in an old family gallery. Here was a cavalier who had ruined the estate in the royal cause; there a fine lady who had reinstated it by contracting a match with a wealthy Roundhead. There hung a gallant who had been in danger for corresponding with the exiled court at St. Germain's; here one who had taken arms for William at the Revolution; and there a third that had thrown his weight alternately into the scale of Whig and Tory.

While Lord Woodville was cramming these words into his guest's ear, "against the stomach of his sense", they gained the middle of the gallery, when he beheld General Browne suddenly start, and assume an attitude of the utmost surprise, not unmixed with fear, as his eyes were caught and suddenly riveted by a portrait of an old lady in a sacque, the fashionable dress of the end of the seventeenth century.

"There she is!" he exclaimed—"there she is, in form and features, though inferior in demoniac expression to the accursed hag who visited me last night."

"If that be the case," said the young nobleman, "there can remain no longer any doubt of the horrible reality of your apparition. That is the picture of a wretched ancestress of mine, of whose crimes a black and fearful catalogue is recorded in a family history in my charter-chest. The recital of them would be too horrible; it is enough to say, that in yon fatal apartment incest and unnatural murder were committed. I will restore it to the solitude to which the better judgement of those who preceded me had consigned it; and never shall anyone, so long as I can prevent it, be exposed to a repetition of the supernatural horrors which could shake such courage as yours."

Thus the friends, who had met with such glee, parted in a very different mood—Lord Woodville to command the Tapestried Chamber to be unmantled and the door built up; and General Browne to seek in some less beautiful country, and with some less dignified friend, forgetfulness of the painful night which he had passed in Woodville Castle.

GHOST STORIES OF THE TILED HOUSE

J. Sheridan Le Fanu

I

Old Sally always attended her young mistress while she prepared for bed—not that Lilias required help, for she had the spirit of neatness and a joyous, gentle alacrity, and only troubled the good old creature enough to prevent her thinking herself growing old and useless.

Sally, in her quiet way, was garrulous, and she had all sorts of old-world tales of wonder and adventure, to which Lilias often went pleasantly to sleep; for there was no danger while old Sally sat knitting there by the fire, and the sound of the rector's mounting upon his chairs, as was his wont, and taking down the putting up his books in the study beneath, though muffled and faint, gave evidence that that good and loving influence was awake and busy.

Old Sally was telling her young mistress, who sometimes listened with a smile, and sometimes lost a good five minutes together of her gentle prattle, how the young gentleman, Mr. Mervyn, had taken that awful old haunted habitation, the Tiled House "beyant at Ballyfermot," and was going to stay there, and wondered no one had told him of the mysterious dangers of that desolate mansion.

It stood by a lonely bend of the narrow road. Lilias had often looked up the short, straight, grass-grown avenue with an awful curiosity at the old house which she had learned in childhood to fear as the abode of shadowy tenants and unearthly dangers.

"There are people, Sally, nowadays, who call themselves free-thinkers, and don't believe in anything—even in ghosts," said Lilias.

"A then the place he's stopping in now, Miss Lilly, 'ill soon cure him of free-thinking, if half they say about it's true," answered Sally.

"But I don't say, mind, *he's* a free-thinker, for I don't know anything of Mr. Mervyn; but if he be not, he must be very brave, or very good, indeed. I know, Sally, I should be horribly afraid indeed, to sleep in it myself," answered Lilias, with a cosy little shudder, as the aerial image of the old house for a moment stood before her, with its peculiar malign, scared, and skulking aspect, as if it had drawn back in shame and guilt among the melancholy old elms and tall hemlock and nettles.

"And now, Sally, I'm safe in bed. Stir the fire, my old darling." For although it was the first week in May, the night was frosty. "And tell me all about the Tiled House again, and frighten me out of my wits."

So good old Sally, whose faith in such matters was a religion, went off over the well-known ground in a gentle little amble—sometimes subsiding into a walk as she approached some special horror, and pulling up altogether—that is to say, suspending her knitting, and looking with a mysterious nod at her young mistress in the four-poster, or lowering her voice to a sort of whisper when the crisis came.

So she told her how when the neighbours hired the orchard that ran up to the windows at the back of the house, the dogs they kept then used to howl so wildly and wolfishly all night among the trees, and prowl under the walls of the house so dejectedly, that they were fain to open the door and let them in at last; and, indeed, small need there was there for dogs; for no one, young or old, dared go near the orchard after nightfall. No, the golden pippins that peeped so splendid through the leaves in the western rays of evening, and made the mouths of the Ballyfermot schoolboys water, glowed undisturbed in the morning sunbeams, and secure in the mysterious tutelage of the night, smiled coyly on their predatory longings. And this was no fanciful reserve and avoidance. Mick Daly, when he had the orchard, used to sleep in the loft over the kitchen; and he swore that within five or six weeks, while he lodged there, he twice saw the same thing, and that was a lady in a hood and a loose dress, her head drooping, and her finger on her lip, walking in silence among the crooked stems, with a little child by the hand, who ran smiling and skipping beside her. And the Widow Cresswell once met them at nightfall on the path through the orchard to the back door, and she did not know what it was until she saw the men looking at one another as she told it.

"It's often she told it to me," said old Sally; "and how she came on them all of a sudden at the turn of the path, just by the thick clump of alder trees; and how she stopped, thinking it was some lady that had a right to be there; and how they went by as swift as the shadow of a cloud, though she only seemed to be walking slow enough, and the little child pulling by her arm, this way and that way, and took no notice of her, nor even raised her head, though she stopped and curtsied. And old Clinton, don't you remember old Clinton, Miss Lilly?"

"I think I do, the old man who limped, and wore the odd black wig?"

"Yes, indeed, acushla, so he did. See how well she remembers? That was by a kick of one of the earl's horses—he was groom then," resumed Sally. "He used to be troubled with hearing the very sounds his master used to make to bring him and old Oliver to the door, when he came back late. It was only on very dark nights when there was no moon. They used to hear, all on a sudden, the whimpering and scraping of dogs at the hall-door, and the sound of the whistle, and the light stroke across the window with the lash of the whip, just like as if the earl himself—may his poor soul find rest—was there. First the wind 'id stop, like you'd be holding your breath, then came these sounds they knew so well, and when they made no sign of stirring or opening the door, the wind 'id begin again with such a hoo-hoo-o-o-high, you'd think it was laughing, and crying, and hooting, all at once."

Here old Sally resumed her knitting, suspended for a moment, as if she were listening to the wind outside the haunted precincts of the Tiled House, and she took up her parable again.

"The very night he met his death in London, old Oliver, the butler, was listening to Clinton—for Clinton was a scholar—reading the letter that came to him through the post that day, telling him to get things ready, for his troubles were nearly over, and he expected to be with them again in a few days, and maybe almost as soon as the letter; and sure enough, while he was reading, there came a frightful rattle to the window, like someone all in a tremble, trying to shake it open, and the earl's voice, as they both conceited, cries from outside, 'Let me in, let me in, let me in!' 'It's him,' says the butler. 'Tis so, bedad,' says Clinton, and they both looked at the windy, and at one another—and then back again—overjoyed and frightened all at onst. Old Oliver was bad with the rheumatiz in his knee, and went lame like. So away goes Clinton to the hall-door, and he calls, 'who's there?' and no answer. Maybe, says Clinton, to himself, 'tis what he's rid round to the back-door; so to the back-door with him, and there he shouts again—and no answer, and not a sound outside—and he began to feel quare, and to the hall-door with him back again. 'Who's there? Do you hear, who's there?' he shouts, and receiving no answer still. 'I'll open the door at any rate,' says he, 'maybe it's what he's made his escape,' for they knew all about his troubles, 'and wants to get in without noise,' so praying all the time—for his mind misgave him, it might not be all right—he shifts the bars and unlocks the door; but neither man, woman, nor child, nor horse, nor any living shape, was standing there, only something or another slipt into the house close by his leg; it might be a dog, or something that way, he could not tell, for he only seen it for a moment with the corner of his eye, and it went in just like as if it belonged to the place. He could not see which way it went, up or down, but the house was never a happy one, or a quiet house after; and Clinton bangs the hall-door, and he took a sort of a turn and a threm-bling, and back with him to Oliver, the butler, looking as white as the blank leaf of his master's letter that was fluttering between his finger and thumb. 'What is it? *What* is it?' says the butler, catching his crutch like a waypon, fastening his eyes on Clinton's white face, and growing almost as pale himself. 'The master's dead,' says Clinton—and so he was, signs on it.

"After the turn she got by what she seen in the orchard, when she came to know the truth of what it was, Jinny Cresswell, you may be sure, did not stay there any longer than she could help; and she began to take notice of things she did not mind before—such as when she went into the big bedroom over the hall that the lord used to sleep in, whenever she went in at one door the other door used to be pulled to very quick, as if someone avoiding her was getting out in haste; but the thing that frightened her most was just this—that sometimes she used to find a long, straight mark from the head to the foot of her bed, as if 'twas made by something heavy lying there, and the place where it was used to feel warm, as if—whoever it was—they only left it as she came into the room.

"But the worst of all was poor Kitty Halpin, the young woman that died of what she seen. Her mother said it was how she was kept awake all the night with the walking about of someone in the next room, tumbling about boxes and pulling open drawers and talking and sighing to himself, and she, poor thing, wishing to go to sleep and wondering who it could be, when in he comes, a fine man, in a sort of loose silk morning-dress an' no wig, but a velvet cap on, and to the windy with him quiet and aisy, and she makes a turn in the bed to let him know there was someone there, thinking he'd go away, but instead of that, over he comes to the side of the bed, looking very bad, and says something to her—but his speech was thick and queer, like a dummy's that 'id be trying to spake—and she grew very frightened, and says she, 'I ask your honour's pardon, sir, but I can't hear you right,' and with that he stretches up his neck high out of his cravat, turning his face up towards the ceiling, and—grace between us and harm!—his throat was cut across like another mouth, wide open, laughing at her; she seen no more, but dropped in a dead faint in the bed, and back to her mother with her in the morning, and she never swallied bit or sup more, only she just sat by the fire holding her mother's hand, crying and trembling, and peepin' over her shoulder, and starting with every sound, till she took the fever and died, poor thing, not five weeks after."

And so on, and on, and on flowed the stream of old Sally's narrative, while Lilias dropped into dreamless sleep, and then the storyteller stole away to her own tidy bedroom and innocent slumbers.

II

I'm sure she believed every word she related, for old Sally was veracious. But all this was worth just so much as such talk commonly is—marvels, fabulæ, what our ancestors call winter's tales—which gathered details from every narrator and dilated in the act of narration. Still it was not quite for nothing that the house was held to be haunted. Under all this smoke there smouldered just a little spark of truth—an authenticated mystery, for the solution of which some of my readers may possibly suggest a theory, though I confess I can't.

Miss Rebecca Chattesworth, in a letter dated late in the autumn of 1753, gives a minute and curious relation of occurrences in the Tiled House, which, it is plain, although at starting she protests against all such fooleries, she has heard with a peculiar sort of interest, and relates it certainly with an awful sort of particularity.

I was for printing the entire letter, which is really very singular as well as characteristic. But my publisher meets me with his *veto*; and I believe he is right. The worthy old lady's letter *is*, perhaps, too long; and I must rest content with a few hungry notes of its tenor.

That year, and somewhere about the 24th October, there broke out a strange dispute between Mr. Alderman Harper, of Highstreet, Dublin, and my Lord Castlemallard, who, in virtue of his cousinship to the young heir's mother, had undertaken for him the management of the tiny estate on which the Tiled or Tyled House—for I find it spelt both ways—stood.

This Alderman Harper had agreed for a lease of the house for his daughter, who was married to a gentleman named Prosser. He furnished it and put up hangings, and otherwise went to considerable expense. Mr. and Mrs. Prosser came there some time in June, after having parted with a good many servants in the interval, she made up her mind that she could not live in the house, and her father waited on Lord Castlemallard and told him plainly that he would not take out the lease because the house was subjected to annoyances which he could not explain. In plain terms, he said it was haunted, and that no servants would live there more than a few weeks, and that after what his son-in-law's family had suffered there, not only should he be excused from taking a lease of it, but that the house itself ought to be pulled down as a nuisance and the habitual haunt of something worse than human malefactors.

Lord Castlemallard filed a bill in the Equity side of Exchequer to compel Mr. Alderman Harper to perform his contract, by taking out the lease. But the alderman drew an answer, supported by no less than seven long affidavits, copies of all which were furnished to his lordship, and with the desired effect; for rather than compel him to place them upon the file of the court, his lordship struck, and consented to release him.

I am sorry the cause did not proceed at least far enough to place upon the records of the court the very authentic and unaccountable story which Miss Rebecca relates.

The annoyances described did not begin till the end of August, when, one evening, Mrs. Prosser, quite alone, was sitting in the twilight at the back parlour window, which was open, looking out into the orchard, and plainly saw a hand stealthily placed upon the stone window-sill outside, as if by someone beneath the window, at her right side, intending to climb up. There was nothing but the hand, which was rather short, but handsomely formed, and white and plump, laid on the edge of the window-sill; and it was not a very young hand, but one aged, somewhere above forty, as she conjectured. It was only a few weeks before that the horrible robbery at Clondalkin had taken place, and the lady fancied that the hand was that of one of the miscreants who was now about to scale the windows of the Tiled House. She uttered a loud scream and an ejaculation of terror, and at the same moment the hand was quietly withdrawn.

Search was made in the orchard, but there was no indications of any person's having been under the window, beneath which, ranged along the wall, stood a great column of flowerpots, which it seemed must have prevented anyone's coming within reach of it.

The same night there came a hasty tapping, every now and then, at the window of the kitchen. The women grew frightened, and the servant-man, taking firearms with him, opened the back-door, but discovered nothing. As he shut it, however, he said "a thump came on it," and a pressure as of somebody striving to force his way in, which frightened *him*; and though the tapping went on upon the kitchen window-panes, he made no further explorations.

About six o'clock on Saturday evening, the cook, "an honest, sober woman, now aged nigh sixty years," being alone in the kitchen, saw, on looking up, it is supposed, the same fat but aristocratic-looking hand laid with its palm against the glass, as if feeling carefully for some inequality in its surface. She cried out, and said something like a prayer, on seeing it. But it was not withdrawn for several seconds after.

After this, for a great many nights, there came at first a low, and afterwards an angry rapping, as it seemed with a set of clenched knuckles, at the back-door. And the servant-man would not open it, but called to know who was there; and there came no answer, only a sound as if the palm of the hand was placed against it, and drawn slowly from side to side, with a sort of soft, groping motion.

All this time, sitting in the back parlour, which, for the time, they used as a drawing-room, Mr. & and Mrs. Prosser were disturbed by rappings at the window, sometimes very low and furtive, like a clandestine signal, and at others sudden and so loud as to threaten the breaking of the pane.

This was all at the back of the house, which looked upon the orchard, as you know. But on a Tuesday night, at about half past nine, there came precisely the same rapping at the hall-door, and went on, to the great annoyance of the master and terror of his wife, at intervals, for nearly two hours.

After this, for several days and nights, they had no annoyance whatsoever, and began to think that the nuisance had expended itself. But on the night of the 13th September, Jane Easterbrook, an English maid, having gone into the pantry for the small silver bowl in which her mistress's posset was served, happening to look up at the little window of only four panes, observed through an auger-hole which was drilled through the window-frame, for the admission of a bolt to secure the shutter, a white pudgy finger—first the tip, and then the two first joints introduced, and turned about this way and that, crooked against the inside, as if in search of a fastening which its owner designed to push aside. When the maid got back into the kitchen, we are told "she fell into 'a swounde,' and was all the next day very weak."

Mr. Prosser being, I've heard, a hard-headed and conceited sort of fellow, scouted the ghost, and sneered at the fears of his family. He was privately of opinion that the whole affair was a practical joke or a fraud, and waited an opportunity of catching the rogue *flagrante delicto*. He did not long keep this theory to himself, but let it out by degrees with no stint of oaths, believing that some domestic traitor held the thread of the conspiracy.

Indeed it was time something were done; for not only his servants, but good Mrs. Prosser herself, had grown to look unhappy and anxious, and kept at home from the hour of sunset, and would not venture about the house after night-fall, except in couples.

The knocking had ceased for about a week; and one night, Mrs. Prosser being in the nursery, her husband, who was in the parlour, heard it begin very softly at the hall-door. The air was quite still, which favoured his hearing distinctly. This was the first time there had been any disturbance at that side of the house, and the character of the summons also was changed.

Mr. Prosser, leaving the parlour door open, it seems, went quietly into the hall. The sound was that of beating on the outside of the stout door, softly and regularly, "with the flat of the hand." He was going to open it suddenly, but changed his mind; and went back very quietly, and on to the head of the kitchen stair, where was "a strong closet" over the pantry, in which he kept his "firearms, swords, and canes."

Here he called his man-servant, whom he believed to be honest; and with a pair of loaded pistols in his own coat-pockets, and giving another pair to him, he went as lightly as he could, followed by the man, and with a stout walking-cane in his hand, forward to the door.

Everything went as Mr. Prosser wished. The besieger of his house, so far from taking fright at their approach, grew more impatient; and the sort of patting which had roused his attention at first, assumed the rhythm and emphasis of a series of double-knocks.

Mr. Prosser, angry, opened the door with his right arm across, cane in hand. Looking, he saw nothing; but his arm was jerked up oddly, as it might be with the hollow of a hand, and something passed under it, with a kind of gentle squeeze. The servant neither saw nor felt anything, and did not know why his master looked back so hastily, and shut the door with so sudden a slam.

From that time, Mr. Prosser discontinued his angry talk and swearing about it, and seemed nearly as averse from the subject as the rest of the family. He grew, in fact, very uncomfortable, feeling an inward persuasion that when, in answer to the summons, he had opened the hall-door, he had actually given admission to the besieger.

He said nothing to Mrs. Prosser, but went up earlier to his bedroom, where "he read a while in his Bible, and said his prayers." I hope the particular relation of this circumstance does not indicate its singularity. He lay awake a good while, it appears; and as he supposed, about a quarter past twelve, he heard the soft palm of a hand patting on the outside of the bedroom door, and then brushed slowly along it.

Up bounced Mr. Prosser, very much frightened, and locked the door, crying, "Who's there?" but receiving no answer but the same brushing sound of a soft hand drawn over the panels, which he knew only too well.

In the morning the housemaid was terrified by the impression of a hand in the dust of the "little parlour" table, where they had been unpacking delft and other things the day before. The print of the naked foot in the sea-sand did not frighten Robinson Crusoe half so much. They were by this time all nervous, and some of them half crazed, about the hand.

Mr. Prosser went to examine the mark, and made light of it, but, as he swore afterwards, rather to quiet his servants than from any comfortable feeling about it in his own mind; however, he had them all, one by one, into the room, and made each place his or her hand, palm downward, on the same table, thus taking a similar impression from every person in the house, including himself and his wife; and his "affidavit" deposed that the formation of the hand so impressed differed altogether from those of the living inhabitants of the house, and corresponded exactly with that of the hand seen by Mrs. Prosser and by the cook.

Whoever or whatever the owner of that hand might be, they all felt this subtle demonstration to mean that it was declared he was no longer out of doors, but had established himself in the house.

And now Mrs. Prosser began to be troubled with strange and horrible dreams, some of which, as set out in detail, in Aunt Rebecca's long letter, are really very appalling nightmares. But one night, as Mr. Prosser closed his bedchamber door, he was struck somewhat by the utter silence of the room, there being no sound of breathing, which seemed unaccountable to him, as he knew his wife was in bed, and his ears were particularly sharp.

There was a candle burning on a small table at the foot of the bed, besides the one he held in one hand, a heavy ledger connected with his father-in-law's business being under his arm. He drew the curtain at the side of the bed, and saw Mrs. Prosser lying, as for a few seconds he mortally feared, dead, her face being motionless, white, and covered with a cold dew; and on the pillow, close beside her head, and just within the curtains, was the same white, fattish hand, the wrist resting on the pillow, and the fingers extended towards her temple with a slow, wavy motion.

Mr. Prosser, with a horrified jerk, pitched the ledger right at the curtains behind which the owner of the hand might be supposed to stand. The hand was instantaneously and smoothly snatched away, the curtains made a great wave, and Mr. Prosser got round the bed in time to see the closet-door, which was at the other side, drawn close by the same white, puffy hand, as he believed.

He drew the door open with a fling, and stared in; but the closet was empty, except for the clothes hanging from the pegs on the wall, and the dressing-table and looking glass facing the windows. He shut it sharply, and locked it, and felt for a minute, he says, "as if he were like to lose his wits"; then, ringing at the bell, he brought the servants, and with much ado they recovered Mrs. Prosser from a sort of "trance," in which, he says, from her looks, she seemed to have suffered "the pains of death"; and Aunt Rebecca adds, "From what she told me of her visions, with her own lips, he might have added 'and of hell also.'"

But the occurrence which seems to have determined the crisis was the strange sickness of their eldest child, a little girl aged between two and three years. It lay awake, seemingly in paroxysms of terror, and the doctors who were called in set down the symptoms to incipient water on the brain. Mrs. Prosser used to sit up with the nurse, by the nursery fire, much troubled in mind about the condition of her child.

Its bed was placed sideways along the wall, with its head against the door of a press or cupboard, which, however, did not shut quite close.

There was a little valance, about a foot deep, round the top of the child's bed, and this descended within some ten or twelve inches of the pillow on which it lay.

They observed that the little creature was quieter whenever they took it up and held it on their laps. They had just replaced it, as it seemed to have grown quite sleepy and tranquil, but it was not five minutes in its bed when it began to scream in one of its frenzies of terror; at the same moment the nurse for the first time detected, and Mrs. Prosser equally plainly saw, following the direction of her eyes, the real cause of the child's sufferings.

Protruding through the aperture of the press, and shrouded in the shade of the valance, they plainly saw the white fat hand, palm downwards, presented towards the head of the child. The mother uttered a scream, and snatched the child from its little bed, and she and the nurse ran down to the lady's sleeping-room, where Mr. Prosser was in bed, shutting the door as they entered; and they had hardly done so, when a gentle tap came to it from the outside.

There is a great deal more, but this will suffice. The singularity of the narrative seems to me to be this, that it describes the ghost of a hand, and no more. The person to whom that hand belonged never once appeared; nor was it a hand separated from a body, but only a hand so manifested and introduced, that its owner was always, by some crafty accident, hidden from view.

In the year 1819, at a college breakfast, I met a Mr. Prosser—a thin, grave, but rather chatty old gentleman, with very white hair, drawn back into a pigtail—and he told us all, with a concise particularity, a story of his cousin, James Prosser, who, when an infant, had slept for some time in what his mother said was a haunted nursery in an old house near Chapelizod, and who, whenever he was ill, over-fatigued, or in anywise feverish, suffered all through his life, as he had done for a time he could scarcely remember, from a vision of a certain gentleman, fat and pale, every curl of whose wig, every button of whose laced clothes, and every feature and line of whose sensual, malignant, and unwholesome face, was as minutely engraven upon his memory as the dress and lineaments of his father's portrait, which hung before him every day at breakfast, dinner, and supper.

Mr. Prosser mentioned this as an instance of a curiously monotonous, individualized, and persistent nightmare, and hinted the extreme horror and anxiety with which his cousin, of whom he spoke in the past tense as "poor Jemmie," was at any time induced to mention it.

I hope the reader will pardon me for loitering so long in the Tiled House, but this sort of lore has always had a charm for me; and people, you know, especially old people, will talk of what most interests themselves, too often forgetting that others may have had more than enough of it.

THE DEAD SMILE

F. Marion Crawford

Sir Hugh Ockram smiled as he sat by the open window of his study, in the late August afternoon, and just then a curiously yellow cloud obscured the low sun, and the clear summer light turned lurid, as if it had been suddenly poisoned and polluted by the foul vapours of a plague. Sir Hugh's face seemed, at best, to be made of fine parchment drawn skintight over a wooden mask, in which two eyes were sunk out of sight, and peered from far within through crevices under the slanting, wrinkled lids, alive and watchful like two toads in their holes, side by side and exactly alike. But as the light changed, then a little yellow glare flashed in each. Nurse Macdonald said once that when Sir Hugh smiled he saw the faces of two women in hell—two dead women he had betrayed. (Nurse Macdonald was a hundred years old.) And the smile widened, stretching the pale lips across the discoloured teeth in an expression of profound self-satisfaction, blended with the most unforgiving hatred and contempt for the human doll. The hideous disease of which he was dying had touched his brain. His son stood beside him, tall, white, and delicate as an angel in a primitive picture, and though there was deep distress in his violet eyes as he looked at his father's face, he felt the shadow of that sickening smile stealing across his own lips and parting them and drawing them against his will. And it was like a bad dream, for he tried not to smile and smiled the more. Beside him, strangely like him in her wan, angelic beauty, with the same shadowy golden hair, the same sad violet eyes, the same luminously pale face, Evelyn Warburton rested one hand upon his arm. And as she looked into her uncle's eyes, and could not turn her own away, she knew that the deathly smile was hovering on her own red lips, drawing them tightly across her little teeth, while two bright tears ran down her cheeks to her mouth, and dropped from the upper to the lower lip while she smiled—and the smile was like the shadow of death and the seal of damnation upon her pure, young face.

"Of course," said Sir Hugh very slowly, and still looking out at the trees, "if you have made up your mind to be married, I cannot hinder you, and I don't suppose you attach the smallest importance to my consent—"

"Father!" exclaimed Gabriel reproachfully.

"No, I do not deceive myself," continued the old man, smiling terribly. "You will marry when I am dead, though there is a very good reason why you had better not—why you had better not," he repeated very emphatically, and he slowly turned his toad eyes upon the lovers.

"What reason?" asked Evelyn in a frightened voice.

"Never mind the reason, my dear. You will marry just as if it did not exist." There was a long pause. "Two gone," he said, his voice lowering strangely, "and two more will be four—all together—for ever and ever, burning, burning, burning bright."

At the last words his head sank slowly back, and the little glare of the toad eyes disappeared under the swollen lids, and the lurid cloud passed from the westering sun, so that the earth was green again and the light pure. Sir Hugh had fallen asleep, as he often did in his last illness, even while speaking.

Gabriel Ockram drew Evelyn away, and from the study they went out into the dim hall, softly closing the door behind them, and each audibly drew breath, as though some sudden danger had been passed.

They laid their hands each in the other's, and their strangely-like eyes met in a long look, in which love and perfect understanding were darkened by the secret terror of an unknown thing. Their pale faces reflected each other's fear.

"It is his secret," said Evelyn at last. "He will never tell us what it is."

"If he dies with it," answered Gabriel, "let it be on his own head!"

"On his head!" echoed the dim hall. It was a strange echo, and some were frightened by it, for they said that if it were a real echo it should repeat everything and not give back a phrase here and there, now speaking, now silent. But Nurse Macdonald said that the great hall would never echo a prayer when an Ockram was to die, though it would give back curses ten for one.

"On his head!" it repeated quite softly, and Evelyn started and looked round.

"It is only the echo," said Gabriel, leading her away.

They went out into the late afternoon light, and sat upon a stone seat behind the chapel, which was built across the end of the east wing. It was very still, not a breath stirred, and there was no sound near them. Only far off in the park a song-bird was whistling the high prelude to the evening chorus.

"It is very lonely here," said Evelyn, taking Gabriel's hand nervously, and speaking as if she dreaded to disturb the silence. "If it were dark, I should be afraid."

"Of what? Of me?" Gabriel's sad eyes turned to her.

"Oh no! How could I be afraid of you? But of the old Ockrams—they say they are just under our feet here in the north vault outside the chapel, all in their shrouds, with no coffins, as they used to bury them."

"As they always will—as they will bury my father, and me. They say an Ockram will not lie in a coffin."

"But it cannot be true—these are fairy tales—ghost stories!" Evelyn nestled nearer to her companion, grasping his hand more tightly, and the sun began to go down.

"Of course. But there is a story of old Sir Vernon, who was beheaded for treason under James II. The family brought his body back from the scaffold in an iron coffin with heavy locks, and they put it in the north vault. But ever afterwards, whenever the vault was opened to bury another of the family, they found the coffin wide open, and the body standing upright against the wall, and the head rolled away in a corner, smiling at it."

"As Uncle Hugh smiles?" Evelyn shivered.

"Yes, I suppose so," answered Gabriel, thoughtfully. "Of course I never saw it, and the vault has not been opened for thirty years—none of us have died since then."

"And if—if Uncle Hugh dies—shall you—" Evelyn stopped, and her beautiful thin face was quite white.

"Yes. I shall see him laid there too—with his secret, whatever it is." Gabriel sighed and pressed the girl's little hand.

"I do not like to think of it," she said unsteadily. "Oh Gabriel, what can the secret be? He said we had better not marry—not that he forbade it—but he said it so strangely, and he smiled—ugh!" Her small white teeth chattered with fear, and she looked over her shoulder while drawing still closer to Gabriel. "And, somehow, I felt it in my own face—"

"So did I," answered Gabriel in a low, nervous voice. "Nurse Macdonald—" He stopped abruptly.

"What? What did she say?"

"Oh—nothing. She has told me things—they would frighten you, dear. Come, it is growing chilly." He rose, but Evelyn held his hand in both of hers, still sitting and looking up into his face.

"But we shall be married, just the same—Gabriel! Say that we shall!"

"Of course, darling—of course. But while my father is so very ill, it is impossible—"

"Oh Gabriel, Gabriel dear! I wish we were married now!" cried Evelyn in sudden distress. "I know that something will prevent it and keep us apart."

"Nothing shall!"

"Nothing?"

"Nothing human," said Gabriel Ockram, as she drew him down to her.

And their faces, that were so strangely alike, met and touched—and Gabriel knew that the kiss had a marvellous savour of evil, but on Evelyn's lips it was like the cool breath of a sweet and mortal fear. And neither of them understood, for they were innocent and young. Yet she drew him to her by her lightest touch, as a sensitive plant shivers and waves its thin leaves, and bends and closes softly upon what it wants, and he let himself be drawn to her willingly, as he would if her touch had been deadly and poisonous; for she strangely loved that half voluptuous breath of fear, and he passionately desired the nameless evil something that lurked in her maiden lips.

"It is as if we loved in a strange dream," she said.

"I fear the waking," he murmured.

"We shall not wake, dear—when the dream is over it will have already turned into death, so softly that we shall not know it. But until then—"

She paused, and her eyes sought his, and their faces slowly came nearer. It was as if they had thoughts in their red lips that foresaw and foreknew the deep kiss of each other.

"Until then—" she said again, very low, and her mouth was nearer to his.

"Dream—till then," murmured his breath.

※　※　※

Nurse Macdonald was a hundred years old. She used to sleep sitting all bent together in a great old leathern arm-chair with wings, her feet in a bag footstool lined with sheepskin, and many warm blankets wrapped about her, even in summer. Beside her a little lamp always burned at night by an old silver cup, in which there was something to drink.

Her face was very wrinkled, but the wrinkles were so small and fine and near together that they made shadows instead of lines. Two thin locks of hair, that was turning from white to a smoky yellow again, were drawn over her temples from under her starched white cap. Every now and then she woke, and her eyelids were drawn up in tiny folds like little pink silk curtains, and her queer blue eyes looked straight before her through doors and walls and worlds to a far place beyond. Then she slept again, and her hands lay one upon the other on the edge of the blanket, the thumbs had grown longer than the fingers with age, and the joints shone in the low lamplight like polished crab-apples.

It was nearly one o'clock in the night, and the summer breeze was blowing the ivy branch against the panes of the window with a hushing caress. In the small room beyond, with the door ajar, the girl-maid who took care of Nurse Macdonald was fast asleep. All was very quiet. The old woman breathed regularly, and her indrawn lips trembled each time as the breath went out, and her eyes were shut.

But outside the closed window there was a face, and violet eyes were looking steadily at the ancient sleeper, for it was like the face of Evelyn Warburton, though there were eighty feet from the sill of the window to the foot of the tower. Yet the cheeks were thinner than Evelyn's, and as white as a gleam, and her eyes stared, and the lips were not red with life, they were dead and painted with new blood.

Slowly Nurse Macdonald's wrinkled eyelids folded themselves back, and she looked straight at the face at the window while one might count ten.

"Is it time?" she asked in her little old, far-away voice.

While she looked the face at the window changed, for the eyes opened wider and wider till the white glared all round the bright violet, and the bloody lips opened over gleaming teeth, and stretched and widened and stretched again, and the shadow golden hair rose and streamed against the window in the night breeze. And in answer to Nurse Macdonald's question came the sound that freezes the living flesh.

That low moaning voice that rises suddenly, like the scream of storm, from a moan to a wail, from a wail to a howl, from a howl to the fear-shriek of the tortured dead—he who had heard knows, and he can bear witness that the cry of the banshee is an evil cry to hear alone in the deep night. When it was over and the face was gone, Nurse Macdonald shook a little in her great chair, and still she looked at the black square of the window, but there was nothing more there, nothing but the night, and the whispering ivy branch. She turned her head to the door that was ajar, and there stood the girl in her white gown, her teeth chattering with fright.

"It is time, child," said Nurse Macdonald. "I must go to him, for it is the end."

She rose slowly, leaning her withered hands upon the arms of the chair, and the girl brought her a woollen gown and a great mantle, and her crutch-stick, and made her ready. But very often the girl looked at the window and was unjointed with fear, and often Nurse Macdonald shook her head and said words which the maid could not understand.

"It was like the face of Miss Evelyn," said the girl at last, trembling.

But the ancient woman looked up sharply and angrily, and her queer blue eyes glared. She held herself by the arm of the great chair with her left hand, and lifted up her crutch-stick to strike the maid with all her might. But she did not.

"You are a good girl," she said, "but you are a fool. Pray for wit, child, pray for wit—or else find service in another house than Ockram Hall. Bring the lamp and help me under my left arm."

The crutch-stick clacked on the wooden floor, and the low heels of the woman's slippers clappered after her in slow triplets, as Nurse Macdonald got towards the door. And down the stairs each step she took was a labour in itself, and by the clacking noise the waking servants knew that she was coming, very long before they saw her.

No one was sleeping now, and there were lights and whisperings and pale faces in the corridors near Sir Hugh's bedroom, and now someone went in, and now someone came out, but every one made way for Nurse Macdonald, who had nursed Sir Hugh's father more than eighty years ago.

The light was soft and clear in the room. There stood Gabriel Ockram by his father's bedside, and there knelt Evelyn Warburton, her hair lying like a golden shadow down her shoulders, and her hands clasped nervously together. And opposite Gabriel, a nurse was trying to make Sir Hugh drink. But he would not, and though his lips were parted, his teeth were set. He was very, very thin and yellow now, and his eyes caught the light sideways and were as yellow coals.

"Do not torment him," said Nurse Macdonald to the woman who held the cup. "Let me speak to him, for his hour is come."

"Let her speak to him," said Gabriel in a dull voice.

So the ancient woman leaned to the pillow and laid the feather-weight of her withered hand, that was like a brown moth, upon Sir Hugh's yellow fingers, and she spoke to him earnestly, while only Gabriel and Evelyn were left in the room to hear.

"Hugh Ockram," she said, "this is the end of your life; and as I saw you born, and saw your father born before you, I am come to see you die. Hugh Ockram, will you tell me the truth?"

The dying man recognized the little far-away voice he had known all his life, and he very slowly turned his yellow face to Nurse Macdonald; but he said nothing. Then she spoke again.

"Hugh Ockram, you will never see the daylight again. Will you tell the truth?"

His toad-like eyes were not dull yet. They fastened themselves on her face.

"What do you want of me?" he asked, and each word struck hollow on the last. "I have no secrets. I have lived a good life."

Nurse Macdonald laughed—a tiny, cracked laugh, that made her old head bob and tremble a little, as if her neck were on a steel spring. But Sir Hugh's eyes grew red, and his pale lips began to twist.

"Let me die in peace," he said slowly.

But Nurse Macdonald shook her head, and her brown, moth-like hand left his and fluttered to his forehead.

"By the mother that bore you and died of grief for the sins you did, tell me the truth!"

Sir Hugh's lips tightened on his discoloured teeth.

"Not on Earth," he answered slowly.

"By the wife who bore your son and died heart-broken, tell me the truth!"

"Neither to you in life, nor to her in eternal death."

His lips writhed, as if the words were coals between them, and a great drop of sweat rolled across the parchment of his forehead. Gabriel Ockram bit his hand as he watched his father die. But Nurse Macdonald spoke a third time.

"By the woman whom you betrayed, and who waits for you this night, Hugh Ockram, tell me the truth!"

"It is too late. Let me die in peace."

The writhing lips began to smile across the set yellow teeth, and the toad eyes glowed like evil jewels in his head.

"There is time," said the ancient woman. "Tell me the name of Evelyn Warburton's father. Then I will let you die in peace."

Evelyn started back, kneeling as she was, and stared at Nurse Macdonald, and then at her uncle.

"The name of Evelyn's father?" he repeated slowly, while the awful smile spread upon his dying face.

The light was growing strangely dim in the great room. As Evelyn looked, Nurse Macdonald's crooked shadow on the wall grew gigantic. Sir Hugh's breath came thick, rattling in his throat, as death crept in like a snake and choked it back. Evelyn prayed aloud, high and clear.

Then something rapped at the window, and she felt her hair rise upon her head in a cool breeze, as she looked around in spite of herself. And when she saw her own white face looking in at the window, and her own eyes staring at her through the glass, wide and fearful, and her own hair streaming against the pane, and her own lips dashed with blood, she rose slowly from the floor and stood rigid for one moment, till she screamed once and fell straight back into Gabriel's arms. But the shriek that answered hers was the fear-shriek of the tormented corpse, out of which the soul cannot pass for shame of deadly sins, though the devils fight in it with corruption, each for their due share.

Sir Hugh Ockram sat upright in his death-bed, and saw and cried aloud:

"Evelyn!" His harsh voice broke and rattled in his chest as he sank down. But still Nurse Macdonald tortured him, for there was a little life left in him still.

"You have seen the mother as she waits for you, Hugh Ockram. Who was this girl Evelyn's father? What was his name?"

For the last time the dreadful smile came upon the twisted lips, very slowly, very surely now, and the toad eyes glared red, and the parchment face glowed a little in the flickering light. For the last time words came.

"They know it in hell."

Then the glowing eyes went out quickly, the yellow face turned waxen pale, and a great shiver ran through the thin body as Hugh Ockram died.

But in death he still smiled, for he knew his secret and kept it still, on the other side, and he would take it with him, to lie with him for ever in the north vault of the chapel where the Ockrams lie uncoffined in their shrouds—all but one. Though he was dead, he smiled, for he had kept his treasure of evil truth to the end, and there was none left to tell the name he had spoken, but there was all the evil he had not undone left to bear fruit.

As they watched—Nurse Macdonald and Gabriel, who held Evelyn still unconscious in his arms while he looked at the father— they felt the dead smile crawling along their own lips—the ancient crone and the youth with the angel's face. Then they shivered a little, and both looked at Evelyn as she lay with her head on his shoulder, and, though she was very beautiful, the same sickening smile was twisting her young mouth too, and it was like the foreshadowing of a great evil which they could not understand.

But by and by they carried Evelyn out, and she opened her eyes and the smile was gone. From far away in the great house the sound of weeping and crooning came up the stairs and echoed along the dismal corridors, for the women had begun to mourn the dead master, after the Irish fashion, and the hall had echoes of its own all that night, like the far-off wail of the banshee among forest trees.

When the time was come they took Sir Hugh in his winding-sheet on a trestle bier, and bore him to the chapel and through the iron door and down the long descent to the north vault, with tapers, to lay him by his father. And two men went in first to prepare the place, and came back staggering like drunken men, and white, leaving their lights behind them.

But Gabriel Ockram was not afraid, for he knew. And he went in alone and saw that the body of Sir Vernon Ockram was leaning upright against the stone wall, and that his head lay on the ground near by with the face turned up, and the dried leathern lips smiled horribly at the dried-up corpse, while the iron coffin, lined with black velvet, stood open on the floor.

Then Gabriel took the thing in his hands, for it was very light, being quite dried by the air of the vault, and those who peeped in from the door saw him lay it in the coffin again, and it rustled a little, like a bundle of reeds, and sounded hollow as it touched the sides and the bottom. He also placed the head upon the shoulders and shut down the lid, which fell to with a rusty spring that snapped.

After that they laid Sir Hugh beside his father, with the trestle bier on which they had brought him, and they went back to the chapel.

But when they saw one another's faces, master and men, they were all smiling with the dead smile of the corpse they had left in the vault, so that they could not bear to look at one another until it had faded away.

❊   ❊   ❊

Gabriel Ockram became Sir Gabriel, inheriting the baronetcy with the half-ruined fortune left by his father, and still Evelyn Warburton lived at Ockram hall, in the south room that had been hers ever since she could remember anything. She could not go away, for there were no relatives to whom she could have gone, and, besides, there seemed to be no reason why she should not stay. The world would never trouble itself to care what the Ockrams did on their Irish estates, and it was long since the Ockrams had asked anything of the world.

So Sir Gabriel took his father's place at the dark old table in the dining-room, and Evelyn sat opposite to him, until such time as their mourning should be over, and they might be married at last. And meanwhile their lives went on as before, since Sir Hugh had been a hopeless invalid during the last year of his life, and they had seen him but once a day for the little while, spending most of their time together in a strangely perfect companionship.

But though the late summer saddened into autumn, and autumn darkened into winter, and storm followed storm, and rain poured on rain through the short days and the long nights, yet Ockram Hall seemed less gloomy since Sir Hugh had been laid in the north vault beside his father. And at Christmastide Evelyn decked the great hall with holly and green boughs, and huge fires blazed on every hearth. Then the tenants were all bidden to a New Year's dinner, and they ate and drank well, while Sir Gabriel sat at the head of the table. Evelyn came in when the port wine was brought, and the most respected of the tenants made a speech to propose her health.

It was long, he said, since there had been a Lady Ockram. Sir Gabriel shaded his eyes with his hand and looked down at the table, but a faint colour came into Evelyn's transparent cheeks. But, said the grey-haired farmer, it was longer still since there had been a Lady Ockram so fair as the next was to be, and he gave the health of Evelyn Warburton.

Then the tenants all stood up and shouted for her, and Sir Gabriel stood up likewise, beside Evelyn. And when the men gave the last and loudest cheer of all there was a voice not theirs, above them all, higher, fiercer, louder—a scream not earthly, shrieking for the bride of Ockram Hall. And the holly and the green boughs over the great chimney-piece shook and slowly waved as if a cool breeze were blowing over them. But the men turned very pale, and many of them set down their glasses, but others let them fall upon the floor for fear. And looking into one another's faces, they were all smiling strangely, a dead smile, like dead Sir Hugh's. One cried out words in Irish, and the fear of death was suddenly upon them all so that they fled in panic, falling over one another like wild beasts in the burning forest, when the thick smoke runs along before the flame, and the tables were overset, and drinking glasses and bottles were broken in heaps, and the dark red wine crawled like blood upon the polished floor.

Sir Gabriel and Evelyn stood alone at the head of the table before the wreck of the feast, not daring to turn to see each other, for each knew that the other smiled. But his right arm held her and his left hand clasped her right as they stared before them, and but for the shadows of her hair one might not have told their two faces apart. They listened long, but the cry came not again, and the dead smile faded from their lips, while each remembered that Sir Hugh Ockram lay in the north vault, smiling in his winding-sheet, in the dark, because he had died with his secret.

So ended the tenants' New Year's dinner. But from that time on Sir Gabriel grew more and more silent, and his face grew even paler and thinner than before. Often without warning and without words, he would rise from his seat, as if something moved him against his will, and he would go out into the rain or the sunshine to the north side of the chapel, and sit on the stone bench, staring at the ground as if he could see through it, and through the vault below, and through the white winding-sheet in the dark, to the dead smile that would not die.

Always when he went out in that way Evelyn came out presently and sat beside him. Once, too, as in summer, their beautiful faces came suddenly near, and their lids drooped, and their red lips were almost joined together. But as their eyes met, they grew wide and wild, so that the white showed in a ring all round the deep violet, and their teeth chattered, and their hands were like hands of corpses, each in the other's for the terror of what was under their feet, and of what they knew but could not see.

Once, also, Evelyn found Sir Gabriel in the chapel alone, standing before the iron door that led down to the place of death, and in his hand there was the key to the door, but he had not put it in the lock. Evelyn drew him away, shivering, for she had also been driven in waking dreams to see that terrible thing again, and to find out whether it had changed since it had lain there.

"I'm going mad," said Sir Gabriel, covering his eyes with his hand as he went with her. "I see it in my sleep, I see it when I am awake—it draws me to it, day and night—and unless I see it I shall die!"

"I know," answered Evelyn, "I know. It is as if threads were spun from it, like a spider's, drawing us down to it." She was silent for a moment, and then she started violently and grasped his arm with a man's strength, and almost screamed the words she spoke. "But we must not go there!" she cried. "We must not go!"

Sir Gabriel's eyes were half shut, and he was not moved by the agony of her face.

"I shall die, unless I see it again," he said, in a quiet voice not like his own. And all that day and that evening he scarcely spoke, thinking of it, always thinking, while Evelyn Warburton quivered from head to foot with a terror she had never known.

She went alone, on a grey winter's morning, to Nurse Macdonald's room in the tower, and sat down beside the great leathern easy-chair, laying her thin white hand upon the withered fingers.

"Nurse," she said, "what was it that Uncle Hugh should have told you, that night before he died? It must have been an awful secret—and yet, though you asked him, I feel somehow that you know it, and that you know why he used to smile so dreadfully."

The old woman's head moved slowly from side to side.

"I only guess—I shall never know," she answered slowly in her cracked little voice.

"But what do you guess? Who am I? Why did you ask who my father was? You know I am colonel Warburton's daughter, and my mother was Lady Ockram's sister, so that Gabriel and I are cousins. My father was killed in Afghanistan. What secret can there be?"

"I do not know. I can only guess."

"Guess what?" asked Evelyn imploringly, and pressing the soft withered hands, as she leaned forward. But Nurse Macdonald's wrinkled lids dropped suddenly over her queer blue eyes, and her lips shook a little with her breath, as if she were asleep.

Evelyn waited. By the fire the Irish maid was knitting fast, and the needles clicked like three or four clocks ticking against each other. And the real clock on the wall solemnly ticked alone, checking off the seconds of the woman who was a hundred years old, and had not many days left. Outside the ivy branch beat the window in the wintry blast, as it had beaten against the glass a hundred years ago.

Then as Evelyn sat there she felt again the waking of a horrible desire—the sickening wish to go down, down to the thing in the north vault, and to open the winding-sheet, and see whether it had changed, and she held Nurse Macdonald's hands as if to keep herself in her place and fight against the appalling attraction of the evil dead.

But the old cat that kept Nurse Macdonald's feet warm, lying always on the bag footstool, got up and stretched itself, and looked up into Evelyn's eyes, while its back arched, and its tail thickened and bristled, and its ugly pink lips drew back in a devilish grin, showing its sharp teeth. Evelyn stared at it, half fascinated by its ugliness. Then the creature suddenly put out one paw with all its claws spread, and spat at the girl, and all at once the grinning cat was like the smiling corpse far down below, so that Evelyn shivered down to her small feet, and covered her face with her free hand lest Nurse Macdonald should wake and see the dead smile there, for she could feel it.

The old woman had already opened her eyes again, and she touched her cat with the end of her crutch-stick, whereupon its back went down and its tail shrunk, and it sidled back to its place on the bag footstool. But its yellow eyes looked up sideways at Evelyn, between the slits of its lids.

"What is it that you guess, nurse?" asked the young girl again.

"A bad thing—a wicked thing. But I dare not tell you, lest it might not be true, and the very thought should blast your life. For if I guess right, he meant that you should not know, and that you two should marry, and pay for his old sin with your souls."

"He used to tell us that we ought not to marry—"

"Yes—he told you that, perhaps—but it was as if a man put poisoned meat before a starving beast and said, "Do not eat," but ever raised his hand to take the meat away. And if he told you that you should not marry, it was because he hoped you would, for of all men living or dead, Hugh Ockram was the falsest man that ever told a cowardly lie, and the cruelest that ever hurt a weak woman, and the worst that ever loved a sin."

"But Gabriel and I love each other," said Evelyn, very sadly.

Nurse Macdonald's old eyes looked far away, at sights seen long ago, and that rose in the grey winter air amid the mists of an ancient youth.

"If you love, you can die together," she said, very slowly. "Why should you live, if it is true? I am a hundred years old. What has life given me? The beginning is fire, the end is a heap of ashes, and between the end and the beginning lies all the pain in the world. Let me sleep, since I cannot die."

Then the old woman's eyes closed again, and her head sank a little lower upon her breast.

So Evelyn went away and left her asleep, with the cat asleep on the bag footstool; and the young girl tried to forget Nurse Macdonald's words, but she could not, for she heard them over and over again in the wind, and behind her on the stairs. And as she grew sick with fear of the frightful unknown evil to which her soul was bound, she felt a bodily something pressing her, and pushing her, and forcing her on, and from the other side she felt the threads that drew her mysteriously, and when she shut her eyes, she saw in the chapel behind the altar, the low iron door through which she must pass to go to the thing.

And as she lay awake at night, she drew the sheet over her face, lest she should see shadows on the wall beckoning her and the sound of her own warm breath made whisperings in her ears, while she held the mattress with her hands, to keep from getting up and going to the chapel. It would have been easier if there had not been a way thither through the library, by a door which was never locked. It would be fearfully easy to take her candle and go softly through the sleeping house. And the key of the vault lay under the altar behind a stone that turned. She knew the little secret. She could go alone and see.

But when she thought of it, she felt her hair rise on her head, and first she shivered so that the bed shook, and then the horror went through her in a cold thrill that was agony again, like myriads of icy needles, boring into her nerves.

❋　　❋　　❋

The old clock in Nurse Macdonald's tower struck midnight.

From her room she could hear the creaking chains and weights in their box in the corner of the staircase, and overhead the jarring of the rusty lever that lifted the hammer. She had heard it all her life. It struck eleven strokes clearly and then came the twelfth, with a dull half stroke, as though the hammer were too weary to go on, and had fallen asleep against the bell.

The old cat got up from the bag footstool and stretched itself, and Nurse Macdonald opened her ancient eyes and looked slowly round the room by the dim light of the night lamp. She touched the cat with her crutch-stick, and it lay down upon her feet. She drank a few drops from her cup and went to sleep again.

But downstairs Sir Gabriel sat straight up as the clock struck, for he had dreamed a fearful dream of horror, and his heart stood still, till he awoke at its stopping, and it beat again furiously with his breath, like a wild thing set free. No Ockram had ever known fear waking, but sometimes it came to Sir Gabriel in his sleep.

He pressed his hands to his temples as he sat up in bed, and his hands were icy cold, but his head was hot. The dream faded far, and in its place there came the master thought that racked his life; with the thought also came the sick twisting of his lips in the dark that would have been a smile. Far off, Evelyn Warburton dreamed that the dead smile was on her mouth, and awoke, starting with a little moan, her face in her hands shivering.

But Sir Gabriel struck a light and got up and began to walk up and down his great room. It was midnight, and he had barely slept an hour, and in the north of Ireland the winter nights are long.

"I shall go mad," he said to himself, holding his forehead. He knew that it was true. For weeks and months the possession of the thing had grown upon him like a disease, till he could think of nothing without thinking first of that. And now all at once it outgrew his strength, and he knew that he must be its instrument or lose his mind—that he must do the deed he hated and feared, if he could fear anything, or that something would snap in his brain and divide him from life while he was yet alive. He took the candlestick in his hand, the old-fashioned heavy candlestick that had always been used by the head of the house. He did not think of dressing, but went as he was, in his silk night-clothes and his slippers, and he opened the door. Everything was very still in the great old house. He shut the door behind him and walked noiselessly on the carpet through the long corridor. A cool breeze blew over his shoulder and blew the flame of his candle straight out from him. Instinctively he stopped and looked round, but all was still, and the upright flame burned steadily. He walked on, and instantly a strong draught was behind him, almost extinguishing the light. It seemed to blow him on his way, ceasing whenever he turned, coming again when he went on—invisible, icy.

Down the great staircase to the echoing hall he went, seeing nothing but the flaring flame of the candle standing away from him over the guttering wax, while the cold wind blew over his shoulder and through his hair. On he passed through the open door into the library, dark with old books and carved bookcases, on through the door in the shelves, with painted shelves on it, and the imitated backs of books, so that one needed to know where to find it—and it shut itself after him with a soft click. He entered the low-arched passage, and though the door was shut behind him and fitted tightly in its frame, still the cold breeze blew the flame forward as he walked. And he was not afraid, but his face was very pale, and his eyes were wide and bright, looking before him, seeing already in the dark air the picture of the thing beyond. But in the chapel he stood still, his hand on the little turning stone tablet in the back of the stone altar. On the tablet were engraved words, *'Clavis sepulchri Clarissimorum Deminorum De Ockram'*—('the key to the vault of the most illustrious lords of Ockram'). Sir Gabriel paused and listened. He fancied that he heard a sound far off in the great house where all had been so still, but it did not come again. Yet he waited at the last, and looked at the low iron door. Beyond it, down the long descent, lay his father uncoffined, six months dead, corrupt, terrible in his clinging shroud. The strangely preserving air of the vault could not yet have done its work completely. But on the thing's ghastly features, with their half-dried, open eyes, there would still be the frightful smile with which the man had died—the smile that haunted—

As the thought crossed Sir Gabriel's mind, he felt his lips writhing, and he struck his own mouth in wrath with the back of his hand so fiercely that a drop of blood ran down his chin and another, and more, falling back in the gloom upon the chapel pavement. But still his bruised lips twisted themselves. He turned the tablet by the simple secret. It needed no safer fastening, for had each Ockram been confined in pure gold, and had the door been wide, there was not a man in Tyrone brave enough to go down to that place, saving Gabriel Ockram himself, with his angel's face and his thin, white hands, and his sad unflinching eyes. He took the great gold key and set it into the lock of the iron door, and the heavy, rattling noise echoed down the descent beyond like footsteps, as if a watcher had stood behind the iron and were running away within, with heavy dead feet. And though he was standing still, the cool wind was from behind him, and blew the flame of the candle against the iron panel. He turned the key.

Sir Gabriel saw that his candle was short. There were new ones on the altar, with long candlesticks, and he lit one, and left his own burning on the floor. As he set it down on the pavement his lip began to bleed again, and another drop fell upon the stones.

He drew the iron door open and pushed it back against the chapel wall, so that it should not shut of itself, while he was within, and the horrible draught of the sepulcher came up out of the depths in his face, foul and dark. He went in, but though the fetid air met him, yet the flame of the tall candle was blown straight from him against the wind while he walked down the easy incline with steady steps, his loose slippers slapping the pavement as he trod.

He shaded the candle with his hand, and his fingers seemed to be made of wax and blood as the light shone through them. And in spite of him the unearthly draught forced the flame forward, till it was blue over the black wick, and it seemed as if it must go out. But he went straight on, with shining eyes.

The downward passage was wide, and he could not always see the walls by the struggling light, but he knew when he was in the place of death by the larger, drearier echo of his steps in the greater space and by the sensation of a distant blank wall. He stood still, almost enclosing the flame of the candle in the hollow of his hand. He could see a little, for his eyes were growing used to the gloom. Shadowy forms were outlined in the dimness, where the biers of the Ockrams stood crowded together, side by side, each with its straight, shrouded corpse, strangely preserved by the dry air, like the empty shell that the locust sheds in summer. And a few steps before him he saw clearly the dark shape of headless Sir Vernon's iron coffin, and he knew that nearest to it lay the thing he sought.

He was as brave as any of those dead men had been, and they were his fathers, and he knew that sooner or later he should lie there himself, beside Sir Hugh, slowly drying to a parchment shell. But he was still alive, and he closed his eyes a moment, and three great drops stood on his forehead.

Then he looked again, and by the whiteness of the winding-sheet he knew his father's corpse, for all the others were brown with age; and, moreover, the flame of the candle was blown towards it. He made four steps till he reached it, and suddenly the light burned straight and high, shedding a dazzling yellow glare upon the fine linen that was all white, save over the face, and where the joined hands were laid on the breast. And at those places ugly stains had spread, darkened with outlines of the features and of the tight-clasped fingers. There was a frightful stench of drying death.

As Sir Gabriel looked down, something stirred behind him, softly at first, then more noisily, and something fell to the stone floor with a dull thud and rolled up to his feet; he started back, and saw a withered head lying almost face upward on the pavement, grinning at him. He felt the cold sweat standing on his face, and his heart beat painfully.

For the first time in all his life that evil thing which men call fear was getting hold of him, checking his heart-strings as a cruel driver checks a quivering horse, clawing at his back-bone with icy hands, lifting his hair with freezing breath, climbing up and gathering in his midriff with leaden weight.

Yet presently he bit his lip and bent down, holding the candle in one hand, to lift the shroud back from the head of the corpse with the other. Slowly he lifted it. Then it clove to the half-dried skin of the face, and his hand shook as if someone had struck him on the elbow, but half in fear and half in anger at himself, he pulled it, so that it came away with a little ripping sound. He caught his breath as he held it, not yet throwing it back, and not yet looking. The horror was working in him, and he felt that old Vernon Ockram was standing up in his iron coffin, headless, yet watching him with the stump of his severed neck.

While he held his breath he felt the dead smile twisting his lips. In sudden wrath at his own misery, he tossed the death-stained linen backward, and looked at last. He ground his teeth lest he should shriek aloud.

There it was, the thing that haunted him, that haunted Evelyn War-burton, that was like a blight on all that came near him.

The dead face was blotched with dark stains, and the thin, grey hair was matted about the discoloured forehead. The sunken lids were half open, and the candlelight gleamed on something foul where the toad eyes had lived.

But yet the dead thing smiled, as it had smiled in life; the ghastly lips were parted and drawn wide and tight upon the wolfish teeth, cursing still, and still defying hell to do its worst—defying, cursing, and always and for ever smiling alone in the dark.

Sir Gabriel opened the winding-sheet where the hands were, and the blackened, withered fingers were closed upon something stained and mottled. Shivering from head to foot, but fighting like a man in agony for his life, he tried to take the package from the dead man's hold. But as he pulled at it the claw-like fingers seemed to close more tightly, and when he pulled harder the shrunken hands and arms rose from the corpse with a horrible look of life following his motion—then as he wrenched the sealed packet loose at last, the hands fell back into their place still folded.

He set down the candle on the edge of the bier to break the seals form the stout paper. And, kneeling on one knee, to get a better light, he read what was within, written long ago in Sir Hugh's queer hand.

He was no longer afraid.

He read how Sir Hugh had written it all down that it might perchance be a witness of evil and of his hatred; how he had loved Evelyn
Warburton, his wife's sister; and how his wife had died of a broken
heart with his curse upon her, and how Warburton and he had fought
side by side in Afghanistan, and Warburton had fallen; but Ockram
had brought his comrade's wife back a full year later, and little Evelyn,
her child, had been born in Ockram Hall. And next, how he had
wearied of the mother, and she had died like her sister with his curse
on her. And then, how Evelyn had been brought up as his niece, and
how he had trusted that his son Gabriel and his daughter, innocent
and unknowing, might love and marry, and the souls of the women he
had betrayed might suffer another anguish before eternity was out.
And, last of all, he hoped that some day, when nothing could be
undone, the two might find his writing and live on, not daring to tell
the truth for their children's sake and the world's word, man and wife.

This he read, kneeling beside the corpse in the north vault, by the
light of the altar candle; and when he had read it all, he thanked God
aloud that he had found the secret in time. But when he rose to his feet
and looked down at the dead face it was changed, and the smile was
gone from it for ever, and the jaw had fallen a little, and the tired, dead
lips were relaxed. And then there was a breath behind him and close
to him, not cold like that which had blown the flame of the candle as
he came, but warm and human. He turned suddenly.

There she stood, all in white, with her shadowy golden hair—for
she had risen from her bed and had followed him noiselessly, and had
found him reading, and had herself read over his shoulder. He started
violently when he saw her, for his nerves were unstrung—and then he
cried out her name in the still place of death:

"Evelyn!"

"My brother!" she answered, softly and tenderly, putting out both
hands to meet his.

THE GHOST OF DOROTHY DINGLEY

Daniel Defoe

In the beginning of this year, a disease happened in this town of Launceston, and some of my scholars died of it. Among others who fell under the malignity then triumphing, was John Elliot, the eldest son of Edward Elliot of Treherse, Esq., a stripling of about sixteen years of age, but of more than common parts and ingenuity. At his own particular request, I preached at the funeral, which happened on the 20th day of June 1665. In my discourse (*ut mos reique locique postulabat*), I spoke some words in commendation of the young gentleman; such as might endear his memory to those that knew him, and, withal, tended to preserve his example to the fry which went to school with him, and were to continue there after him. An ancient gentleman, who was then in the church, was much affected with the discourse, and was often heard to repeat, the same evening, an expression I then used out of Virgil:

Et puer ipse fuit cantari dignus.

The reason why this grave gentleman was so concerned at the character, was a reflection he made upon a son of his own, who being about

125

the same age, and, but a few months before, not unworthy of the like character I gave of the young Mr. Elliot, was now, by a strange accident, quite lost as to his parent's hopes and all expectation of any further comfort by him.

The funeral rites being over, I was no sooner come out of the church, but I found myself most courteously accosted by this old gentleman; and with an unusual importunity almost forced against my humour to see his house that night; nor could I have rescued myself from his kindness, had not Mr. Elliot interposed and pleaded title to me for the whole of the day, which, as he said, he would resign to no man.

Hereupon I got loose for that time, but was constrained to leave a promise behind me to wait upon him at his own house the Monday following. This then seemed to satisfy, but before Monday came I had a new message to request me that, if it were possible, I would be there on the Sunday. The second attempt I resisted by answering that it was against my convenience, and the duty which mine own people expected from me.

Yet was not the gentleman at rest, for he sent me another letter on the Sunday, by no means to fail on the Monday, and so to order my business as to spend with him two or three days at least. I was indeed startled at so much eagerness, and so many dunnings for a visit, without any business; and began to suspect that there must needs be some design in the bottom of all this excess of courtesy. For I had no familiarity, nor could I imagine whence should arise such a flush of friendship on the sudden.

On the Monday I went, and paid my promised devoir, and met with entertainment as free and plentiful as the invitation was importunate. There also I found a neighbouring minister who pretended to call in accidentally, but by the sequel I suppose it otherwise. After dinner this brother of the coat undertook to show me the gardens, where, as we were walking, he gave me the first discovery of what was mainly intended in all this treat and compliment.

First he began to tell the infortunity of the family in general, and then gave an instance in the youngest son. He related what a hopeful, sprightly lad he lately was, and how melancholic and sottish he was now grown. Then did he with much passion lament, that this ill-humour should so incredibly subdue his reason; for, says he, the poor boy believes himself to be haunted with ghosts, and is confident that he meets with an evil spirit in a certain field about half a mile from this place, as often as he goes that way to school.

In the midst of our twaddle, the old gentleman and his lady (as observing their cue exactly) came up to us. Upon their approach, and pointing me to the arbour, the parson renews the relation to me; and they (the parents of the youth) confirmed what he said, and added many minute circumstances, in a long narrative of the whole. In fine, they all three desired my thoughts and advise in the affair.

I was not able to collect thoughts enough on the sudden to frame a judgement upon what they had said, only I answered, that the thing which the youth reported to them was strange, yet not incredible, and that I knew not then what to think or say of it; but if the lad would be free to me in talk, and trust me with his counsels, I had hopes to give them a better account of my opinion the next day.

I had no sooner spoken so much, but I perceived myself in the springe their courtship had laid for me; for the old lady was not able to hide her impatience, but her son must be called immediately. This I was forced to comply with and consent to, so that drawing off from the company to an orchard near by, she went herself and brought him to me, and left him with me.

It was the main drift of all these three to persuade me that either the boy was lazy, and glad of any excuse to keep from the school, or that he was in love with some wench and ashamed to confess it; or that he had a fetch upon his father to get money and new clothes, that he might range to London after a brother he had there; and therefore they begged of me to discover the root of the matter, and accordingly to dissuade, advise, or reprove him, but chiefly, by all means, to undeceive him as to the fancy of ghosts and spirits.

I soon entered into a close conference with the youth, and at first was very cautious not to displease him, but by smooth words to ingratiate myself and get within him, for I doubted he would be too distrustful or too reserved. But we had scarcely passed the first situation, and begun to speak to the business, before I found that there needed no policy to screw myself into his breast; for he most openly and with all obliging candour did aver, that he loved his book, and desired nothing more than to be bred a scholar; that he had not the least respect for any of womankind, as his mother gave out; and that the only request he would make to his parents was, that they would but believe his constant assertions concerning the woman he was disturbed with, in the field called the Higher-Broom Quartils. He told me with all naked freedom, and a flood of tears, that his friends were unkind and unjust to him, neither to believe nor pity him; and that if any man (making a bow to me) would but go with him to the place, he might be convinced that the thing was real, etc.

By this time he found me apt to compassionate his condition, and to be attentive to his relation of it, and therefore he went on in this way:

"This woman which appears to me," said he, "lived a neighbour here to my father, and died about eight years since; her name, Dorothy Dingley, of such a stature, such age, and such complexion. She never speaks to me, but passeth by hastily, and always leaves the footpath to me, and she commonly meets me twice or three times in the breadth of the field.

"It was about two months before I took any notice of it, and though the shape of the face was in my memory, yet I did not recall the name of the person, but without more thereabout, and had frequent occasion that way. Nor did I imagine anything to the contrary before she began to meet me constantly, morning and evening, and always in the same field, and sometimes twice or thrice in the breadth of it.

"The first time I took notice of her was about a year since, and when I first began to suspect and believe it to be a ghost, I had courage enough not to be afraid, but kept it to myself a good while, and only wondered very much about it. I did often speak to it, but never had a word in answer. Then I changed my way, and went to school the Under Horse Road, and then she always met me in the narrow lane, between the Quarry Park and the Nursery, which was worse.

"At length I began to be terrified at it, and prayed continually that God would either free me from it or let me know the meaning of it. Night and day, sleeping and waking, the shape was ever running in my mind, and I often did repeat these places of Scripture (with that he takes a small Bible out of his pocket), Job vii. 14: 'Thou scarest me with dreams, and terrifiest me through visions.' And Deuteronomy xxviii. 67: 'In the morning, thou shalt say, Would God it were even; and at even thou shalt say, Would God it were morning; for the fear of thine heart, wherewith thou shalt fear, and for the sight of thine eyes, which thou shalt see.'"

I was very much pleased with the lad's ingenuity in the application of these pertinent Scriptures to his condition, and desired him to proceed.

"When," says he, "by degrees, I grew very pensive, inasmuch that it was taken notice of by all our family; whereupon, being urged to it, I told my brother William of it, and he privately acquainted my father and mother, and they kept it to themselves for some time.

"The success of this discovery was only this; they did sometimes laugh at me, sometimes chide me, but still commanded me to keep to my school, and put such fopperies out of my head. I did accordingly go to school often, but always met the woman in the way."

This, and much more to the same purpose, yea, as much as held a dialogue of near two hours, was our conference in the orchard, which ended with my proffer to him, that without making any privy to our intents, I would next morning walk with him to the place, about six o'clock. He was even transported with joy at the mention of it, and replied, "But will you, sure, sir? Will you, sure, sir? Thank God! Now I hope I shall be relieved."

From this conclusion we retired into the house.

The gentleman, his wife, and Mr. Sam were impatient to know the event, insomuch that they came out of the parlour into the hall to meet us; and seeing the lad look cheerfully, the first compliment from the old man was, "Come, Mr. Ruddle, you have talked with him; I hope now he will have more wit. An idle boy! An idle boy!"

At these words, the lad ran up the stairs to his own chamber, without replying, and I soon stopped the curiosity of the three expectants by telling them I had promised silence, and was resolved to be as good as my word; but when things were riper they might know all. At present, I desired them to rest in my faithful promise, that I would do my utmost in their service, and for the good of their son. With this they were silenced; I cannot say satisfied.

The next morning before five o'clock, the lad was in my chamber, and very brisk. I arose and went with him. The field he led me to I guessed to be twenty acres, in an open country, and about three furlongs from any house. We went into the field, and had not gone about a third part, before the spectrum, in the shape of a woman, with all the circumstances he had described her to me in the orchard the day before (as much as the suddenness of its appearance and evanition would permit me to discover), met us and passed by. I was a little surprised at it, and though I had taken up a firm resolution to speak to it, yet I had not the power, nor indeed durst I look back; yet I took care not to show any fear to my pupil and guide, and therefore only telling him that I was satisfied in the truth of his complaint, we walked to the end of the field and returned, nor did the ghost meet us that time above once. I perceived in the young man a kind of boldness, mixed with astonishment: the first caused by my presence, and the proof he had given of his own relation, and the other by the sight of his persecutor.

In short, we went home: I somewhat puzzled, he much animated.

At our return, the gentlewoman whose inquisitiveness had missed us, watched to speak with me. I gave her a convenience, and told her that my opinion was that her son's complaint was not to be slighted, nor altogether discredited; yet, that my judgement in his case was not settled. I gave her caution, moreover, that the thing might not take wind, lest the whole country should ring with what we had yet no assurance of.

In this juncture of time I had business which would admit no delay; wherefore I went for Launceston that evening, but promised to see them again next week. Yet I was prevented by an occasion which pleaded a sufficient excuse, for my wife was that week brought home from a neighbour's house very ill. However, my mind was upon the adventure. I studied the case, and about three weeks after went again, resolving, by the help of God, to see the utmost.

The next morning, being the 27th day of July 1665, I went to the haunted field by myself, and walked the breadth of the field without any encounter. I returned and took the other walk, and then the spectrum appeared to me, much about the same place where I saw it before, when the young gentleman was with me. In my thoughts, it moved swifter than the time before, and about ten feet distance from me on my right hand insomuch that I had not time to speak, as I had determined with myself beforehand.

The evening of this day, the parents, the son, and myself being in the chamber where I lay, I propounded to them our going all together to the place next morning, and after some asseveration that there was no danger in it, we all resolved upon it. The morning being come, lest we should alarm the family of servants, they went under the pretence of seeing a field of wheat, and I took my horse and fetched a compass another way, and so met at the stile we had appointed.

Thence we all four walked leisurely into the Quartils, and had passed above half the field before the ghost made appearance. It then came over the stile just before us, and moved with that swiftness that by the time we had gone six or seven steps it passed by. I immediately turned head and ran after it, with the young man by my side; we saw it pass over the stile by which we entered, but no farther. I stepped upon the hedge at one place, he at another, but could discern nothing; whereas, I dare aver, that the swiftest horse in England could not have conveyed himself out of sight in that short space of time. Two things I observed in this day's appearance. I. That a spaniel dog, who followed the company unregarded, did bark and run away as the spectrum passed by; whence it is easy to conclude that it was not our fear or fancy which made the apparition. 2. That the motion of the spectrum was not gradation, or by steps, and moving of the feet, but a kind of gliding, as children upon the ice, or a boat down a swift river, which punctually answers the description that ancients gave of the *Lemures,* which was Κατὰ ῥύμτω ἀέριον καὶ ὁρμὴν ἀπξαποδισν (Heliodorus).

But to proceed. This ocular evidence clearly convinced, but, withal, strangely frightened the old gentleman and his wife, who knew this Dorothy Dingley in her lifetime, were at her burial, and now plainly saw her features in this present apparition. I encouraged them as well as I could, but after this they went no more. However, I was resolved to proceed, and use such lawful means as God hath discovered, and learned men have successfully practised in these irregular cases.

The next morning being Thursday, I went out very early by myself, and walked for about an hour's space in meditation and prayer in the field next adjoining to the Quartils. Soon after five I stepped over the stile into the disturbed field, and had not gone above thirty or forty paces before the ghost appeared at the farther stile. I spoke to it with a loud voice, in some such sentences as the way of these dealings directed me, whereupon it approached, but slowly, and when I came near, it moved not. I spake again, and it answered, in a voice neither very audible nor intelligible. It was not in the least terrified, and therefore persisted until it spake again, and gave me satisfaction. But the work could not be finished at this time; wherefore the same evening, an hour after sunset, it met me again near the same place, and after a few words on each side, it quietly vanished, and neither doth appear since, nor ever will more to any man's disturbance. The discourse in the morning lasted about a quarter of an hour.

These things are true, and I know them to be so, with as much certainty as eyes and ears can give me; and until I can be persuaded that my senses do deceive me about their proper object, and by that persuasion deprive myself of the strongest inducement to believe the Christian religion, I must and will assert that these things in this paper are true.

As for the manner of my proceeding, I find no reason to be ashamed of it, for I can justify it to men of good principles, discretion, and recondite learning, though in this case I choose to content myself in the assurance of the thing, rather than be at the unprofitable trouble to persuade others to believe it; for I know full well with what difficulty relations of so uncommon a nature and practice obtain relief. He that tells such a story may expect to be dealt withal as a traveller in Poland by the robbers, viz., first murdered and then searched—first condemned for a liar, or superstitious, and then, when it is too late, have his reasons and proofs examined. This incredulity may be attributed:

1. To the infinite abuses of the people, and impositions upon their faith by the cunning monks and friars, etc., in the days of darkness and popery; for they made apparitions as often as they pleased, and got both money and credit by quieting the *terriculamenta vulgi,* which their own artifice had raised.

2. To the prevailing of Somatism and the Hobbean principle in these times, which is a revival of the doctrine of the Sadducees; and as it denies the nature, so it cannot consist with the apparition of spirits; of which, see *Leviathan,* p. I. c. 12.

3. To the ignorance of men in our age, in this peculiar and mysterious part of philosophy and of religion, namely, the communication between spirits and men. Not one scholar in ten thousand (though otherwise of excellent learning) knows anything of it or the way how

to manage it. This ignorance breeds fear and abhorrence of that which otherwise might be of incomparable benefit to mankind.

But I being a clergyman and young, and a stranger in these parts, do apprehend silence and secrecy to be my best security.

In rebus abstrusissimis abundans cautela non nocet.

THE DEAD MAN OF VARLEY GRANGE

Anonymous

"Hallo, Jack! Where are you off to? Going down to the governor's place for Christmas?"

Jack Darent, who was in my old regiment, stood drawing on his doeskin gloves upon the 23rd of December the year before last. He was equipped in a long ulster and top hat, and a hansom, already loaded with a gun-case and portmanteau, stood awaiting him. He had a tall, strong figure, a fair, fresh-looking face, and the merriest blue eyes in the world. He held a cigarette between his lips, and late as was the season of the year there was a flower in his buttonhole. When did I ever see handsome Jack Darent and he did not look well dressed and well fed and jaunty? As I ran up the steps of the Club he turned round and laughed merrily.

"My dear fellow, do I look the sort of man to be victimized at a family Christmas meeting? Do you know the kind of business they have at home? Three maiden aunts and a bachelor uncle, my eldest brother and his insipid wife, and all my sister's six noisy children at dinner. Church twice a day, and snapdragon between the services! No, thank you! I have a great affection for my old parents, but you don't catch me going in for that sort of national festival!"

"You irreverent ruffian!" I replied, laughing. "Ah, if you were a married man . . ."

"Ah, if I were a married man!" replied Captain Darent with something that was almost a sigh, and then lowering his voice, he said hurriedly, "How is Miss Lester, Fred?"

"My sister is quite well, thank you," I answered with becoming gravity; and it was not without a spice of malice that I added, "She has been going to a great many balls and enjoying herself very much."

Captain Darent looked profoundly miserable.

"I don't see how a poor fellow in a marching regiment, a younger son too, with nothing in the future to look to, is ever to marry nowadays," he said almost savagely; "when girls, too, are used to so much luxury and extravagance that they can't live without it. Matrimony is at a deadlock in this century, Fred, chiefly owing to the price of butcher's meat and bonnets. In fifty years' time it will become extinct and the country be depopulated. But I must be off, old man, or I shall miss my train."

"You have never told me where you are going to, Jack."

"Oh, I am going to stay with old Henderson, in Westernshire; he has taken a furnished house, with some first-rate pheasant shooting, for a year. There are seven of us going—all bachelors, and all kindred spirits. We shall shoot all day and smoke half the night. Think what you have lost, old fellow, by becoming a Benedick!"

"In Westernshire, is it?" I inquired. "Whereabouts is this place, and what is the name of it? For I am a Westernshire man by birth myself, and I know every place in the county."

"Oh, it's a tumbledown sort of old house, I believe," answered Jack carelessly. "Gables and twisted chimneys outside, and uncomfortable spindle-legged furniture inside—you know the sort of thing; but the shooting is capital, Henderson says, and we must put up with our quarters. He has taken his French cook down, and plenty of liquor, so I've no doubt we shan't starve."

"Well, but what is the name of it?" I persisted, with a growing interest in the subject.

"Let me see," referring to a letter he pulled out of his pocket. "Oh, here it is—Varley Grange."

"Varley Grange!" I repeated, aghast. "Why, it has not been inhabited for years."

"I believe not," answered Jack unconcernedly. "The shooting has been let separately; but Henderson took a fancy to the house too and thought it would do for him, furniture and all, just as it is. My dear Fred, what are you looking so solemnly at me for?"

"Jack, let me entreat of you not to go to this place," I said, laying my hands on his arm.

"Not go! Why, Lester, you must be mad! Why on earth shouldn't I go there?"

"There are stories—uncomfortable things said of that house." I had not the moral courage to say, "It is haunted," and I felt myself how weak and childish was my attempt to deter him from his intended visit; only—I knew all about Varley Grange.

I think handsome Jack Darent thought privately that I was slightly out of my senses, for I am sure I looked unaccountably upset and dismayed by the mention of the name of the house that Mr. Henderson had taken.

"I dare say it's cold and draughty and infested with rats and mice,' he said laughingly; "and I have no doubt the creature-comforts will not be equal to Queen's Gate; but I stand pledged to go now, and I must be off this very minute, so have no time, old fellow, to inquire into the meaning of your sensational warning. Goodbye, and . . . and remember me to the ladies."

He ran down the steps and jumped into the hansom.

"Write to me if you have time!" I cried out after him; but I don't think he heard me in the rattle of the departing cab. He nodded and smiled at me and was swiftly whirled out of sight.

As for me, I walked slowly back to my comfortable house in Queen's Gate. There was my wife presiding at the little five o'clock tea-table, our two fat, pink and white little children tumbling about upon the hearthrug amongst dolls and bricks, and two utterly spoilt and overfed pugs; and my sister Bella—who, between ourselves, was the prettiest as well as dearest girl in all London—sitting on the floor in her handsome brown, velvet gown, resigning herself gracefully to be trampled upon by the dogs, and to have her hair pulled by the babies.

"Why, Fred, you look as if you had heard bad news," said my wife, looking up anxiously as I entered.

"I don't know that I have heard of anything very bad; I have just seen Jack Darent off for Christmas," I said, turning instinctively towards my sister. He was a poor man and a younger son, and of course a very bad match for the beautiful Miss Lester; but for all that I had an inkling that Bella was not quite indifferent to her brother's friend.

"Oh!" says that hypocrite. "Shall I give you a cup of tea, Fred!"

It is wonderful how women can control their faces and pretend not to care a straw when they hear the name of their lover mentioned. I think Bella overdid it, she looked so supremely indifferent.

"Where on earth do you suppose he is going to stay, Bella?"

"Who? Oh, Captain Darent! How should I possibly know where he is going? Archie, pet, please don't poke the doll's head quite down Ponto's throat; I know he will bite it off if you do."

This last observation was addressed to my son and heir.

"Well, I think you will be surprised when you hear: he is going to Westernshire, to stay at Varley Grange."

"*What!*" No doubt about her interest in the subject now! Miss Lester turned as white as her collar and sprang to her feet impetuously, scattering dogs, babies and toys in all directions away from her skirts as she rose.

"You cannot mean it, Fred! Varley Grange, why, it has not been inhabited for ten years; and the last time—Oh, do you remember those poor people who took it? What a terrible story it has!" She shuddered.

"Well, it is taken now," I said, "by a man I know, called Henderson—a bachelor; he has asked down a party of men for a week's shooting, and Jack Darent is one of them."

"For Heaven's sake prevent him from going!" cried Bella, clasping her hands.

"My dear, he is gone!"

"Oh, then write to him—telegraph—tell him to come back!" she urged breathlessly.

"I am afraid it is no use," I said gravely. "He would not come back; he would not believe me; he would think I was mad."

"Did you tell him anything?" she asked faintly.

"No, I had not time. I did say a word or two, but he began to laugh."

"Yes, that is how it always is!" she said distractedly. "People laugh and pooh-pooh the whole thing, and then they go there and see for themselves, and it is too late!"

She was so thoroughly upset that she left the room. My wife turned to me in astonishment; not being a Westernshire woman, she was not well up in the traditions of that venerable county.

"What on earth does it all mean, Fred?" she asked me in amazement. "What is the matter with Bella, and why is she so distressed that Captain Darent is going to stay at that particular house?"

"It is said to be haunted, and . . ."

"You don't mean to say you believe in such rubbish, Fred?" interrupted my wife sternly, with a side-glance of apprehension at our firstborn, who, needless to say, stood by, all eyes and ears, drinking in every word of the conversation of his elders.

"I never know what I believe or what I don't believe," I answered gravely. "All I can say is that there are very singular traditions about that house, and that a great many credible witnesses have seen a very strange thing there, and that a great many disasters have happened to the persons who have seen it."

"What has been seen, Fred? Pray tell me the story! Wait, I think I will send the children away."

My wife rang the bell for the nurse, and as soon as the little ones had been taken from the room she turned to me again.

"I don't believe in ghosts or any such rubbish one bit, but I should like to hear your story."

"The story is vague enough," I answered.

"In the old days Varley Grange belonged to the ancient family of Varley, now completely extinct. There was, some hundred years ago, a daughter, famed for her beauty and her fascination. She wanted to marry a poor, penniless squire, who loved her devotedly. Her brother, Dennis Varley, the new owner of Varley Grange, refused his consent and shut his sister up in the nunnery that used to stand outside his park gates—there are a few ruins of it left still. The poor nun broke her vows and ran away in the night with her lover. But her brother pursued her and brought her back with him. The lover escaped, but the lord of Varley murdered his sister under his own roof, swearing that no scion of his race should live to disgrace and dishonour his ancient name.

"Ever since that day Dennis Varley's spirit cannot rest in its grave—he wanders about the old house at night time, and those who have seen him are numberless. Now and then the pale, shadowy form of a nun flits across the old hall, or along the gloomy passages, and when both strange shapes are seen thus together misfortune and illness, and even death, is sure to pursue the luckless man who has seen them, with remorseless cruelty."

"I wonder you believe in such rubbish," says my wife at the conclusion of my tale.

I shrug my shoulders and answer nothing, for who are so obstinate as those who persist in disbelieving everything that they cannot understand?

❋ ❋ ❋

It was little more than a week later that, walking by myself along Pall Mall one afternoon, I suddenly came upon Jack Darent walking towards me.

"Hallo, Jack! Back again? Why, man, how odd you look!"

There was a change in the man that I was instantly aware of. His frank, careless face looked clouded and anxious, and the merry smile was missing from his handsome countenance.

"Come into the Club, Fred," he said, taking me by the arm. "I have something to say to you."

He drew me into a corner of the Club smoking-room.

"You were quite right. I wish to Heaven I had never gone to that house."

"You mean—have you seen anything?" I inquired eagerly.

"I have seen *everything*," he answered with a shudder. "They say one dies within a year—"

"My dear fellow, don't be so upset about it," I interrupted; I was quite distressed to see how thoroughly the man had altered.

"Let me tell you about it, Fred."

He drew his chair close to mine and told me his story, pretty nearly in the following words:

"You remember the day I went down you had kept me talking at the Club door; I had a race to catch the train; however, I just did it. I found the other fellows all waiting for me. There was Charlie Wells, the two Harfords, old Colonel Riddell, who is such a crack shot, two fellows in the Guards, both pretty fair, a man called Thompson, a barrister, Henderson and myself—eight of us in all. We had a remarkably lively journey down, as you may imagine, and reached Varley Grange in the highest possible spirits. We all slept like tops that night.

"The next day we were out from eleven till dusk among the coverts, and a better day's shooting I never enjoyed in the whole course of my life, the birds literally swarmed. We bagged a hundred and thirty brace. We were all pretty well tired when we got home, and did full justice to a very good dinner and first-class Perrier-Jouet. After dinner we adjourned to the hall to smoke. This hall is quite the feature of the house. It is large and bright, panelled half-way up with somber old oak, and vaulted with heavy carved oaken rafters. At the farther end runs a gallery, into which opened the door of my bedroom, and shut off from the rest of the passages by a swing door at either end.

"Well, all we fellows sat up there smoking and drinking brandy and soda, and jawing, you know—as men always do when they are together—about sport of all kinds, hunting and shooting and salmon-fishing; and I assure you not one of us had a thought in our heads beyond relating some wonderful incident of a long shot or big fence by which we could each cap the last speaker's experiences. We were just, I recollect, listening to a long story of the old Colonel's, about his experiences among bisons in Cachemire, when suddenly one of us—I can't remember who it was—gave a sort of shout and started to his feet, pointing up to the gallery behind us. We all turned round, and there—I give you my word of honour, Lester—stood a man leaning over the rail of the gallery, staring down upon us.

"We all saw him. Every one of us. Eight of us, remember. He stood there full ten seconds, looking down with horrible glittering eyes at us. He had a long tawny beard, and his hands, that were crossed together before him, were nothing but skin and bone. But it was his face that was so unspeakably dreadful. It was livid—the face of a dead man!"

"How was he dressed?"

"I could not see; he wore some kind of a black cloak over his shoulders, I think, but the lower part of his figure was hidden behind the railings. Well, we all stood perfectly speechless for, as I said, about ten seconds; and then the figure moved, backing slowly into the door of the room behind him, which stood open. It was the door of my bedroom! As soon as he had disappeared our senses seemed to return to us. There was a general rush for the staircase, and, as you may imagine, there was not a corner of the house that was left unsearched; my bedroom especially was ransacked in every part of it. But all in vain; there was not the slightest trace to be found of any living being. You may suppose that not one of us slept that night. We lighted every candle and lamp we could lay hands upon and sat up till daylight, but nothing more was seen.

"The next morning, at breakfast, Henderson, who seemed very much annoyed by the whole thing, begged us not to speak of it any more. He said that he had been told, before he had taken the house, that it was supposed to be haunted; but, not being a believer in such childish follies, he had paid but little attention to the rumour. He did not, however, want it talked about, because of the servants, who would be so easily frightened. He was quite certain, he said, that the figure we had seen last night must be somebody dressed up to practice a trick upon us, and he recommended us all to bring our guns down loaded after dinner, but meanwhile to forget the startling apparition as far as we could.

"We, of course, readily agreed to do as he wished, although I do not think that one of us imagined for a moment that nay amount of dressing-up would be able to simulate the awful countenance that we had all of us seen too plainly. It would have taken a Hare or an Arthur Cecil, with all the theatrical appliances known only to those two talented actors, to have 'made-up' the face, that was literally that of a corpse. Such a person could not be amongst us—actually in the house—without our knowledge.

"We had another good day's shooting, and by degrees the fresh air and exercise and the excitement of the sport obliterated the impression of what we had seen in some measure from the minds of most of us. That evening we all appeared in the hall after dinner with our loaded guns beside us; but, although we sat up till the small hours and looked frequently up at the gallery at the end of the hall, nothing at all disturbed us that night.

"Two nights thus went by and nothing further was seen of the gentleman with the tawny beard. What with the good company, the good cheer and the pheasants, we had pretty well forgotten all about him.

"We were sitting as usual upon the third night, with our pipes and our cigars; a pleasant glow from the bright wood fire in the great chimney lighted up the old hall, and shed a genial warmth about us; when suddenly it seemed to me as if there came a breath of cold, chill air behind me, such as one feels when going down into some damp, cold vault or cellar.

"A strong shiver shook me from head to foot. Before even I saw it I *knew* that it was there.

"It leant over the railing of the gallery and looked down at us all just as it had done before. There was no change in the attitude, no alteration in the fixed, malignant glare in those stony, lifeless eyes; no movement in the white and bloodless features. Below, amongst the eight of us gathered there, there arose a panic of terror. Eight strong, healthy, well-educated nineteenth-century Englishmen, and yet I am not ashamed to say that we were paralysed with fear. Then one, more quickly recovering his senses than the rest, caught at his gun, that leant against the wide chimney-corner, and fired.

"The hall was filled with smoke, but as it cleared away every one of us could see the figure of our supernatural visitant slowly backing, as he had done on the previous occasion, into the chamber behind him, with something like a sardonic smile of scornful derision upon his horrible, death-like face.

"The next morning it is a singular and remarkable fact that four out of the eight of us received by the morning post—so they stated—letters of importance which called them up to town by the very first train! One man's mother was ill, another had to consult his lawyer, whilst pressing engagements, to which they could assign no definite name, called away the other two.

"There were left in the house that day but four of us—Wells, Bob Harford, our host, and myself. A sort of dogged determination not to be worsted by a scare of this kind kept us still there. The morning light brought a return of common sense and natural courage to us. We could manage to laugh over last night's terrors whilst discussing our bacon and kidneys and hot coffee over the late breakfast in the pleasant morning-room, with the sunshine streaming cheerily in through the diamond-paned windows.

'It *must* be a delusion of our brains,' said one.

'Our host's champagne,' suggested another.

'A well-organized hoax,' opined a third.

'I will tell you what we will do,' said our host. 'Now that those other fellows have all gone—and I suppose we don't any of us believe much in those elaborate family reasons which have so unaccountably summoned them away—we four will sit up regularly night after night and watch for this thing, whatever it may be. I do not believe in ghosts. However, this morning I have taken the trouble to go out before breakfast to see the Rector of the parish, and old gentleman who is well up in all the traditions of the neighbourhood, and I have learnt from him the whole of the supposed story of our friend of the tawny beard, which, if you will, I will relate to you.'

"Henderson then proceeded to tell us the tradition concerning the Dennis Varley who murdered his sister, the nun—a story which I will not repeat to you, Lester, as I see you know it already."

The clergyman had furthermore told him that the figure of the murdered nun was also sometimes seen in the same gallery, but that this was a very rare occurrence. When both the murderer and his victim are seen together, terrible misfortunes are sure to assail the unfortunate living man who sees them; and if the nun's face is revealed, death within the year is the doom of the ill-fated person who has seen it.

'Of course,' concluded our host, 'I consider all these stories to be absolutely childish. At the same time I cannot help thinking that some human agency—probably a gang of thieves or housebreakers—is at work, and that we shall probably be able to unearth an organized system of villainy by which the rogues, presuming on the credulity of the persons who have inhabited the place, have been able to plant themselves securely among some secret passages and hidden rooms in the house, and have carried on their depredations undiscovered and unsuspected. Now, will all of you help me to unravel this mystery?'

"We all promised readily to do so. It is astonishing how brave we felt at eleven o'clock in the morning; what an amount of pluck and courage each man professed himself to be endued with; how lightly we jested about the 'old boy with the beard,' and what jokes we cracked about the murdered nun!

'She would show her face oftener if she was good-looking. No fear of her looking at Bob Harford, he was too ugly. It was Jack Darent who was the showman of the party; she'd be sure to make straight for him if she could, he was always run after by the women,' and so on, till we were all laughing loudly and heartily over our own witticisms. That was eleven o'clock in the morning.

"At eleven o'clock at night we could have given a very different report of ourselves.

"At eleven o'clock at night each man took up his appointed post in solemn and somewhat depressed silence.

"The plan of our campaign had been carefully organized by our host. Each man was posted separately with about thirty yards between them, so that no optical delusion, such as an effect of fire-light upon the oak paneling, nor any reflection from the circular mirror over the chimney-piece, should be able to deceive more than one of us. Our host fixed himself in the very centre of the hall, facing up the short, straight flight of steps; Harford was at the top of the stairs upon the gallery itself; I was opposite to him at the further end. In this manner, whenever the figure—ghost or burglar—should appear, it must necessarily be between two of us, and be seen from both the right and the left side. We were prepared to believe that one amongst us might be deceived by his senses or by his imagination, but it was clear that two persons could not see the same object from a different point of view and be simultaneously deluded by any effect of light or any optical hallucination.

"Each man was provided with a loaded revolver, a brandy and soda and a sufficient stock of pipes or cigars to last him through the night. We took up our positions at eleven o'clock exactly, and waited."

"At first we were all four very silent and, as I have said before, slightly depressed; but as the hour wore away and nothing was seen or heard we began to talk to each other. Talking, however, was rather a difficulty. To begin with, we had to shout—at least we in the gallery had to shout to Henderson, down in the hall; and though Harford and Wells could converse quite comfortably, I, not being able to see the latter at all from my end of the gallery, had to pass my remarks to him second-hand through Harford, who amused himself in mis-stating every intelligent remark that I entrusted him with; added to which natural impediments to the 'flow of the soul,' the elements thought fit to create such a hullabaloo without that conversation was rendered still further a work of difficulty.

"I never remember such a night in all my life. The rain came down in torrents; the wind howled and shrieked wildly amongst the tall chimneys and the bare elm trees without. Every now and then there was a lull, and then, again and again, a long sobbing moan came swirling round and round the house, for all the world like the cry of a human being in agony. It was a night to make one shudder, and thank heaven for a roof over one's head.

"We all sat on at our separate posts hour after hour, listening to the wind and talking at intervals; but as the time wore on insensibly we became less and less talkative, and a sort of depression crept over us.

"At last we relapsed into a profound silence; then suddenly there came upon us all that chill blast of air, like a breath from a charnel-house, that we had experienced before, and almost simultaneously a hoarse cry broke from Henderson in the body of the hall below, and from Wells half-way up the stairs. Harford and I sprang to our feet, and we too saw it.

"The dead man was slowly coming up the stairs. He passed silently up with a sort of still, gliding motion, within a few inches of poor Wells, who shrank back, white with terror, against the wall. Henderson rushed wildly up the staircase in pursuit, whilst Harford and I, up on the gallery, fell instinctively back at his approach.

"He passed between us.

"We saw the glitter of his sightless eyes—the shriveled skin upon his withered face—the mouth that fell away, like the mouth of a corpse. Beneath his tawny beard. We felt the cold death-like blast that came with him, and the sickening horror of his terrible presence. Ah! Can I ever forget it?"

With a strong shudder Jack Darent buried his face in his hands, and seemed too much overcome for some minutes to be able to proceed.

"My dear fellow, are you *sure?*" I said in an awe-struck whisper.

He lifted his head.

"Forgive me, Lester; the whole business has shaken my nerves so thoroughly that I have not yet been able to get over it. But I have not yet told you the worst."

"Good Heavens—is there worse?" I ejaculated.

He nodded.

"No sooner," he continued, "had this awful creature passed us than Harford clutched at my arm and pointed to the farther end of the gallery.

'Look!" he cried hoarsely, 'the nun!'

There, coming towards us from the opposite direction, was the veiled figure of a nun.

There were the long, flowing black and white garments—the gleam of the crucifix at her neck—the jangle of her rosary-beads from her waist; but her face was hidden.

A sort of desperation seized me. With a violent effort over myself, I went towards this fresh apparition.

"It *must* be a hoax," I said to myself, and there was a half-formed intention in my mind of wrenching aside the flowing draperies and of seeing for myself who and what it was. I strode towards the figure—I stood—within half a yard of it. The nun raised her head slowly—and, Lester—*I saw her face!*"

There was a moment's silence.

"What was it like, Jack?" I asked him presently.

He shook his head.

"That I can never tell to any living creature."

"Was it so horrible?"

He nodded assent, shuddering.

"And what happened next?"

"I believe I fainted. At all events I remembered nothing further. They made me go to the vicarage the next day. I was so knocked over by it all—I was quite ill. I could not have stayed in the house. I stopped there all yesterday, and I got up to town this morning. I wish to Heaven I had taken your advice, old man, and had never gone to the horrible house."

"I wish you had, Jack," I answered fervently.

"Do you know that I shall die within the year?" he asked me presently.

I tried to pooh-pooh it.

"My dear fellow, don't take the thing so seriously as all that. Whatever may be the meaning of these horrible apparitions, there can be nothing but an old wives' fable in *that* saying. Why on earth should you die—you of all people, a great strong fellow with a constitution of iron? You don't look much like dying!"

"For all that I shall die. I cannot tell you why I am so certain—but I know that it will be so," he answered in a low voice. "And some terrible misfortune will happen to Harford—the other two never saw her—it is he and I who are doomed."

✳   ✳   ✳

A year has passed away. Last summer fashionable society rang for a week or more with the tale of poor Bob Harford's misfortune. The girl whom he was engaged to, and to whom he was devotedly attached—young, beautiful and wealthy—ran away on the eve of her wedding-day with a drinking, swindling villain who had been turned out of ever so many clubs and tabooed for ages by every respectable man in town, and who had nothing but a handsome face and a fascinating manner to recommend him, and who by dint of these had succeeded in gaining a complete ascendancy over the fickle heart of poor Bob's lovely fiancée. As to Harford, he sold out and went off to the backwoods of Canada, and has never been heard of since.

And what of Jack Darent? Poor, handsome Jack, with his tall figure and his bright, happy face, and the merry blue eyes that had wiled Bella Lester's heart away! Alas! Far away in Southern Africa, poor Jack Darent lies in an unknown grave—slain by a Zulu assegai on the fatal plain of Isandula!

And Bella goes about clad in sable garments, heavy-eyed and stricken with sore grief. A widow in heart, if not in name.

JOHN CHARRINGTON'S WEDDING

E. Nesbit

No one ever thought that May Forster would marry John Charrington; but he thought differently, and things which John Charrington intended had a queer way of coming to pass. He asked her to marry him before he went up to Oxford. She laughed and refused him. He asked her again next time he came home. Again she laughed, tossed her dainty blonde head, and again refused. A third time he asked her; she said it was becoming a confirmed bad habit, and laughed at him more than ever.

John was not the only man who wanted to marry her: she was the belle of our village *coterie,* and we were all in love with her more or less; it was a sort of fashion, like heliotrope ties or Inverness capes. Therefore we were as much annoyed as surprised when John Charrington walked into our little local Club—we held it in a loft over the saddler's, I remember—and invited us all to his wedding.

"Your wedding?"

"You don't mean it?"

"Who's the happy fair? When's it to be?"

John Charrington filled his pipe and lighted it before he replied. Then he said:

"I'm sorry to deprive you fellows of your only joke—but Miss Forster and I are to be married in September."

"You don't mean it?"

"He's got the mitten again, and it's turned his head."

"No," I said, rising, "I see it's true. Lend me a pistol someone—or a first-class fare to the other end of Nowhere. Charrington has bewitched the only pretty girl in our twenty-mile radius. Was it mesmerism, or a love-potion, Jack?"

"Neither, sir, but a gift you'll never have—perseverance—and the best luck a man ever had in this world."

There was something in his voice that silenced me, and all chaff of the other fellows failed to draw him further.

The queer thing about it was that when we congratulated Miss Forster, she blushed and smiled and dimpled, for all the world as though she were in love with him, and had been in love with him all the time. Upon my word, I think she had. Women are strange creatures.

We were all asked to the wedding. In Brisham everyone who was anybody knew everybody else who was anyone. My sisters were, I truly believe, more interested in the *trousseau* than the bride herself, and I was to be best man. The coming marriage was much canvassed at afternoon tea-tables, and at our little Club over the saddler's, and the question was always asked: "Does she care for him?"

I used to ask that question myself in the early days of their engagement, but after a certain evening in August I never asked it again. I was coming home from the Club through the churchyard. Our church is on a thyme-grown hill, and the turf about it is so thick and soft that one's footsteps are noiseless.

I made no sound as I vaulted the low lichened wall, and threaded my way between the tombstones. It was at the same instant that I heard John Charrington's voice, and saw Her. May was sitting on a low flat gravestone, her face turned towards the full splendour of the western sun. Its expression ended, at once and for ever, any question of love for him; it was transfigured to a beauty I should not have believed possible, even to that beautiful little face.

John lay at her feet, and it was his voice that broke the stillness of the golden August evening.

"My dear, my dear, I believe I should come back from the dead if you wanted me!"

I coughed at once to indicate my presence, and passed on into the shadow fully enlightened.

The wedding was to be early in September. Two days before I had to run up to town on business. The train was late, of course, for we are on the South-Eastern, and as I stood grumbling with my watch in my hand, whom should I see but John Charrington and May Forster. They were walking up and down the unfrequented end of the platform, arm in arm, looking into each other's eyes, careless of the sympathetic interest of the porters.

Of course I knew better than to hesitate a moment before burying myself in the booking-office, and it was not till the train drew up at the platform, that I obtrusively passed the pair with my Gladstone, and took the corner in a first-class smoking-carriage. I did this with as good an air of not seeing them as I could assume. I pride myself on my discretion, but if John were travelling alone I wanted his company. I had it.

"Hullo, old man," came his cheery voice as he swung his bag into my carriage; "here's luck; I was expecting a dull journey!"

"Where are you off to?" I asked, discretion still bidding me turn my eyes away, though I saw, without looking, that hers were red-rimmed.

"To old Brandbridge's," he answered, shutting the door and leaning out for a last word with his sweetheart.

"Oh, I wish you wouldn't go, John," she was saying in a low, earnest voice. "I feel certain something will happen."

"Do you think I should let anything happen to keep me, and the day after tomorrow our wedding day?"

"Don't go," she answered, with a pleading intensity which would have sent my Gladstone on to the platform and me after it. But she wasn't speaking to me. John Charrington was made differently; he rarely changed his opinions, never his resolutions.

He only stroked the little ungloved hands that lay on the carriage door.

"I must, May. The old boy's been awfully good to me, and now he's dying I must go and see him, but I shall come home in time for—" the rest of the parting was lost in a whisper and in the rattling lurch of the starting train.

"You're sure to come?" she spoke as the train moved.

"Nothing shall keep me." He answered; and we steamed out. After he had seen the last of the little figure on the platform he leaned back in his corner and kept silence for a minute.

When he spoke it was to explain to me that his godfather, whose heir he was, lay dying at Peasmarsh Place, some fifty miles away, and had sent for John, and John had felt bound to go.

"I shall surely be back tomorrow," he said, "or, if not, the day after, in heaps of time. Thank Heaven, one hasn't to get up in the middle of the night to get married nowadays!"

"And suppose Mr. Branbridge dies?"

"Alive or dead I mean to be married on Thursday!" John answered, lighting a cigar and unfolding *The Times*.

At Peasmarsh station we said goodbye, and he got out, and I saw him ride off; I went on to London, where I stayed the night.

When I got home the next afternoon, a very wet one, by the way, my sister greeted me with:

"Where's Mr. Charrington?"

"Goodness knows," I answered testily. Every man, since Cain, has resented that kind of question.

"I thought you might have heard from him," she went on, "as you're to give him away tomorrow."

"Isn't he back?" I asked, for I had confidently expected to find him at home.

"No, Geoffrey,"—my sister Fanny always had a way of jumping to conclusions, especially such conclusions as were least favourable to her fellow-creatures—"he has not returned, and, what is more, you may depend upon it he won't. You mark my words, there'll be no wedding tomorrow."

My sister Fanny has a power of annoying me which no other human being possesses.

"You mark my words," I retorted with asperity, "you had better give up making such a thundering idiot of yourself. There'll be more wedding tomorrow than ever you'll take the first part in." A prophecy which, by the way, came true.

But though I could snarl confidently to my sister, I did not feel so comfortable when late that night, I, standing on the doorstep of John's house, heard that he had not returned. I went home gloomily through the rain. Next morning brought a brilliant blue sky, gold sun, and all such softness of air and beauty of cloud as go to make up a perfect day. I woke with a vague feeling of having gone to bed anxious, and of being rather averse to facing that anxiety in the light of full wakefulness.

But with my shaving-water came a note from John which relieved my mind and sent me up to the Forsters' with a light heart.

May was in the garden. I saw her blue gown through the hollyhocks as the lodge gates swung to behind me. So I did not go up to the house, but turned aside down the tufted path.

"He's written to you too," she said, without preliminary greeting, when I reached her side.

"Yes, I'm to meet him at the station at three, and come straight on to the church."

Her face looked pale, but there was a brightness in her eyes, and a tender quiver about the mouth that spoke of renewed happiness.

"Mr. Branbridge begged him so to stay another night that he had not the heart to refuse," she went on. "He is so kind, but I wish he hadn't stayed."

I was at the station at half past two. I felt rather annoyed with John. It seemed a sort of slight to the beautiful girl who loved him, that he should come as it were out of breath, and with the dust of travel upon him, to take her hand, which some of us would have given the best years of our lives to take.

But when the three o'clock train glided in, and glided out again having brought no passengers to our little station, I was more than annoyed. There was no other train for thirty-five minutes; I calculated that, with much hurry, we might just get to the church in time for the ceremony; but, oh, what a fool to miss that first train! What other man could have done it?

That thirty-five minutes seemed a year, as I wandered round the station reading the advertisements and the timetables, and the company's bye-laws, and getting more and more angry with John Charrington. This confidence in his own power of getting everything he wanted the minute he wanted it was leading him too far. I hate waiting. Everyone does, but I believe I hate it more than anyone else. The three-thirty-five was late, of course.

I ground my pipe between my teeth and stamped with impatience as I watched the signals. Click. The signal went down. Five minutes later I flung myself into the carriage that I had brought for John.

"Drive to the church!" I said, as someone shut the door. "Mr. Charrington hasn't come by this train."

Anxiety now replaced anger. What had become of the man? Could he have been taken suddenly ill? I had never known him have a day's illness in his life. And even so he might have telegraphed. Some awful accident must have happened to him. The thought that he had played her false never—no, not for a moment—entered my head. Yes, something terrible had happened to him, and on me lay the task of telling his bride. I almost wished the carriage would upset and break my head so that someone else might tell her, not I, who—but that's nothing to do with this story.

It was five minutes to four as we drew up at the church-yard gate.

A double row of eager onlookers lined the path from lychgate to porch. I sprang from the carriage and passed up between them. Our gardener had a good front place near the door. I stopped.

"Are they waiting still, Byles?" I asked, simply to gain time, for of course I knew they were by the waiting crowd's attentive attitude.

"Waiting, sir? No, no, sir; why, it must be over by now."

"Over! Then Mr. Charrington's come?"

"To the minute, sir; must have missed you somehow, and, I say, sir," lowering his voice, "I never see Mr. John the least bit so afore, but my opinion is he's been drinking pretty free. His clothes was all dusty and his face like a sheet. I tell you I didn't like the looks of him at all, and the folks inside are saying all sorts of things. You'll see, something's gone very wrong with Mr. John, and he's tried liquor. He looked like a ghost, and in he went with his eyes straight before him, with never a look or a word for none of us: him that was always such a gentleman!"

I had never heard Byles make so long a speech. The crowd in the churchyard were talking in whispers and getting ready rice and slippers to throw at the bride and bridegroom. The ringers were ready with their hands on the ropes to ring out the merry peal as the bride and bridegroom should come out.

A murmur from the church announced them; out they came. Byles was right. John Charrington did not look himself. There was dust on his coat, his hair was disarranged. He seemed to have been in some row, for there was a black mark above his eyebrow. He was deathly pale. But his pallor was not greater than that of the bride, who might have been carved in ivory—dress, veil, orange blossoms, face and all.

As they passed out the ringers stooped—there were six of them—and then, on the ears expecting the gay wedding peal, came the slow tolling of the passing bell.

A thrill of horror at so foolish a jest from the ringers passed through us all. But the ringers themselves dropped the ropes and fled like rabbits out into the sunlight. The bride shuddered, and grey shadows came about her mouth, but the bridegroom led her on down the path where the people stood with the handfuls of rice; but the handfuls were never thrown, and the wedding-bells never rang. In vain the ringers were urged to remedy their mistake: they protested with many whispered expletives that they would see themselves further first.

In a hush like the hush in the chamber of death the bridal pair passed into their carriage and its door slammed behind them.

Then the tongues were loosed. A babel of anger, wonder, conjecture from the guests and the spectators.

"If I'd seen his condition, sir," said old Forster to me as we drove off, "I would have stretched him on the floor of the church, sir, by Heaven I would, before I'd have let him marry my daughter!"

Then he put his head out of the window.

"Drive like hell," he cried to the coachman; "don't spare the horses."

He was obeyed. We passed the bride's carriage. I forbore to look at it, and old Forster turned his head away and swore. We reached home before it.

We stood in the hall doorway, in the blazing afternoon sun, and in about half a minute we heard wheels crunching the gravel. When the carriage stopped in front of the steps old Forster and I ran down.

"Great Heaven, the carriage is empty! And yet—

I had the door open in a minute, and this is what I saw—

No sign of John Charrington; and of May, his wife, only a huddled heap of white satin lying half on the floor of the carriage and half on the seat.

"I drove straight here, sir," said the coachman, as the bride's father lifted her out; "and I'll swear no one got out of the carriage."

We carried her into the house in her bridal dress and drew back her veil. I saw her face. Shall I ever forget it? White, white and drawn with agony and horror, bearing such a look of terror as I have never seen since except in dreams. And her hair, her radiant blonde hair, I tell you it was white like snow.

As we stood, her father and I, half mad with the horror and mystery of it, a boy came up the avenue—a telegraph boy. They brought the orange envelope to me. I tore it open.

> *"Mr. Charrington was thrown from the dogcart on his way to the station at half past one. Killed on the spot!"*

And he was married to May Forster in our parish church at *half past three,* in presence of half the parish.

"I shall be married, dead or alive!"

What had passed in that carriage on the homeward drive? No one knows—no one will ever know. Oh, May! Oh, my dear!

Before a week was over they laid her beside her husband in our little churchyard on the thyme-covered hill—the churchyard where they had kept their love-trysts.

Thus was accomplished John Charrington's wedding.

THE NIGHT WALKERS

Sydney J. Bounds

"You're drinking too much again."

Roger Bateson glanced across the table as his wife's furious whisper echoed around the canal-side pub. She had pushed back her plate with the remains of lunch, fat trimmed off cold meat and a tired leaf of lettuce. Her mouth was turned down at the corners.

He looked back at the large-scale map spread out on the table, his finger still on the junction where two cuts met. He had been working out time and distance to their next mooring, when he spotted the branch and the name of the lock a few miles along it: Deadmen's Lock.

"Look at this, Jan."

"I'm not interested."

"Then you'd better get interested, because this is where we're going."

He swallowed the rest of his pint and rose abruptly, tall and willowy and black-haired, dressed in faded jeans and a check shirt. He carried the map across to a corner where two local men sat sucking on pipes over empty glasses.

"Can I get you a refill?" Roger's brilliant smile switched on like the charm of a con-man.

"With pleasure, sir. Us has never been known to turn down free beer."

"We're on a holiday cruise—I suppose that's obvious?" Roger displayed his map of the waterways and pointed out the junction, a few miles north of the Swan inn. "I'd like to know if this branch is navigable."

"Aye, we know un . . . your health, sir, and my advice is, stick to the main line. That branch ain't nice and that's fact. The lock's dangerous, been a few drowned there, 's how it got its name."

"'Tis true what Harry says." The second oldster wiped his moustache. "But there's more to it. Local folk avoid Deadmen's Lock, and with reason. Only visitors use that stretch of cut, and they don't happen back to tell any tales."

"Rumours, Tom—"

"Aye, and the Night Walkers be only rumour? I'll wager you a quid you don't fancy walking along the towing path after dark. You know same as everyone in these parts 'tis a cruel haunting, a plague spot best avoided."

Roger stared at them. "Ghosts, you mean? You're serious?"

"Ghosts? In a manner o speaking. I don't say they mean harm, but it must get powerful lonely down there. And the Night Walkers, well, they like company."

"So it's best to give that branch a miss, sir. If you'll take my advice."

"Time, gen'lemen, please!"

Jan rose promptly and started towards the door. "Are you coming, Roger?"

He finished his beer, folded the map and followed her out into late summer sunlight. He walked just a trifle unsteadily across the jetty where *Sister Rose* was tied up. But now the idea of cruising the branch was fixed, like an immovable object, in his mind.

As Jan, blonde and dumpy, stepped aboard their hire cruiser, she turned to give him a hard look.

"If I know you, we're going all the same. No matter that it's dangerous. You won't consider my feelings—either keep straight on, or turn back?"

"You're dead right, I won't," Roger agreed. "Sounds like a lot of old cod to me. But if other people avoid this cut, good—we'll have it all to ourselves. That's the whole point of a holiday on the canals, to get away from the rat-race and enjoy a quiet life in the backwaters."

Jan laughed harshly. "The quiet life, yeah, stuck in a cramped cabin cooking on a paraffin stove, slogging away at rusted-up locks. I'm fed up with it."

Roger ignored her; she reminded him of a needle stuck in a groove. Her idea of a holiday was a first-class hotel on the sea front with waiters to fetch and carry. It had been his idea to spend a fortnight on the canals and he didn't back down to anybody, least of all his wife.

He started the engine and slipped the mooring ropes and eased *Sister Rose* out into the middle of the canal. She cruised along at a steady three miles and hour, leaving the Swan behind. Ahead was an empty horizon where blue sky met silver water; on each side, beyond thick green hedges, open countryside.

Jan changed into a bikini and sun-bathed on the cabin roof.

It could have been a marvellous holiday last year, Roger thought; but in their second year of marriage, the glamour had worn thin. They seemed to spend more time rowing than anything else.

And it was hard work at times, winding sluice paddles and pushing heavy wooden beams to work lock gates.

He reached the junction marked on his map and nosed the cruiser into it. There was a screen of low branches and overgrown hedge, but he forced a way through; the foliage sprang back, isolating them from the rest of the world.

The only sound was the noise of their engine. Roger was just a bit apprehensive; this cut was narrow, the banks high and green, and patches of weed floated on the surface.

Presently the boat slowed as the engine took up the strain. He leaned over the side to use the boat hook.

"Give me a hand, Jan."

"You can do it yourself—it was your idea to come up here, so get on with it."

Her voice was shrill. How had he ever imagined she had a soft country burr? It grated like a buzz-saw and he shouted back:

"Bitch!"

He reversed, then poked away with the boat hook, clearing the propeller.

The boat moved forward again. The trees grew in close and dense foliage cut off any view beyond. They chugged along, the engine protesting; and again he had to stop to get rid of the weed.

Roger glanced from his map to the sinking sun. Deadmen's Lock wasn't far now. He'd reach it before dark, and that was far enough for one day. An old disused lock wouldn't be easy to work; he'd leave that till morning. Maybe Jan would be in a better mood then.

Sister Rose plodded on until, ahead, the ancient timbers of the lock reared out of the canal.

Roger slowed the boat and took her in close to the tow-path, searching for a mooring. Not that he expected much traffic; he hadn't seen another boat since he left the main line. It was a lonely spot, quiet, with no sign of life anywhere.

Jan sat up suddenly. "Please, Roger, let's go on. I don't like it here."

"That's too bad. You wouldn't help with the boat, and I'm dead tired."

"It's always what you want."

"I'm mooring. You get supper ready."

She stamped into the cabin and he heard her banging things about as he tied up.

Strangely, the tow-path looked as though it were still in use. It was wide and clear where it ran along the bank, from the lock and past the boat. A damp mist was forming over the canal, turning the evening air chill. A breeze moved the gathering mist in eddies, first hiding, then revealing the gaunt framework of lock gates and balance beams.

He went into the cabin. Jan had changed into slacks and sweater, and there was cold tinned meat and bread and butter and tomatoes on the fold-out table between their bunks.

"We only had a cold lunch," he grumbled.

"If you want something hot, cook it yourself!"

Roger scowled and reached for a can of beer. He pulled off the tab.

"Drinking again? Your breath stinks enough already."

"Ah, shut up."

They ate in silence, darkness coming down like a shroud, and Roger lit an oil lamp. Water dripped monotonously somewhere, and a rope creaked as the boat shifted fractionally.

He glowered at his wife. A year ago she'd been a dolly-bird, now . . . well, there wasn't anyone else available.

"How about it tonight?"

She sniffed. "That's all you think about. Suppose you do the washing-up for once?"

She left the table and went out on deck. Roger pushed back his chair and followed.

The night was dark and moonless. A few stars shone through banks of cloud and a chill wind blew across dark water, rippling its surface and stirring the mist. Deadmen's Lock had an eerie appearance by starlight, sagging timbers shrouded in greenish weed; a steady drip-drip of water leaked from the sluices and an unpleasant smell, like rotting vegetation, came on the breeze.

On impulse, he voiced his thoughts. "Remember what the locals told us? A haunted place, where the drowned walk."

Wind moaned through the trees and Jan shivered. "It sounds like the dead wailing," she whispered, and came into his arms for comfort.

"It's only the wind," Roger said, refusing to admit his own unease.

He stared at the mist hanging over the lock. Muffled splashing sounds came from there. Rats? He wondered. Jan was warm and scented in his arms. "Let's go inside."

"Okay, Rog."

He knew by her tone of voice that it was going to be all right, and smiled in the night, remembering their courting; how she'd been willing after a horror film.

Then the mist parted, like a stage curtain, and the stars shone on indistinct shapes, vaguely man-like, with just a hint of transparency.

Jan gave a choking sob and Roger's arms tightened about her.

"It's nothing," he muttered. "A trick of the light."

His brain refused to accept what his eyes recorded. This could not possibly be happening, yet his scalp lifted.

Grotesque figures, bloated and pallid, heaved themselves up from the water in the lock chamber. The drowned climbed laboriously on to the tow-path, trailing weeds like green slime.

Starlight shone on and through the Night Walkers as, in seeming slow motion, they drifted towards the *Sister Rose*.

A wave of paralyzing cold struck. The wind roared, battering at their ears, and Jan's mouth opened in a silent scream.

Clothed in mist, the Night Walkers moved along the embankment, water-logged flesh swollen and pulpy. They squelched as they came, dripping water. Dead eyes stared avidly.

Roger suddenly remembered: *they like company* . . . and pushed Jan from him. He stumbled across the deck and fumbled at the mooring ropes with hands that shook. He couldn't loosen the knots and his teeth rattled in his head. Oh God, he prayed, let us get away, please let us get away . . .

The Night Walkers reached the boat and clambered aboard. Jan shrank back as one of the leprous shapes reached out to embrace her. She tried to jump to the opposite bank, but the gap was too wide; she vanished into the pond with a splash, crying out in her distress.

Roger gave up on the ropes; his hands were useless. One of the corpse-shapes stalked him. He flung up an arm that apparently went through the figure, and his arm felt as numb as if he'd stuck it in a refrigerator.

He jumped after his wife, into the canal.

"Jan!"

He glimpsed a head, hair spread out and floating on the surface, then she went under again as he stroked towards her.

Something curled around his ankle, dragging him back, pulling him under. He spluttered as water filled his mouth and nostrils. It's only weeds, he told himself, don't panic; but it felt like a hand gripping him, pulling him down, down . . .

He choked, lungs filling, and couldn't break free of the relentless hold. He struggled to reach the surface in his last moments of consciousness. Weeds like hands or hands like weeds, they wouldn't let go. Despair came, and darkness, and the roar in his ears gradually faded . . .

Sister Rose rocked gently at her mooring. The mist lifted and the stars shone on the still and silent water of Deadmen's Lock. After a decent interval, Roger and Jan, too, joined the Night Walkers.

BRICKETT BOTTOM

Amyas Northcote

The Reverend Arthur Maydew was the hard-working incumbent of a large parish in one of our manufacturing towns. He was also a student and a man of no strong physique, so that when an opportunity was presented to him to take an annual holiday by exchanging parsonages with an elderly clergyman, Mr. Roberts, the Squarson of the Parish of Overbury, and an acquaintance of his own, he was glad to avail himself of it.

Overbury is a small and very remote village in one of our most lovely and rural counties, and Mr. Roberts had long held the living of it.

Without further delay we can transport Mr. Maydew and his family, which consisted only of two daughters, to their temporary home. The two young ladies, Alice and Maggie, the heroines of this narrative, were at that time aged twenty-six and twenty-four years respectively. Both of them were attractive girls, fond of such society as they could find in their own parish and, the former especially, always pleased to extend the circle of their acquaintance. Although the elder in years, Alice in many ways yielded place to her sister, who was the more energetic and practical and upon whose shoulders the bulk of the family cares and responsibilities rested. Alice was inclined to be absent-minded and emotional and to devote more of her thoughts and time to speculations of an abstract nature than her sister.

Both of the girls, however, rejoiced at the prospect of a period of quiet and rest in a pleasant country neighbourhood, and both were gratified at knowing that their father would find in Mr. Roberts' library much that would entertain his mind, and in Mr. Roberts' garden an opportunity to indulge freely in his favourite game of croquet. They would have, no doubt, preferred some cheerful neighbours, but Mr. Roberts was positive in his assurances that there was no one in the neighbourhood whose acquaintance would be of interest to them.

The first few weeks of their new life passed pleasantly for the Maydew family. Mr. Maydew quickly gained renewed vigour in his quiet and congenial surroundings, and in the delightful air, while his daughters spent much of their time in long walks about the country and in exploring its beauties.

One evening late in August the two girls were returning from a long walk along one of their favourite paths, which led along the side of the Downs. On their right, as they walked, the ground fell away sharply to a narrow glen, named Brickett Bottom, about three-quarters of a mile in length, along the bottom of which ran a little-used country road leading to a farm, known as Blaise's Farm, and then onward and upward to lose itself as a sheep track on the higher Downs. On their side of the slope some scattered trees and bushes grew, but beyond the lane and running up over the farther slope of the glen was a thick wood, which extended away to Carew Court, the seat of a neighbouring magnate, Lord Carew. On their left the open Down rose above them and beyond its crest lay Overbury.

The girls were walking hastily, as they were later than they had intended to be and were anxious to reach home. At a certain point at which they had now arrived the path forked, the right hand branch leading down into Brickett Bottom and the left hand turning up over the Down to Overbury.

Just as they were about to turn into the left hand path Alice suddenly stopped and pointing downwards exclaimed:

"How very curious, Maggie! Look, there is a house down there in the Bottom, which we have, or at least I have, never noticed before, often as we have walked up the Bottom."

Maggie followed with her eyes her sister's pointing finger.

"I don't see any house," she said.

"Why, Maggie," said her sister, "can't you see it! A quaint-looking, old-fashioned red brick house, there just where the road bends to the right. It seems to be standing in a nice, well-kept garden too."

Maggie looked again, but the light was beginning to fade in the glen and she was short-sighted to boot.

"I certainly don't see anything," she said, "but then I am so blind and the light is getting bad; yes, perhaps I do see a house," she added, straining her eyes.

"Well, it is there," replied her sister, "and to-morrow we will come and explore it."

Maggie agreed readily enough, and the sisters went home, still speculating on how they had happened not to notice the house before and resolving firmly on an expedition thither the next day. However, the expedition did not come off as planned, for that evening Maggie slipped on the stairs and fell, spraining her ankle in such a fashion as to preclude walking for some time.

Notwithstanding the accident to her sister, Alice remained possessed by the idea of making further investigations into the house she had looked down upon from the hill the evening before; and the next day, having seen Maggie carefully settled for the afternoon, she started off for Brickett Bottom. She returned in triumph and much intrigued over her discoveries, which she eagerly narrated to her sister.

Yes. There was a nice, old-fashioned red brick house, not very large and set in a charming, old-world garden in the Bottom. It stood on a tongue of land jutting out from the woods, just at the point where the lane, after a fairly straight course from its junction with the main road half a mile away, turned sharply to the right in the direction of Blaise's Farm. More than that, Alice had seen the people of the house, whom she described as an old gentleman and a lady, presumably his wife. She had not clearly made out the gentleman, who was sitting in the porch, but the old lady, who had been in the garden busy with her flowers, had looked up and smiled pleasantly at her as she passed. She was sure, she said, that they were nice people and that it would be pleasant to make their acquaintance.

Maggie was not quite satisfied with Alice's story. She was of a more prudent and retiring nature than her sister; she had an uneasy feeling that, if the old couple had been desirable or attractive neighbours, Mr. Roberts would have mentioned them, and knowing Alice's nature she said what she could to discourage her vague idea of endeavouring to make acquaintance with the owners of the red brick house.

On the following morning, when Alice came to her sister's room to inquire how she did, Maggie noticed that she looked pale and rather absent-minded, and, after a few commonplace remarks had passed, she asked:

"What is the matter, Alice? You don't look yourself this morning."

Her sister gave a slightly embarrassed laugh.

"Oh, I am all right," she replied, "only I did not sleep very well. I kept on dreaming about the house. It was such an odd dream too: the house seemed to be home, and yet to be different."

"What, that house in Bricket Bottom?" said Maggie. "Why, what is the matter with you, you seem to be quite crazy about the place?"

"Well, it is curious, isn't it, Maggie, that we should have only just discovered it, and that it looks to be lived in by nice people? I wish we could get to know them."

Maggie did not care to resume the argument of the night before and the subject dropped, nor did Alice again refer to the house or its inhabitants for some little time. In fact, for some days the weather was wet and Alice was forced to abandon her walks, but when the weather once more became fine she resumed them, and Maggie suspected that Brickett Bottom formed one of her sister's favourite expeditions. Maggie became anxious over her sister, who seemed to grow daily more absent-minded and silent, but she refused to be drawn into any confidential talk, and Maggie was nonplussed.

One day, however, Alice returned from her afternoon walk in an unusually excited state of mind, of which Maggie sought an explanation. It came with a rush. Alice said that, that afternoon, as she approached the house in Brickett Bottom, the old lady, who as usual was busy in her garden, had walked down to the gate as she passed and had wished her good day.

Alice had replied and, pausing, a short conversation had followed. Alice could not remember the exact tenor of it, but, after she had paid a compliment to the old lady's flowers, the latter had rather diffidently asked her to enter the garden for a closer view. Alice had hesitated, and the old lady had said: "Don't be afraid of me, my dear, I like to see young ladies about me and my husband finds their society quite necessary to him." After a pause she went on: "Of course nobody has told you about us. My husband is Colonel Paxton, late of the Indian Army, and we have been here for many, many years. It's rather lonely, for so few people ever see us. Do come in and meet the Colonel."

"I hope you didn't go in," said Maggie rather sharply.

"Why not?" replied Alice.

"Well, I don't like Mrs. Paxton asking you in that way," answered Maggie.

"I don't see what harm there was in the invitation," said Alice. "I didn't go in because it was getting late and I was anxious to get home; but—"

"But what?" asked Maggie.

Alice shrugged her shoulders.

"Well," she said, "I have accepted Mrs. Paxton's invitation to pay her a little visit to-morrow." And she gazed defiantly at Maggie.

Maggie became distinctly uneasy on hearing of this resolution. She did not like the idea of her impulsive sister visiting people on such slight acquaintance, especially as they had never heard them mentioned before. She endeavoured by all means, short of appealing to Mr.

Maydew, to dissuade her sister from going, at any rate until there had been time to make some inquiries as to the Paxtons. Alice, however, was obdurate.

What harm could happen to her? She asked. Mrs. Paxton was a charming old lady. She was going early in the afternoon for a short visit. She would be back for tea and croquet with her father and, anyway, now that Maggie was laid up, long solitary walks were unendurable and she was not going to let slip the chance of following up what promised to be a pleasant acquaintance.

Maggie could do nothing more. Her ankle was better and she was able to get down the garden and sit in a long chair near her father, but walking was still quite out of the question, and it was with some misgivings that on the following day she watched Alice depart gaily for her visit, promising to be back by half-past four at the very latest.

The afternoon passed quietly till nearly five, when Mr. Maydew, looking up from his book, noticed Maggie's uneasy expression and asked:

"Where is Alice?"

"Out for a walk," replied Maggie; and then after a short pause she went on: "And she has also gone to pay a call on some neighbours whom she has recently discovered."

"Neighbours," ejaculated Mr. Maydew, "what neighbours? Mr. Roberts never spoke of any neighbours to me."

"Well, I don't know much about them," answered Maggie. "Only Alice and I were out walking the day of my accident and saw or at least she saw, for I am so blind I could not quite make it out, a house in Brickett Bottom. The next day she went to look at it closer, and yesterday she told me that she had made the acquaintance of the people living in it. She says that they are a retired Indian officer and his wife, a Colonel and Mrs. Paxton, and Alice describes Mrs. Paxton as a charming old lady, who pressed her to come and see them. So she has gone this afternoon, but she promised me she would be back long before this."

Mr. Maydew was silent for a moment and then said:

"I am not well pleased about this. Alice should not be so impulsive and scrape acquaintance with absolutely unknown people. Had there been nice neighbours in Brickett Bottom, I am certain Mr. Roberts would have told us."

The conversation dropped; but both father and daughter were disturbed and uneasy and, tea having been finished and the clock striking half-past five, Mr. Maydew asked Maggie:

"When did you say Alice would be back?"

"Before half-past four at the latest, father."

"Well, what can she be doing? What can have delayed her? You say you did not see the house," he went on.

"No," said Maggie, "I cannot say I did. It was getting dark and you know how short-sighted I am."

"But surely you must have seen it at some other time," said her father.

"That is the strangest part of the whole affair," answered Maggie. "We have often walked up the Bottom, but I never noticed the house, nor had Alice till that evening. I wonder," she went on after a short pause, "if it would not be well to ask Smith to harness the pony and drive over to bring her back. I am not happy about her—I am afraid—"

"Afraid of what?" said her father in the irritated voice of a man who is growing frightened. "What can have gone wrong in this quiet place? Still, I'll send Smith over for her."

So saying he rose from his chair and sought out Smith, the rather dull-witted gardener-groom attached to Mr. Roberts' service.

"Smith," he said, "I want you to harness the pony at once and go over to Colonel Paxton's in Brickett Bottom and bring Miss Maydew home."

The man stared at him.

"Go where, sir?" he said.

Mr. Maydew repeated the order and the man, still staring stupidly, answered:

"I never heard of Colonel Paxton, sir. I don't know what house you mean."

Mr. Maydew was now growing really anxious.

"Well, harness the pony at once," he said; and going back to Maggie he told her of what he called Smith's stupidity, and asked her if she felt that her ankle would be strong enough to permit her to go with him and Smith to the Bottom to point out the house.

Maggie agreed readily and in a few minutes the party started off. Brickett Bottom, although not more than three-quarters of a mile away over the Downs, was at least three miles by road; and as it was nearly six o'clock before Mr. Maydew left the Vicarage, and the pony was old and slow, it was getting late before the entrance to Brickett bottom was reached. Turning into the lane the cart proceeded slowly up the Bottom, Mr. Maydew and Maggie looking anxiously from side to side, whilst Smith drove stolidly on looking neither to the right nor left.

"Where is the house?" said Mr. Maydew presently.

"At the bend of the road," answered Maggie, her heart sickening as she looked out through the failing light to see the trees stretching their ranks in unbroken formation along it. The cart reached the bend. "It should be here," whispered Maggie.

They pulled up. Just in front of them the road bent to the right round a tongue of land, which, unlike the rest of the right hand side of the road, was free from trees and was covered only by rough grass and stray bushes. A closer inspection disclosed evident signs of terraces having once been formed on it, but of a house there was no trace.

"Is this the place?" said Mr. Maydew in a low voice.

Maggie nodded.

"But there is no house here," said her father. "What does it all mean? Are you sure of yourself, Maggie? Where is Alice?"

Before Maggie could answer a voice was heard calling "Father! Maggie!" The sound of the voice was thin and high and, paradoxically, it sounded both very near and yet as if it came from some infinite distance. The cry was thrice repeated and then silence fell. Mr. Maydew and Maggie stared at each other.

"That was Alice's voice," said Mr. Maydew huskily, "she is near and in trouble, and is calling us. Which way did you think it came from, Smith?" he added turning to the gardener.

"I didn't hear anybody calling," said the man.

"Nonsense!" answered Mr. Maydew.

And then he and Maggie both began to call "Alice. Alice. Where are you?" There was no reply and Mr. Maydew sprang from the cart, at the same time bidding Smith to hand the reins to Maggie and come and search for the missing girl. Smith obeyed him and both men, scrambling up the turfy bit of ground, began to search and call through the neighbouring wood. They heard and saw nothing, however, and after an agonized search Mr. Maydew ran down to the cart and begged Maggie to drive to Blaise's Farm for help leaving himself and Smith to continue the search. Maggie followed her father's instructions and was fortunate enough to find Mr. Rumbold, the farmer, his two sons and a couple of labourers just returning from the harvest field. She explained what had happened, and the farmer and his men promptly volunteered to form a search party, though Maggie, in spite of her anxiety, noticed a queer expression on Mr. Rumbold's face as she told him her tale.

The party, provided with lanterns, now went down the Bottom, joined Mr. Maydew and Smith and made an exhaustive but absolutely fruitless search of the woods near the bend of the road. No trace of the missing girl was to be found, and after a long and anxious time the search was abandoned, one of the young Rumbolds volunteering to ride into the nearest town and notify the police.

Maggie, though with little hope in her own heart, endeavoured to cheer her father on their homeward way with the idea that Alice might have returned to Overbury over the Downs whilst they were going by road to the Bottom, and that she had seen them and called to them in jest when they were opposite the tongue of land.

However, when they reached home there was no Alice and, though the next day the search was resumed and full inquiries were instituted by the police, all was to no purpose. No trace of Alice was ever found, the last human being that saw her having been an old woman, who had met her going down the path into the Bottom on the afternoon of her disappearance, and who described her as smiling but looking "queerlike."

This is the end of the story, but the following may throw some light upon it.

The history of Alice's mysterious disappearance became widely known through the medium of the Press and Mr. Roberts, distressed beyond measure at what had taken place, returned in all haste to Overbury to offer what comfort and help he could give to this afflicted friend and tenant. He called upon the Maydews and, having heard their tale, sat for a short time in silence. Then he said:

"Have you ever heard any local gossip concerning this Colonel and Mrs. Paxton?"

"No," replied Mr. Maydew, "I never heard their names until the day of my poor daughter's fatal visit."

"Well," said Mr. Roberts, "I will tell you all I can about them, which is not very much, I fear." He paused and then went on: "I am now nearly seventy-five years old, and for nearly seventy years no house has stood in Bricket Bottom. But when I was a child about five there was an old-fashioned, red brick house standing in a garden at the bend of the road, such as you have described. It was owned and lived in by a retired Indian soldier and his wife, a Colonel and Mrs. Paxton. At the time I speak of, certain events having taken place at the house and the old couple having died, it was sold by their heirs to Lord Carew, who shortly after pulled it down on the ground that it interfered with his shooting. Colonel and Mrs. Paxton were well known to my father, who was the clergyman here before me, and to the neighbourhood in general. They lived quietly and were not unpopular, but the Colonel was supposed to possess a violent and vindictive temper.

Their family consisted only of themselves, their daughter and a couple of servants, the Colonel's old Army servant and his Eurasian wife. Well, I cannot tell you details of what happened, I was only a child; my father never liked gossip and in later years, when he talked to me on the subject, he always avoided any appearance of exaggeration or sensationalism. However, it is known that Miss Paxton fell in love with and became engaged to a young man to whom her parents took a strong dislike. They used every possible means to break off the match, and many rumours were set on foot as to their conduct—undue influence, even cruelty were charged against them. I do not know the truth, all I can say is that Miss Paxton died and a very bitter feeling against her parents sprang up. My father, however, continued to call, but was rarely admitted. In fact, he never saw Colonel Paxton after his daughter's death and only saw Mrs. Paxton once or twice. He described her as an utterly broken woman, and was not surprised at her following her daughter to the grave in about three months' time. Colonel Paxton became, if possible, more of a recluse than ever after his wife's death and himself died not more than a month after her under circumstances which pointed to suicide. Again a crop of rumours sprang up, but there was no one in particular to take action, the doctor certified Death from Natural Causes, and Colonel Paxton, like his wife and daughter, was buried in this churchyard. The property passed to a distant relative, who came down to it for one night shortly afterwards; he never came again, having apparently conceived a violent dislike to the place, but arranged to pension off the servants and then sold the house to Lord Carew, who was glad to purchase this little island in the middle of his property. He pulled it down soon after he had bought it, and the garden was left to relapse into a wilderness."

Mr. Roberts paused.

"Those are all the facts," he added.

"But there is something more," said Maggie.

Mr. Roberts hesitated for a while.

"You have a right to know all," he said almost to himself; then louder he continued: "What I am now going to tell you is really rumour, vague and uncertain; I cannot fathom its truth or its meaning. About five years after the house had been pulled down a young maid-servant at Carew Court was out walking one afternoon. She was a stranger to the village and a newcomer to the Court. On returning home to tea she told her fellow-servants that as she walked down Brickett Bottom, which place she described clearly, she passed a red brick house at the bend of the road and that a kind-faced old lady had asked her to step in for a while. She did not go in, not because she had any suspicions of there being anything uncanny, but simply because she feared to be late for tea.

"I do not think she ever visited the Bottom again and she had no other similar experience, so far as I am aware.

"Two or three years later, shortly after my father's death, a traveling tinker with his wife and daughter camped for the night at the foot of the Bottom. The girl strolled away up the glen to gather blackberries and was never seen or heard of again. She was searched for in vain—of course, one does not know the truth—and she may have run away voluntarily from her parents, although there was no known cause for her doing so.

"That," concluded Mr. Roberts, "is all I can tell you of either facts or rumours; all that I can do is to pray for you and for her."

THE WATER GHOST OF HARROWBY HALL

John Kendrick Bangs

The trouble with Harrowby Hall was that it was haunted, and, what was worse, the ghost did not merely appear at the bedside of a person, but remained there for one mortal hour before it disappeared.

It never appeared except on Christmas Eve, and then as the clock was striking twelve. The owners of Harrowby hall had tried their hardest to rid themselves of the damp and dewy lady who rose up out of the best bedroom floor at midnight, but they had failed. They had tried stopping the clock, so that the ghost would not know when it was midnight; but she made her appearance just the same, and there she would stand until everything about her was thoroughly soaked.

Then the owners of Harrowby Hall closed up every crack in the floor with hemp, and over this were placed layers of tar and canvas; the walls were made waterproof, and the doors and windows likewise, in the hope that the lady would find it difficult to leak into the room, but even this did no good.

The following Christmas Eve she appeared as promptly as before, and frightened the guest of the room quite out of his senses by sitting down beside him, and gazing with her cavernous blue eyes into his. In her long, bony fingers bits of dripping seaweed were entwined, the ends hanging down, and these ends she drew across his forehead until he fainted away. He was found unconscious in his bed the next morning, simply saturated with sea-water and fright.

The next year the master of Harrowby Hall decided not to have the best spare bedroom opened at all, but the ghost appeared as usual in the room—that is, it was supposed she did, for the hangings were dripping wet the next morning. Finding no one there, she immediately set out to haunt the owner of Harrowby himself. She found him in his own cosy room, congratulating himself upon having outwitted her.

All of a sudden the curl went out of his hair, and he was as wet as if he had fallen into a rain barrel. When he saw before him the lady of the cavernous eyes and seaweed fingers he too fainted, but immediately came to, because the vast amount of water in his hair, trickling down over his face, revived him.

Now it so happened that the master of Harrowby was a brave man. He intended to find out a few things he felt he had a right to know. He would have liked to put on a dry suit of clothes first, but the ghost refused to leave him for an instant until her hour was up. In an effort to warm himself up he turned to the fire; it was an unfortunate move, because it brought the ghost directly over the fire, which immediately was extinguished.

At this he turned angrily to her, and said: "Far be it from me to be impolite to a woman, madam, but I wish you'd stop your visits to this house. Go and sit out on the lake, if you like that sort of thing; soak in the rain barrel, if you wish; but do not come into a gentleman's house and soak him and his possessions in this way, I beg of you!"

"Henry Hartwick Oglethorpe," said the ghost, in a gurgling voice, "you don't know what you are talking about. You do not know that I am compelled to haunt this place year after year by my terrible fate. It is no pleasure for me to enter this house, and ruin everything I touch. I never aspired to be a shower bath, but it is my doom. Do you know who I am?"

"No, I don't," returned the master of Harrowby. "I should say you were the Lady of the Lake!"

"No, I am the Water Ghost of Harrowby Hall, and I have held this highly unpleasant office for two hundred years tonight."

"How the deuce did you ever come to get elected?" asked the master.

"Through a mistake," replied the spectre. "I am the ghost of that fair maiden whose picture hangs over the mantelpiece in the drawing-room."

"But what made you get the house into such a spot?"

"I was not to blame, sir," returned the lady. "It was my father's fault. He built Harrowby Hall, and the room I haunt was to have been mine. My father had it furnished in pink and yellow, knowing well that blue and grey was the only combination of colours I could bear. He did it to spite me, and I refused to live in the room. Then my father said that I could live there or on the lawn, he didn't care which. That night I ran from the house and jumped over the cliff into the sea."

"That was foolish," said the master of Harrowby.

"So I've heard," returned the ghost, "but I really never realized what I was doing until after I was drowned. I had been drowned a week when a sea nymph came to me. She informed me that I was to be one of her followers, and that my doom was to haunt Harrowby Hall for one hour every Christmas Eve throughout the rest of eternity. I was to haunt that room on such Christmas Eves as I found it occupied; and if it should turn out not to be occupied I was to spend that hour with the head of the house."

"I'll sell the place."

"That you cannot do, for then I must appear to any purchaser, and reveal to him the awful secret of the house."

"Do you mean to tell me that on every Christmas Eve that I don't happen to have somebody in that guest-chamber, you are going to haunt me wherever I may be, taking all the curl out of my hair, putting out my fire and soaking me through to the skin?" demanded the master.

"Yes, Oglethorpe. And what is more," said the water ghost, "it doesn't make the slightest difference where you are. If I find that room empty, wherever you may be I shall douse you with my spectral pres . . ."

Here the clock struck one, and immediately the ghost faded away. It was perhaps more a trickle than a fading, but as a disappearance it was complete.

"By St. George and his Dragon!" cried the master of Harrowby, "I swear that next Christmas there'll be someone in the spare room, or I spend the night in a bathtub."

But when Christmas Eve came again the master of Harrowby was in his grave. He never recovered from the cold he caught that awful night. Harrowby Hall was closed, and the heir to the estate was in London. And there to him in his apartment came the water ghost at the appointed hour. Being younger and stronger, however, he survived the shock. Everything in his rooms was ruined—his clocks were rusted; a fine collection of watercolour drawings was entirely washed out. And because the apartments below his were drenched with water soaking through the floors, he was asked by his landlady to leave the apartment immediately.

The story of his family's ghost had gone about; no one would invite him to any party except afternoon teas and receptions, and fathers of daughters refused to allow him to remain in their houses later than eight o'clock at night.

So the heir of Harrowby Hall determined that something must be done.

The thought came to him to have the fireplace in the room enlarged, so that the ghost would evaporate at its first appearance. But he remembered his father's experience. Then he thought of steampipes. These, he remembered, could lie hundreds of feet deep in water, and still be hot enough to drive the water away in vapour. So the haunted room was heated by steam to a withering degree.

The scheme was only partially successful. The water ghost appeared at the specified time, but hot as the room was, it shortened her visit by no more than five minutes in the hour. And during this time the young master was a nervous wreck, and the room itself was terribly cracked and warped. And worse than this, as the last drop of the water ghost was slowly sizzling itself out on the floor, she whispered that there was still plenty of water where she came from, and that next year would find her as exasperatingly saturating as ever.

It was then that, going from one extreme to the other, the heir of Harrowby hit upon the means by which the water ghost was ultimately conquered, and happiness came once more to the house of Oglethorpe.

The heir provided himself with a warm suit of fur underclothing. Wearing this with the furry side in, he placed over it a tight-fitting rubber garment like in a jersey. On top of this he drew on another set of woolen underclothing, and over this was a second rubber garment like the first. Upon his head he wore a light and comfortable diving helmet; and so clad, on the following Christmas Eve he awaited the coming of his tormentor.

It was a bitterly cold night that brought to a close this twenty-fourth day of December. The air outside was still, but the temperature was below zero. Within all was quiet; the servants of Harrowby Hall awaited with beating hearts the outcome of their master's campaign against his supernatural visitor.

The master himself was lying on the bed in the haunted room, dressed as he had planned and then . . .

The clock clanged out the hour of twelve.

There was a sudden banging of doors. A blast of cold air swept through the halls. The door leading into the haunted chamber flew open, a splash was heard, and the water ghost was seen standing at the side of the heir of Harrowby. Immediately from his clothing there streamed rivulets of water, but deep down under the various garments he wore he was as dry and warm as he could have wished.

"Ha!" said the young master of Harrowby, "I'm glad to see you."

"You are the most original man I've met, if that is true," returned the ghost. "May I ask where did you get that hat?"

"Certainly, madam," returned the master, courteously. "It is a little portable observatory I had made for just such emergencies as this. But tell me, is it true that you are doomed to follow me about for one mortal hour—to stand where I stand, to sit where I sit?"

"That is my happy fate," returned the lady.

"We'll go out on the lake," said the master, starting up.

"You can't get rid of me that way," returned the ghost. "The water won't swallow me up; in fact, it will just add to my present bulk."

"Nevertheless," said the master, "we will go out on the lake."

"But my dear sir," returned the ghost, "it is fearfully cold out there. You will be frozen hard before you've been out ten minutes."

"Oh, no, I'll not," replied the master. "I am very warmly dressed. Come!" This last in a tone of command that made the ghost ripple.

And they started.

They had not gone far before the water ghost showed signs of distress.

"You walk too slowly," she said, "I am nearly frozen. I beg you, hurry!"

"I should like to oblige a lady," returned the master courteously, "but my clothes are rather heavy, and a hundred yards an hour is about my speed. Indeed, I think we had better sit down on this snowdrift, and talk matters over."

"Do not! Do not do so, I beg!" cried the ghost. "Let us move on. I feel myself growing rigid as it is. If we stop here, I shall be frozen stiff."

"That, madam" said the master slowly, seating himself on an ice cake . . . "that is why I have brought you here. We have been on this spot just ten minutes; we have fifty more. Take your time about it, madam, but freeze. That is all I ask of you."

"I cannot move my right leg now," cried the ghost, in despair, "and my overskirt is a solid sheet of ice. Oh, good, kind Mr. Oglethorpe, light a fire, and let me go free from these icy fetters."

"Never, madam. It cannot be. I have you at last."

"Alas!" cried the ghost, a tear trickling down her frozen cheek. "Help me, I beg, I congeal!"

"Congeal, madam, congeal!" returned Oglethorpe coldly. "You are drenched and have drenched me for two hundred and three years, madam. Tonight, you have had your last drench."

"Ah, but I shall thaw out again, and then you'll see. Instead of the comfortably warm, genial ghost I have been in the past, sir, I shall be ice water," cried the lady, threateningly.

"No, you won't either," returned Oglethorpe; "for when you are frozen quite stiff, I shall send you to a cold-storage warehouse, and there shall you remain an icy work of art for evermore."

"But warehouses burn."

"So they do, but this warehouse cannot burn. It is made of asbestos and surrounding it are fireproof walls, and within those walls the temperature is now and shall be 416 degrees below the zero point; low enough to make an icicle of any flame in this world—or the next," the master added, with a chuckle.

"For the last time I beseech you. I would go on my knees to you, Oglethorpe, if they were not already frozen. I beg of you do not do . . ."

Here even the words froze on the water ghost's lips and the clock struck one. There was a momentary tremor throughout the ice-bound form, and the moon, coming out from behind a cloud, shone down on the rigid figure of a beautiful woman sculptured in clear, transparent ice. There stood the ghost of Harrowby Hall, conquered by the cold, a prisoner of all time.

The heir of Harrowby had won at last, and today in a large storage house in London stands the frigid form of one who will never again flood the house of Oglethorpe with woe and sea-water.

THE REAPER'S IMAGE

Stephen King

"We moved it last year, and quite an operation it was, too," Mr. Carlin said as they mounted the stairs. "Had to move it by hand, of course. No other way. We insured it against accident with Lloyds before we even took it out of the case in the drawing-room. Only firm that would insure for the sum we had in mind."

Spangler said nothing. The man was a fool. Johnson Spangler had learned a long time ago that the only way to talk to a fool was to ignore him.

"Insured it for a quarter of a million dollars," Mr. Carlin resumed when they reached the second-floor landing. His mouth quirked in a half-bitter, half-humorous line. "And a pretty penny it cost, too." He was a little man, not quite fat, with rimless glasses and a bald head that shone like a varnished volleyball. A suit of armour, guarding the mahogany shadows of the second-floor corridor, stared at them impassively.

It was a long corridor, and Spangler eyed the walls and hangings with a cool professional eye. Samuel Claggert had bought in copious quantities, but he had not bought well. Like so many of the self-made industry emperors of the late 1800s, he had been little more than a pawnshop rooter masquerading in collector's clothing, a connoisseur of canvas monstrosities, trashy novels and poetry collections in expensive cowhide bindings, and atrocious pieces of sculpture, all of which he considered Art.

Up here the walls were hung—festooned was perhaps a better word—with imitation Moroccan drapes, numberless (and, no doubt, anonymous) Madonnas holding numberless haloed babes while numberless angels flitted hither and thither in the background, grotesque scrolled candelabra, and one monstrous and obscenely ornate chandelier surmounted by a salaciously grinning nymphet.

Of course the old pirate had come up with a few interesting items; the law of averages demanded it. And if the Samuel Claggert Memorial Private Museum (Guided Tours on the Hour—Admission $1.00 Adults, $.50 Children—nauseating) was ninety-eight percent blatant junk, there was always that other two per cent, things like the Coombs long rifle over the hearth in the kitchen, the strange little *camera obscura* in the parlour, and of course the—

"The Delver looking-glass was removed after a rather unfortunate . . . incident," Mr. Carlin said abruptly, motivated apparently by a ghastly glaring portrait of no one in particular at the base of the next staircase. "There have been others, harsh words, wild statements, but this was an attempt to actually destroy the mirror. The woman, a Miss Sandra Bates, came in with a rock in her pocket. Fortunately her aim was bad and she only cracked a corner of the case. The mirror was unharmed. The Bates girl had a brother—"

"No need to give me the dollar tour," Spangler said quietly. "I'm conversant with the history of the Delver glass."

"Fascinating, isn't it?" Carlin cast him an odd, oblique look. "There was that English duchess in 1709 . . . and the Pennsylvania rug-merchant in 1746 . . . not to mention—"

"I'm conversant with the history," Spangler repeated quietly. "It's the workmanship I'm interest in. And then, of course, there's the question of authenticity—"

"Authenticity!" Mr. Carlin chuckled, a dry sound, as if bones had stirred in the cupboard below the stairs. "It's been examined by experts, Mr. Spangler."

"So was the Lemlier Stradivarius."

"So true," Mr. Carlin said. "But no Stradivarius ever had quite the ... the unsettling effect of the Delver glass."

"Yes, quite," Spangler said in his softly contemptuous voice. "Quite."

They climbed the third and fourth flights of stairs in silence. As they drew closer to the roof of the rambling structure, it became oppressively hot in the dark upper galleries. With the heat came a creeping stench that Spangler knew well, for he had spent all his adult life working in it—the smell of long-dead flies in shadowy corners, of wet rot and creeping wood lice behind the plaster. The smell of age. It was a smell common only to museums and mausoleums. He imagined much the same smell might arise from the grave of a virginal young girl, forty years dead.

Up here the relics were piled helter-skelter in true junk-shop profusion; Mr. Carlin led Spangler through a maze of statuary, frame-splintered portraits, pompous gold-plated birdcages, the dismembered skeleton of an ancient tandem bicycle. He led him to the far wall where a stepladder had been set up beneath a trapdoor in the ceiling. A dusty padlock hung from the trap.

Off to the left, an imitation Adonis stared at them pitilessly with blank pupil-less eyes. One arm was outstretched, and a yellow sign hung on the wrist which read: ABSOLUTELY NO ADMITTANCE.

Mr. Carlin produced a keyring from his jacket pocket, selected one, and mounted the stepladder. He paused on the third rung, his bald head gleaming faintly in the shadows. "I don't like that mirror," he said. "I never did. I'm afraid to look into it. I'm afraid I might look into it one day and see ... what the rest of them saw."

"They saw nothing but themselves," Spangler said.

Mr. Carlin began to speak, stopped, shook his head, and fumbled

191

above him, craning his neck to fit the key properly into the lock. "Should be replaced," he muttered. "It's—damn!" The lock sprung suddenly and swung out of the hasp. Mr. Carlin made a fumbling grab for it, and almost fell off the ladder. Spangler caught it deftly and looked up at him. He was clinging shakily to the top of the stepladder, face white in the brown semi-darkness.

"You *are* nervous about it, aren't you?" Spangler said in a mildly wondering tone.

Mr. Carlin said nothing. He seemed paralysed.

"Come down," Spangler said, "Please."

Carlin descended the ladder slowly, clinging to each rung like a man tottering over a bottomless chasm. When his feet touched the floor he began to babble, as if the floor contained some current that had turned him on, like an electric light.

"A quarter of a million," he said. "A quarter of a million dollars' worth of insurance to take that . . . *thing* from down there to up here. That goddamn *thing*. They had to rig a special block and tackle to get it into the gable store-room up there. And I was hoping—almost praying—that someone's fingers would be slippery . . . that the rope would be the wrong test . . . that the thing would fall and be shattered into a million pieces—"

"Facts," Spangler said. "Facts, Carlin. Number one: John Delver was an English craftsman of Norman descent who made mirrors in what we call the Elizabethan period of England's history. He lived and died uneventfully. No pentacles scrawled on the floor for the house-keeper to rub out, no sulphur-smelling documents with a splotch of blood on the dotted line. Number two: His mirrors have become collectors' items due principally to fine craftsmanship and to the fact that a form of crystal was used that has a mildly magnifying and distorting effect upon the eye of the beholder—a rather distinctive trademark. Number three: Only five Delvers remain in existence, to our present knowledge—two of them in America. They are priceless. Number four: This Delver and one other that was destroyed in the London

Blitz have gained a rather spurious reputation due largely to falsehood, exaggeration, and coincidence—"

"Number five," Mr. Carlin said. "Supercilious bastard, aren't you?"

Spangler looked with mild detestation at the blind-eyed Adonis.

"I was guiding the tour that Sandra Bates's brother was a part of when he got his look into your precious mirror, Spangler. He was perhaps sixteen, part of a high-school group. I was going through the history of the glass and had just got to the part *you* would appreciate—extolling the flawless craftsmanship, the perfection of the glass itself, when the boy raised his hand. "But what about that black splotch in the upper left-hand corner?" he asked. "That looks like a mistake."

"And one of his friends asked him what he meant, so the Bates boy started to tell him, then stopped. He looked at the mirror very closely, pushing right up to the red velvet guard-rope around the case—*then he looked behind him as if what he had seen had been the reflection of someone—of someone in black—standing at his shoulder.* "It looked like a man," he said. "But I couldn't see the face. It's gone now." And that was all."

"Go on," Spangler said. "You're itching to tell me it was the Reaper—I believe that is the common explanation, isn't it? That occasional chosen people see the Reaper's image in the glass? Get it out of your system, man. Tell me about the horrific consequences and defy me to explain it. Was he later hit by a car? Jump out of a window? What?"

Mr. Carlin chuckled a forlorn little chuckle. "You should know better, Spangler. Haven't you told me twice that you are . . . ah . . . conversant with the history of the DeIver glass? There were no horrific consequences. There never have been. That's why the DeIver glass isn't Sunday supplementized like the Koh-i-Noor Diamond or the curse on King Tut's tomb. It's mundane compared to those. You think I'm a fool, don't you?"

"Yes," Spangler said. "Can we go up now?"

"Certainly," Mr. Carlin said passionlessly. He climbed the ladder and pushed the trapdoor. There was a clickety-clickety-bump as it was drawn up into the shadows by a counter-weight, and then Mr. Carlin disappeared into the shadows. Spangler followed. The blind Adonis stared unknowingly after them.

✵　✵　✵

The gable-room was explosively hot, lit only by one cobwebby, many-angled window that filtered the hard outside light into a dirty milky glow. The Delver looking-glass was propped at an angle to the light, catching most of it and reflecting a pearly patch on to the far wall. It had been bolted securely into a wooden frame. Mr. Carlin was not looking at it. Quite studiously not looking at it.

"You haven't even put a dust-cloth over it," Spangler said, visibly angered for the first time.

"I think of it as an eye," Mr. Carlin said. His voice was still drained, perfectly empty. "If it's left open, always open, perhaps it will go blind."

Spangler paid no attention. He took off his jacket, folded the buttons carefully in, and with infinite gentleness he wiped the dust from the convex surface of the glass itself. Then he stood back and looked at it.

It was genuine. There was no doubt about it, never had been, really. It was a perfect example of Delver's particular genius. The cluttered room behind him, his own reflection, Carlin's half-turned figure—they were all clear, sharp, almost three-dimensional. The faint magnifying effect of the glass gave everything a slightly curved effect that added an almost fourth-dimensional distortion. It was—

His thought broke off, and he felt another wave of anger.

"Carlin."

Carlin said nothing.

"Carlin, you damned fool, I thought you said that girl didn't harm the mirror."

No answer.

Spangler stared at him icily in the glass. "There is a piece of friction tape in the upper left-hand corner. Did she crack it? For God's sake, man, speak up!"

"You're seeing the Reaper," Carlin said. His voice was deadly and without passion. "There's no friction tape on the mirror. Put your hand over it . . . dear God . . . "

Spangler wrapped the upper sleeve of his coat carefully around his hand, reached out, and pressed it gently against the mirror. "You see? Nothing supernatural. It's gone. My hand covers it."

"Covers it? Can you feel the tape? Why don't you pull it off?"

Spangler took his hand away carefully and looked into the glass. Everything in it seemed a little more distorted; the room's odd angles seemed to yaw crazily as if on the verge of sliding off into some unseen eternity. There was no dark spot in the mirror. It was flaw-less. He felt a sudden unhealthy dread rise in him and despised him-self for feeling it.

"It looked like him, didn't it?" Mr. Carlin asked. His face was very pale, and he was looking directly at the floor. A muscle twitched spas-modically in his neck. "Admit it, Spangler. It looked like a hooded figure standing behind you, didn't it?"

"It looked like friction tape masking a short crack," Spangler said very firmly. "Nothing more, nothing less—"

"The Bates boy was very husky," Carlin said rapidly. His words seemed to drop into the hot, still atmosphere like stones into a quarry full of sullen dark water. "Like a football player. He was wearing a letter sweater and dark green chinos. We were halfway to the upper hall exhibits when—"

"The heat is making me feel ill," Spangler said a little unsteadily. He had taken out a handkerchief and was wiping his neck. His eyes searched the convex surface of the mirror in small, jerky movements.

"When he said he wanted a drink of water . . . a drink of water, for God's sake!"

Carlin turned and stared wildly at Spangler. "How was I to know? How was I to know?"

"Is there a lavatory? I think I'm going to—"

"His sweater . . . I just caught a glimpse of his sweater going down the stairs . . . then . . . "

"—be sick."

Carlin shook his head, as if to clear it, and looked at the floor again. "Of course. Third door on your left, second floor, as you go toward the stairs." He looked up appealingly. "How was I to *know*?"

But Spangler had already stepped down on to the ladder. It rocked under his weight and for a moment Carlin thought—hoped—that he would fall. He didn't. Through the open square in the floor Carlin watched him descend, holding his mouth lightly with one hand.

"Spangler—?"

But he was gone.

※　※　※

Carlin listened to his footfalls fade to echoes, then die away. When they were gone, he shivered violently. He tried to move his own feet to the trapdoor, but they were frozen. Just that last, hurried glimpse of the boy's sweater . . . God! . . .

It was as if huge invisible hands were pulling his head, forcing it up. Not wanting to look, Carlin stared into the glimmering depths of the Delver looking-glass.

There was nothing there.

The room was reflected back to him faithfully in its glimmering confines. A snatch of a half-remembered Tennyson poem occurred to him, and he muttered it aloud: "'I'm half-sick of shadows,' said the Lady of Shallott . . . "

And still he could not look away, and the breathing stillness held him. Behind the mirror a moth-eaten buffalo head peered at him with flat obsidian eyes.

The boy had wanted a drink of water, and the fountain was in the first-floor lobby. He had gone downstairs and—

And had never come back.

Ever.

Anywhere.

Like the duchess who had paused after primping before her glass for a soirée and decided to go into the sitting-room for her pearls. Like the rug-merchant who had gone for a carriage ride and had left behind him only an empty carriage and two close-mouthed horses.

And the DeIver glass had been in New York from 1897 until 1920, had been there when Judge Crater—

Carlin stared as if hypnotized into the shallow depths of the mirror. Below, the blind-eyed Adonis kept watch.

He waited for Spangler much like the Bates family must have waited for their son, much like the duchess's coachman must have waited for his mistress to return from the sitting-room. He stared into the mirror and waited.

And waited.

And waited.

CHRISTMAS EVE IN THE BLUE CHAMBER

Jerome K. Jerome

"I don't want to make you fellows nervous," began my uncle in a peculiarly impressive, not to say bloodcurdling, tone of voice, "and if you would rather that I did not mention it, I won't; but, as a matter of fact, this very house, in which we are now sitting, is haunted."

"You don't say that!" exclaimed Mr. Coombes.

"What's the use of your saying I don't say it when I have just said it?" retorted my uncle somewhat annoyed. "You talk so foolishly. I tell you the house is haunted. Regularly on Christmas Eve the Blue Chamber" (they call the room next to the nursery the 'Blue Chamber' at my uncle's) "is haunted by the ghost of a sinful man—a man who once killed a Christmas carol singer with a lump of coal."

"How did he do it?" asked Mr. Coombes, eagerly. "Was it difficult?"

"I do not know how he did it," replied my uncle; "he did not explain the process. The singer had taken up a position just inside the front gate, and was singing a ballad. It is presumed that, when he opened his mouth for B flat, the lump of coal was thrown by the sinful man from one of the windows, and that it went down the singer's throat and choked him."

"You want to be a good shot, but it is certainly worth trying," murmured Mr. Coombes thoughtfully.

"But that was not his only crime, alas!" added my uncle. "Prior to that he had killed a solo cornet player."

"No! Is that really a fact?" exclaimed Mr. Coombes.

"Of course it's a fact," answered my uncle testily. "At all events, as much a fact as you can expect to get in a case of this sort."

"The poor fellow, the cornet player, had been in the neighbourhood barely a month. Old Mr. Bishop, who kept the 'Jolly Sand Boys' at the time, and from whom I had the story, said he had never known a more hard-working and energetic solo cornet player. He, the cornet player, only knew two tunes, but Mr. Bishop said the man could not have played with more vigour, or for more hours a day, if he had known forty. The two tunes he did play were 'Annie Laurie' and 'Home, Sweet Home'; and as regards his performance of the former melody, Mr. Bishop said that a mere child could have told what it was meant for.

"This musician—this poor, friendless artist—used to come regularly and play in this street just opposite for two hours every evening. One evening he was seen, evidently in response to an invitation, going into this very house, *but was never seen coming out of it!*"

"Did the townsfolk try offering any reward for his recovery?" asked Mr. Coombes.

"Not a penny," replied my uncle.

"Another summer," continued my uncle, "a German band visited here, intending—so they announced on their arrival—to stay till the autumn.

"On the second day after their arrival, the whole company, as fine and healthy a body of men as one would wish to see, were invited to dinner by this sinful man, and, after spending the whole of the next twenty-four hours in bed, left the town a broken and dyspeptic crew; the parish doctor, who had attended them, giving it as his opinion that it was doubtful if they would, any of them, be fit to play an air again."

"You—you don't know the recipe, do you?" asked Mr. Coombes.

"Unfortunately I do not," replied my uncle; "but the chief ingredient was said to have been railway dining-room hash."

"I forget the man's other crimes," my uncle went on; "I used to know them all at one time, but my memory is not what it was. I do not, however, believe I am doing his memory an injustice in believing that he was not entirely unconnected with the death, and subsequent burial, of a gentleman who used to play the harp with his toes; and that neither was he altogether unresponsible for the lonely grave of an unknown stranger who had once visited the neighbourhood, an Italian peasant lad, a performer upon the barrel-organ.

"Every Christmas Eve," said my uncle, cleaving with low impressive tones the strange awed silence that, like a shadow, seemed to have slowly stolen into and settled down upon the room, "the ghost of this sinful man haunts the Blue Chamber, in this very house. There, from midnight until cock-crow, amid wild muffled shrieks and groans and mocking laughter and the ghostly sound of horrid blows, it does fierce phantom fight with the spirits of the solo cornet player and the murdered carol singer, assisted at intervals by the shades of the German band; while the ghost of the strangled harpist plays mad ghostly melodies with ghostly toes on the ghost of a broken harp."

Uncle said the Blue Chamber was comparatively useless as a sleeping apartment on Christmas Eve.

"Hark!" said my uncle, raising a warning hand towards the ceiling, while we held our breath, and listened: "Hark! I believe they are at it now—in the Blue Chamber!"

I rose up and said that *I* would sleep in the Blue Chamber.

"Never!" cried my uncle, springing up. "You shall not put yourself in this deadly peril. Besides, the bed is not made."

"Never mind the bed," I replied. "I have lived in furnished apartments for gentlemen, and have been accustomed to sleep on beds that have never been made from one year's end to the other. I am young, and have had a clear conscience now for a month. The spirits will not harm me. I may even do them some little good, and induce them to be quiet and go away. Besides, I should like to see the show."

They tried to dissuade me from what they termed my foolhardy enterprise, but I remained firm and claimed my privilege. I was "the guest." "The guest" always sleeps in the haunted chamber on Christmas Eve; it is his right.

They said that if I put it on that footing they had, of course, no answer, and they lighted a candle for me and followed me upstairs in a body.

Whether elevated by the feeling that I was doing a noble action or animated by a mere general consciousness of rectitude is not for me to say, but I went upstairs that night with remarkable buoyancy. It was as much as I could do to stop at the landing when I came to it; I felt I wanted to go on up to the roof. But, with the help of the banisters, I restrained my ambition, wished them all good-night and went in and shut the door.

Things began to go wrong with me from the very first. The candle tumbled out of the candlestick before my hand was off the lock. It kept on tumbling out again; I never saw such a slippery candle. I gave up attempting to use the candlestick at last and carried the candle about in my hand, and even then it would not keep upright. So I got wild and threw it out the window, and undressed and went to bed in the dark.

I did not go to sleep; I did not feel sleepy at all; I lay on my back looking up at the ceiling and thinking of things. I wish I could remember some of the ideas that came to me as I lay there, because they were so amusing.

I had been lying like this for half an hour or so, and had forgotten all about the ghost, when, on casually casting my eyes round the room, I noticed for the first time a singularly contented-looking phantom sitting in the easy-chair by the fire smoking the ghost of a long clay pipe.

I fancied for the moment, as most people would under similar circumstances, that I must be dreaming. I sat up and rubbed my eyes. No! It was a ghost, clear enough. I could see the back of the chair through his body. He looked over towards me, took the shadowy pipe from his lips and nodded.

The most surprising part of the whole thing to me was that I did not feel in the least alarmed. If anything I was rather pleased to see him. It was company.

I said: "Good evening. It's been a cold day!"

He said he had not noticed it himself, but dared say I was right.

We remained silent for a few seconds, and then, wishing to put it pleasantly, I said: "I believe I have the honour of addressing the ghost of the gentleman who had the accident with the carol singer?"

He smiled and said it was very good of me to remember it. One singer was not much to boast of, but still every little helped.

I was somewhat staggered at his answer. I had expected a groan of remorse. The ghost appeared, on the contrary, to be rather conceited over the business. I thought that as he had taken my reference to the singer so quietly perhaps he would not be offended if I questioned him about the organ grinder. I felt curious about that poor boy.

"Is it true," I asked, "that you had a hand in the death of that Italian peasant lad who came to the town with a barrel-organ that played nothing but Scotch airs?"

He quite fired up. "Had a hand in it!" he exclaimed indignantly. "Who has dared to pretend that he assisted me? I murdered the youth myself. Nobody helped me. Alone I did it. Show me the man who says I didn't."

I calmed him. I assured him that I had never, in my own mind, doubted that he was the real and only assassin, and I went on and asked him what he had done with the body of the cornet player he had killed.

He said: "To which one may you be alluding?"

"Oh, were there any more then?" I inquired.

He smiled and gave a little cough. He said he did not like to appear to be boasting, but that, counting trombones, there were seven.

"Dear me!" I replied, "you must have had quite a busy time of it, one way and another."

He said that perhaps he ought not to be the one to say so; but that really, speaking of ordinary middle-class society, he thought there were few ghosts who could look back upon a life of more sustained usefulness.

He puffed away in silence for a few seconds while I sat watching him. I had never seen a ghost smoking a pipe before, that I could remember, and it interested me.

I asked him what tobacco he used, and he replied: "The ghost of cut Cavendish as a rule."

He explained that the ghost of all the tobacco that a man smoked in life belong to him when he became dead. He said he himself had smoked a good deal of cut Cavendish when he was alive, so that he was well supplied with the ghost of it now.

I thought I would join him in a pipe, and he said, "Do, old man"; and I reached over and got out the necessary paraphernalia from my coat pocket and lit up.

We grew quite chummy after that, and he told me all his crimes. He said he had lived next door once to a young lady who was learning to play the guitar, while a gentleman who practiced on the bass-viol lived opposite. And he, with fiendish cunning, had introduced these two unsuspecting young people to one another, and had persuaded them to elope with each other against their parents' wishes, and take their musical instruments with them; and they had done so, and before the honeymoon was over, *she* had broken his head with the bass-viol, and *he* had tried to cram the guitar down her throat, and had injured her for life.

My friend said he used to lure muffin-men into the passage and then stuff them with their own wares till they burst. He said he had quieted eighteen that way.

Young men and women who recited long and dreary poems at evening parties, and callow youths who walked about the streets late at night, playing concertinas, he used to get together and poison in batches of ten, so as to save expenses, and park orators and temperance lecturers he used to shut up six in a small room with a glass of water and a collection-box apiece, and let them talk each other to death.

It did one good to listen to him.

I asked him when he expected the other ghosts—the ghosts of the singer and the cornet player, and the German band that Uncle John had mentioned. He smiled, and said they would never come again, any of them.

I said, "Why, isn't it true, then, that they meet you here every Christmas Eve for a row?"

He replied that it was true. Every Christmas Eve, for twenty-five years, had he and they fought in that room; but they would never trouble him or anybody else again. One by one had he laid them out, spoiled and made them utterly useless for all haunting purposes. He had finished off the last German band ghost that very evening, just before I came upstairs, and had thrown what was left of it out through the slit between the window sashes. He said it would never be worth calling a ghost again.

"I suppose you will still come yourself, as usual?" I said. "They would be sorry to miss you, I know."

"Oh, I don't know," he replied; "there's nothing much to come for now; unless," he added kindly, "*you* are going to be here. I'll come if you will sleep here next Christmas Eve."

"I have taken a liking to you," he continued; "you don't fly off, screeching, when you see a party, and your hair doesn't stand on end. You've no idea," he said, "how sick I am of seeing people's hair standing on end."

He said it irritated him.

Just then a slight noise reached us from the yard below, and he started and turned deathly black.

"You are ill," I cried, springing towards him; "tell me the best thing to do for you. Shall I drink some brandy, and give you the ghost of it?"

He remained silent, listening intently for a moment, and then he gave a sigh of relief, and the shade came back to his cheek.

"It's all right," he murmured; "I was afraid it was the cock."

"Oh, it's too early for that," I said. "Why, it's only the middle of the night."

"Oh, that doesn't make any difference to those cursed chickens," he replied bitterly. "They would just as soon crow in the middle of the night as at any other time—sooner, if they thought it would spoil a chap's evening out. I believe they do it on purpose."

He said a friend of his, the ghost of a man who had killed a tax collector, used to haunt a house in Long Acre, where they kept fowls in the cellar, and every time a policeman went by and flashed his searchlight down the grating, the old cock there could fancy it was the sun, and start crowing like mad, when, of course, the poor ghost had to dissolve, and it would, in consequence, get back home sometimes as early as one o'clock in the morning, furious because it had only been out for an hour.

I agreed that it seemed very unfair.

"Oh, it's an absurd arrangement altogether," he continued, quite angrily. "I can't imagine what our chief could have been thinking of when he made it. As I have said to him, over and over again, 'Have a fixed time, and let everybody stick to it—say four o'clock in summer, and six in winter. Then, one would know what one was about.'"

"How do you manage when there isn't any clock handy?" I enquired.

He was on the point of replying, when again he started and listened. This time I distinctly heard Mr. Bowles's cock, next door, crow twice.

"There you are," he said, rising and reaching for his hat; "that's the sort of thing we have to put up with. What *is* the time?"

I looked at my watch, and found it was half-past three.

"I thought as much," he muttered. "I'll wring that blessed bird's neck if I get hold of it." And he prepared to go.

"If you can wait half a minute," I said, getting out of bed, "I'll go a bit of the way with you."

"It's very good of you," he replied, pausing, "but it seems unkind to drag you out."

"Not at all," I replied, "I shall like a walk." And I partially dressed myself, and took my umbrella; and he put his arm through mine, and we went out together, the best of friends.

HOUSEWARMING

Steve Rasnic Tem

Judith glanced around the living room once before starting up to bed. Boxes of books and glassware still crowded much of the floor and filled the seats of many of the overstuffed chairs, but at least she'd got the heavy curtains up over the large front windows. She was suddenly startled as two brilliant spots of light blossomed in the cloth, as if a car had turned off the highway and were headed straight across her front yard and into the house.

She laughed lightly to herself. There was a driveway across the road; her neighbours were merely backing up into their garage. She wondered, briefly, if people would be able to see through her curtains, but no, they were too thick, she was sure.

Something scratched at the door and her laughter died. Her nerves jangled as she struggled for control. What was wrong with her? She seemed to be forgetting where she lived now; she acted as if this were her old place, downtown in the inner city. After all, she'd moved into this quiet neighbourhood in the suburbs for her nerves, so why couldn't she relax and enjoy it? She heard the two cats mewling at the door and went to let them in.

The black cat came through first. "Edge!" she whispered, "You scared the wits out of me!" Then the grey cat, Myra, slipped through.

Judith closed the door behind them, turned, then looked back over her shoulder at the door once more. She reached over and slid the dead bolt home, then latched the chain lock. It didn't matter she'd found a new place; old habits die hard. Besides, it made her feel better.

The cats had already found their place atop a basket full of towels. They curled together like two fat commas. Judith smiled and opened the door to the stairwell. She stepped inside, then slipped her hand out to switch off the light.

When the door closed she was in a dim yellow darkness, the only light for the stairwell that of a streetlight somewhere north of the house, some of its illumination caught by a small narrow window just above head-level, on the first and only landing. There was a wall lamp at this landing but it didn't work. Judith planned to have it fixed first thing the next day, she hated the dark.

She allowed her fingers to stray to the walls as she ascended the staircase, reminded once more of how lucky she'd been to find such a place out of the congestion of the city but still within easy commuting distance. It was an old house, well-made. The stairwell walls and steps were a beautiful maple, the same maple she thought must be all through the house, although much of it was coated with what was probably a century's accumulation of paint. She'd begun restoring some of that woodwork to its original splendour this very first day, and she knew she wouldn't be happy until it had all been refinished, and the dull, light-absorbing surfaces replaced with shiny wood.

She knew already that redoing the old house wouldn't be easy. It had taken her hours just to chisel away at the first layer of paint. After several coatings of the strongest paint remover she could find the paint still stubbornly adhered. It was almost as if the house were fighting her, holding on to its covering. But apparently her frustration had given her new strength, however, for just as she was ready to give up the scraper had taken away several layers of paint at once, and the old blue carpet was soon covered with large, multicoloured flakes of paint. One brownish layer remained beneath all that, but that had been comparatively easy to strip.

The wood beneath was a brilliant orange-rose, shiny and like new. Judith was startled. She imagined that was exactly as the wood had looked for the first tenants.

Sleep did not come easily. Judith couldn't help mulling over all the things she needed to do the next few days to get the house into shape. She'd have to call the plumber; all the fixtures appeared to be locked up tight. She hadn't even been able to take a bath. She couldn't understand it; the previous tenants had left only a month before.

The furnace was almost as stubborn. It was also quite old, and although she had been able to start a fire, it seemed to give up its heat grudgingly. All the windows on the bottom floor were stuck solid, but then, that mattered little since it was winter. But several of the cupboards seemed to have similar problems, even though for the life of her Judith could find no excuse for their being stuck. They weren't locked, the plunger moved freely back and forth, there was no paint or anything else between the door and the frame—in fact, there seemed to be more than enough clearance all the way around. There just seemed to be no reason for those doors not to open. So most of her things had to remain in boxes; it made her uncomfortable, the house less than home-like when she couldn't at least get her cupboards straightened away. It was as if someone were holding on for dear life to the doorknobs within the cupboards, fighting her.

Many of the lights wouldn't work, storage jars were so jammed into the narrow basement shelves she couldn't budge any of them, and the gas oven's operation was so sporadic she was afraid to use it—the gas seeming to come and go at will. The list seemed endless, and grew longer and longer even as Judith attempted to fall asleep.

A creaking, as if the living-room floor were slowly splitting lengthwise, began somewhere near the window beneath her, and seemed to travel all the way to the bathroom at the rear of the first floor. Judith shifted nervously; she couldn't remember ever hearing a sound of quite that character.

Quickly she began listing all the things it could be: the cats chasing each other, a mouse beneath the floorboards, or most likely the movements of an old house that is in the process of resettling even after a hundred years. She had learned this exercise of list-making as a little girl. It always seemed to calm her a bit, although never completely.

It embarrassed her, being twenty-eight years old and still frightened of sounds in the darkness like a six-year-old. But at least she didn't give in to the fears as she once had.

As a small child she had gone through a period in which she was convinced someone was trying to get in through her bedroom window. Each night she'd covered herself over completely with sheets, blankets, heavy quilts—even in the warmest weather. For a while she'd tried to ignore the sounds coming from her window: the creakings, slidings, tappings, whisperings. But each time she'd eventually have to face those noises, and then her list-making would begin. It could be just a tree branch, but no, it didn't sound like a tree branch scratching. It could be the wind rattling at the pane. But no, the wind wasn't that rhythmical. So maybe it was a bird, blown in by the wind. Or a wasp. Or the blind had come loose.

But inevitably those years, she lost. And began screaming and sobbing as loudly as she could.

And every time her father had come and turned on the light, and explained to her that actually it had been a branch, the blind, or a small bird blown in against the pane. But each time he had seemed angrier, more impatient, until that last time he'd slapped her and called her a baby, and she'd never screamed for him again, but bit and bit on her lip until she'd thought she'd bitten it through.

It occurred to her some years later that she had always heard more noises, that the dark had been much more frightening, when her father had been angry with her. Then the house hadn't seemed a safe place. She hadn't felt as if she'd belonged. The house hadn't wanted her there.

Something slid on the floor below her. It sounded like a chair, one of the heavy, overstuffed chairs. It could be just a book sliding from its precarious perch. But no, it didn't sound like a book sliding at all.

When she'd first moved into the city she'd made a big mistake taking that apartment downtown. She knew that now, even if it had been cheaper. There were street crimes nearly every day, burglaries, rapes. Not the sort of thing to make one feel secure, especially someone with all her fears. She'd been foolish not to consider that. The apartment was dingy, ill-kept, the years of progressively worse tenants clearly recorded in the walls and furniture. She hadn't belonged there; it could never have felt like home. And she had heard the noises more than ever; she got little sleep living there.

Something, somewhere, rolled then fell a short distance. It could be just a log, but no, it didn't sound anything like a log dropping in the fireplace.

Obviously, just moving hadn't been enough to solve the problem. Here were the noises, the sounds that had always let Judith know she wasn't at home, that she wasn't wanted here, and it was only her first night in the house.

She felt foolish. It was a problem she was going to have to beat if she were to be happy living anywhere. She breathed deeply, fully, trying to remain calm and rational. Sounds were everywhere; they couldn't be avoided. She thought about how one could hear things even in white noise, static, hear almost anything. Judith had left the television on one night, fallen asleep in front of it, and had been sure her father was there in the room, lecturing her about her silly, irrational fears. But it had been the static from the television, that was all. Nothing else.

A few fast creaks in succession. Someone stepping quickly across the living room, reaching for the stairwell door? It could be the cat, one of the cats. But no, it didn't sound anything like a cat.

She'd been a bit apprehensive when she'd first looked at the house, but mainly because she'd just simply never visualized herself as a homeowner. It didn't fit her picture of the future. It had always been difficult for her to imagine living in a house she was totally responsible for, or one that other people had lived and died here before? Countless numbers? In the face of all that, how could she ever feel that she *owned* such a place? How was she to feel at home here, with all those other presences at the back of her mind, evident in every nook and cranny of the house?

Something seemed to snap downstairs, wood from the doorframe, or a window being pried loose? It could have been the works of the cuckoo clock on the dining-room wall, but no, it didn't sound like clockworks.

She had checked the neighbourhood out quite carefully. Most of the residents were elderly, had been here a long time, and claimed they'd never had any trouble, even though a poorer and more violent section of the city was only a few blocks away. Some younger couples had recently moved into houses at both corners, and were spending so much time revitalizing their properties Judith sensed the beginnings of a change in the neighbourhood. Judith was lucky, the real estate agent had told her. She was getting the place before the property values skyrocketed. And although that section of the city but a short distance away made her nervous sometimes, Judith was convinced she'd chosen one of the safest places in the city to make her home.

The door was apparently rattling on its hinges.

A window suddenly banged.

But no, it didn't' sound like a tree branch. No, it didn't sound like the wind.

Something heavy slid on the floor below. Something banged the wall as one of her cats screeched.

Without thinking Judith was screaming with her cat, racing down the stairs, her arms tensed and raised. She slammed open the stairwell door and hit the light-switch sobbing.

The sudden glare shocked her system. She looked around the living room wide-eyed, as if she'd suddenly awakened from a bad nightmare and had difficulty adjusting to her bland surroundings.

A few books lay on the floor. One edge of the rug had been curled up. The arm covers of her chairs were all scattered about the floor like empty skins. Typical tricks her cats pulled all the time.

"Edge? Myra?" she called.

The black cat, Edge, came around the side of one of the chairs, crying. Judith picked him up and began stroking his sleek, dark coat. "Where's your sister, Edge? Where's Myra?"

Judith called for Myra several times. No answer. She finally gave up, hugged Edge to her. "Guess I'm not the only scaredy cat, huh, Edge?" She chuckled, turned out the light, and carried Edge up to bed with her.

In the darkness a picture suddenly tilted on the wall. A lamp crept to the edge of a table. Several books fell out of their box.

A heavy overstuffed chair slid back from the wall to its original position. The muted yellow glare from a passing car illuminated the green-papered wall behind it, and the matted grey fur speckled with red.

THE FERRIES

Ramsey Campbell

When Berry reached Parkgate promenade he heard the waves. He couldn't recall having heard them during his stroll down the winding road from Neston Village, between banks whispering with grass, past the guarded lights of infrequently curtained windows. Beneath clouds diluted by moonlight, the movement of the waves looked indefinably strange. They sounded faint, not quite like water.

The promenade was scarcely two cars wide. Thin lanterns stood on concrete stalks above the sea wall, which was overlooked by an assortment of early Victoria Buildings: antique shops, cafés that in the afternoons must be full of ladies taking tea and cakes, a nursing home, a private school that looked as though it had been built as something else. In the faltering moonlight all of them looked black and white. Some were Tudor-striped.

As he strolled—the June night was mild, he might as well enjoy himself as best he could now he was here—he passed the Marie Celeste Hotel. That must have appealed to his uncle. He was still grinning wryly when he reached his uncle's address.

Just then the moon emerged from the clouds, and he saw what was wrong with the waves. There was no water beyond the sea wall, only an expanse of swaying grass that stretched as far as he could see. The sight of the grass, overlooked by the promenade buildings as though it was still the River Dee, made him feel vaguely but intensely expectant, as though about to glimpse something on the pale parched waves.

Perhaps his uncle felt this too, for he was sitting at the black bow window on the first floor of the white house, gazing out beyond the sea wall. His eyes looked colourless as moonlight. It took three rings of the bell to move him.

Berry shouldn't feel resentful. After all, he was probably his uncle's only living relative. Nevertheless there were decisions to be made in London, at the publishers: books to be bought or rejected—several were likely to be auctioned. He'd come a long way hurriedly, by several trains; his uncle's call had sounded urgent enough for that, as urgent as the pips that had cut him off. Berry only wished he knew why he was here.

When at last his uncle opened the door, he looked unexpectedly old. Perhaps living ashore had aged him. He had always been small, but now he looked dwindled, though still tanned and leathery. In his spotless black blazer with its shining silvery buttons, and his tiny gleaming shoes, he resembled a doll of himself.

"Here we are again." Though he sounded gruff, his handshake was firm, and felt grateful for company. When he'd toiled upstairs, using the banisters as a series of walking-sticks, he growled, "Sit you down."

There was no sense of the sea in the flat, not even maritime prints to enliven the timidly patterned wallpaper. Apart from a couple of large old trunks, the flat seemed to have nothing to do with his uncle. It felt like a waiting-room.

"Get that down you, James." His uncle's heartiness seemed faded; even the rum was a brand you could buy in supermarkets, not one of the prizes he'd used to bring back from voyages. He sat gazing beyond the promenade, sipping the rum as though it was as good as any other.

"How are you, uncle? It's good to see you." They hadn't seen each other for ten years, and Berry felt inhibited; besides, his uncle detested effusiveness. When he'd finished his rum he said, "You sounded urgent on the phone."

"Aye." The years had made him even more taciturn. He seemed to resent being reminded of his call.

"I wouldn't have expected you to live so far from everything," Berry said, trying a different approach.

"It went away." Apparently he was talking about the sea, for he continued: "There used to be thirteen hotels and a pier. All the best people came here to bathe. They said the streets were as elegant as Bath. The private school you passed, that was the old Assembly Rooms."

Though he was gazing across the sea wall, he didn't sound nostalgic. He sat absolutely still, as though relishing the stability of the room. He'd used to pace restlessly when talking, impatient to return to the sea.

"Then the Dee silted up," he was saying. "It doesn't reach here now, except at spring tides and in storms. That's when the rats and voles flee onto the promenade—hordes of them, they say. I haven't seen it, and I don't mean to."

"You're thinking of moving?"

"Aye." Frowning at his clenched fists, he muttered, "Will you take me back with you tomorrow and let me stay until I find somewhere? I'll have my boxes sent on."

He mustn't want to make the journey alone in case he was taken ill. Still, Berry couldn't help sounding a little impatient. "I don't live near the sea, you know."

"I know that." Reluctantly he added, "I wish I lived farther away."

Perhaps now that he'd had to leave the sea, his first love, he wanted to forget about it quickly. Berry could tell he'd been embarrassed to ask for help—a captain needing help from a nephew who was seasick on hovercraft! But he was a little old man now, and his tan was only a patina; all at once Berry saw how frail he was. "All right, uncle," he said gently. "It won't be any trouble."

His uncle was nodding, not looking at him, but Berry could see he was moved. Perhaps now was the time to broach the idea Berry had had on the train. "On my way here," he said carefully, "I was remembering some of the tales you used to tell."

"You remember them, do you?" The old man didn't sound as though he wanted to. He drained a mouthful of rum in order to refill his glass. Had the salt smell that was wafting across the grass reminded him too vividly?

Berry had meant to suggest the idea of a book of his uncle's yarns, for quite a few had haunted him: the pigmies who could carry ten times their own weight, the flocks of birds that buried in guano any ships that ventured into their territory, the light whose source was neither sun nor moon but that outlined an island on the horizon, which receded if ships made for it. Would it be a children's book, or a book that tried to trace the sources? Perhaps this wasn't the time to discuss it, for the smell that was drifting through the window was stagnant, very old.

"There was one story I never told you."

Berry's head jerked up; he had been nodding off. Even his uncle had never begun stories as abruptly—as reluctantly—as this.

"Some of the men used to say it didn't matter if you saw it so long as you protected yourself." Was the old man talking to himself, to take his mind off the desiccated river, the stagnant smell? "One night we all saw it. One minute the sea was empty, the next that thing was there, close enough to swim to. Some of the men would almost have done that, to get it over with." He gulped a mouthful of rum and stared sharply out across the pale dry waves. "Only they could see the faces watching. None of us forgot that, ever. As soon as we got ashore all of us bought ourselves protection. Even I did," he said bitterly, "when I'd used to say civilized men kept pictures on walls."

Having struggled out of his blazer, which he'd unbuttoned carefully and tediously, he displayed his left forearm. Blinking sleepily, Berry made out a tattoo, a graceful sailing ship surrounded by a burst of light. Its masts resembled almost recognizable symbols.

"The younger fellows thought that was all we needed. We all wanted to believe that would keep us safe. I wonder how they feel now they're older." The old man turned quickly toward the window; he seemed angry that he'd been distracted. Something had changed his attitudes drastically, for he had hated tattooes. It occurred to Berry, too late to prevent him from dozing, that his uncle had called him because he was afraid to be alone.

Berry's sleep was dark and profound. Half-submerged images floated by, so changed as to be unrecognizable. Sounds reached him rather as noise from the surface might try to reach the depths of the sea. It was impossible to tell how many times his uncle had cried out before the calls woke him.

"James . . ." The voice was receding, but at first Berry failed to notice this; he was too aware of the smell that filled the room. Something that smelled drowned in stagnant water was near him, so near that he could hear its creaking. At once he was awake, and so afraid that he thought he was about to be sick.

"James . . ." Both the creaking and the voice were fading. Eventually he managed to persuade himself that despite the stench, he was alone in the room. Forcing his eyes open, he stumbled to the window. Though it was hard to focus his eyes and see what was out there, his heart was already jolting.

The promenade was deserted, the buildings gleamed like bone. Above the sea wall the lanterns glowed thinly. The wide dry river was flooded with grass, which swayed in the moonlight, rustling and glinting. Over the silted river, leaving a wake of grass that looked whiter than the rest, a ship was receding.

It seemed to be the colour and the texture of the moon. Its sails looked stained patchily by mould. It was full of holes, all of which were misshapen by glistening vegetation. Were its decks crowded with figures? If so, he was grateful that he couldn't see their faces, for their movements made him think of drowned things lolling underwater, dragged back and forth by currents.

Sweat streamed into his eyes. When he'd blinked them clear, the moon was darkening. Now the ship looked more like a mound from which a few trees sprouted, and perhaps the crowd was only swaying bushes. Clouds closed over the moon, but he thought he could see a pale mass sailing away, overtopped by lurid sketches that might be masts. Was that his uncle's voice, its desperation overwhelmed by despair? When moonlight flooded the landscape a few moments later, there was nothing but the waves of grass, from which a whiter swathe was fading.

He came to himself when he began shivering. An unseasonably chill wind was clearing away the stench of stagnant water. He gazed in dismay at his uncle's blazer, draped neatly over the empty chair.

❋ ❋ ❋

There wasn't much that he could tell the police. He had been visiting his uncle, whom he hadn't seen for years. They had both had a good deal to drink, and his uncle, who had seemed prematurely aged, had begun talking incoherently and incomprehensibly. He'd woken to find that his uncle had wandered away, leaving his blazer, though it had been a cold night.

Did they believe him? They were slow and thorough, these policemen; their thoughts were as invisible as he meant his to be. Surely his guilt must be apparent, the shame of hiding the truth about his uncle, of virtually blackening his character. In one sense, though, that seemed hardly to matter: He was sure they wouldn't find his uncle alive. Eventually, since Berry could prove that he was needed in London, they let him go.

He trudged along the sweltering promenade. Children were scrambling up and down the sea wall, old people on sticks were being promenaded by relatives. In the hazy sunshine, most of the buildings were still black and white. Everywhere signs said FRESH SHRIMPS. In a shop that offered 'Gifts and bygones', ships were stiff in bottles. Waves of yellowing grass advanced, but never very far.

He ought to leave, and be grateful that he lived inland. If what he'd seen last night had been real, the threat was far larger than he was. There was nothing he could do.

But suppose he had only heard his uncle's voice on the silted river, and had hallucinated the rest? He'd been overtired, and confused by his uncle's ramblings; how soon had he wakened fully? He wanted to believe that the old man had wandered out beyond the promenade and had collapsed, or even that he was alive out there, still wandering.

There was only one way to find out. He would be in sight of the crowded promenade. Holding his briefcase above his head as though he was submerging, he clambered down the sea wall.

The grass was tougher than it looked. Large patches had to be struggled through. After five hundred yards he was sweating, yet he seemed to be no closer to the far bank, nor to anything else. Ahead through the haze he could just distinguish the colours of fields in their frames of trees and hedges. Factory chimneys resembled grey pencils. All this appeared to be receding.

He struggled onward. Grass snagged him, birds flew up on shrill wings, complaining. He could see no evidence of the wake he'd seen last night: nothing but the interminable grass, the screeching birds, the haze. Behind him the thick heat had blurred the promenade, the crowds were pale shadows. Their sounds had been swallowed by the hissing of grass.

He'd been tempted several times to turn back, and was on the point of doing so, when he saw a gleam in the dense grass ahead. It was near the place where he'd last glimpsed the ship, if he had done so. The gleaming object looked like a small shoe.

He had to persuade himself to go forward. He remembered the swaying figures on the decks, whose faces he'd dreaded to see. Nevertheless he advanced furiously, tearing a path through the grass with his briefcase. He was almost there before he saw that the object wasn't a shoe. It was a bottle.

When inertia carried him forward, he realized that the bottle wasn't empty. For an unpleasant moment he thought it contained the skeleton of a small animal. Peering through the grime that coated the glass, he made out a whitish model ship with tattered sails. Tiny overgrown holes gaped in it. Though its decks were empty, he had seen it before.

He stood up too quickly, and almost fell. The heat seemed to flood his skull. The ground underfoot felt unstable; a buzzing of insects attacked him; there was a hint of a stagnant smell. He was ready to run, dizzy as he was, to prevent himself from thinking.

Then he remembered his uncle's despairing cry: 'James . . . James . . . ' Even then, if he had been able to run, he might have done nothing—but his dizziness both hindered him and gave him time to feel ashamed. If there was a chance of helping his uncle, however impossible it seemed— He snatched up the bottle and threw it into his briefcase. Then, trying to forget about it, he stumbled back toward the crowds.

❋   ❋   ❋

His uncle was calling him. He woke to the sound of a shriek. Faces were sailing past him, close enough to touch if he could have reached through the glass. It was only a train on the opposite line, rushing away from London. Nevertheless he couldn't sleep after that. He finished reading the typescript he'd brought with him, though he knew by now he didn't want to buy the book.

The state of his desk was worse than he'd feared. His secretary had answered most of his letters, but several books had piled up, demanding to be read. He was stuffing two of them into his briefcase, to be read on the bus and, if he wasn't too tired, at home, when he found he was holding the grimy bottle. At once he locked it in a drawer. Though he wasn't prepared to throw it away until he understood its purpose, he was equally reluctant to take it home.

That night he could neither sleep nor read. He tried strolling in Holland Park, but while that tired him further, it failed to calm him.

The moonlit clouds that were streaming headlong across the sky made everything beneath them look unstable. Though he knew that the lit houses beyond the swaying trees were absolutely still, he kept feeling that the houses were rocking slyly, at anchor.

He lay trying to relax. Beyond the windows of his flat, Kensington High Street seemed louder than ever. Nervous speculations kept him awake. He felt he'd been meant to find the bottle, but for what purpose? Surely it couldn't harm him; after all, he had only once been to sea. How could he help his uncle? His idea of a book of stories was nagging him; perhaps he could write it himself, as a kind of monument to his uncle—except that the stories seemed to be drifting away into the dark, beyond his reach, just like the old man. When eventually he dozed, he thought he heard the old man calling.

In the morning his desk looked even worse; the pile of books had almost doubled. He managed to sort out a few that could be trusted to readers for reports. Of course, a drain must have overflowed outside the publishers; that was why only a patch of pavement had been wet this morning—he knew it hadn't rained. He consulted his diary for distractions.

Sales conference 11:00 a.m.: he succeeded in being coherent, and even in suggesting ideas, but his thoughts were elsewhere. The sky resembled sluggish smoke, as though the oppressive day was smouldering. His mind felt packed in grey stuffing. The sound of cars outside seemed unnaturally rhythmic, almost like waves.

Back at his desk he sat trying to think. Lack of sleep had isolated him in a no-man's-land of consciousness, close to hallucination. He felt cut off from whatever he was supposed to be doing. Though his hand kept reaching out impulsively, he left the drawer locked. There was no point in brooding over the model ship until he'd decided what to do.

Beyond the window his uncle cried out. No, someone was shouting to guide a lorry; the word wasn't 'James' at all. But he still didn't know how to help his uncle, assuming that he could, assuming that it wasn't too late. Would removing the ship from the bottle achieve something?

In any case, could one remove the ship at all? Perhaps he could consult an expert in such matters. "I know exactly whom you want," his secretary said, and arranged for them to meet tomorrow.

Dave Peeples lunch 12:30: ordinarily he would have enjoyed the game, especially since Peeples liked to discuss books in pubs, where he tended to drink himself into an agreeable state. Today's prize was attractive: a best-selling series that Peeples wanted to take to a new publisher. But today he found Peeples irritating—not only his satyr's expressions and postures, which were belied by his paunch, but also the faint smirk with which he constantly approved of himself. Still, if Berry managed to acquire the books, the strain would have been worthwhile.

They ate in the pub just round the corner from the publishers. Before long Berry grew frustrated; he was too enervated by lack of sleep to risk drinking much. Nor could he eat much, for the food tasted unpleasantly salty. Peeples seemed to notice nothing, and ate most of Berry's helping before he leaned back, patting his paunch.

"Well now," he said when Berry raised the subject of the books. "What about another drink?" Berry was glad to stand up, to feel the floor stable underfoot, for the drinkers at the edge of his vision had seemed to be swaying extravagantly.

"I'm not happy with the way my mob are promoting the books," Peeples admitted. "They seem to be letting them just lie there." Berry's response might have been more forceful if he hadn't been distracted by the chair that someone was rocking back and forth with a steady rhythmic creaking.

When Berry had finished making offers Peeples said, "That doesn't sound bad. Still, I ought to tell you that several other people are interested." Berry wondered angrily whether he was simply touring publishers in search of free meals. The pub felt damp, the dimness appeared to be glistening. No doubt it was very humid.

Though the street was crowded, he was glad to emerge. "I'll be in touch," Peeples promised grudgingly, but at that moment Berry didn't care, for on the opposite pavement the old man's voice was crying, "James!" It was only a newspaper-seller naming his wares, which didn't sound much like James. Surely a drain must have overflowed where the wet patch had been, for there was a stagnant smell.

Editors meeting 3:00 p.m.: he scarcely had time to gulp a mug of coffee beforehand, almost scalding his throat. Why did they have to schedule two meetings in one day? When there were silences in which people expected him to speak, he managed to say things that sounded positive and convincing. Nevertheless he heard little except for the waves of traffic, advancing and withdrawing, and the desperate cries in the street. What was that crossing the intersection, a long pale shape bearing objects like poles? It had gone before he could jerk his head round, and his colleagues were staring only at him.

It didn't matter. If any of these glimpses weren't hallucinations, surely they couldn't harm him. Otherwise, why hadn't he been harmed that night in Parkgate? It was rather a question of what he could do to the glimpses. "Yes, that's right," he said to a silence. "Of course it is."

Once he'd slept he would be better able to cope with everything. Tomorrow he would consult the expert. After the meeting he slumped at his desk, trying to find the energy to gather books together and head for home.

His secretary woke him. "Okay," he mumbled, "you go on." He'd follow her in a moment, when he was more awake. It occurred to him that if he hadn't dozed off in Parkgate, his uncle might have been safe. That was another reason to try to do something. He'd get up in a few moments. It wasn't dark yet.

When he woke again, it was.

He had to struggle to raise his head. His elbows had shoved piles of books to the edge of the desk. Outside, the street was quiet except for the whisper of an occasional car. Sodium lamps craned their necks toward his window. Beyond the frosted glass of his office cubicle, the maze of the open-plan office looked even more crowded with darkness than the space around his desk. When he switched on his desk-lamp, it showed him a blurred reflection of himself trapped in a small pool of brightness. Hurriedly he switched on the cubicle's main light.

Though he was by no means awake, he didn't intend to wait. He wanted to be out of the building, away from the locked drawer. Insomnia had left him feeling vulnerable, on edge. He swept a handful of books into the briefcase—God, they were becoming a bad joke—and emerged from his cubicle.

He felt uncomfortably isolated. The long angular room was lifeless; none of the desks seemed to retain any sense of the person who sat there. The desertion must be swallowing his sounds, which seemed not only dwarfed but robbed of resonance, as though surrounded by an emptiness that was very large.

His perceptions must be playing tricks. Underfoot the floor felt less stable than it ought to. At the edge of his vision the shadows of desks and cabinets appeared to be swaying, and he couldn't convince himself that the lights were still. He mustn't let any of this distract him. Time enough to think when he was home.

It took him far too long to cross the office, for he kept teetering against desks. Perhaps he should have taken time to waken fully, after all. When eventually he reached the lifts, he couldn't bring himself to use one; at least the stairs were open, though they were very dark. He groped, swaying, for the light-switch. Before he'd found it, he recoiled. The wall he had touched felt as though it were streaming with water.

A stagnant stench welled up out of the dark. When he grabbed the banister for support, that felt wet too. He mustn't panic: a door or window was open somewhere in the building, that was all he could hear creaking; its draught was making things feel cold—not wet—and was swinging the lights back and forth. Yes, he could feel the draught blustering at him, and smell what must be a drain.

He forced himself to step onto the stairs. Even the darkness was preferable to groping for the light-switch, when he no longer knew what he might touch. Nevertheless, by the time he reached the half-landing he was wishing for light. His vertigo seemed to have worsened, for he was reeling from side to side of the staircase. Was the creaking closer? He mustn't pause, plenty of time to feel ill once he was outside in a taxi; he ought to be able to hold off panic so long as he didn't glimpse the ship again—

He halted so abruptly that he almost fell. Without warning he'd remembered his uncle's monologue. Berry had been as dopey then as he was now, but one point was all at once terribly clear. Your first glimpse of the ship meant only that you would see it again. The second time, it came for you.

He hadn't yet seen it again. Surely he still had a chance. There were two exits from the building; the creaking and the growing stench would tell him which exit to avoid. He was stumbling downstairs because that was the alternative to falling. His mind was a grey void that hardly even registered the wetness of the banisters. The foyer was in sight now at the foot of the stairs, its linoleum gleaming; less than a flight of stairs now, less than a minute's stumbling—

But it was not linoleum. The floorboards were bare, when there ought not even to be boards, only concrete. Shadows swayed on them, cast by objects that, though out of sight for the moment, seemed to have bloated limbs. Water sloshed from side to side of the boards, which were the planks of a deck.

He almost let himself fall, in despair. Then he began to drag himself frantically up the stairs, which perhaps were swaying, after all. Through the windows he thought he saw the cityscape rising and falling. There seemed to be no refuge upstairs, for the stagnant stench was everywhere—but refuge wasn't what he was seeking.

He reeled across the office, which he'd darkened when leaving, into his cubicle. Perhaps papers were falling from desks only because he had staggered against them. His key felt ready to snap in half before the drawer opened.

He snatched out the bottle, in which something rattled insect-like, and stumbled to the window. Yes, he had been meant to find the bottle—but by whom, or by what? Wrenching open the lock of the window, he flung the bottle into the night.

He heard it smash a moment later. Whatever was inside it must certainly have smashed too. At once everything felt stable, so abruptly that he grew dizzier. He felt as though he'd just stepped onto land after a stormy voyage.

There was silence except for the murmur of the city, which sounded quite normal—or perhaps there was another sound, faint and receding fast. It might have been a gust of wind, but he thought it resembled a chorus of cries of relief so profound it was appalling. Was one of them his uncle's voice?

Berry slumped against the window, which felt like ice against his forehead. There was no reason to flee now, nor did he think he would be capable of moving for some time. Perhaps they would find him here in the morning. It hardly mattered, if he could get some sleep—

All at once he tried to hold himself absolutely still, in order to listen. Surely he needn't be nervous any longer, just because the ship in the bottle had been deserted, surely that didn't mean— But his legs were trembling, and infected the rest of his body until he couldn't even strain his ears. By then, however, he could hear far better than he would have liked.

Perhaps he had destroyed the ship, and set free its captives; but if it had had a captain, what else might Berry have set loose? The smell had grown worse than stagnant—and up the stairs, and now across the dark office, irregular but purposeful footsteps were sloshing.

❋ ❋ ❋

Early next morning several people reported glimpses of a light, supposedly moving out from the Thames into the open sea. Some claimed the light had been accompanied by sounds like singing. One old man tried to insist that the light had contained the outline of a ship. The reports seemed little different from tales of objects in the skies, and were quickly dismissed, for London had a more spectacular mystery to solve: how a publisher's editor could be found in a first-floor office, not merely dead but drowned.

THE FETCH

Tina Rath

"You really should have a ghost," said Felicity, tilting her long-stemmed wine glass so that the yellow wine glittered in the candlelight.

"Do you mean we should buy one? Can you recommend a reliable stockist?" Ambrose asked lightly.

"Harrods, I should think. I'm sure they'd get you one, even if they don't carry a stock. Or you could try Habitat for something trendier but more middle-market. If you did go to them, of course, you'd have to be prepared to find a copy of your ghost in someone else's Blue Room. Like seeing endless replicas of your pine veneer dresser in other people's kitchens."

Emily had been listening admiring, but bewildered to the nonsense her friend and her husband were talking. She said, rather plaintively: "But we haven't got a pine veneer dresser," and realized at once that it was the wrong thing.

Felicity smiled at Ambrose and glanced again at the exquisite dresser that they did have, a perfect piece of furniture, polished by generations of farm wives to a rare blue bloom. She envied Emily her new house, her money, her jewels and her clothes, though never her looks or her husband, but she felt she could have killed her just for that dresser. She made herself say: "That's just what I mean. You have everything so perfect here, so right that you must have a really special ghost. A unique spectre. If you haven't got one, you must advertise."

"I'm sure there's an agency that could help us," Ambrose said. "They can probably be found in *Time Out*, calling themselves Renta Wraith, or Ghouls a'Plenty."

"But we have got a ghost," Emily said softly.

Conversation stopped abruptly. Felicity watched Ambrose's big, deceptively jovial red face become almost black with a sudden rush of dark blood. He seized the wine bottle and filled their glasses. She noticed that his hand was shaking.

"How exciting," said Felicity. "What sort of ghost, Emily?"

"It's all rubbish. A delusion. People will think—all sorts of things if you start describing your hallucinations, you know," said Ambrose.

Emily often told Felicity that she liked to have guests because Ambrose was so nice to her if other people were there. Felicity wondered how badly he behaved when they were not. There had been a scandal not long after he married. Easily hushed up, with his money, and Emily's, but very nasty. Something about a girl and violence that stopped only just short of murder. And there had been that unpleasant business with the hunt saboteur. Lucky for both of them that there had been someone to stop him . . .

There had also been a death, once. A younger boy had been killed while Ambrose was at school, and he had left very soon afterwards. Ambrose had never officially been blamed for that. At the worst it had been rough horseplay, perhaps a little bullying that went too far . . . But the school did not want to keep him.

Felicity wondered if he ever hit Emily. She found the idea rather exciting. She smiled encouragingly at Emily who was looking quite crushed by merely verbal violence, and said: "What sort of ghost is it? A headless nun? Or something utterly non-human with green and dripping scales?"

"No," said Ambrose, answering for his wife as he so often did. "She's rather a disappointment even if you choose to believe in her."

"It's a female ghost then?"

"Yes, so they say. Rather pathetic, really. She stands under the pines at the end of the garden. It's supposed to be a youngish woman with brown hair pulled back or piled up, wearing a long blue dress with a high neck. The funny thing is, she's supposed to look a bit like Emily. I think she was some dim little Victorian slavey who used to wait for her boyfriend there, under the pines, and he stood her up. In the end, she pined away and died, as they did in those days, and she's just too dim to move on. That is, if there really is anything there, which I strongly doubt."

Felicity suddenly thought: "But he has seen her too." Aloud she said: "Perhaps the boyfriend went off to the war and got killed. One evening the ghost of a soldier in a red coat will come limping up the lane and they'll float off together, hand in hand."

Emily struck in, sounding more confident than usual. "I'm not so sure that she did just die. Naturally, I mean. There's something round her neck. It could be a red ribbon, but it could be—something else."

"D'you mean you've really seen her?" Felicity squeaked.

Emily nodded. Her slightly bulging eyes bulged still more with importance. "Several times. The first time I thought she was real. You know, those Victorian dresses used to be fashionable. Well, I went up to her and I was going to ask what she wanted, tell her she was on private property, but when I got right up to her she wasn't there."

"You mean, she vanished?" Ridiculously Felicity felt gooseflesh creep up her bare arms.

"No," Emily frowned, trying to explain. "It was like one of those puzzle pictures. You know, one way it's just blobs and splashes of paint, but if you catch it from the right angle it's a face. Or sometimes," she added, to herself, "it's a face but if you look again, it's a skull. Suddenly I was at another angle and she wasn't there."

"But did you know there was a ghost before you saw her? Had

you heard any local stories about her that could make you, well, imagine things?"

"But there were no stories," said Emily. "No one ever saw anything until we came here."

For some reason that seemed the weirdest thing of all. There was a short uneasy silence and then Ambrose said: "Our char's seen her."

Felicity felt this was a neat way of devaluing Emily's psychic pretensions, but Emily accepted the supporting testimony, with one mild protest. "Mrs. Beecham doesn't like being called a char, dear. But she has seen her. She thought it was me, she said, until she got close, and then, suddenly she wasn't there any more."

"It's all your imagination," said Ambrose roughly, "you haven't got enough to do."

Emily, who ran a large house and an extensive programme of entertaining for Ambrose's business friends, with the assistance of Mrs. Beecham three mornings a week, smiled and said nothing.

Felicity swallowed the last of her wine and stood up. "Well, it's been lovely, but now I must catch my beastly train."

"Ambrose will drive you to the station," said Emily. "Can't you stay a bit longer?"

"No, really, I have to be up early, you know."

They talked themselves into the hall and Felicity gathered up her wrap and her bag.

"You must really come and stay with us," said Emily, "for a nice rest. We've got masses of room."

"I tell you what," said Felicity, leaning forward to kiss her friend. "I've got some holiday owing to me. I'll come down and organize a lovely housewarming party for you. You remember my famous parties!"

No doubt Emily did remember from the days when they had shared a flat. She looked uneasy as she remembered, but Felicity smiled and got into the car beside Ambrose. "A lovely party for a lovely house!" she called to Emily as the car swept her out of sight.

"You really do like the house, don't you?" Ambrose said. He sounded amused.

"It's beautiful," Felicity agreed. Envy almost choked her.

"More your sort of place than Emily's, really," Ambrose said, twisting the knife. "Funny that. Her having the money and you having the style. Not to mention the expensive tastes."

"Very funny," she said resentfully. But she let her shoulder and thigh drift against his.

"Sometimes, you know, I ask myself how long I can go on with Emily."

He might have meant to sound pathetic, to give a new twist to the old line 'My wife doesn't understand me.' In fact, he sounded violently angry. Dangerous. Felicity wondered what he might do, some day, if he got angry enough.

"What time does your train really leave?" he asked.

"In forty-five minutes," she replied precisely. "You can always tell Emily it was late and you had to wait with me on the platform."

"Why should I tell Emily anything?" He sounded genuinely puzzled.

Felicity did not answer. He turned off the main road into a tree-lined lane. She endured the interlude that followed by thinking of Emily's money, the money that must come to Ambrose if she should die. Of the house. And the housewarming.

※　※　※

It was late when Felicity got back to her London flat. She shared it with two other girls, who were in bed and asleep when she got in, but she rattled about the kitchen, making herself tea, not caring if she woke them. She hated them, hated the flat that never felt warm, never looked tidy or even clean, hated Emily who had everything she wanted, hated Ambrose who had handled her very roughly. Most of all she hated herself.

She had always envied Emily, ever since they had met at that very expensive boarding school where Felicity's aunt had taught English. When Felicity was left an orphan, and a very poor orphan at that, her aunt had persuaded the headmistress to give her a place at the school, where she could keep an eye on her. She was not, of course, a boarder. She alone of all the girls had gone, well, not home, but to her aunt's flat, to sleep. She alone of all the girls did not have rich parents. Under those circumstances it was very difficult to make friends, which is how she had come to be involved with Emily. Emily was plain and shy, so shy that it cancelled out any advantage in having rich parents. The only girl who could be bothered with her was her fellow outcast.

When they left school, Emily's parents had bought her a flat in London, and for a while Felicity was reasonably happy. She shared with Emily, paying no rent, borrowing her clothes, and giving parties with her money. Emily was quite happy with this arrangement. She hated the parties, but it was a nice big flat and she could always go to bed with a book. Then her parents took her to meet Ambrose.

At first Felicity could not understand why both families seemed so anxious for Emily and Ambrose to marry. They were both so rich. It seemed such a waste, to hoard money like that when they could make two poor people very happy. And Emily obviously had no appeal for Ambrose at all. It was only later, as she got to know him, and to hear the gossip about him, that Felicity realized what a drag on the marriage market Ambrose had been. He had been lucky to get Emily, a nice quiet girl, who would give him at least the appearance of a respectable marriage, tell lies for him when necessary, and bail him out whenever his taste for violence got too much for him. He had been lucky, too, in being born rich. Amongst the poorer classes, who have little influence with the law, and a distressing tendency to call a spade a spade, Ambrose might have been called a dangerous madman. He might even have been locked up.

Sitting at the sticky kitchen table, sipping her tea, Felicity thought about Emily. She thought about the ghost, hallucination, apparition, that Emily (*and* the char) had seen in the garden. And she made a decision.

Next day, after work, she went to see a friend. Felicity was one of those people who always knew where to find an expert, and this friend was an expert in what some people call paranormal phenomena and others call black magic. She outlined the situation to him crisply, giving all the details but no names.

"What you have there," he told her, "is a fetch. A co-walker. For reasons I shall never understand it's quite often called a Doppelgänger, even in England. It's the ghost of a living person. Of your friend in fact. There was a case in the eighteenth century, I think. A young girl met herself one evening, walking in her father's grounds. It's Holland Park now, by the way. The apparition was just like her, in every detail, except that it was very pale, and I think it was carrying withered flowers. She died soon afterwards."

"Then," Felicity suggested, hesitantly, "it could mean death. It's dangerous."

"Yes, I think it probably is. Not in itself, but it does suggest that a rather nasty psychic field has been set up."

"Could it be a warning?"

"Yes, indeed, yes."

"So, if my—friend—did something to change her fate, left her husband, or got him to move house, something like that, then she could save herself?"

"Perhaps."

"But if, on the other hand, she did something really crazy, like dressing like the apparition and walking under the pines herself she could—make the disaster happen."

"If she was crazy enough to try it, yes. Almost certainly. Has she got a dress like the one she described?"

"No."

"Good. If she had I would have advised her to burn it."

Felicity frowned. "*Can* you avoid your fate?"

"Perhaps. Perhaps not. I would certainly advise her to move right away from the neighbourhood, leave her husband, who sounds a boor anyway, and hope for the best."

"Yes," said Felicity. "I see."

She finished her tea, thanked him, and went home. Once there she sat down to make a list. It began with a reminder to buy a length of blue material, either form Laura Ashley or from Liberty's.

❋   ❋   ❋

It took more than one visit to persuade Emily that a combined house-warming and Halloween party, with all the guests in fancy dress was a good idea. But Felicity was all girlish enthusiasm and Ambrose quite encouraging and in the end they brought her round. Felicity was to do all the decorations, the pumpkins with grinning faces, the plastic cobwebs and the polystyrene bats, and she would provide costumes for herself and for Emily. No one, she promised as she took Emily's distressingly ample measurements, would know about them until the evening of the party.

"I feel quite excited, really," Emily lied timidly, trying to enter into the spirit of things, as they sent invitations and made the necessary follow-up phone calls.

"It's got to be fancy dress," Felicity insisted, making call after call at Emily's expense. "If you're not in costume, I promise they won't let you in."

"That's right, Felicity, you tell them," said Ambrose, almost cheerfully.

It was a pity that just before the event Felicity had to go back to her office for three days so that the bulk of the preparations suddenly fell on Emily. Ambrose lost a lot of his good humour while Felicity was away, and when she came back, with her parcels and her bottle of wine, on the night of the party, she found her friend almost tearful.

"Never mind," she told her, "the house looks lovely. Quite terrifying. Come and put your costume on."

She unwrapped the parcels in Emily's bedroom. Hers held a white filmy nightdress, and a phial of stage blood to dab round her mouth; Emily's a blue print dress, long skirted and high necked, complete with a piece of red neck-ribbon.

Emily leaped back, as if from a snake. "Oh no, I couldn't wear that!" she exclaimed. "I really couldn't."

Felicity let her mouth droop. "But I thought it was ideal! Your very own ghost! I made it specially for you."

"I just couldn't, Felicity," said Emily with uncharacteristic firmness. "I'd feel awful."

Felicity held up her vampire costume, so the light shone through it. "We could swap," she suggested.

Emily gasped at the thought of exhibiting herself to her guests in a nightdress and gave in. Indeed she caved in completely, putting herself passively into Felicity's hands, as if she had no will left. Felicity buttoned her into the dress, tied her sash, fastened the red ribbon round her neck and then sat her in front of the mirror, to pile up her hair in a fanciful Victorian style. As Felicity studied her friend's reflected face she wondered just what she was doing. Perhaps Emily had been doomed from the start like the girl who met herself in Holland Park, with her bunch of withered flowers. Perhaps after all Felicity was doing no more than give a nudge to something quite inevitable. She smiled at Emily's reflection.

"It's going to be a lovely party," she said.

"You've been very clever with your make-up," said the innocent Emily. "You look just like a real vampire. Really wicked!"

Felicity, who had made no change in her make-up, smiled again.

The party went with a real swing. Felicity, who had carried realism to the extent of wearing nothing at all but her nightdress and a few dabs of blood, was very popular. Some people may have noticed that their host was drinking rather a lot and seemed in a worse temper than usual. But perhaps that was because his blood-stained knife sticking out of his pocket proved less original than he had thought it would. There were at least four other Jacks. How careless of Felicity to have suggested the same idea to so many people. The hostess, too, seemed unhappy. As her friend Felicity said in her sworn statement, later, she had complained of a headache at around midnight and gone for a stroll.

She was not seen again by anyone at the party until the next morning when they found her under the pines at the end of the garden. There was a red ribbon of blood round her throat.

There was quite a lot of scandal about that.

One or two of the guests, those who sold their stories to the Sunday papers, gave quite a wrong impression of the kind of party it had been. The police somehow gained the idea that there had been some sort of drug orgy going on. They never, ever managed to trace the movements of all the guests, some invited, some not, some masked and all in some sort of disguise. The fact that five people were in identical costumes did not help. The story of the ghost got out, and a prominent psychic announced that poor Emily had been struck down by forces from the beyond because of her foolish mockery of that pathetic revenant.

Ambrose helped the police with their enquiries for a few days, but his previous experience with such affairs was a positive advantage and eventually they had to let him go. He got a small flat in town, and Felicity moved in with him. In the summer they got married, and began to think of what they should do about the house.

Felicity was quite determined that they should live there. After all, all that she had done (if she had done anything; she was not prepared to admit even to herself that she had) had been done to get the house. And a murder and a haunting made the place virtually unsaleable. Besides, moving in would be an excellent way to face down scandal.

Fortified by these and other rationalizations, she drove down one summer's day to see what would have to be done before they could move back. A quick look round told her that it would be perfectly habitable after a good clean and she decided to call on Mrs. Beecham in the village to see if she would oblige.

As she left the house, she glanced, almost without intention, at the pines. What she saw sent her running down the drive and out into the lane, too frightened even to think of trying to get into her car. It took a lot of deep breathing, and the repetition of her mantra "there's nothing there, there can't be anything there," before she could go back. This time there was nothing. She got into the car and drove to the village.

She had pulled herself together by the time she got there, but Mrs. Beecham's sharp eyes detected signs of shock.

"You've been up to the house then?" she said.

"Yes," said Felicity. "We shall be moving in shortly. So we'd be very grateful if you could see your way to going in and giving everything a thorough clean." Under Mrs. Beecham's knowing gaze she began to babble. "You'll probably want to take someone with you . . . to help . . . it's a big job . . . I'll pay you what you like, of course . . . "

"I don't want paying no more than the going rate," said Mrs. Beecham. "*I* don't have cause to worry about any ghost."

"Mrs. Beecham," said Felicity, trying to control her trembling lips, "there is no ghost there."

"Well, maybe it isn't exactly a ghost, yet. It's not the last Mrs. Edwards, that's for sure. It looks more like a blonde lady, though it could be a redhead."

She looked steadily at Felicity, who lowered her eyes, knowing that Mrs. Beecham had seen what she had seen.

It was Felicity herself who now stood under the pines, blood running through her long blonde hair.

GUESTS FROM GIBBET ISLAND

Washington Irving

Whoever has visited the ancient and renowned village of Communipaw may have noticed an old stone building of most ruinous and sinister appearance. The doors and window-shutters are ready to drop from their hinges; old clothes are stuffed in the broken panes of glass; while legions of half-starved dogs prowl about the premises, and rush out and bark at every passer-by; for your beggarly house in a village is most apt to swarm with profligate and ill-conditioned dogs. What adds to the sinister appearance of this mansion is a tall frame in front, not a little resembling a gallows, and which looks as if waiting to accommodate some of the inhabitants with a well-merited airing. It is not a gallows, however, but an ancient signpost; for this dwelling in the golden days of Communipaw was one of the most orderly and peaceful of village taverns, where public affairs were talked and smoked over. In fact, it was in this very building that Oloffe the Dreamer, and his companions, concerted that great voyage of discovery and colonization, in which they explored Buttermilk Channel, were nearly shipwrecked in the Strait of Hell-gate, and finally landed on the Island of Manhattan, and founded the great city of New Amsterdam.

Even after the province had been cruelly wrested from the sway of their High Mightinesses by the combined forces of the British and the Yankees, this tavern continued its ancient loyalty. It is true, the head of the Prince of Orange disappeared from the sign, a strange bird being painted over it, with the explanatory legend of *Die Wilde Gans,* or The Wild Goose; but this all the world knew to be a sly riddle of the landlord, the worthy Teunis Van Gieson, a knowing man in a small way, who laid his finger beside his nose and winked when any one studied the signification of his sign and observed that his goose was hatching, but would join the flock whenever they flew over the water; an enigma which was the perpetual recreation and delight of the loyal but fatheaded burghers of Communipaw.

Under the sway of this patriotic, though discreet and quiet publican, the tavern continued to flourish in primeval tranquillity, and was the resort of true-hearted Nederlanders, from all parts of Pavonia, who met here quietly and secretly to smoke and drink the downfall of Briton and Yankee, and success to Admiral Van Tromp.

The only drawback on the comfort of the establishment was a nephew of mine host, a sister's son, Yan Yost Vanderscamp by name, and a real scamp by nature. This unlucky whipster showed an early propensity to mischief, which he gratified in a small way by playing tricks upon the frequenters of the Wild Goose: putting gunpowder in their pipes, or squibs in their pockets, and astonishing them with an explosion, while they sat nodding round the fireplace in the bar-room; and if perchance a worthy burgher from some distant part of Pavonia lingered until dark over his potation, it was odds but young Vanderscamp would slip a brier under his horse's tail, as he mounted, and send him clattering along the road, in neck-or-nothing style, to the infinite astonishment and discomfiture of the rider.

It may be wondered at that mine host of the Wild Goose did not turn such a graceless varlet out of doors, but Teunis Van Gieson was an easy-tempered man, and having no child of his own, looked upon his nephew with almost parental indulgence. His patience and good nature were doomed to be tried by another intimate of his mansion. This was a cross-grained curmudgeon of a negro, named Pluto, who was a kind of enigma in Communipaw. Where he came from, nobody knew. He was found one morning, after a storm, cast like a sea-monster on the strand, in front of the Wild Goose, and lay there, more dead than alive. The neighbours gathered round, and speculated on this production of the deep; whether it were fish or flesh, or a compound of both, commonly yclept a merman. The kind-hearted Teunis Van Gieson, seeing that he wore the human form, took him into this house, and warmed him into life. By degrees, he showed signs of intelligence, and even uttered sounds very much like language, but which no one in Communipaw could understand. Some thought him a negro just from Guinea, who had either fallen overboard, or escaped from a slave-ship. Nothing, however, could ever draw from him any account of his origin. When questioned on the subject, he merely pointed to Gibbet Island, a small rocky islet, which lies in the open bay, just opposite Communipaw, as if that were his native place, though everybody knew it had never been inhabited.

In the process of time, he acquired something of the Dutch language, that is to say, he learnt all its vocabulary of oaths and maledictions, with just words sufficient to string them together. "Donder en Blicksem!" (thunder and lightning), was the gentlest of his ejaculations. For years he kept about the Wild Goose, more like one of those familiar spirits or household goblins we read of, than like a human being. He acknowledged allegiance to no one, but performed various domestic offices, when it suited his humour: waiting occasionally on the guests; grooming the horses; cutting wood; drawing water; and all this without being ordered. Lay any command on him, and the stubborn sea-urchin was sure to rebel. He was never so much at home, however, as when on the water, plying about in skiff or canoe, entirely alone, fishing, crabbing, or grabbing for oysters, and would bring home quantities for the larder of the Wild Goose, which he would throw down at the kitchen-door, with a growl. No wind nor weather deterred him from launching forth on his favourite element: indeed, the wilder the weather, the more he seemed to enjoy it. If a storm was brewing, he was sure to put off from shore; and would be seen far out in the bay, his light skiff dancing like a feather on the waves, when sea and sky were in a turmoil, and the stoutest ships were fain to lower their sails. Sometimes on such occasions he would be absent for days together. How he weathered the tempest, and how and where he subsisted, no one could divine, nor did any one venture to ask, for all had an almost superstitious awe of him. Some of the Communipaw oystermen declared they had more than once seen him suddenly disappear, canoe and all, as if plunged beneath waves, and after a while come up again, in quite a different part of the bay; whence they concluded that he could live under water like that notable species of wild duck, commonly called the hell-diver. All began to consider him in the light of a foul-weather bird, like the Mother Carey's Chicken, or petrel; and whenever they saw him putting far out in his skiff, in cloudy weather, made up their minds for a storm.

The only being for whom he seemed to have any liking, was Yan Yost Vanderscamp, and him he liked for his very wickedness. He in a manner took the boy under his tutelage, prompted him to all kinds of mischief, aided him in every wild harum-scarum freak, until the lad became the complete scapegrace of the village: a pest to his uncle, and to every one else. Nor were his pranks confined to the land; he soon learned to accompany old Pluto on the water. Together these worthies would cruise about the broad bay, and all the neighbouring straits and rivers; poking around in skiffs and canoes; robbing the set and nets of the fishermen; landing on remote coasts, and laying waste orchards and water-melon patches; in short, carrying on a complete system of piracy, on a small scale. Piloted by Pluto, the youthful Vanderscamp soon became acquainted with all the bays, rivers, creeks, and inlets of the watery world around him; could navigate from the Hook to Spiting-Devil on the darkest night, and learned to set even the terrors of Hell-gate at defiance.

At length, negro and boy suddenly disappeared, and days and

weeks elapsed, but without tidings of them. Some said they must have run away and gone to sea; others jocosely hinted that old Pluto, being no other than his namesake in disguise, had spirited away the boy to the nether regions. All, however, agreed in one thing, that the village was well rid of them.

In the process of time, the good Teunis Van Gieson slept with his fathers, and the tavern remained shut up, waiting for a claimant, for the next heir was Yan Yost Vanderscamp, and he had not been heard of for years. At length, one day, a boat was seen pulling for shore, from a long, black, rakish-looking schooner that lay at anchor in the bay. The boat's crew seemed worthy of the craft from which they debarked. Never had such a set of noisy, roistering, swaggering varlets landed in peaceful Communipaw. They were outlandish in garb and demeanour, and were headed by a rough, burly, bully ruffian, with fiery whiskers, a copper nose, a scar across his face, and a great Flaundrish beaver slouched on one side of his head, in whom, to their dismay, the quiet inhabitants were made to recognize their early pest, Yan Yost Vanderscamp. The rear of this hopeful gang was brought up by old Pluto, who had lost an eye, grown grizzly-headed, and looked more like a devil than ever. Vanderscamp renewed his acquaintance with the old burghers, much against their will, and in a manner not at all to their taste. He slapped them familiarly on the back, gave them an iron grip of the hand, and was hail fellow well met. According to his own account, he had been all the world over; had made money by bags full; had ships in every sea, and now meant to turn the Wild Goose into a country-seat, where he and his comrades, all rich merchants from foreign parts, might enjoy themselves in the interval of their voyages.

Sure enough, in a little while there was a complete metamorphose of the Wild Goose. From being a quiet, peaceful Dutch public house, it became a most riotous, uproarious private dwelling; a complete rendezvous for boisterous men of the seas, who came here to have what they called a 'blow out' on dry land, and might be seen at all hours, lounging about the door, or lolling out of the windows, swearing among themselves, and cracking rough jokes on every passer-by. The house was fitted up, too, in so strange a manner; hammocks slung to the walls, instead of bedsteads; odd kinds of furniture, of foreign fashion: bamboo couches, Spanish chairs; pistols, cutlasses, and blunderbusses, suspended on every peg, silver crucifixes on the mantel-pieces, silver candlesticks and porringers on the tables, contrasting oddly with the pewter and Delft ware of the original establishment. And then the strange amusements of these sea-monsters! Pitching Spanish dollars, instead of quoits; firing blunderbusses out of the window; shooting at a mark, or at any unhappy dog, or cat, or pig, or barn-door fowl, that might happen to come within reach.

The only being who seemed to relish their rouch waggery was old Pluto; and yet he led but a dog's life of it, for they practiced all kinds of manual jokes upon him: kicked him about like a football; shook him by his grizzly mop of wool; and never spoke to him without coupling a curse by way of adjective to his name, and consigning him to the infernal regions. The old fellow, however, seemed to like them better, the more they cursed him, though his utmost expression of pleasure never amounted to more than the growl of a petted bear, when his ears are rubbed.

Old Pluto was the ministering spirit at the orgies of the Wild Goose; and such orgies as took place there! Such drinking, singing, whooping, swearing; with an occasional interlude of quarrelling and fighting. The noisier grew the revel, the more old Pluto plied the potations, until the guests would become frantic in their merriment, smashing everything to pieces, and throwing the house out of the windows. Sometimes, after a drinking bout, they sallied forth and scoured the village, to the dismay of the worthy burghers, who gathered their women within doors, and would have shut up the house. Vanderscamp, however, was not to be rebuffed. He insisted on renewing acquaintance with his old neigh-bours, and on introducing his friends, the merchants, to their families; swore he was on the look-out for a wife, and meant, before he stopped, to find husbands for all their daughters. So, will-ye, nill-ye, sociable he was; swaggered about their best parlours, with his hat on one side of his head; sat on the good wife's nicely-waxed mahogany table, kicking his heels against the carved and polished legs; kissed and tousled the young vrouws; and if they frowned and pouted, gave them a gold rosary, or a sparkling cross, to put them in good humour again.

Sometimes nothing would satisfy him, but he must have some of his old neighbours to dinner at the Wild Goose. There was no refusing him, for he had the complete upper hand of the community, and the peaceful burghers all stood in awe of him. But what a time would the quiet, worthy men have, among these rakehells, who would delight to astound them with the most extravagant gunpowder tales, embroidered with all kinds of foreign oaths; clink the can with them; pledge them in deep potations; bawl drinking songs in their ears, and occasionally fire pistols over their heads, or under the table, and then laugh in their faces, and ask them how they liked the smell of gunpowder.

Thus was the little village of Communipaw for a time like the unfortunate wight possessed with devils; until Vanderscamp and his brother merchants would sail on another trading voyage, when the Wild Goose would be shut up, and everything relapse into a quiet, only to be disturbed by his next visitation.

The mystery of all these proceedings gradually dawned upon the tardy intellects of Communipaw. These were the times of the notorious Captain Kidd, when the American harbours were the resorts of piratical adventurers of all kinds, who, under pretext of mercantile voyages, scoured the West Indies, made plundering descents upon the Spanish Main, visited even the remote Indian Seas, and then came to dispose of their booty, have their revels, and fit out new expeditions, in the English colonies.

Vanderscamp had served in this hopeful school, and, having risen to importance among the buccaneers, had pitched upon his native village, and early home, as a quiet, out-of-the-way, unsuspected place, where he and his comrades, while anchored at New York, might have their feasts, and concert their plans, without molestation.

At length the attention of the British government was called to these piratical enterprises, that were becoming so frequent and outrageous. Vigorous measures were taken to check and punish them. Several of the most noted freebooters were caught and executed, and three of Vanderscamp's chosen comrades, the most riotous swashbucklers of the Wild Goose, were hanged in chains on Gibbet Island, in full sight of their favourite resort. As to Vanderscamp himself, he and his man Pluto again disappeared, and it was hoped by the people of Communipaw that he had fallen in some foreign brawl, or been swung on some foreign gallows.

For a time, therefore, the tranquility of the village was restored; the worthy Dutchmen once more smoked their pipes in peace, eyeing, with peculiar complacency, their old pests and terrors, the pirates, dangling and drying in the sun, on Gibbet Island.

This perfect calm was doomed at length to be ruffled. The fiery persecution of the pirates gradually subsided. Justice was satisfied with the examples that had been made, and there was no more talk of Kidd, and the other heroes of like kidney. On a calm summer evening, a boat, somewhat heavily laden, was seen pulling into Communipaw. What was the surprise and disquiet of the inhabitants, to see Yan Yost Vanderscamp seated at the helm, and his man Pluto tugging at the oar! Vanderscamp, however, was apparently an altered man. He brought home with him a wife, who seemed to be a shrew, and to have the upper hand of him. He no longer was the swaggering, bully ruffian, but affected the regular merchant, and talked of retiring from business, and settling down quietly, to pass the rest of his days in his native place.

The Wild Goose mansion was again opened, but with diminished splendour, and no riot. It is true, Vanderscamp had frequently nautical visitors, and the sound of revelry was occasionally overheard in his house; but everything seemed to be done under the rose; and old Pluto was the only servant that officiated at these orgies. The visitors, indeed, were by no means of the turbulent stamp of their predecessors; but quiet, mysterious traders, full of nods, and winks, and hieroglyphic signs, with whom, to use their cant phrase, 'everything was snug'. Their ships came to anchor at night, in the lower bay; and, on a private signal, Vanderscamp would launch his boat, and accompanied solely by his man Pluto, would make them mysterious visits. Sometimes boats pulled in at night, in front of the Wild Goose, and various articles of merchandise were landed in the dark, and spirited away, nobody knew whither. One of the more curious of the inhabitants kept watch, and caught a glimpse of the features of some of these night visitors, by the casual glance of a lantern, and declared that he recognized more than one of the freebooting frequenters of the Wild Goose in former times; whence he concluded that Vanderscamp was at his old game, and that this mysterious merchandise was nothing more nor less than piratical plunder. The more charitable opinion, however, was that Vanderscamp and his comrades, having been driven from their old line of business by the 'oppressions of government', had resorted to smuggling to make both ends meet.

Be that as it may: I come now to the extraordinary fact, which is the butt-end of this story. It happened late one night, that Yan Yost Vanderscamp was returning across the broad bay, in his light skiff, rowed by his man Pluto. He had been carousing on board of a vessel newly arrived, and was somewhat obfuscated in intellect by the liquor he had imbibed. It was a still, sultry night; a heavy mass of lurid clouds was rising in the west, with the low muttering of distant thunder. Vanderscamp called on Pluto to pull lustily, that they might get home before the gathering storm. The old negro made no reply, but shaped his course so as to skirt the rocky shores of Gibbet Island. A faint creaking overhead caused Vanderscamp to cast up his eyes, when to his horror he beheld the bodies of three pot companions and brothers in iniquity dangling in the moonlight, their rags fluttering, and their chains creaking, as they were slowly swung backward and forward by the rising breeze.

"What do you mean, you blockhead!" cried Vanderscamp, "by pulling so close to the island?"

"I thought you'd be glad to see your old friends once more," growled the negro: "you were never afraid of a living man, what do you fear from the dead?"

"Who's afraid?" hiccupped Vanderscamp, partly heated by liquor, partly nettled by the jeer of the negro; "who's afraid! Hang me, but I would be glad to see them once more, alive or dead, at the Wild Goose. Come, my lads in the wind!" continued he, taking a draught, and flourishing the bottle above his head, "here's fair weather to you in the other world; and if you should be walking the rounds tonight, odds fish! But I'll be happy if you will drop in to supper."

A dismal creaking was the only reply. The wind blew loud and shrill, and as it whistled round the gallows, and among the bones, sounded as if they were laughing and gibbering in the air. Old Pluto chuckled to himself, and now pulled home. The storm burst over the voyagers, while they were yet far from shore. The rain fell in torrents, the thunder crashed and pealed, and the lightning kept up an incessant blaze. It was stark midnight before they landed in Communipaw.

Dripping and shivering, Vanderscamp crawled homeward. He was completely sobered by the storm; the water soaked from without having diluted and cooled the liquor within. Arrived at the Wild Goose, he knocked timidly and dubiously at the door, for he dreaded the reception he was to receive from his wife. He had reason to do so. She met him at the threshold, in a precious ill-humour.

"Is this a time," said she, "to keep people out of their beds, and to bring home company, to turn the house upside down?'

"Company?" said Vanderscamp, meekly; "I have brought no company with me, wife."

"No, indeed! They have got here before you, but by your invitation; and blessed-looking company they are, truly!"

Vanderscamp's knees smote together. "For the love of heaven, where are they, wife?"

"Where?—why in the blue-room, upstairs; making themselves as much at home as if the house were their own."

Vanderscamp made a desperate effort, scrambled up to the room, and threw open the door. Sure enough, there, at a table, on which burned a light as blue as brimstone, sat the three guests from Gibbet Island, with halters round their necks, and bobbing their cups together, as they were hob-a-nobbing, and trolling the old Dutch freebooters' glee, since translated into English:

> For *three merry lads be we,*
> And *three merry lads be we:*
> I *on the land, and thou on the sand,*
> And *Jack on the gallows-tree.*

Vanderscamp saw and heard no more. Starting back with horror, he missed his footing on the landing-place, and fell from the top of the stairs to the bottom. He was taken up speechless, and, either from the fall or the fright, was buried in the yard of the little Dutch church at Bergen on the following Sunday.

From that day forward, the fate of the Wild Goose was sealed. It was pronounced a *haunted house,* and avoided accordingly. No one inhabited it but Vanderscamp's shrew of a window, and old Pluto, and they were considered but little better than its hobgoblin visitors. Pluto grew more and more haggard and morose, and looked more like an imp of darkness than a human being. He spoke to no one, but went about muttering to himself, or, as some hinted, talking with the devil, who, though unseen, was ever at his elbow. Now and then he was seen pulling about the bay alone in his skiff in dark weather, or at the approach of nightfall: nobody could tell why, unless on an errand to invite more guests from the gallows. Indeed it was affirmed that the Wild Goose still continued to be a house of entertainment for such guests, and that on stormy nights, the blue chamber was occasionally illuminated, and sounds of diabolical merriment were overheard, mingling with the howling of the tempest. Some treated these as idle stories, until on one such night, it was about the time of the equinox, there was a horrible uproar in the Wild Goose, that could not be mistaken. It was not so much the sound of revelry, however, as strife, with two or three piercing shrieks that pervaded every part of the village. Nevertheless, no one thought of hastening to the spot. On the contrary, the honest burghers of Communipaw drew their nightcaps over their ears, and buried their heads under the bedclothes, at the thoughts of Vanderscamp and his gallows companions.

The next morning, some of the bolder and more curious undertook to reconnoiter. All was quiet and lifeless at the Wild Goose. The door yawned wide open, and had evidently been open all night, for the storm had beaten into the house. Gathering more courage from the silence and apparent desertion, they gradually ventured over the threshold. The house had indeed the air of having been possessed by devils. Everything was topsy-turvy; trunks had been broken open, and chests of drawers and corner cupboards turned inside out, as in a time of general sack and pillage; but the most woeful sight was the widow of Yan Yost Vanderscamp, extended a corpse on the floor of the blue chamber, with the marks of a deadly gripe on the windpipe.

All now was conjecture and dismay at Communipaw; and the disappearance of old Pluto; who was nowhere to be found, gave rise to all kinds of wild surmises. Some suggested that the negro had betrayed the house to some of Vanderscamp's buccaneering associates, and that they had decamped together with the booty; other surmised that the negro was nothing more nor less than a devil incarnate, who had now accomplished his ends, and made off with his dues.

Events, however, vindicated the negro from this last imputation. His skiff was picked up, drifting about the bay, bottom upward, as if wrecked in a tempest; and his body was found, shortly afterwards, by some Communipaw fishermen, stranded among the rocks of Gibbet Island, near the foot of the pirates' gallows. The fishermen shook their heads, and observed that old Pluto had ventured once too often to invite guests from Gibbet Island.

THE TRYST

Garry Kilworth

Rebecca stopped the car. The signpost was weathered and the print had peeled away in places but she could just make out the name of the village. BEECHWALD 4M. She shook her head in an attempt to clear it of the muzziness that had surrounded it since the previous night's party. *A scratchin' and breakin'* gig, the host had called it. *Scratchin'* involved physically regrooving a record with a stylus several times so that when you came to play it properly, the most godawful, weird sounds came out of the speakers; and then the *breakin'* would start. She could only describe the latter as a gymnastic display performed by disco athletes. It had been a fascinating party, spoiled only by a piece of fudge that Steven had slipped her in the early hours of the morning. The fudge had been spiked with grass and had induced successive waves of nausea and panic in her. The adverse effect of what Steven had wanted, of course. She was a virgin, a little afraid of committing herself, and Steven had thought to release her from her inhibitions. Afterwards, there had been a fight between them and eventually she had agreed to spend the weekend at the cottage. Steven was to drive down later in the evening, after closing his office.

She stared beyond the signpost into a damp spinney that hung shadows like dark rags from its branches. She felt a sense of unease: it was almost as if the copse were enticing her to leave the car and enter its semi-penetrable, dark environment, yet at the same time, it threatened her with its decaying aspect. She shuddered. Out here, in the country, her imagination—*her fanciful* imagination as Steven would have it—seemed to unfold like a black-paper beast into something barely recognizable, but still elusive in its precise identification. In the city she could cope with her nightmares, surrounded by hard, substantial concrete and the appliances of modern life. Once in the countryside, however, the external, natural forms induced the awakening of inherent, unnatural fears. The asymmetrical shapes of nature had other vague, indefinable forms lurking within them that startled her imagination into activity. She would catch the silhouette of a half-human face trapped in the darknesses of trees growing into each other. Or hear the thrashing of a forbidden creature fighting its way from the supernatural place into the real world. What frightened her most was her fixed fascination with these agents of her own fancy. It was as if she were creating terror so that it could feed on itself, a horrible cycle that, once self-cannibalizing had begun, grew in size and intensity as it gorged upon its own grey amorphous body.

Rebecca continued along the straight road, an avenue lined by poplars. The low October sun shone obliquely through the file of trees, and the car cut through the bars of sunlight that lay across the tarmac, the shadows of their trunks slicing rapidly across the windscreen like the phantom blades of a repetitive executioner. It caused her head to spin again and she had to concentrate hard to keep the car on the left. Her hands were shaking badly and her mouth felt dry as she came out the other end of the gauntlet run. Finally, she could see the lone cottage, a mile before the village church, on a low hill.

The cottage belonged to one of Steven's friends.

"Three hundred years old," Steven had told her on handing her the keys. "There's a story goes with it. Apparently it was built by some woodsman for himself and his bride, only the bride ran away on her wedding night with some other swain—the blacksmith's son or some-thing. This woodsman guy—Druit his name was—used to fell beech trees for the local furniture industry. You can imagine—he must have been a hulk. Muscles of iron and that sort of thing . . ."

Steven had said the last sentence very quickly. Rebecca knew he was sensitive about his slim build. "Anyway," Steven had continued, "he found the couple in a shack in the woods and . . . dispatched them with his axe in a terrible fit of rage." Steven had brought the edge of his hand down lightly on the side of her neck at these words. He enjoyed teasing her.

"Why are you telling me this?" she had asked him, knowing full well the reasons.

"Just thought you'd be interested."

"What happened to . . . Druit? The woodsman?"

"He went back to his cottage and hung himself." Steven grinned. "Oh, come on, Becky. It's only a story. Probably isn't even true. Here, give me a hug. It's going to be all right—really. We're adults."

"I wasn't thinking of that," she had said. "That poor man . . ."

"He was a murderer, for Christ's sake. What do you think hap-pened to murderers in those days, anyway? Becky, you know, I almost love you."

"You can't almost love someone. You either do or you don't."

He had smiled. "Okay, so I was lying."

"What? What were you lying about?"

"I do love you . . . completely."

He had folded her into his arms and she had felt his sharp elbows cut-ting into her sides, but, unfortunately, she was fond of him. He was exciting, he knew lots of exciting people and she felt good when she was with him. He had an easy smile and a grace that could not be found in many men. Steven, when he wanted to, which was most of the time, could make her feel alive. He had laughed when she told him that. He had an easy laugh, which was infectious.

The car entered an autumnal tunnel of bushes and trees that

smothered the roadway just before the hill. Just as she was thinking about switching on the lights, she came out at the other side, into a blinding swathe of sunlight. In another week or two that gold and russet arch would have disappeared, leaving an upturned wickerwork basket.

She stopped the car and switched off the engine, staying in the warmth for a few moments. The cottage was not unattractive; set well back off the road; there was an unkempt garden without a path, leading to the grey stone frontage. Two windows burned in the evening sunlight: the eyes of a man on the point of death. (What made her think of that? Of course: Dylan Thomas: *Rage, rage at the dying of the light* . . . Steven had read it to her a few evenings ago.) The slate roof had been smothered by moss but . . . well, it was only for two nights, anyway. If it leaked, they could cuddle up before the fire and . . . well, she knew what. Her legs started to shake a little but she tried to turn her mind to other things. Hell, what was she being so schoolgirlish about anyway? She did want Steven. That was the cause of the trembling, after all. It would be good, once the first time was over and she knew what it was all about . . . what was expected of her.

The sun had been sliced in half, severed by the sharp horizon.

She got out of the car and opened the boot of the Mini to extract her bags. Then she walked the length of the spongy lawn to the front door. One or two chrysanthemums were still in bloom in a small untidy plot beneath the living-room window. They looked a little bedraggled but they loaned a bit of colour to the rather drab exterior. She used a worn footscraper set in a block of concrete by the low door before putting the key in the lock. The mechanism was resistant and she had to use both hands to turn the key. It finally gave way with a solid 'thunk'. The woodwork was damp and the door was difficult to open—even then it would only give a yard.

"Someone doesn't like visitors," she said. The sound of her own voice was hollow and she hoped Steven would arrive soon. At least a prowler would have the same problems. Presumably there was a back door and she could escape that way while he was fighting to get in the front. Once inside, she heaved the door shut and switched on the light: the room she entered was tiny and gloomy, with only the one small window, but it owned a wide, inviting inglenook. There was a door with a step up, presumably to the kitchen. She turned her attention to the fire. That was the first task. It would give the room some friendly warmth and she would have something on which to concentrate. She put her bags on the wooden staircase that twisted upstairs and went into the kitchen to look for fuel. Under the sink unit was a stack of logs and some old newspapers. Kindling. She needed something to start the blaze with. She looked in the pantry and eventually found some fire lighters. Perversely, she was disappointed. The newspapers were superfluous after all. There would have been more satisfaction in lighting the fire without the devices of the modern world, but short of trying to hack at one of the logs with an old breadknife, there was nothing for it but to use the devices of the modern world. Modern? She laughed. Back in her Holborn flat she would have switched on the electric fire.

In quite a short time the logs were flaring in the grate and she began to feel very pleased with herself. Hell, this country life was not so difficult. She had brought some bread with her. Once the logs had burned down a bit she would make some toast. She glanced towards the front window. It was dark now. No trace of light outside. Should she leave the rather tatty curtain open so that she could see the headlamps of Steven's car winding up the hill? The window was like a black mirror with reflected flames dancing inside it. She quickly crossed the room and tugged the curtain over the panes. Then she sat on the stone seat inside the inglenook, enjoying the sensation of keeping close company with an open fire, and waited, listening for the sound of an engine in the wind outside.

She awoke some time later with a start. The flames had died to a red glow. Only one hot charcoal revealed any life whatsoever. Her limbs ached, especially her legs, and there was a small depression on her temple where it had rested against the corner of a stone. She looked at her watch. 11:30. Where the hell was Steven? She rubbed her forehead and staggered into the kitchen for some more logs.

Once the fire was going again, Rebecca took a novel out of her travelling bag. *Middlemarch*. George Eliot and her village societies were appropriate to the scene. For some reason, she did not want to go upstairs before Steven arrived. It was not something she wanted to analyse. She just did not want to, and that was that. The hearthrug was comfortable enough in any case. *Come on, come on!* She thought to herself as she tried to concentrate on Dorothea's frustrated desire to become a learned lady in a time when knowledge was considered to be superfluous to female requirements.

Suddenly, the pages grew brighter and brighter before her eyes. Her breath caught in her throat. *What was happening?* Looking up, through the effulgence, she saw that the single bulb was burning with an increasingly greater intensity, until it was as white as a blacksmith's forge. The effect was blinding. The whole room shone with a luminosity that hurt her eyes wherever she looked. Then followed a noise like a thin scream coming from the centre of the room and the bulb exploded, sending a spray of fine, hot glass into her face. Rebecca cried out as vivid colours danced before her eyes. Finally, when she could focus again, she could make out the shape of a huge man standing in the middle of the room. His beard and hair were alive with a supernatural radiance. She could see his large-honed hands held a long-handled axe. The blade seemed to draw into itself the brilliance of the eradiating fire in curving bands, so that, as he swung it to and fro, the beams snaked around her head to play upon the sharp cutting-edge of the bright metal.

The man's shouts mingled with her screams. His eyes were full of rage and glowed with hatred. A ridged nerve twisted down from his hairline to scar his brow.

He raised the axe and brought it down with a tremendous blow aimed at her head. Rebecca cowered and the axe-head missed, striking the stonework of the inglenook with a deafening ring, sending a shower of sparks onto her cheek. She scrambled towards the kitchen and managed to crawl inside and kick the door shut.

Jumping to her feet and babbling hysterically, she pulled at the back door but it would not yield. The window was as fixed, and too small to crawl through anyway. She was trapped. Completely terrified, she slid to the greasy kitchen floor and lay whimpering and sobbing in the draught that blew beneath the door.

After a long while she realized the intruder had not followed her into the kitchen and she began to recover some of her composure. She listened intently for sounds coming from the front room but there was nothing but the occasional crackle and hiss of burning logs. An hour later she eased open the door to the living-room and looked inside. Nothing but the shadowy flames of the firelight leaping up the white-washed walls. Had he gone? Carefully, she inspected all the corners of the room. The only place she could not see was inside the inglenook itself. Should she make a dash for the front door? She remembered that it was still locked. She could see the key glinting softly in the reflected glow of the fire. If he was in the inglenook he would take her head off before she could even turn the key. She waited for another half an hour, then eased herself round the corner to get a better view of the fireplace. Just then a log exploded, sending bits of flaming bark onto the hearthrug, and, instinctively, she ducked back into the kitchen. But she had seen the interior of the inglenook. It was empty.

Rebecca picked up the breadknife and walked unsteadily towards the front door. *She had to get out.* That was all. If he could not follow her into the kitchen, he certainly could not follow her outside. Just before she reached the door, she paused. In the knotted patterns of the natural wood she could just make out the image of a man. Was that a trick of the light, or was it? . . . She was undecided. Suddenly, something inside her snapped, and she slashed at the face of the figure with the breadknife, feeling the blade cut deep into the soft, damp wood. The knife fell to the floor as she staggered backwards, heaving for breath, the effort had cost her so.

There was a deep groove in the door, about a third of the way down the bizarre head of the strange, warped stain. She stared at its grotesque shape. It was as if it had been burned into the grain of the wood, heat flung at it in the silhouette of a man. She remembered the shining axe and the scintillating hair. This . . . manifestation had the power to attract light and possibly transform it into psychic energy, giving it a solid three-dimensional form and animation. If it got out again, it would kill her, she was sure. Did she dare try to pass it or should she wait for the sanity of the daytime? While she stood, still undecided, the fire flared into brilliance with the sound of rushing air and the figure in the door became alive again, stepping out into the room.

Rebecca fell backwards onto the rug. The man took one step forward and let the axe drop to his feet. It clattered on the stones. He gave a single, hoarse, pitiful cry, and Rebecca could only just understand the word.

"Blind!"

He stood there, unmoving. No longer did his face coruscate with incandescent fire. It merely shone with the normal paleness of human flesh, like a moon trimmed with textured darkness. Rebecca held her breath, keeping as still as death and holding down the sound of her heartbeat by sheer willpower. He moved his head, slowly, to one side, and she knew he was listening. Gradually his face turned towards her again and he knelt down before her. She stifled a scream as hands reached out and then she could feel his rough, calloused palms on the sides of her face. She stared into his sightless eyes and a surge of pity mingled with her fear. He was blind and she had been the cause. Her knife had robbed him of his sight.

The fingers began to close together round her head and she knew in that moment that he was going to crush her skull. She felt the enormous strength, the power behind the hands as they tensed for the final pressure that would crack her head like an eggshell. A vein in her temple pulsed against his warm palm with the quickness of a frightened rabbit's heart. The pressure stopped and she reached up to touch his cheek with her fingertips. His hands slipped away and she took his head, cradling it naturally in her lap and rocking gently to and fro. A series of emotions went through her breast, each locked tightly to the other. Fear was linked with pity, for his blindness, and pity with tenderness. She could sense—no, more than that, she could *feel* the agony of unhappiness that inhabited the heart of this man. His melancholy filled the room with its atmosphere and she wanted the warmth she felt in her own heart to waft away his dreadful sadness in a wave of sympathetic love. There was no passion here, no high fever of emotion, only the gentle, charitable love of a human being for a creature of the night. Druit had been blind before—blind with rage. Should not this new blindness be visited by an unchaotic emotion, one that created, not destroyed? Not just an emotion, an act? She had the means to move his grief nearer to flames, where it could dry its wings. His strong arms moved about her and her heart pulsed quickly against his resting brow . . .

"Don't worry," she said, "don't worry. There's no one here. Just the two of us. No one else. Just the two of us." Her thighs were damp with his tears where he had cried, soundlessly, from those sightless eyes, into the lap of her cotton dress. She buried her face in warm hair that smelled of straw dust and her own tears came coursing softly down her cheeks. The thick curls caught her fingers as she tried to stroke his head, and she rocked him, rocked with him, rocking in him . . . A log in the grate sloughed its bark, slowly, revealing the white, naked wood beneath, soon to be consumed by the flames.

Finally, they lay in each other's arms before the fire, secure in the glow from its deep, red heart.

❊   ❊   ❊

When Rebecca woke in the morning, there was nothing but cold, grey ashes in the grate. She rose from the rug and gazed at the door. The woodwork was devoid of any inherent shape: no sinister artistry, no dark stain, no image of a man, just plain, varnished beech. The restraining influence that had held him to the world had been removed. The woodsman had gone. She knew why and she knew that light had not been the only energy source . . . not entirely. There had been an intrinsic power within her that had drawn him out of his centuries-old retreat. That power had now been consumed before the fire when the woodsman had finally used the only key that could unlock his worldly fetters.

The sound of an engine broke the stillness of the morning. She gathered together her bags. Steven was just getting out of his car as she walked the length of the lawn and climbed into the Mini. He came running across to her as she started the motor. She wound down the window and looked into his flushed features.

"I'm sorry, Becky. Got held up. The car lights failed."

"You're too late, Steven."

He stared at her, half-angry, half-puzzled.

"Too late for what?"

"Too late for me."

"I don't understand . . . why are you leaving?"

She hesitated, then replied, "I had a visitor. Druit. He spent the night with me. I'm sure you understand *that.*"

"Druit?" He looked genuinely puzzled, as if she were playing a game with him. Then he gave a nervous laugh. "Oh, that! Becky, that was just a story. I was teasing. I made it up . . ." He laughed again. "The cottage is only eighty years old, for heaven's sakes. There was no Druit. Can't you take a joke?"

Rebecca stared at him, gauging the depth of his words. He was telling the truth this time, and, strangely, truth was more satisfying than the lie. Her reply was definite, delivered in measured tones. "In that case, I *certainly* don't need you." She pulled away from him and began the descent, down into the foliage of the tunnel at the bottom of the slope. The darkness closed around her with welcome, comfortable folds.

AN APPARITION

Guy De Maupassant

We had been talking about sequestration in connection with a recent lawsuit. It was towards the end of an evening spent among friends, at an old house in the Rue de Grenelle, and every one of us had told a story—a story supposed to be true. Eventually, the aged Marquis de la Tour Samuel, who was eighty-two, got to his feet and, leaning against the mantelpiece, said, in a rather tremulous voice:

I too have experienced something strange, so strange in fact that I have been haunted by it all my life. It is more than half a century since the incident happened, but not a month has passed without my seeing it all again in a dream. The impression, the imprint of terror, if you can follow me, has stayed with me ever since that day. For ten minutes I underwent such a ghastly fright that ever since a kind of perpetual fear has remained in my soul. Unexpected noises make me tremble to the bottom of my heart and things obscurely seen in the darkness almost impel me irresistibly to flee. In brief, at night I am afraid.

I wouldn't have confessed to that when I was younger! But now I can say anything. At eighty-two I don't feel obliged to be courageous in the presence of imaginary dangers. I have never given way before any real danger.

But the affair disturbed me so utterly and caused me such profound, mysterious and awful distress, that I never mentioned it to anyone. I have suppressed it in the depths of my being, those depths in which tormented secrets are hidden, the secrets and frailties we are ashamed of. I shall tell it to you precisely as it happened, without any attempt at explanation. Undoubtedly it can be explained—unless I were mad at the time. But I wasn't mad and I will prove it. You are at liberty to think what you choose. But these are the plain facts.

It was in the year 1827, in July. I was stationed at Rouen. One day, as I was strolling along the quay, I came across a man whom I thought I knew—without being able to remember exactly who he was. Impulsively, I made as if to stop; the stranger noticed this, glanced at me . . . and embraced me.

He was a friend of my youth whom I had liked immensely. It was five years since I had set eyes on him and he seemed to be fifty years older. His hair was completely white and he moved with a stoop as if utterly worn out. He saw my astonishment and told me what had happened to shatter his life.

He had fallen desperately in love with a young girl and had married her. But, after a single year of supreme love and happiness, she had died suddenly—of heart trouble—perhaps of love. On the day she was buried, he abandoned his château and went to live in his house in Rouen. There he existed, desperate and lonely, eaten up by grief, and so unhappy that he contemplated suicide.

"Now I have met you again," he said, "I shall ask you to do me an important favour: to go to my former home and obtain for me, from the bureau in my bedroom—our bedroom—certain documents which I urgently require. I can't send a servant or even a lawyer, as utter discretion and complete secrecy are needed. For my own part, nothing on earth would persuade me to go into that house again. I will give you the key of the room—which I myself locked on departing—and the key of the bureau and also a note to my gardener, instructing him to open up the château for you. But come and have breakfast with me tomorrow morning and we will arrange everything."

I agreed to do him this small favour. It wouldn't be much of a trip, for his property was only a few miles out of Rouen, and could easily be reached in an hour by horse. So at ten o'clock next day I went round to his house and we had breakfast together . . . yet he hardly spoke a word.

He asked me to forgive him, but the idea of the visit I was going to make to the bedroom in the château, the scene of his past happiness, overwhelmed him. Certainly he was strangely disturbed and preoccupied, as if some unknown conflict were going on in his soul.

Eventually he told me in detail what I must do. It was quite simple. I was to obtain two bundles of letters and a roll of documents from the first drawer on the right-hand side of the bureau to which I had the key. He added, "I do not need to request you not to look at them."

I was offended by that and told him so in no uncertain manner. "Do forgive me, I am suffering so much," he said brokenly and began to weep.

At about one o'clock I left him and set off on my mission.

The weather was splendid and I rode across the fields listening to the larks singing and to the rhythmical tapping of my sword against my boot. Presently I came to the forest and walked my horse. Branches of trees brushed my face as I rode and, every now and then, I caught a leaf in my teeth and chewed it eagerly, for the sheer joy of being alive that sometimes fills one with intense happiness.

As I drew near the château, I took the letter for the gardener out of my pocket to have a look at it and was surprised to find it was sealed. I was so astonished and vexed by this that I was on the point of returning without having carried out my promise; but decided this would show too much sensitiveness. Quite possibly my friend had sealed the envelope unthinkingly, he had been so upset.

The château had the appearance of having been neglected for a score of years. The gate was open wide and so derelict it was a wonder it was still hanging; the paths were smothered in weeds and the flowerbeds and the lawn were all one.

My loud knocking aroused the old man who emerged from a side-door. He seemed bewildered with astonishment at my visit. He read the letter I gave him, examined it again and again, surveyed me suspiciously, put the letter in a pocket and eventually demanded: "Well, then, what do you want?"

"As you have only just read your master's instructions, you should know what I want. I wish to enter the château."

He was flabbergasted. "You mean . . . you propose to go into . . . her room?"

I was beginning to lose patience. "Look here! Are you going to stand there cross-questioning me?"

"No, monsieur," he said in confusion; "it's only . . . well, it's only because the room hasn't been open since . . . since she died. If you don't mind waiting for a few minutes I'll go myself to see . . . if . . ."

I interrupted him angrily: "Look, what are you talking about? You can't get into the room, as I have the key!"

"All right, monsieur, I will show you the way," was all he could say at that.

"Just show me the staircase and then leave me. I will find the way without you."

"But, monsieur . . ."

I was really angry by now. "Shut up or I'll give you something to think about." I brushed past him and entered the château.

I made my way first through the kitchen; then a couple of rooms occupied by the caretaker and his wife; next, through a spacious hall by which I came to the staircase. I went up the stairs . . . and soon recognized the door described by my friend.

I opened it without difficulty and went in. The room was so dark that to begin with I couldn't make out a thing. I came to a halt, my nostrils assailed by the unpleasant, mouldering smell of untenanted rooms, of dead rooms. Presently, as my eyes grew used to the darkness,

I could see quite clearly a large untidy bedroom, the bed covered only by mattress and pillows—on one of which was the obvious impression of an arm or a head, as if somebody had been resting there recently.

The chairs were all out of place. I noticed that a door, probably leading to an ante-room, had been left half-open.

I went straight to the window, which I opened to let in the daylight. But the clasps of the shutters had become so rusty I couldn't make them budge. I even attempted to break them with my sword, but couldn't. As I was becoming vexed by my unavailing efforts and anyhow could see quite well in the gloom, I gave up the idea of obtaining more light and went across to the bureau.

I sat down in a chair, undid the lid of the bureau and opened the drawer in question. It was crammed full. I required only three bundles of papers, which I knew how to identify, and started to look for them.

I was peering closely in an attempt to make out the writing on them, when I seemed to hear—feel, rather—something rustling behind me. I took no notice, thinking that draught from the window was causing the movement. But, the next moment, a similar movement, barely perceptible, made me shiver unaccountably and disturbingly. I felt so stupid at this, that pride prevented my turning round. By now I had located the second bundle of documents and was on the point of picking up the third when a long, poignant sigh, coming from near my shoulder, made me leap like a madman from my chair and land several feet away. As I leapt, I turned round, my hand on the hilt of my sword, and, in truth, if I hadn't felt it at my side, I would have fled like a coward.

A tall woman, clad in white, stood looking at me from behind the chair where I had been sitting a moment ago. I almost collapsed with the tremor that passed through me. No one could appreciate that fearful terror unless he had experienced it! The mind grows blank; the heart stands still; the whole body becomes limp as a sponge, as if life itself were ebbing.

I don't believe in ghosts, yet I surrendered utterly to a dreadful fear of the dead; and I endured more in those few moments than in the rest of my life, simply from that overwhelming terror of the supernatural. If she hadn't spoken, I think I would have died. But she spoke, she spoke in a gentle, sad voice, that set my nerves tingling. I daren't say I had regained control of myself and come to my senses. No! I was so scared I hardly knew what I was doing; but a certain innate pride, a shred of soldierly instinct, caused me, in spite of myself, to maintain some kind of bold front. I was keeping up appearances to myself, I suppose, and to her, whoever she might be, woman or ghost. It was only afterwards I realized all this, for I can tell you, when the apparition appeared, I thought of nothing. I was afraid.

She said: "Oh, monsieur! You can do me a great service."

I endeavoured to reply, but I couldn't utter a word. Nothing but a vague sound issued from my throat.

She went on: "Will you? You can save me, cure me. I am suffering fearfully. I am suffering, oh, how I suffer!" and she sat down slowly in the chair.

"Will you?" she asked, regarding me.

I signified assent by nodding, for I was still voiceless.

Thereupon she held out to me a tortoiseshell comb and murmured: "Comb my hair, please comb my hair! That will cure me. It must be combed. Look at my head—how I suffer. My hair burns me so!"

Her hair, unplaited, was very long and very black. It hung over the back of the chair and reached to the floor. Why did I take that comb with a shudder, why did I take that long, black hair that made my skin creep as if I were handling snakes? I don't know.

That feeling has stayed in my fingers to this day and I still shiver when I think of it.

I combed her hair. I handled—I don't know how—those ice-cold tresses. I untangled them, loosened them. She sighed and bowed her head, appearing to be content. All at once she exclaimed "Thank you!" and snatched the comb from my hand and fled through the half-open door.

AN APPARITION

Left to myself, I went through the terrified agitation of a person who wakes up from a nightmare. At last I came to my senses; I hastened to the window and with a great effort broke open the shutters, letting in a flood of light. At once I ran to the door through which she had gone. I found it closed and immovable!

Then a frantic wish to flee overcame me in the kind of panic soldiers experience in battle. I clutched the three bundles of letters on the open bureau; ran from the room, rushed down the stairs four at a time, found myself outside, I don't know how, and seeing my horse a few paces away leaped into the saddle and galloped off.

I only halted on reaching Rouen and my own house. Flinging the bridle to my groom, I hurried to my room, where I locked myself in to think. For an hour I speculated anxiously whether I had been the victim of an hallucination. Surely I must have had one of those mysterious nervous shocks, one of those mental disturbances that give rise to miracles, to which the supernatural owes its influence.

I was almost convinced I had seen a vision, experienced an hallucination, when I went to the window. I happened to glance at my chest. My military cape was covered with hairs; the long hair of a woman, which had got caught in the buttons! One by one, with trembling fingers, I plucked them off and flung them away.

Then I summoned my groom. I was too distressed to go and see my friend that day; moreover, I wanted to consider more fully what I ought to tell him. I sent him his letters, for which he gave the groom a receipt. He enquired after me very particularly. He was told I was unwell, that I had had sunstroke or some such thing. He appeared to be exceedingly anxious. At daybreak next morning I visited him, determined to tell him the truth. He had gone out on the previous evening and had not yet returned. I called again during the course of the day. My friend was still absent. I waited a whole week. He did not appear. At length I informed the authorities. A search was started, but not the least trace of his whereabouts or the manner of his disappearance was discovered.

A thorough examination was made of the derelict château. Nothing of a suspicious nature came to light. There was no sign that a woman had been concealed there.

The enquiries led to nothing and the search was abandoned. For more than half a century I have heard nothing. I know no more than before.

AUNT HESTER

Brian Lumley

I suppose my Aunt Hester Lang might best be described as the 'black sheep' of the family. Certainly no one ever spoke to her, or of her—none of the elders of the family, that is—and if my own little friendship with my aunt had been known I am sure that would have been stamped on too; but of course that friendship was many years ago.

I remember it well: how I used to sneak around to Aunt Hester's house in hoary Castle-Ilden, not far from Harden on the coast, after school when my folks thought I was at Scouts, and Aunt Hester would make me cups of cocoa and we would talk about newts ('efts', she called them), frogs, conkers, and other things—things of interest to small boys—until the local Scouts' meeting was due to end, and then I would hurry home.

We (father, mother, and myself) left Harden when I was just twelve years old, moving down to London where the Old Man had got himself a good job. I was twenty years old before I got to see my aunt again. In the intervening years I had not sent her so much as a post-card (I've never been much of a letter-writer) and I knew that during the same period of time my parents had neither written nor heard from

273

her; but still that did not stop my mother warning me before I set out for Harden not to 'drop in' on Aunt Hester Lang.

No doubt about it, they were frightened of her, my parents—well, if not frightened, certainly they were apprehensive.

Now to me a warning has always been something of a challenge. I had arranged to stay with a friend for a week, a school pal from the good old days, but long before the northbound train stopped at Harden my mind was made up to spend at least a fraction of my time at my aunt's place. Why shouldn't I? Hadn't we always got on famously? Whatever it was she had done to my parents in the past, I could see no good reason why *I* should shun her.

She would be getting on in years a bit now. How old, I wondered? Older than my mother, her sister, by a couple of years—the same age (obviously) as her twin brother, George, in Australia—but of course I was also ignorant of his age. In the end, making what calculations I could, I worked it out that Aunt Hester and her distant brother must have seen at least one hundred and eight summers between them. Yes, my aunt must be about fifty-four years old. It was about time someone took an interest in her.

It was a bright Friday night, the first after my arrival in Harden, when the ideal opportunity presented itself for visiting Aunt Hester. My school friend, Albert, had a date—one he did not really want to put off—and though he had tried his best during the day it had early been apparent that his luck was out regards finding, on short notice, a second girl for me. It had been left too late. But in any case, I'm not much on blind dates—and most dates are 'blind' unless you really know the girl—and I go even less on doubles; the truth of the matter was that I had wanted the night for my own purposes. And so, when the time came for Albert to set out to meet his girl, I walked off in the opposite direction, across the autumn fences and fields to ancient Castle-Ilden.

I arrived at the little old village at about eight, just as dusk was making its hesitant decision whether or not to allow night's onset, and went straight to Aunt Hester's thatch-roofed bungalow. The place stood (just as I remembered it) at the Blackhill end of cobbled Main Street, in a neat garden framed by cherry trees with the fruit heavy in their branches. As I approached the gate the door opened and out of the house wandered the oddest quartet of strangers I could ever have wished to see.

There was a humped-up, frenetically mobile and babbling old chap, ninety if he was a day; a frumpish fat woman with many quivering chins; a skeletally thin, incredibly tall, ridiculously wrapped-up man in scarf, pencil-slim overcoat and fur gloves; and finally, a perfectly delicate old lady with a walking-stick and ear-trumpet. They were shepherded by my Aunt Hester, no different it seemed than when I had last seen her, to the gate and out into the street. There followed a piped and grunted hubbub of thanks and general genialities before the four were gone, in the direction of the leaning village pub, leaving my aunt at the gate finally to spot me where I stood in the shadow of one of her cherry trees. She knew me almost at once, despite the interval of nearly a decade.

"Peter?"

"Hello, Aunt Hester."

"Why, Peter Norton! My favourite young man—and tall as a tree! Come in, come in!"

"It's bad of me to drop in on you like this," I answered, taking the arm she offered, "all unannounced and after so long away, but I—"

"No excuses required," she waved an airy hand before us and smiled up at me, laughter lines showing at the corners of her eyes and in her unpretty face. "And you came at just the right time—my group has just left me all alone."

"Your group'?"

"My séance group! I've had it for a long time now, many a year. Didn't you know I was a bit on the psychic side? No, I suppose not; your parents wouldn't have told you about *that,* now would they? That's what started it all originally—the trouble in the family, I mean."

We went on into the house.

"Now I had meant to ask you about that," I told her. "You mean my parents don't like you messing about with spiritualism? I can see that they wouldn't, of course—not at all the Old Man's cup of tea—but still, I don't really see what it could have to do with them."

"Not *your* parents, Love" (she had always called me 'Love'), "mine—and yours later; but especially George, your uncle in Australia. And not just spiritualism, though that has since become part of it. Did you know that my brother left home and settled in Australia because of me?" A distant look came into her eyes. "No, of course you didn't, and I don't suppose anyone else would ever have become aware of my power if George hadn't walked me through a window . . ."

"Eh?" I said, believing my hearing to be out of order. "Power? Walked you through a window?"

"Yes," she answered, nodding her head, "he walked me through a window! Listen, I'll tell you a story from the beginning."

By that time we had settled ourselves down in front of the fire in Aunt Hester's living-room and I was able to scan, as she talked, the paraphernalia her 'group' had left behind. There were old leather-bound tomes and treatises, tarot cards, a ouija board, shiny brown with age, oh, and several other items beloved of the spiritualist. I was fascinated, as ever I had been as a boy, by the many obscure curiosities in Aunt Hester's cottage.

"The first I knew of the link between George and myself," she began, breaking in on my thoughts, "as apart from the obvious link that exists between all twins, was when we were twelve years old. Your grandparents had taken us, along with your mother, down to the beach at Seaton Carew. It was July and marvellously hot. Well, to cut a long story short, your mother got into trouble in the water."

"She was quite a long way out and the only one anything like close to her was George—who couldn't swim! He'd waded out up to his neck, but he didn't dare go any deeper. Now, you can wade a long way out at Seaton. The bottom shelves off very slowly. George was at least fifty yards out when we heard him yelling that Sis was in trouble . . ."

"At first I panicked and started to run out through the shallow water, shouting to George that he should swim to Sis, which of course he couldn't—*but he did!* Or at least, *I did!* Somehow I'd swapped places with him, do you see? Not physically but mentally. I'd left him behind me in the shallow water, in my body, and I was swimming for all I was worth for Sis in his! I got her back to the shallows with very little trouble—she was only a few inches out of her depth—and then, as soon as the danger was past, I found my consciousness floating back into my own body.

"Well, everyone made a big fuss of George; he was the hero of the day, you see? How had he done it?—they all wanted to know, and all he was able to say was that he'd just seemed to stand there watching himself save Sis. And of course he *had* stood there watching it all—through my eyes!"

"I didn't try to explain it, no one would have believed or listened to me anyway, and I didn't really understand it myself—but George was always a bit wary of me from then on. He said nothing, mind you, but I think that even as early as that first time he had an idea . . ."

Suddenly she looked at me closely, frowning. "You're not finding all this a bit too hard to swallow, Love?"

"No," I shook my head. "Not really. I remember reading somewhere of a similar thing between twins—a sort of Corsican Brothers situation."

"Oh, but I've heard of many such!" she quickly answered. "I don't suppose you've read Joachim Feery on the *Necronomicon?*"

"No," I answered. "I don't think so."

"Well, Feery was the illegitimate son of Baron Kant, the German, 'witch-hunter.' He died quite mysteriously in 1934 while still a comparatively young man. He wrote a number of occult limited editions—mostly published at his own expense—the vast majority of which religious and other authorities bought up and destroyed as fast as they appeared. Unquestionably—though it has never been discovered where he saw or read them—Feery's source books were very rare and sinister volumes; among them the *Cthaat Aquadingen,* the *Necronom-icon,* von Junzt's *Unspeakable Cults,* Prinn's *De Vermis Mysteriis,* and others of that sort. Often Feery's knowledge in respect of such books has seemed almost beyond belief. His quotes, while apparently gen-uine and authoritative, often differ substantially when compared with the works from which they were supposedly culled. Regarding such discrepancies, Feery claimed that most of his occult knowledge came to him 'in dreams'!" She paused, then asked: "Am I boring you?"

"Not a bit of it," I answered. "I'm fascinated."

"Well, anyhow," she continued, "as I've said, Feery must some-where have seen one of the very rare copies of Abdul Alhazred's *Necro-nomicon,* in one translation or another, for he published a slim volume of notes concerning that book's contents. I don't own a copy myself but I've read one belonging to a friend of mine, an old member of my group. Alhazred, while being reckoned by many to have been a madman, was without doubt the world's foremost authority on black magic and the horrors of alien dimensions, and he was vastly interested in every facet of freakish phenomena, physical and metaphysical."

She stood up, went to her bookshelf and opened a large modern volume of Aubrey Beardsley's fascinating drawings, taking out a number of loose white sheets bearing lines of her own neat hand-writing.

"I've copied some of Feery's quotes, supposedly from Alhazred. Listen to this one:

> Tis a veritable & attestable Fact, that between certain
> related Persons there exists a Bond more powerful
> than the strongest Ties of Flesh & Family, whereby
> one such Person may be *aware* of all the Pains or Pas-
> sions of one far distant; & further, there are those
> whose skills in such Matters are aided by forbidden
> Knowledge or Intercourse through dark Magic with
> Spirits & Beings of outside Spheres. Of the latter: I

278

have sought them out, both Men & Women, & upon
Examination have in all Cases discovered them to be
Users of Divination, observers of Times, Enchanters,
Witches, Charmers, or Necromancers. All claimed to
work their Wonders through Intercourse with dead &
departed Spirits, but I fear that often such Spirits
were evil Angels, the Messengers of the Dark one &
yet more ancient Evils. Indeed, among them were
some whose Powers were prodigious, who might at
will *inhabit* the Body of another even at a great distance & against the Will & often unbeknown to the
Sufferer of such outrage . . .

She put down the papers, sat back and looked at me quizzically.

"That's all very interesting," I said after a moment, "but hardly
applicable to yourself."

"Oh, but it is, Love," she protested. "I'm George's twin, for one
thing, and for another—"

"But you're no witch or necromancer!"

"No, I wouldn't say so—but I am a 'User of Devinations', and I do
'work my Wonders through Intercourse with dead and departed
Spirits'. That's what spiritualism is all about."

"You mean you actually take this, er, Alhazred and spiritualism and
all seriously?" I deprecated.

She frowned. "No, not Alhazred, not really," she answered after a
moment's thought. "But he is interesting, as you said. As for spiritualism: yes, I *do* take it seriously. Why, you'd be amazed at some of the
vibrations I've been getting these last three weeks or so. *Very* disturbing, but so far rather incoherent; frantic, in fact. I'll track him
down eventually, though—the spirit, I mean . . ."

We sat quietly then, contemplatively for a minute or two. Frankly,
I didn't quite know what to say; but then she went on. "Anyway, we
were talking about George and how I believed that even after that first

279

occasion he had a bit of an idea that I was at the root of the thing. Yes, I really think he did. He said nothing, and yet . . .

"And that's not all, either. It was some time after that day on the beach before Sis could be convinced that she hadn't been saved by me. She was sure it had been me, not George, who pulled her out of the deep water.

"Well, a year or two went by, and school-leaving exams came up. I was all right, a reasonable scholar—I had always been a bookish kid—but poor old George . . ." She shook her head sadly. My uncle, it appeared, had not been too bright.

After a moment she continued. "Dates were set for the exams and two sets of papers were prepared, one for the boys, another for the girls. I had no trouble with my paper, I knew even before the results were announced that I was through easily—but before that came George's turn. He'd been worrying and chewing, cramming for all he was worth, biting his nails down to the elbows and getting nowhere. I was in bed with flu when the day of his exams came round, and I remember how I just lay there fretting over him. He was my brother, after all.

"I must have been thinking of him just a bit too hard, though, for before I knew it there I was, staring down hard at an exam paper, sitting in a class full of boys in the old school!"

" . . . An hour later I had the papers all finished, and then I concentrated myself back home again. This time it was a definite effort for me to find my way back to my own body."

"The house was in an uproar. I was downstairs in my dressing-gown; mother had an arm around me and was trying to console me; father was yelling and waving his arms about like a lunatic. 'The girl's gone *mad!*' I remember him exploding, red faced and a bit frightened."

"Apparently I had rushed downstairs about an hour earlier. I had been shouting and screaming tearfully that I'd miss the exam, and I had wanted to know what I was doing home. And when they had called me *Hester* instead of *George*—! Well, then I had seemed to go completely out of my mind!

"Of course, I had been feverish with flu for a couple of days. That was obviously the answer: I had suddenly reached the height of hitherto unrecognized delirious fever, and now the fever had broken I was going to be all right. That was what they said . . ."

"George eventually came home with his eyes all wide and staring, frightened-looking, and he stayed that way for a couple of days. He avoided me like the plague! But the next week—when it came out about how good his marks were, how easily he had passed his examination papers—well . . ."

"But surely he must have known," I broke in. What few doubts I had entertained were now gone forever. She was plainly not making all of this up.

"But why should he have known, Love? He knew he'd had two pretty nightmarish experiences, sure enough, and that somehow they had been connected with me; but he couldn't possibly know that they had their origin *in* me—that I formed their focus."

"Did he find out, though?"

"Oh, yes, he did," she slowly answered, her eyes seeming to glisten jut a little in the homely evening glow of the room. "And as I've said, that's why he left home in the end. It happened like this:

"I had never been a pretty girl—no, don't say anything, Love. You weren't even a twinkle in your father's eye then, he was only a boy himself, and so you wouldn't know. But at a time of life when most girls only have to pout to set the boys on fire, well, I was only very plain, and I'm probably giving myself the benefit of the doubt at that."

"Anyways, when George was out nights, walking his latest girl, dancing, or whatever, I was always at home on my own with my books. Quite simply, I came to be terribly jealous of my brother. Of course, you don't know him, he had already been gone something like fifteen years when you were born, but George was a handsome lad. Not strong, mind you, but long and lean and a natural for the girls."

"Eventually he found himself a special girlfriend and came to spend all his time with her. I remember being furious because he wouldn't tell me anything about her . . ."

She paused and looked at me and after a while I said, "Uh-huh?" inviting her to go on.

"It was one Saturday night in the spring, I remember, not long after our nineteenth birthday, and George had spent the better part of an hour dandying himself up for this unknown girl. That night he seemed to take a sort of stupid, well, *delight* in spiting me; he refused to answer my questions about his girl or even mention her name. Finally, after he had set his tie straight and slicked his hair down for what seemed like the thousandth time, he dared to wink at me—maliciously, I thought, in my jealousy—as he went out into the night."

"That did it. Something *snapped!* I stamped my foot and rushed upstairs to my room for a good cry. And in the middle of crying I had my idea—"

"You decided to, er, swap identities with your brother, to have a look at his girl for yourself," I broke in. "Am I right?"

She nodded in answer, staring at the fire; ashamed of herself, I thought, after all this time. "Yes I did," she said. "For the first time I used my power for my own ends. And mean and despicable ends they were.

"But this time it wasn't like before. There was no instantaneous, involuntary flowing of my psyche, as it were. No immediate change of personality. I had to force it, to concentrate and concentrate and *push* myself. But in a short period of time, before I even knew it, well, there I was."

"There you were? In Uncle George's body?"

"Yes, in his body, looking out through his eyes, holding in his hand the cool, slender hand of a very pretty girl. I had expected the girl, of course, and yet . . ."

"Confused and blustering, letting go of her hand, I jumped back and bumped into a man standing behind me. The girl was saying:

"George, what's wrong?" in a whisper, and people were staring. We were in a second-show picture-house queue. Finally I managed to mumble an answer, in a horribly hoarse, unfamiliar, frightened voice— George's voice, obviously, and my fear—and then the girl moved closer and kissed me gently on the cheek!

"She did! But of course she would, wouldn't she, if I were George? 'Why, you jumped then like you'd been stung—' she started to say; but I wasn't listening, Peter, for I had jumped again, even more violently, shrinking away from her in a kind of horror. I must have gone crimson, standing there in that queue, with all those unfamiliar people looking at me—*and I had just been kissed by a girl!*"

"You see, I wasn't thinking like George at all! I just wished with all my heart that I hadn't interfered, and before I knew it I had George's body in motion and was running down the road, the picture-house queue behind me and the voice of this sweet little girl echoing after me in pained and astonished disbelief."

"Altogether my spiteful adventure had taken only a few minutes, and, when at last I was able to do so, I controlled myself—or rather, George's self—and hid in a shop doorway. It took another minute or two before I was composed sufficiently to manage a, well, a 'return trip', but at last I made it and there I was back in my room."

"I had been gone no more than seven or eight minutes all told, but I wasn't back to *exactly* where I started out from. Oh, George hadn't gone rushing downstairs again in a hysterical fit, like that time when I sat his exam for him—though of course the period of transition had been a much longer one on that occasion—but he had at least moved off the bed. I found myself standing beside the window . . ." She paused.

"And afterwards?" I prompted her, fascinated.

"Afterwards?" she echoed me, considering it. "Well, George was very quiet about it . . . No, that's not quite true. It's not that he was quiet, rather that he avoided me more than ever, to such an extent that I hardly ever saw him, no more than a glimpse at a time as he came and went. Mother and father didn't notice George's increased coolness towards me, but I certainly did. I'm pretty sure it was then that he had finally recognized the source of this thing that came at odd times like some short-lived insanity to plague him. Yes, looking back, I can see how I might easily have driven George completely insane! But of course, from that time on he was forewarned . . ."

"Forewarned?" I repeated her. "And the next time he—"

"The next time?" She turned her face so that I could see the fine scars on her otherwise smooth left cheek. I had always wondered about those scars. "I don't remember a great deal about the next time, shock, I suppose, a 'mental block', you might call it, but anyway, the next time was the *last* time . . . !"

"There was a boy who took me out once or twice, and I remember that when he stopped calling for me it was because of something George had said to him. Six months had gone by since my shameful and abortive experiment, and now I deliberately put it out of my mind as I determined to teach George a lesson. You must understand, Love, that this boy I mentioned, well . . . he meant a great deal to me.

"Anyway, I was out to get my own back. I didn't know how George had managed to make it up with his girl, but he had. I was going to put an end to their little romance once and for all."

"It was a fairly warm, early October, I remember, when my chance eventually came. A Sunday afternoon, and George was out walking with his girl. I had planned it minutely. I knew exactly what I must say, how I must act, what I must do. I could do it in two minutes flat, and be back in my own body before George knew what was going on. For the first time my intentions were *deliberately* malicious . . ."

I waited for my aunt to continue, and after a while again prompted her: "And? Was this when—"

"Yes, this was when he walked me through the window. Well, he didn't exactly walk me through it, I believe I leapt, or rather, he leapt me, if you see what I mean. One minute I was sitting on a grassy bank with the same sweet little girl, and the next there was this awful pain— my whole body hurt, and it was *my* body, for my consciousness was suddenly back where it belonged. Instantaneously, inadvertently, I was—myself!"

"But I was lying crumpled on the lawn in front of the house! I remember seeing splinters of broken glass and bits of yellow painted wood from my shattered bedroom window, and then I went into a faint with the pain."

"George came to see me in the hospital—once. He sneered when my parents had their backs turned. He leaned over my bed and said: '*Got* you, Hester!' Just that, nothing more.

"I had a broken leg and collarbone. It was three weeks before they let me go home. By then George had joined the Merchant Navy and my parents knew that somehow I was to blame. They were never the same to me from that time on. George had been the apple of the Family Eye, if you know what I mean. They knew that his going away, in some unknown way, had been my fault. I did have a letter from George—well, a note. It simply warned me 'never to do it again', that there were worse things than falling through windows!"

"And you never did, er, do it again?"

"No, I didn't dare; I haven't dared since. There *are* worse things, Love, than being walked through a window! And if George hates me still as much he might . . ."

"But I've often *wanted* to do it again. George has two children, you know?"

I nodded an affirmation: "Yes, I've heard mother mention them. Joe and Doreen?"

"That right," she nodded. "They're hardly children any more, but I think of them that way. They'll be in their twenties now, your cousins. George's wife wrote to me once many years ago. I've no idea how she got my address. She did it behind George's back, I imagine. Said how sorry she was that there was 'trouble in the family'. She sent me photographs of the kids. They were beautiful children. For all I know there may have been other children later—even grandchildren."

"I don't think so," I told her. "I think I would have known. They're still pretty reserved, my folks, but I would have learned that much, I'm sure. But tell me: how is it that you and mother aren't closer? I mean, she never talks about you, my mother, and yet you are her sister."

"Your mother is two years younger than George and me: my aunt informed me. "She went to live with her grandparents down South when she was thirteen. Sis, you see, was the brilliant one. George was a bit dim; I was clever enough; but Sis, she was really clever. Our parents sent Sis off to live with Granny, where she could attend a school worthy of her intelligence. She stayed with Gran from then on. We simply drifted apart . . ."

"Mind you, we'd never been what you might call close, not for sisters. Anyhow, we didn't come together again until she married and came back up here to live, by which time George must have written to her and told her one or two things. I don't know what or how much he told her, but—well, she never bothered with me—and anyway I was working by then and had a flat of my own."

"Years passed, I hardly ever saw Sis, her little boy came along— you, Love—I fell in with a spiritualist group, making real friends for the first time in my life; and, well, that was that. My interest in spiritualism, various other ways of mine that didn't quite fit the accepted pattern, the unspoken *thing* I had done to George, we drifted apart. You understand?"

I nodded. I felt sorry for her, but of course I could not say so. Instead I laughed awkwardly and shrugged my shoulders. "Who needs people?"

She looked shocked. "We all do, Love!" Then for a while she was quiet, staring into the fire.

"I'll make a brew of tea," she suddenly said, then looked at me and smiled in a fashion I well remembered. "Or should we have cocoa?"

"Cocoa!" I instinctively laughed, relieved at the change of subject.

She went into the kitchen and I lit a cigarette. Idle, for the moment, I looked about me, taking up the loose sheets of paper that Aunt Hester had left on her occasional table. I saw at once that many of her jottings were concerned with extracts from exotic books. I passed over the piece she had read out to me and glanced at another sheet. Immediately my interest was caught; the three passages were all from the Holy Bible:

> Regard not them that have familiar spirits, neither seek after wizards, to be defiled by them." Lev. 19:31.

> "Then said Saul unto his servants, Seek me a woman that hath a familiar spirit, that I may go to her and enquire of her. And his servants said to him, Behold, there is a woman that hath a familiar spirit at En-dor." 1 Sam. 28:6,7.

> "Many of them also which used curious arts brought their books together, and burned them before all men." Acts 19:19.

The third sheet contained a quote from *Today's Christian:*

> To dabble in matters such as these is to reach within demoniac circles, and it is by no means rare to discover scorn and skepticism transformed to hysterical possession in persons whose curiosity has led them merely to attend so-called 'spiritual séances'. These things of which I speak are of a nature as serious as any in the world today, and I am only one among many to utter a solemn warning against any intercourse with 'spirit forces' or the like, whereby the unutterable evil of demonic possession could well be the horrific outcome.

Finally, before she returned with a steaming jug of cocoa and two mugs, I read another of Aunt Hester's extracts, this one again from Feery's *Notes on the Necronomicon:*

> Yea, & I discovered how one might, be he an Adept
> & his familiar Spirits powerful enough, control the
> Wanderings or Migration of his Essence into all
> manner of Beings & Persons—even from beyond the
> Grave of Sod or the Door of the Stone Sepulchre . . .

I was still pondering this last extract an hour later, as I walked Harden's night streets towards my lodgings at the home of my friend. Three evenings later, when by arrangement I returned to my aunt's cottage in old Castle-Ilden, she was nervously waiting for me at the gate and whisked me breathlessly inside. She sat me down, seated herself opposite and clasped her hands in her lap almost in the attitude of an excited young girl.

"Peter, Love, I've had an idea, such a simple idea that it amazes me I never thought of it before."

"An idea? How do you mean, Aunt Hester, what sort of idea? Does it involve me?"

"Yes, I'd rather it were you than any other. After all, you know the story now . . ."

I frowned as an oddly foreboding shadow darkened latent areas of my consciousness. Her words had been innocuous enough as of yet, and there seemed no reason why I should suddenly feel so— *uncomfortable,* but—

"The story?" I finally repeated her. "You mean this idea of yours concerns—Uncle George?"

"Yes, I do!" she answered. "Oh, Love, I can *see* them; if only for a brief moment or two, I can see my nephew and niece. You'll help me? I know you will."

The shadow thickened darkly, growing in me, spreading from hidden to more truly conscious regions of my mind. "Help you? You mean you intend to—" I paused, then started to speak again as I saw for sure what she was getting at and realized that she meant it: "But haven't you said that this stuff was too dangerous? The last time you—"

"Oh, yes, I know," she impatiently argued, cutting me off. "But now, well, it's different. I won't stay more than a moment or two—just long enough to see the children—and then I'll get straight back . . . *here*. And there'll be precautions. It can't fail, you'll see."

"Precautions?" Despite myself I was interested.

"Yes," she began to talk faster, growing more excited with each passing moment. "The way I've worked it out, it's perfectly safe. To start with, George will be asleep—he won't know anything about it. When his sleeping mind moves into my body, why, it will simply stay asleep! On the other hand, when *my* mind moves into *his* body, then I'll be able to move about and—"

"And use your brother as a keyhole!" I blurted, surprising even myself. She frowned, then turned her face away. What she planned was wrong. I knew it and so did she, but if my outburst had shamed her it certainly had not deterred her—not for long.

When she looked at me again her eyes were almost pleading. "I know how it must look to you, Love, but it's not so. And I know that I must seem to be a selfish woman, but that's not quite true either. Isn't it natural that I should want to see my family? They are mine, you know. George, my brother; his wife, my sister-in-law; their children, my nephew and niece. Just a—yes—a 'peep', if that's the way you see it. But, Love, I *need* that peep. I'll only have a few moments, and I'll have to make them last me for the rest of my life."

I began to weaken. "How will you go about it?"

"First, a glance," she eagerly answered, again reminding me of a young girl. "Nothing more, a mere glance. Even if he's awake he won't ever know I was there; he'll think his mind wandered for the merest second. If he *is* asleep, though, then I'll be able to, well, 'wake him up', see his wife—and, if the children are still at home, why, I'll be able to see them too. Just a glance."

"But suppose something does go wrong?" I asked bluntly, coming back to earth. "Why, you might come back and find your head in the gas oven! What's to stop him from slashing your wrists? That only takes a second, you know."

"That's where you come in, Love." She stood up and patted me on the cheek, smiling cleverly. "You'll be right here to see that nothing goes wrong."

"But—"

"And to be doubly sure," she cut me off, "why, *I'll be tied in my chair!* You can't walk through windows when you're tied down, now can you?"

❋ ❋ ❋

Half an hour later, still suffering inwardly from that as yet unspecified foreboding, I had done as Aunt Hester directed me to do, tying her wrists to the arms of her cane chair with soft but fairly strong bandages from her medicine cabinet in the bathroom.

She had it all worked out, reasoning that it would be very early morning in Australia and that her brother would still be sleeping. As soon as she was comfortable, without another word, she closed her eyes and let her head fall slowly forward onto her chest. Outside, the sun still had some way to go to setting; inside, the room was still warm—yet I shuddered oddly with a deep, nervous chilling of my blood.

It was then that I tried to bring the thing to a halt, calling her name and shaking her shoulder, but she only brushed my hand away and hushed me. I went back to my chair and watched her anxiously.

As the shadows seemed visibly to lengthen in the room and my skin cooled, her head sank even deeper onto her chest, so that I began to think she had fallen asleep. Then she settled herself more comfortably yet and I saw that she was still awake, merely preparing her body for her brother's slumbering mind.

In another moment I knew something had changed. Her position was as it had been; the shadows crept slowly still; the ancient clock on the wall ticked its regular chronological message; but I had grown inexplicably colder, and there was this feeling that *something* had changed . . .

Suddenly there flashed before my mind's eye certain of those warning jottings I had read only a few nights earlier, and there and then I was determined that this thing should go no further. Oh, she had warned me not to do anything to frighten or disturb her, but this was different. Somehow I knew that if I didn't act now—

"Hester! Aunt Hester!" I jumped up and moved towards her, my throat dry and my words cracked and unnatural-sounding. And she lifted her head and opened her eyes.

For a moment I thought that everything was all right—then . . .

She cried out and stood up, ripped bandages falling in tatters from strangely strong wrists. She mouthed again, staggering and patently disorientated. I fell back in dumb horror, knowing that something was very wrong and yet unable to put my finger on the trouble.

My aunt's eyes were wide now and bulging, and for the first time she seemed to see me, stumbling towards me with slack jaw and tongue protruding horribly between long teeth and drawn-back lips. It was then I knew what was wrong, that this frightful *thing* before me was not my aunt, and I was driven backward before its stumbling approach, warding it off with waving arms and barely articulate cries.

Finally, stumbling more frenziedly now, clawing at empty air inches in front of my face, she—it—spoke: "No!" the awful voice gurgled over its wriggling tongue. "No, Hester, you . . . you *fool!* I warned you . . ."

And in that same instant I saw not an old woman, but the horribly alien figure of *a man in a woman's form!*

More grotesque than any drag artist, the thing pirouetted in grim, constricting agony, its strange eyes glazing even as I stared in a paralysis of horror. Then it was all over and the frail scarecrow of flesh, purple tongue still protruding from frothing lips, fell in a crumpled heap to the floor.

❈   ❈   ❈

That's it, that's the story—not a tale I've told before, for there would have been too many questions, and it's more than possible that my version would not be believed. Let's face it, who *would* believe me? No, I realized this as soon as the thing was done, and so I simply got rid of the torn bandages and called in a doctor. Aunt Hester died of a heart attack, or so I'm told, and perhaps she did—straining to do that which, even with her powers, should never have been possible.

During this last fortnight or so since it happened, I've been trying to convince myself that the doctor was right (which I was quite willing enough to believe at the time), but I've been telling myself lies. I think I've known the real truth ever since my parents got the letter from Australia. And lately, reinforcing that truth, there have been the dreams and the daydreams—*or are they?*

This morning I woke up to a lightless void, a numb, black, silent void, wherein I was incapable of even the smallest movement, and I was horribly, hideously frightened. It lasted for only a moment, that's all, but in that moment it seemed to me that I was dead, or that the living Me inhabited a dead body!

Again and again I find myself thinking back on the mad Arab's words as reported by Joachim Feery: '. . . even from beyond the Grave of Sod . . .' And in the end I know that this is indeed the answer.

That is why I'm flying tomorrow to Australia. Ostensibly I'm visiting my uncle's wife, my Australian aunt; but really I'm only interested in him, in Uncle George himself. I don't know what I'll be able to do, or even if there is anything I *can* do. My efforts may well be completely useless, and yet I must try to do something.

I *must* try, for I know now that it's that or find myself once again, perhaps permanently, locked in that hellish, knighted—place?—of black oblivion and insensate silence. In the dead and rotting body of my Uncle George, already buried three weeks when Aunt Hester put her mind in his body—*the body she's now trying to vacate in favour of mine!*

OUR LADY OF
THE SHADOWS

Tony Richards

In any other city in the world, the discovery of Mary-Jane Palmer's body floating in the river would have been sad, and disquieting, that was all. A four-line filler on the inside pages of the daily newspapers. A minor tragedy passed over like a dead bird in the road. But this was Paris, the river was the Seine, and because of that the proceedings were tinted with a vague gothic suggestion of romance. A small crowd gathered—middle-aged businessmen in their sleek, well-filled suits; art students and booksellers in striped t-shirts and wrap-around sunglasses, hair combed back like solid strands of crude oil; a few tourists; a few old women with faces wrinkled like contour maps. The gendarmerie arrived in a buzzing blue van and kept their siren going long after it was necessary, as though to add to the occasion. Plump, moustachioed, holsters gleaming, they walked around the body and gazed at it through squinted eyes.

L'amour, they muttered.
L'amour.
Until they turned her over.
And saw her face . . .

�֎   ✷   ✷

She was lost. Well and truly so. There is an area on the right bank of the city, wedged between the République and L'Ile de la Cité, which is quite comprehensible by day, yet which becomes beyond nightfall an insufficiently-lit mesh of narrow dank streets and cobbled alleys. Every shutter remains tightly closed, and small gargoyles leer, from the roofs of the eighteenth-century houses, at anyone who scurries by. They leered now at Mary-Jane Palmer. She tried to avoid their gaze.

She had seen no one since she had left the main road. It must have been quarter of an hour now.

Her camera swung uselessly at her side.

Her blonde hair was dropping across her forehead in damp, lank strands.

All she could hear were her own uncomfortable high heels marking time on the ancient cobbles. She wished, wished to God, that Ginny was there.

She and Ginny Layner had completed their first year at Berkeley that summer, had decided to go with the money they'd saved on a three-month tour of Europe. They had loved Athens, revelled in Spain, breathed the ice-and-pine thin oxygen of Switzerland as though it were the world's most expensive perfume. And fallen out in Turin over some ludicrous argument. Ginny had tried to fix her up with an obese, sweaty, oversexed perhaps-millionaire, as a joke. Mary-Jane had continued on her own to Paris.

After arriving at seven o'clock, and dining slowly at an overpriced café, she had decided, at eleven ten, to walk to Notre Dame Cathedral and take a few pictures before the floodlights were turned out. And now . . .

She turned another corner. Then another.

And saw the grey-cloaked woman.

She stopped dead. Her mouth hung open like a slack elastic band. She could hear the words forming in her mind, *Pardon, madame, mais*

. . . yet some instinct halted her, the words would not come out. Could not. The woman in the cloak seemed as unassailable by the outside world as though she had been screened by sheets of two-inch glass.

The kind of glass scientists watched dangerous experiments through.

The kind of glass Hitler had crouched behind in his bullet-proof limousine.

That enclosed. That encysted. That oblivious.

For Mary-Jane Palmer, the night was just beginning.

※　※　※

It repeated itself, with stark cinematographic perfection, three times in her nightmares before dawn. As though, even while her body sought the foetal escape of sleep, her mind was still working like a stupid, quiet computer, trying to understand what it had seen.

Deep down in the cellar.

Before she had turned and run.

Repeat—

The woman floating by like a grey patch of mist suspended just above the cobblestones, moving in a direct straight line towards the most ancient of all the houses, at the far end of the street.

Mary-Jane, standing in the shadows by the corner like a rigid doll, watching. And then . . . breaking loose, deciding she was being ridiculous, going to follow the woman and ask her the way. Except the woman was far ahead by now.

The house, raising itself like an animal, looming to devour the suddenly tiny figure of the woman as she glided towards the front door. She turned aside at the final moment, slipped through a gate in the iron railings fronting the house and hurried down the stone stairs. At this distance, Mary-Jane could not tell whether her shoes made any sound or not. The area was silent, the street was tall and narrow, echoey; she *should* have been able to tell.

Pardon, *madame*. Concentrate on that, Mary-Jane Palmer, idiot, nervous American tourist from Idaho. *Pardon, madame, mais je suis perdue.*

Deep in the darkness below the house, a door came open, then swung sharply closed.

Mary-Jane got to the railings half a minute after that, followed her softly down. There were windows down there, with grilles across, but no light had appeared in them in all that time.

How can she *live* like this? By the time Mary-Jane had reached the bottom, she was walking not on stone but on a caked-solid mass of garbage and dead leaves. It had not rained in Europe all that month, and yet here it remained sewer-moist, the smell was unbelievable. The entire façade of the house, she noted, was rotted as a cheap wooden mask.

She was just about to lose her nerve when the light appeared inside and she found herself—edging across to the first pane of glass—wiping aside the dust—staring in at—the six cloaked figures grouped around the altar—the single candle on it—the far blank wall of solid brick—except—the light must have been playing tricks— there *must* have been a door—*had* to—because—suddenly there was a seventh figure in the room—shorter than the rest—cloak the black of vacuums—who—raised her head. Eyes like dust pits, face as white as maggots. And then there was the turning and the running and the panicked flight, and

Mary-Jane Palmer awoke.

She was in her Parisian hotel room in bed, the sheets soaked with sweat and her neck twisted against the bolster. The morning sunlight was pouring in through her curtains. Traffic was humming beyond them. Yet the after-image of that face remained. She went to the bathroom, and was sick.

※　※　※

Breakfast was fresh croissants and black chicoried coffee, served on a gleaming white tablecloth by a respectful concierge. She felt more human by the time she was brushing the crumbs off her napkin; the incident of the night before had paled into a semi-dream experience to be stored away under *inexplicable happenings abroad*. She caught a glimpse of her own reflection in the silvered coffee pot, a healthy college girl at the end of her teens with long flaxen hair and beautiful extreme blue eyes looked back at her, smiling. The camera was lying on the table next to her empty cup. She snatched it up, slung it over her shoulder and went, almost at a run, to catch the nearest bus. She was going to see Notre Dame properly this time.

Paris burned under a sun like white sheet metal. The shops were bursting, the traffic snarled, and by the time the bus had rattled and jostled down to the Seine, Mary-Jane felt that the city had taken her in its great frantic stride and accepted her. She walked face on into a cooling breeze along the riverbank. Old men were playing cards beneath the shadow of a clump of trees and, somewhere far away, a busker with a clarinet could be heard above the traffic. A plane soared high towards the east, leaving a white plume of smoke against the cloudless azure sky.

And then it loomed in sight beyond the next parade of trees. Notre Dame. The Cathedral of Our Lady of the City of Paris. Even on this most brilliant of summer days, it seemed to snatch and absorb the light with cold disdainful grandeur.

Mary-Jane stopped a moment, sucked in a breath, before the tourist in her took over; then she was hugging the camera to her eye, snapping off half a dozen pictures, dimly aware that not one of them could recreate the building's incredible first impact. She hurried across the short bridge to the island, found the cathedral's main entrance.

Stepped inside.

Into a dim coolness that had persisted, enclosed from the sun, for eight hundred years. Into a temple so created by a people who believed in an awesome, omnipotent, terrifying God that the great stone pillars lanced up into impenetrable shadow long before they reached the roof, the candles flickering in the alcoves seemed to cast no light at all, each tiny footstep echoed back like the tread of something inhumanly vast. The air seemed as chill and damp as an undersea cavern. The shadows seemed to breathe.

She had seen the homes of dead gods in Athens and Rome. But nothing, *nothing,* to challenge this. As her eyes adjusted, she could see scattered amongst the pews a few local people praying. All of them women, middle-aged or old. They seemed tiny as infants in the vastness of the place. She thought, *If God truly does exist—*

"—then he lives in Notre Dame," completed a quiet voice behind her.

She spun around, bewildered.

The man she ended up facing was at least six foot two, slim, early thirties, smiling at her beneath the opaque black of his sunglasses. Hair pale as though it had come out of a bottle; dressed in a morning-grey suit, navy tie, crisp white shirt; cufflinks gleamed. Only the black plastic discs over his eyes seemed forbidding.

"How did you know what I was thinking?"

"Same thing I think every time I come here. Besides, your lips were moving."

She smiled gently. "I do that every time I think something important."

Why was she telling him this?

"My name is Michael Levant," he was saying. "I was born in Calgary, in Canada, but I've lived here the last ten years. I know this city inside out, and I love it. You can call me Everyman. As in," and the statement became a question, "Everyman, I will go with thee, and be thy guide?"

She leaned against a pillar. "That's the smoothest pick up I've ever heard."

"No strings. Promise."

"Even smoother. In a cathedral, for God's sake!"

She said that last piece far too loud. Close by, a kneeling, shawled old woman turned savagely around and shushed her, eyes blazing.

"That's the look," Michael Levant said, "you'll get all over Paris.

Just another foreign tourist, bumbling around the major sights, making a nuisance of herself, and never, ever, getting close to the heartbeat of the city unless . . ." He let the sentence hang.
Extended his hand.
And said quietly:
"Shall we go?"

⁂   ⁂   ⁂

She did not like him. She realized that in the first half hour. He had a small yellow Citroën which he drove like a maniac, dodging furiously, stamping on the brake at every light. When they walked, he strode ahead and she had to hurry to keep up with him. And he would not look at what she wanted to see. But by that time she had told him her name, age, where she had come from. And the hotel she was staying at. Why? Why had she come with him at all? Perhaps because he fascinated her at first. Perhaps too, because of the vague sensation she had felt first looking at him, that she had seen him somewhere before. Curiosity.

It persisted. Cool and tall as an icicle, he seemed to have a drawing effect on other people but herself. Not the Parisian young. He was just another executive type to them, fashion or advertising maybe, on his way to his forties and a duodenal ulcer to prove it. But old enough to remember, perhaps, the last war, like the crooked old man who kept his eyes averted as he served them coffee in the Tulleries. Like, in the cigarette kiosk, the gaunt grey-haired woman who had snapped at her last three customers, slammed their change down. Who handed Levant his pack of *disque bleu* carefully as though it were glass. Curiosity. Ginny would have laughed.

And abruptly stopped laughing when they were walking along the Champs Elysées, towards the Place de L'Etoile. She saw the sneer on Levant's face even before he spoke, and *knew* it was going to be something nasty.

"Look at that."

Across the way was a McDonald's burger stand hemmed in by two cinemas. *Bruce Lee—Fist of Fury*, read one placard, and *Goldie Hawn est 'Private Benjamin'* the other.

"This city's changed, even in the time I've lived here. Give it another twenty years and it'll look like downtown Dallas. Fast food, fast culture, everything the same and bland. The great American disease, spreading across the world like a neon plague."

And Mary-Jane, who had been looking for an excuse to get really angry for the past hour, practically shouted, "*I'm* American."

"You're different."

Oh my *God*.

"You have such beautiful blue eyes."

She backed away from him, made a pretence of looking at her wristwatch. It was already noon. "Look, Mr. Levant, thanks all the same, but I really have to be going."

"Where? You're alone."

"I just . . ."

She turned and started to walk away. And he grabbed hold of her wrist.

His grip was very cool and smooth, as though his hand had been cast out of metal. He was hurting her. Mary-Jane struggled, could not break free. Subsided, staring at him numbly. No one had ever grabbed her like that before.

"I'm sorry," he said, gently. "I've offended you."

"It's okay. Please just—"

"I really do like you, you know. I ought to make it up to you somehow."

She had never looked at him quite so hard before. He had never stood so straight, his shoulders set at such an angle, his body poised expectantly. Again, the feeling came that she had seen him before. A crazy idea stole into the margins of her consciousness.

"I'll pick you up at eight from your hotel," he said. "Take you out for a *real* Parisian dinner."

She nodded quickly, *anything* to get rid of him. "Fine. Great."

"You promise you'll be there?"

"Sure, I promise."

And then there was the turning and the hurrying away, for the second time in twenty-four hours. She seemed to spend her entire life in this city turning and running. I'm *sure* I've seen him. *Sure.*

By eight o'clock she was left in no doubt. Towards evening, a thunderstorm had gathered over Paris, the rain came down in great tumbling warm drops and when, hiding at the rear of the lobby, she saw Michael Levant walk in, he was wearing a long grey trenchcoat draped over the shoulders of his suit. He looked around puzzledly, went to the desk and had her room buzzed, waited for another fifteen minutes. From behind, with the coat draped around him, she was certain.

The cloak. The cellar. The huddled people. He was one of them.

※　※　※

In the dream, she was not alone in the hotel room that night.

A black shape resolving itself from the walls—the same black shape she had seen the night before—the woman—shorter than the rest— wrapped in black cloaks—bat black—death black—moving towards her—gliding towards her—staring—out of—eyes like dust pits—face as white as maggots—closer now—and the eyes—some nocolour thing whirling in their depths—bottomless—and the face—ghastly crawling ancient—and diseased—and corrupted—held together only by its expression   of—something—deeper—than—pain—something— worse—than—agony—the face of a prisoner locked in a centuries old cell—of an explorer lost forever underground—forever—looming closer—and—the woman—reached out one hand—fingers like white worms—nails sharp as blades—and—touched her on the arm.

Mary-Jane Palmer snapped back into wakefulness.

She sat up in bed. The travel alarm on the cabinet clicked towards three in the morning. It was unaccountably chill in the room; there was the faint smell of something gone bad, of formaldehyde and ozone and dead meat. Mary-Jane got up and went to the window. She twitched back the curtain, peered out. A car was going by on the street below, and in the sudden pale sweep of its headlights, Mary-Jane saw them, all six of them. Dressed in grey. Immobile in the shadows between the age old streetlamps. Smiling. Staring up at her.

※　※　※

When the concierge came to open her desk at six thirty, Mary-Jane was already there waiting, cases packed.

"I'm checking out. I'd like my passport, please."

"Mademoiselle—?"

"My passport, dammit! *Passeport! Maintenant!* NOW!"

The concierge eyed her strangely and made tiny movements with her hands. "Mademoiselle, that is impossible. You did not hear? We have an—*voleur*—a burglary last night. Everything from the safety-box is gone. No passport."

"That's ridiculous! You're *lying!*"

"Mademoiselle?"

"What the hell am I supposed to *do?*"

"I am sorry, mademoiselle."

"You *are* lying, aren't you? Oh, for God's sake, can I at least, *please,* use your phone?"

Her hand was trembling as she dialled the first number. The concierge was standing at the far end of the desk, watching, her face a mask, until Mary-Jane glared at her and she sniffed and went away. The conversation with the American Consulate was brief. A provisional exit visa would take four days to prepare, and did she *know* how many tourists got into a bind this time of year? Four days! She slammed down the handset. There were tears starting in her eyes. For a moment she contemplated phoning Idaho, *Mom? Dad? Come and take me home!* But they had been silently against this trip, and if she came running to them now like a frightened little girl, she would never, ever, be totally independent again, she would shrink in her eyes and theirs to the size of a freckled helpless moppet, and that would remain with her all of her life. She rubbed her eyes, took a deep breath, and phoned the police.

It took two hours for the detective to arrive. His name was Duconnchamp; a man in his fifties, face, beneath his thinning hair, as shapeless as his raincoat. When Mary-Jane saw him approach, her first thought was, *No! Not an older man. Not someone Levant can get at.*

Now he was sitting opposite her in the lobby, sucking on the gnawed end of his pencil. He regarded her through bored brown eyes.

"This man Levant?" he asked her in good English. "He spoke to you for how long, in the cathedral?"

"I'm not sure. I think, a couple of minutes."

"Do you always go off with strange men after just a couple of minutes?"

She became acutely aware of the other people in the lobby. She wanted to hide, to disappear. *She* had become the guilty one. There was no way to explain. "I don't know. I—he—had this kind of *drawing* effect, I couldn't look away from him. He spoke so quietly. He—I just don't know. Are you *implying* something?"

Duconnchamp's gaze flickered back down to his notebook. "And you say that he came here to the hotel at eight, and then again at three o'clock?"

"He was outside at three, with the others."

"On the pavement?"

"Yes."

"At three in the morning?"

"*Yes!*"

He jotted something down. What was the French for *hysterical?* Mary-Jane wondered coldly.

"*Six* of them . . . What did this Levant tell you about himself?"

"Nothing, really. Just that he came from Calgary ten years ago."

"From Calgary? He is Jesus come down from the cross, perhaps?"

"From Calgary in *Canada,* for God's sake! Look, I know you think I'm crazy, but could you at least check him out? That shouldn't be too difficult, should it?"

Duconnchamp seemed to consider that a moment. Then he heaved himself out of the worn leather armchair, wandered across to the phone and spent ten minutes talking on it, punctuating his conversation with wary glances at Mary-Jane. When he finally came back, he was shaking his head.

"There is no record of a Michael Levant being admitted to this country."

"So what are you going to do? What am *I* going to do?"

He shrugged. "Change your hotel. Be careful of strangers. Give me a call if you see him again." His gaze became almost benign, paternal. "May I make a suggestion? Paris is the most beautiful city in the world if you give it half a chance. Of course, you are alone, and far from home, and things tend to get—in your mind, *you* know, but one unpleasant man does not make an unpleasant city. It is only fear which makes it so. And there is nothing to be afraid of."

"I'll make a note of that," said Mary-Jane.

※　※　※

It was becoming warm and bright again, the rainwater of the previous evening quietly vanishing away until only the deepest puddles remained and the city smelled freshly-laundered. Rejuvenated, Mary-Jane thought, from the window of her new hotel room on the Avenue de L'Opéra. She had planned to remain hidden in her room until the exit visa showed. But it was a tiny room, decorated in drab brown with a ghastly cast iron cross over the bed, and leaning over the window ledge she could see—an old woman selling balloons; a busker, complete with tame monkey, grinding an original barrel-organ; three young women so beautiful, so stylishly dressed, that they *had* to be models on the way to an assignment; a gendarme arguing with a motorist; thirty, she counted, tiny schoolchildren walking double file; scurrying businessmen; lounging students; life. The street was awash with sunlight. Trees rustled in the breeze. And perhaps Duconnchamp had been right, and there wasn't that much to be afraid of. What if she had only *dreamt* going to the window?

By one o'clock, she was out on the street again. Moving quickly, glancing around her timid as a deer, but out nonetheless.

And, as she walked, as she toured the sights, something Michael Levant had said came back to her. Three schoolchildren hurried by wearing plastic masks, Chewbacca and R2-D2 and Luke Skywalker. There were posters everywhere, now she looked, advertising Coca-Cola and Dr. Pepper's and Ronald McDonald and Marlboro and Kellog's and Hubba-Bubba bubble gum. A hot dog stall outside the Sorbonne. A video shop—Burt Reynolds swaggered across the display screen.

Down by the river, half a block of grey, beautiful hundred-year-old houses had been cleared to provide space for a featureless glass tower block.

"Like downtown Dallas," Michael Levant had said.

It was as though a silent, deadly war were being waged between ancient and modern, old and new. And if there was a war, who were the soldiers? Who the generals?

In the square in front of the Eiffel Tower, a large crowd had gathered to watch a street-theatre company perform. Mary-Jane was approaching it, hoping she was not too late to watch the act, when a ripple passed through the massed people, they were parting for someone who moved as smooth and fluidly as though there were no one blocking the way. Mary-Jane caught a glimpse of coiffed red hair, a pale grey blouse and skirt, before the woman was lost from sight.

And on the Pont Royal, she glanced to the next bridge to see a shorter, dark, grey-suited man standing against the far railings, staring in the opposite direction across Paris as if, by staring hard enough, he

305

could devour it. He was one of the six she had seen last night—she was positive.

She confined her tour to the churches now, as though some medieval race-memory impelled her towards sanctuary. Large or small, the pattern was the same in each. Rows of slim red candles, smoking faintly, barely making an impression on the gloom. The altar, cold and lifeless as a gravestone. The priest, weary looking, gazing out of tired eyes for a vision which would not manifest itself. And the women, the ageing, praying women.

At last, Mary-Jane found herself in a tiny chapel off the Avenue Montaigne. She stared at the plaster statue of the Virgin Mary, but it was just a statue, that was all. And the cross above it—nothing more than a powerless piece of brass. The sad, exhausted old women were in their pews, kneeling, fumbling their prayer-beads, muttering. Muttering. *Who are you praying to?* Mary-Jane wanted to shout. *What are you praying for? The return of an age that's gone forever? The resurgence of quiet and gentility and accordions on the street and Maurice goddamn Chevalier? Well they won't help you! The gods here couldn't grant your wishes if they tried! You need new gods! Different gods!*

And she could not get it out of her mind.

Different gods. Different rites and rituals and holy places.

The altar, in the cellar beneath the ancient house.

Different holy places. Different cathedrals and churches and chapels and—crypts.

The altar, beneath the house.

※   ※   ※

It was drawing towards evening when Mary-Jane stepped out of the taxicab onto the cobbled street. She paid the young driver, she had specifically chosen a *young* driver, and tipped him heavily for his effort; he had been tirelessly scouring every street for the past hour. The cab made a puttering noise as it moved away. The shadows were lengthening in the dying, ochre sunlight, enveloping the cobbles like a closing fist.

The house loomed, massively, above her.

Mary-Jane wavered a moment, listening to the hoots and rumble of the homegoing traffic, far away. Then she descended the steps towards the cellar.

The carpet of refuse had turned to mud by now; it slopped around her ankles. The door was firmly locked. Mary-Jane went to the space on the window she had wiped clean the night before, widened the smear and looked in. The cellar was featureless and empty save for the altar. The candle on it, melted to stub, was black. She went back up, and around to the side of the house.

And found a window where the shutter was hanging loose, there was a smash in the pane just wide enough to allow her hand through to the latch. She slipped off her shoes before she crawled inside, so as to not leave muddy footprints on the floor.

Her mother would have been proud of her, she reflected.

She had expected the inside of the house to be as featureless as the cellar. Instead, she found herself in a completely furnished room. Louis Quinze, she thought the style was called. *Original* Louis Quinze, blanketed beneath a layer of dust and cobwebs which only allowed the most occasional glimpse of rich red velvet, sparkling gold brocade. A crystal chandelier, made, if that were possible, even more ornate by the attentions of over a hundred years of spiders, tinkled softly overhead, casting shadows. The huge Turkish carpet was coated with grey powder. Mary-Jane could tell from the smell in the air, even before she noticed that the only footprints were her own, that the lounge had not been entered in decades. Perhaps centuries.

She opened the door very slowly, trembling as it creaked. The marbled hallway was deserted. The house was as dangerously still as a predatory animal holding its breath. Her shoes still dangling from her hand, she crept through into the next room down the passageway.

Which had been used. Which had been cleaned. Which contained a smell far worse than the one in the lounge. The same odour she had noticed in her hotel room last night. Formaldehyde and ozone and dead meat. At least, that was what her senses registered, trying to break into comprehensible form an odour so alien it set every alarm in her body screaming. The room was heavy with it. She could feel it start clinging to her clothes and hair the moment she walked in.

It was a library.

Except . . . the walls were painted black. The slats of light coming in through the shutters seemed like bars across some ghastly Bastille cell.

There were seven of the portraits, there against the far wall of the room. One was the red-haired woman, one was the shorter, dark man. Three were the three others she had seen from her hotel window.

The sixth—

—She found herself closing the door behind her without knowing why. She felt as though she were moving through syrup. Time had turned to syrup. The world had slowed its spinning to a crawl—

The sixth was Michael Levant.

If you removed the wig. If you removed the eighteenth-century clothing. The same went for the others. Devoid of their pale grey, modern clothes, they were fanatical peacocks, embroidered in silk, hardened at the edges by jewellery and rings, massive flashing gems. Whoever the long-dead artist had been, he had managed to capture their grandeur and stark arrogance perfectly—or perhaps, like a physical force, it had simply imprinted itself on the canvas. That strong. That overwhelming.

But if Mary-Jane had shrunk before any of them, it would have been the seventh, at the direct centre with Michael Levant to its right. A woman. Incredibly beautiful. High cheekbones. Full lips. Skin wondrously pale. Green eyes which stared out of that inhuman beauty like the eyes of a tiger staring from the undergrowth, like the eyes of a closing shark. Mary-Jane Palmer felt sick.

She dragged herself away from the portraits, to another wall filled with books. Dragged one of the largest from its shelf and, dropping her shoes, put it down on a desk. She flipped through the brittle yellow, handwritten pages quickly. And perhaps she was mistaken, her poor French was to blame. But it seemed to be some kind of ledger, taxes, levies, payments, dues, records of properties owned, establishments controlled, debts to be collected, and if it *was* that, then these people had secretly once owned half of Paris. She practically strained her shoulders returning it to its place. When she opened the next, a much smaller black one, she saw that it was printed and illustrated. The illustrations were obscene. She closed it quickly. And repeated the pattern most of the way along the shelf. Someone might have paid a fortune for such a large collection on the single subject of black magic.

La Force de la Vie, read one spine high above which caught her eye.

The Force of Life.

By Michel Le Vant.

The insane ramblings of a man who should have been dead centuries ago. Mary-Jane picked through it as best she could.

It is not the (something) *of the heart, the movement of the* (lungs?), *the* (untranslatable) *which makes the difference between life and death. Rather, it is a* (power?) *which* (untranslatable) *and solid. If this is true, if this* (untranslatable), *then* (surely?) *it is possible to make a—'*

Out in the hallway, there was the rattling of a key in the front door.

The black room seemed to narrow in on Mary-Jane. Squeezed her. Trapped her. And it was not so much that she froze—she was incapable of movement. God, if she could only hear something but her own thumping heart.

Footsteps on the marble.

Two voices began a conversation. Both men spoke perfect French, but one of them she recognized as Michael Levant.

"Are you sure?"

"Of course I'm sure," Levant said. "She's the one. She has the—"

What was that word? Flame?

They were coming closer to the library door.

The men were speaking too quickly now, Mary-Jane could not translate. All she caught was something from Levant about the cathedral. *We shall see Notre Dame again,* or perhaps she had got it wrong. She could not think straight, was almost fainting. Her consciousness was curling up and hiding where her body could not. She was going to die.

The footsteps paused a few yards from the library door. Then, she could hear both men going up the marble stairs. She caught two more words from Levant.

Cette nuit.

Tonight.

After that, she was moving for the window, fumbling with the shutters. And then there was the turning and the running. Harder, and faster, and more furiously, than she had ever run in her life.

❖ ❖ ❖

Running. The city swirled around her, blind as a tornado. Running.

"What do you *mean*, the bus is full?"

The balding man in the ticket office stared at her with eyes of stone, shifted his cigar from one cheek to the other. Then he reached up, and pulled a black blind down across the front of the booth.

Running.

"I have to be out of this city *tonight!*"

There was an air traffic controllers' strike. There had been no strike this afternoon, but now there was one. The bespectacled lady at the information desk shrugged and turned away from her.

Running.

She hurried towards the Gare du Nord. Rounded the corner, and slid to a sudden halt. The red-haired woman and the short, dark man were casually waiting one either side of the station's entrance. She paused a moment, numb with fear and desperation, before moving back into the shadows.

The night had closed in around Mary-Jane, stealing up on her while she was not looking. Paris glowed like a swarm of fireflies, like a shoal of iridescent fish beneath some deep grey sea. The Champs Elysées glittered like a vast tiara; Sacré Coeur, high on its hilltop, burned pure white against its floodlights. The most beautiful city in the world. The City of Light. And yet, between the individual lights which made up that one vast brightness, there were insular patches of dark. And it was to that dark that Mary-Jane confined herself, scuttling like a crab along the crowded sidewalks. Running.

Throngs of people jostled past. Those who noticed her at all shied away, detoured around her. She was wild-faced by now, straggle-haired, she had no coat or luggage. Or even shoes. She had left them behind in the house. The passing faces became a seamless blur out of which she expected that of Michael Levant to resolve itself any moment. The cars swished by like luminous brush marks.

And then . . . there was the cab, coming towards her. The driver was young, with curly blond hair. There was a Snoopy sticker on the windscreen, like a religious emblem.

She rushed out in front of it and it screeched to a halt an instant from hitting her. She was at the passenger door and scrambling in before the driver even had time to complain.

"I want to get out of Paris, now. Take me out. Please."

"American?"

He had turned around in his seat, was smiling at her, taking in her slimness and her bright blue eyes, a cigarette dangling from between his lips.

"Yes. Please will you—"

"I watch all the movies. My English is good, yes?"

"Yes! Now will you please get me out of here! Anywhere!"

He nodded curiously, dropping ash, and then turned to the wheel, shifted into gear. They began to move. They began to speed, whisking into the outside lane, cutting through the traffic like a knife. He was trying to impress her, drive like they did in the movies. She was glad of that.

She did not relax till they neared the outskirts of Paris. Only then did she begin to slide back against the leather upholstery, body sagging, eyes narrowing towards exhaustion. She could see the road funneling ahead of her through her slitted eyes. She could see—

The lorry suddenly roaring out of the turning.

The driver going rigid, clinging to the wheel.

The side of the lorry looming up like a tidal wave.

And then there was a deafening roar, and a spinning, and then only silence. She swam up from the deep place she had retreated to, and managed to open her eyes. The cab was upside down. The driver was dead, his face turned to pulp. She felt gentle hands lifting her, moving her, and she prayed that ambulancemen here wore pale grey uniforms, and she prayed that she was safe at last.

And she was still semi-conscious when they carried her into the cellar of the house.

The altar pressed cold against her back. Michael Levant loomed over her. He was holding his book.

"You read." He was smiling. "You saw. Not flesh and blood and bone and heart that mark the difference between dead and living. Not that. The power. The flame. You have it strong. She needs it."

The black shape resolved itself next to him. Face as white as maggots, eyes like dust pits. It moved towards her, to drink deeply of the flame.

It would be in the newspapers the following evening. A young girl found with a completely dead face. As white as maggots. Eyes like dust pits. Similar bodies had been found—one of a Canadian tourist ten years ago, five others, but none had been dumped so openly as in the Seine. As though to announce, the task is completed.

The work is done.

❈   ❈   ❈

Michael Levant smiled, that following evening, and set the newspaper down beside him on the rear seat of the limousine, then turned to gently kiss his wife. How beautiful she was. High cheekbones. Full lips. Skin wondrously pale.

And beautiful extreme blue eyes.

The limousine sped on like an arrow, carrying her into the thundering, whirling traffic.

Into the heart of Paris.

Into a city which had known her once.

Would know her once again.

Notre Dame des Ombres.

Our Lady of the Shadows.

SHE WALKS ON DRY LAND

R. Chetwynd-Hayes

If eccentricity is a sign of greatness, then verily I, Charles Edward Devereux, Fourth Earl of Montcalm, must be among the greatest in the three kingdoms. During the length of a long life I have always been prone to follow that line of conduct that is least amenable to convention and thus brought down upon my unbowed head the unmerited disapproval of my contemporaries. But I have never understood why wealth and position should stop any man doing that which pleased him, so long as his conduct did not result in harm or discomfort to his fellow beings.

In the year of our Lord 1812, early on the morning of October 5th, being tired of the excesses practiced at the Regent's court, I ordered my body servant Patrick to saddle two horses, and after informing my people I would be absent for an unspecified period, departed for an unknown destination.

I travelled east, leaving London by way of the Strand, then proceeded into the county of Essex, determined to follow the coastline until a whim prompted me to do otherwise. Calling myself Charles Beverley (this being my mother's maiden name) I put up at various inns and places of entertainment and on the fifth day after my departure from London arrived at the small fishing village I will call Den-ham.

This was nothing more than a row of small cottages that seemed to be an extension of the old grey-stone church, plus one inn that bore the sign THE LIMPING SAILOR on a creaking board over its main doorway. I ordered Patrick to take charge of the horses and entered this establishment, half determined to spend a few days in this retreat, for I was much taken by its brooding atmosphere of isolation, the thudding music of restless waves and the sad dirge of wheeling gulls.

There was one saloon, if the single room furnished only by a long bar and a few crude benches can be so designated, and several men—mainly hard of feature and somber of mien—greeted my entrance with the undisguised curiosity of their kind. A large, red-faced man who I assumed to be the landlord, knuckled his forehead (for even plainly dressed I could never be mistaken for other than a person of quality) and asked:

"What be your pleasure, sir?"

I slapped a gold coin down upon the bar and smiled benignly.

"A tankard of sack. Also let any present who would partake of my hospitality be served with what pleases them best."

Instantly there was much movement of feet, a mass surge towards the bar and I became the centre of flattering attention, for the way to reach your yokel's heart is through his gullet. When all were supplied with their needs and I had half-drained my pewter tankard, I broached the matter of accommodation.

"Could you put me up for a day or so?" I asked the landlord. "Two rooms and simple fare is all that will be required."

To my surprise the fellow shook his head and an abrupt silence stilled tongues that had been loosened by my largesse.

"This is a small house, sir, and I have no means of entertaining such a gentleman as yourself. Few travellers pass this way, you understand."

Although when making my enquiry I was of two minds if I really wanted to stay in this miserable hovel, a direct refusal had the immediate result of arousing my ire. Neither was I appeased when those who had been partaking of my liberality withdrew and began muttering among themselves. I raised my voice and again addressed the landlord.

"I would remind you that this is a place of public entertainment and you are compelled by law to provide accommodation for any traveller who requests it."

The fellow rubbed his hands, then spread them wide in a gesture of apparent helplessness, even while I detected a gleam of fear in his small, deep-set eyes.

"I have no vacant room, sir, Ipswich is but a few miles inland . . ."

"I have no mind to ride a few miles inland at this advanced hour. There must be at least two upper rooms. I will settle for one and my fellow can sleep on the floor."

I watched the heavy face assume a sullen expression and my rage rose to a level that was out of all proportion to the ridiculous situation, but I am not accustomed to having my will thwarted. When he spoke again his voice was no longer respectful.

"There's no room and that's final. Be gone and ride where you will. But you'll no stay here."

I struck him with my riding crop and he fell back, clutching a mighty gash on his forehead; but before the others could reach me I was covering them with my horse pistol, nigh choking with rage. The door flew open and there was Patrick, a towering figure with a blunderbuss clasped firmly in his great hands—and they slunk back like rats confronted by two savage dogs. My anger is a flame that burns fiercely for a short space of time, but soon fades when opposition to my will is overcome. When next I spoke my voice was gentle.

"Come, my friends, there is no reason for us to quarrel. Some nefarious activity doubtless makes you resent the presence of strangers. Smuggling perhaps. Do not worry on my account, for I can be both blind and deaf when I so wish. But understand this, I am determined to stay in this place for so long as the fancy takes me and it will ill become any man to say otherwise. Now, I care not if I spend the night in this inn or another, more accommodating abode, but some roof will provide shelter. I am prepared to be a generous guest, but a ferocious outcast. So—who is ready to be my host?"

An old man with stooped shoulders ventured to advance a few steps and after saluting me, proceeded to speak.

"Sir, I am Josiah Woodward, the elder of this law-abiding community and humbly crave your indulgence when I say you do wrong to commit violence when no man's hand was raised against you. Fear for your safety, sir, forces us to be inhospitable, not evil doing. Come nightfall it bodes ill for any stranger found within the confines of this village and I implore you to ride from hence and give thanks to Almighty God that you do so with body and soul intact."

I laughed softly for now I realized that here was one of those isolated communities where superstition bemused the minds of its inhabitants, although I was impressed by their mien and mode of speech, which would have done justice to many a Whitehall gallant. I lowered my pistol and said gently:

"Now I understand. You are trying to frighten me with some bogie that moans beyond tightly closed windows, or a demon horseman who comes galloping across the moonlit moor. Have no fear for my safety, my good fellow, I am more than a match for any adversary, be he from this world or the next."

Their voices rose up and created a chorus of horrified rebuke and the landlord, who had by now somewhat recovered from my admonishing blow, crossed himself vigorously. The old man shook his head.

"It ill becomes you, sir, to treat with levity advice given by those who speak from bitter experience. We who live here have nothing to fear and if so inclined could take pleasure from watching your sinful pride crumble before the wind of abject terror. A year or so ago there came one like unto yourself, who refused to heed our well-intentioned warning, and now his bones lie rotting in the churchyard. Ask not why, sir, but get you gone with our blessing."

I experienced a thrill of excitement, for here was a situation to guarantee some diversion, even though it more than probably had a mundane explanation. An ancient folk tale, embellished by imagination and retelling round winter fires, based perhaps on some actual event, the origins of which were now lost in the mists of time. I chuckled and said: "But I insist on knowing why, old man. You cannot expect a person of my standing to flee from a shadow I have yet to see, to say nothing of unsatisfied curiosity that would pester me for the rest of my life. What dreadful fate strikes down the stranger, but leaves the inhabitants unscathed?"

The old fellow positively glared at me.

"It is doubtful if words of mine will do more than evoke scorn, but if so be your wish, I will tell you what I know, which is little, for there is no man living who can do more than repeat what his father told him, as indeed did his father before him. But you must accept that long ago, perhaps during the reign of him they now call Charles the martyr, there lived in this place a maiden called Elizabeth Coldwell. 'Tis said she was possessed of great beauty, with black hair and white skin and a face to tempt a man to sin."

"A stranger came to these shores. One of noble birth, in a ship that anchored off Needles Point and he did what no fisherman, be he master of his own vessel or a humble caster of nets, had ever hoped to do. He enslaved her heart with fine promises and fulsome words. No one knew what took place on the sleek white ship. Maybe after satisfying his own lust, he gave her to the crew, or again perhaps she stumbled across some secret that threatened his safety and so was murdered. But one fact is certain. After his ship had sailed, her body was washed up on the beach yonder, so mutilated, no man could look upon it unmoved."

The old man paused, whether to regain his breath or reinforce his imagination, I could not determine, but I nodded and said:

"Very sad. But I wager some variation of that tale is related in every inn along this coast. And now I suppose you will tell me her unhappy shade comes drifting over the rocks on a moonlit night and he who sees it will die within a year and a day."

The old man shook his head sadly.

"No, sir. We never see her from one year's end to the next. But let a stranger spend one night within the boundaries of this village, then, sir—she comes up from the sea and walks on dry land."

"For what purpose?" I enquired.

"To show him her face, sir. No man can look upon it without going mad—a singular madness, for he'll run screaming down to the sea and drown himself."

I called back over one shoulder.

"Patrick, are you willing to risk your sanity for a sight of this lady? I'm thinking she'll have her hands full with the two of us."

Patrick shrugged and spoke with the familiarity that had come into being over the years.

"If you had any sense you'd do what they say and ride out of here. But if stay you must, then so will I. And I can't see how any wraith can steal our sanity, seeing there's not a spoonful between us."

I straightened up and put away my pistol.

"So, that's settled. Now in which house do I spend the night?"

The landlord growled like a wounded hound and pointed a shaking forefinger in my direction.

"We wash our hands of you and that black-visaged minion and may Elizabeth Coldwell drive you both to her sea-girt grave. But no man here will give you succour. There's an empty cottage at the far end of the street. Take that and hark you—no one will pay heed to your screams, save maybe to pray for your damned souls."

"And food?" I asked. "Surely you will not let us go mad on an empty stomach."

He nodded, albeit reluctantly. "Aye, there's victuals for the payment."

※　※　※

The cottage was unfurnished and had clearly not been lived in for some time, thereby confirming my suspicion that the village was dying. In another ten years the entire place would be merely a collection of deserted houses, breeding dens for any number of wailing ghosts. Patrick had managed to acquire four blankets, how I did not enquire, and these he laid out on the floor, so that I at least could enjoy a modicum of comfort. The landlord had supplied two loaves, a slab of strong cheese and two bottles of wine (at an exorbitant price) and this sparse fare blunted the edge of our appetites while we waited for something to happen.

"Well, Patrick," I asked, "do you think we'll pass a peaceful night, or will our inhospitable friends put on a show for our benefit?"

He laid the barrel of his blunderbuss over the sill of the open window and smiled grimly.

"There'll be a few more ghosts around if they try it on. But I'm thinking your lordship's as cracked as an old jug to play a game like this. You were flashing your gold around in there and that's enough reason for us to be quickly dispatched and our bodies thrown to the fishes. And I doubt if your pistol and old Betsy here would do more than account for a few."

I reflected on his words then shook my head.

"No. They're law-abiding enough, just warped by superstitious fear. And this adventure is one after my own heart, for who can say if there may not be a basis of truth to the old fellow's story. Violent death may leave scars on the road of time."

"Surely your lordship isn't really expecting a moaning ghost to come up from the sea?"

I pointed to the scene laid out before us.

"From such a setting one must expect anything—or nothing."

A rough road separated the row of cottages from the beach; from there on there was nothing more than a mass of jutting rocks, over which the incoming tide rolled and retreated, the waves tinted with silver moonlight, while on both sides towering cliffs curved gently inwards to form a vast bay. To our right a long wooden pier had been erected and to this several fishing boats were moored, each one jogging up and down as the waves lapped their black hulls. The scene was bleak, but at the same time not without an element of wild beauty and I pondered on the possibility of building a small retreat on this isolated coast, a place to which I could escape when the mood took me.

Then a black, seething cloud bank came drifting high up over the east cliff and veiled the face of the moon. I went back to my couch of blankets and yawned.

"Maybe we shall have to content ourselves with hearing the lady, not seeing her."

Patrick lit a tall tallow candle and cast an uneasy glance at the open window.

"I'd be just as pleased if we did neither. If your lordship cares to sleep, I'll keep watch and maybe take a little walk outside. I'm mindful there's a back entrance to this place and I'd not put it past those spalpeens to send their ghost in through the back door."

I uncorked a bottle and poured a generous measure into a tankard.

"Do what you please. But call out if you catch a glimpse of the vengeful lady. That's not a sight you must keep to yourself."

I did not intend to sleep, but we had ridden far that day and the wine, though distasteful to the palate, was strong and not conducive to relentless vigilance. How long I slept I have no idea, but I was abruptly hurled back into complete consciousness by the hoarse scream of a man, surely one of the most terrifying sounds on earth. For a moment I sat perfectly still and stared blankly round the bare room, that now seemed to be filled with grotesque leaping shadows that were trying to put the candle out.

Then my head jerked round and there was the open window, a black square that refused to admit so much as a spark of light and I *knew*—knew with unquestioning certainty—that something—someone—was standing just beyond that darkness, looking in. And all the while that hoarse scream went on and on, gradually receding, accompanied by the crunch-crunch of pounding feet, until both sounds finally merged with the endless murmur of waves surging over rocks.

But I was wrapped in a mantle of fear that drained the last vestige of warmth from my body and I could only stare at the black screen that was the window, sick to my very soul, knowing that the mere sight of whatever was watching me would shatter my sanity and send me, like poor Patrick, screaming down to the beach to seek oblivion in the restless sea.

The candle flickered and the shadows leapt up the walls, did a mad dance over the ceiling, then froze into terrifying immobility when the wind died and the world seemed to be holding its breath. I caught a suggestion of movement in the window-frame, before I closed my eyes and prayed that I might have the strength of will not to open them again until the danger had passed—if it ever did.

Then—she was there. A few feet to my left; an unseen presence that was as real as the floorboards beneath my trembling legs, the dim candlelight that flickered through my closed eyelids and the fear that held me in its icy grip. But even in the midst of my terror, I realized in some inexplicable way, that that which stood looking down at me was only a part of the being that had perished so long ago—the worse part. A personality fragment that derived some kind of obscene life from undying hate. The arrival of a stranger (or strangers), a disturbing pattern of fresh thought waves, was sufficient to energize something that was neither flesh nor spirit, but possibly formed from the essence of both.

There was a nigh overwhelming urge to open my eyes and satisfy an illogical curiosity. Like a man poised on the top of a high building, who says: "Let me jump, it's the quickest way down," so I toyed with the mad notion that to *see* would put an end to horrific conjecture. Might it not be better to go mad suddenly, than to sit for another eight or nine hours of darkness, knowing that something so dreadful it had sent poor, unimaginative Patrick shrieking down to the sea, was standing a bare two feet to my left, looking down at me.

For let me make one point clear—I knew its exact location, a rough idea of its shape and size and even the manner of its attire. I sensed the likeness of a young woman, some five feet six inches high, with long black hair and dressed in a torn, white gown. Only the face and eyes escaped me, but I realized that here was the crux of the matter. Poor Patrick had seen the face, maybe looked into the eyes—and in an instant became a screaming madman.

After a while I managed to move an arm and felt strangely disappointed when no cold hand tried to restrain me. I digested a tiny scrap of knowledge. Quite possibly if I got up and walked it would just follow me—or retreat in front of me—but always careful to keep the face turned towards mine. Walk! Walk out of this room, out of the cottage and not stop until I had reached the confines of the village!

Then surely I would be beyond her jurisdiction. Once I had stepped over the village boundary, I might as well be in London or the wilds of Africa. But I would have to walk with closed eyes, knowing that stark horror accompanied me, and that a stumble or a moment's distraction could result in my seeing the indescribable.

I got up—very, very slowly—and for one moment sensed the face was at a level with my own, then lurched across the room, not daring to put my arms out, lest my hands touch something it was best not to think about. I blundered into a wall, edged my way along it until an open space told me I had reached the doorway, then stumbled out into the narrow passage.

Sound returned when I came to the front door. The sighing wind, the menacing murmur of waves breaking on the rock-girt shore, the distant hoot of an owl. I turned right and, determined now to retain full control of my senses, carefully lowered one foot before raising the other. But—oh, merciful God—it knew what I was about, for could I not sense it in front?—the face all but pressed against my own and once—once—there was the faint suggestion of a cold kiss on my lips, and the merest hint of hands being laid on my shoulders.

Then did I Charles Edward Devereux, Earl of Montcalm, who had often boasted that he feared neither man nor devil, scream out my terror and run with all speed that labouring heart and gasping lungs would permit; eyes tight shut, mouth gaping, unmindful of the brambles that tore at my hands and clothes, the rock that tripped, the low wall that had to be surmounted, for I had the ridiculous notion that my very soul was in peril.

And she—she not it—whimpered like a frustrated child, clutched at my closed eyes with insubstantial hands and finally sent out a long, despairing cry.

Then I collapsed, rolled into a ditch and surrendered to the burning need to open my eyes, at that moment not caring if a dozen sanity-murdering faces were looking down at me, so long as I were permitted one last glimpse of the night sky. My head was below ground level and I could indeed see the sky where clouds were moving away, leaving the moon free to illuminate the surrounding countryside and turn the grey waves to sparkling silver.

After a while I found the courage to stand up and look back towards the row of cottages, and then to the rock-studded beach, and was just in time to see a white figure drift down to the shoreline, before dispersing into a cloud of fast retreating mist.

By luck—or God's mercy—I had stumbled across the village boundary and cheated Elizabeth Coldwell of her second victim.

※   ※   ※

I returned to the village next morning and was greeted (if that is the right word) by its inhabitants who appeared to view my continued existence as a major miracle. The old man laid a shaking hand on my arm as though to make sure I was still intact, then asked in a tremulous voice:

"How did you escape her, sir? Your man was discovered cold and stiff, but an hour since."

"I closed my eyes," I answered briefly. "That which cannot be seen, can be endured. Just. Where have you put my servant?"

I was taken to an outhouse at the back of the inn and looked down upon all that remained of my friend and servant. His face was a mask of frozen terror. I gave the old man two gold coins.

"See that he gets a Christian burial."

"That we will, sir. Within the hour, lest tonight he too walks on dry land."

I collected the two horses and rode away, sadder and wiser than when I came, and determined never again to venture forth into isolated places.

But it is an indisputable fact that even to this day, I cannot close my eyes without feeling there is something standing a few feet to my left watching me.

ABOUT THE EDITORS

R. CHETWYND-HAYES had a publishing career that lasted more than forty years. He produced thirteen novels, twenty-five collections of stories, and edited twenty-four anthologies. In 1989 both the Horror Writers of America and the British Fantasy Society presented him with Life Achievement Awards, and he was the Special Guest at the 1997 World Fantasy Convention in London. His stories have been adapted for film, television, radio and comic strips, and have been translated into numerous languages around the world. He died in 2001.

STEPHEN JONES is the winner of three World Fantasy Awards, three Horror Writers Association Bram Stoker Awards and three International Horror Guild Awards, as well as being a Hugo Award nominee and a fifteen-times recipient of the British Fantasy Award. One of Britain's most acclaimed anthologists of horror and dark fantasy, he has more than seventy books to his credit. You can visit his web site at: http://www.herebedragons.co.uk/jones